T0154709

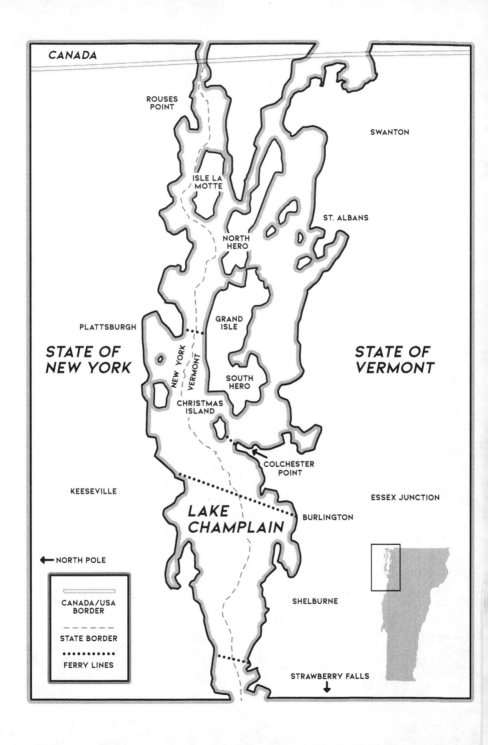

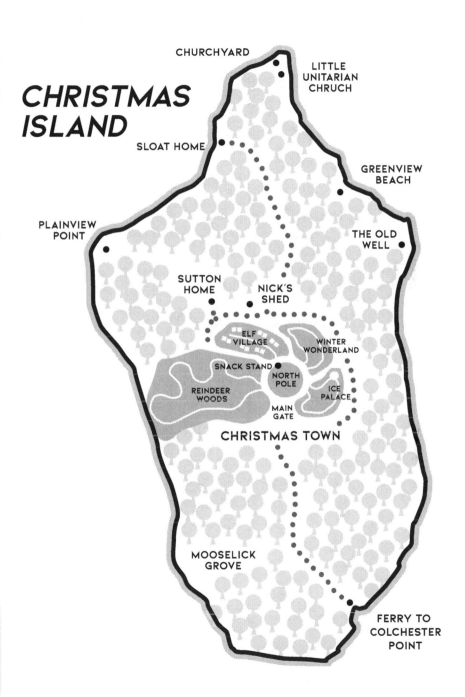

CHRISTMAS ISLAND

CHURCHYARD

LITTLE
UNITARIAN
CHRUCH

SLOAT HOME

GREENVIEW
BEACH

PLAINVIEW
POINT

THE OLD
WELL

SUTTON
HOME

NICK'S
SHED

ELF
VILLAGE

WINTER
WONDERLAND

SNACK STAND

NORTH
POLE

REINDEER
WOODS

ICE
PALACE

MAIN
GATE

CHRISTMAS TOWN

MOOSELICK
GROVE

FERRY TO
COLCHESTER
POINT

GARRETT COUNTY PRESS

DESIGNED BY KEVIN STONE

Garrett County Press books are distributed to the trade by National Book Network, 800-462-6420.

www.gcpress.com

Photo by Jennifer Baumstein from Pexels

THE ONION RING LOVERS

(GUIDE TO VERMONT)

A NOVEL

KEVIN STONE

FOR DEBBI

The best thing that came out of my Vermont journey

& OLIVIA

*Who at nine is a better writer than I could
ever hope to be.*

TAKE THE HIGH ROAD

2000

"Here we go."

An insignificant maroon Ford Festiva hatchback, rusted and wheezing, wound its way down a steep hill. For the umpteenth time, Jim Sutton said a silent prayer as he pressed the brake pedal. Relieved to feel the brakes respond, Jim winced at the whine as the worn pads engaged the drum. They were long overdue to be replaced, but you try to find the time or the funds when you're a public-school English teacher.

"Atta girl…" Jim soothed his car as he slalomed the hill. Since he had started the trip, he had developed the affectation of speaking to himself. Mostly to pass the time, partly just to hear another voice, even if it was his own. His thoughts were interrupted by the keening wail of a car horn. Jim looked in the rear-view mirror. Reflected in reverse he could see the driver of an obnoxiously orange SUV gesticulating wildly. He supposed he was going a little slow down the steep hill. Jim could see the two-lane road up ahead became a four lane. He struggled to roll down the window while steering his little automobile. Jim stuck his hand out and made a waving motion for the orange monstrosity to pass.

Jim could hear the SUV engine rev as it sped to pass him on the left. "Fuck off, asshole!" The driver shouted as he sped off. Jim looked up to see the custom New York State plate as he drove off.

WL-HNG

Jim shook his head as he cranked the window up, looking over at the green sign on the side of the road that read:

1

BORDER TO VERMONT 50

Jim could feel himself getting tense. He had been driving for a while up through New York state. Of course he knew this was his destination.

"At least it's not fall," Jim mumbled, looking across the green valleys around him.

Jim hated autumn in Vermont. Spring was Jim's favorite season. Spring, when the new leaves opened, fresh, new and alive…light, lush, green, verdant, and vibrant. Jim felt at home and at peace under canopies. He would stand and stare up at the boughs, watching the new leaves ripple in the wind, moved by unseen eddies and currents. In those rare moments, Jim could lose his sense of self. He felt part of something bigger, more connected to nature than to other people. The colorful displays of fall in New England were just a prelude to winter. With winter, of course, came Christmas.

Just the thought of that holiday made Jim shudder. It's not like he was anti-religion, or anti-Christian. He was none of those things. If anything, Jim was anti-Christmas. The holiday itself. The pageantry, the symbols, the overwhelming omnipresence of it. He had grown up with a strange perspective on the holiday. So, some latitude could be granted to Jim Sutton in his dislike of the holiday and the season of winter that heralded its arrival.

Fall is the quintessential time of the year to visit the Green Mountain State. Thousands vacation in the small, unassuming state every year. *Leaf peepers*, the locals call them, in a mix of fondness and derision, or flatlanders, the catch–all designation for those whom God did not give the good sense to have been born a Vermonter.

Jim Sutton's parents did not have the foresight to birth their brood in Vermont, but rather in the city of Boston in the adjoining state of Massachusetts. If New England were its own country, Boston would be its financial and cultural capital. Boston holds a special, sometimes mystical place in New Englanders' hearts. The Red Sox may play in Fenway Park, right in the middle of the big city of Boston, but in the furthest rural areas, they were THE team of the land, held in the highest esteem.

The same could not be said for how New Englanders felt about New York City. Perhaps it was a remnant of colonial times when New York laid claim to half of the state, but Vermonters do not trust New Yorkers. You could live in Vermont for fifty years after moving from New York, and you'd still be a damned New Yorker. Your kids would be as well. Some say it takes three full generations to become a true Vermonter.

The only New Yorkers Vermont ever embraced and claimed as their own were Ben & Jerry, the ice cream entrepreneurs and Bernie Sanders, the Democratic Socialist Brooklynite. Ben Cohen and Jerry Greenfield helped put Vermont on the map with their ice cream, Bernie's adoption as native son said more about the state's fierce independent streak than anything else. Vermont had for generations been staunchly Republican, but the rise of Bernie Sanders from carpetbagger to Mayor of Burlington to (almost) Democratic candidate for President of the United States, coincided with the progressive awakening of the state. Political shifts and realignments notwithstanding, Bernie's main appeal could be said that he was an unrepentant pain in the ass—a trait that Vermonters recognized and acknowledged as one they not only admired but one they aspired to embody as well.

The whims and laws of provincialism are intricate, delicate and resolute, and Bob and Linda Sutton wandered right into them, like a fly drawn to a field of genuine home-grown Vermont manure.

GOOD NEWS. BAD NEWS.

1968–1977

Linda and Bob, met in graduate school at Boston College in 1968.

Bob Sutton migrated from Minnesota to study Latin American Studies. Linda Boyd hailed from Seaford Delaware and was studying for a master's degree in education. She hoped to become a Spanish teacher.

Bob and Linda's romance was not typical. Bob noticed her in their mutual Spanish class. Linda noticed his unimpressive opinions on Latin American geo-politics. She was more interested in academics than in socializing, and certainly not dating. Linda had staunchly decided before she graduated high school that she would not limit herself by settling for a comfortable marriage. *Family may happen, or it may not.* SHE held her own fate. She wasn't in school to land a husband or start a family.

Linda had felt off for the better part of a week. Halfway through Professor Carlson's lecture, her stomach growled ominously. She had cooked pasta Carbonara the night before and it was sitting leaden in her belly. She quickly excused herself. Linda had hardly made it out of the lecture hall before the contents of her stomach came lurching up, splattering on the floor like some ersatz Jackson Pollock creation. Linda's roommate, Missy McNight convinced her to visit to the campus nurse. Linda initially objected, but after being harangued, relented.

Linda sat on the examining table, the white paper crinkled under her as she swung her bell-bottomed jeans legs back and forth.

"I took your temperature, everything is alright." The nurse said entering the room, smiling.

4

"I'm sure its just food poisoning" Linda replied. *Stupid Missy, this is a waste of time.* She though ruefully, *My paper isn't going to write itself.*

The nurse smiled and took Linda's hand. Then the nurse handed her a pamphlet on *"The Miracle of Motherhood"* and escorted her out the door.

Linda shuffled back to her dorm room in a daze. Looking up, she saw Bob walking across the quad. Seeing her, he waved and started walking toward her. She waved back weakly.

"I'm so glad I ran into you!" Bob exclaimed. "I just came from the most amazing meeting. We're going to organize a protest against the war." Bob looked at her, his eyes shining.

"That's great." Linda said blankly.

"Isn't it?" Bob replied, oblivious to Linda's blasé response. "If we all come together, I really think we can end this fascist aggression against the people of Vietnam by next year. Are we still on for tonight?"

"Tonight?" Linda replied.

"Dinner. My place? I'm cooking." Bob furrowed his brow, then laughed.

"Oh yes. Of course." Linda managed a weak smile.

"See you then!" Bob kissed Linda on the forehead and trotted away. He turned around. "Seven!" He shouted.

She knocked on the door.

"Hey, there's my girl" Bob purred as he opened the door. Steamy food smells filled the hall. Bob was making his patented "Stew a-la Bob" which meant stew with twice as many carrots. Linda didn't really care for carrots, but she always pretended to love it when he made it for her.

Bob ushered her in. She had been to his dorm room many times for "dinner" which really was just a prelude to fooling around. His roommate was gone, as usual. Bob reached past Linda and tied a red handkerchief to the doorknob.

"Come in," Bob said. "Dinner's almost ready."

"Bob, I'm late." Linda said.

"It's only seven fifteen, you're just on time." Bob said looking at his watch. "Actually, for *you*, you're early"

"No Bob, I'm *late.*"

Bob's brow furrowed in confusion. Then his jaw went slack with realization.

"Late? You. But we, but you…" Bob's face was a road map of confusion "You said you were on something."

"I was. I am" Linda stammered.

"I thought the pill was ninety-nine percent effective," Bob said. "Wow. So, what do we do now?"

"I don't know."

"I have a buddy who told me of a doctor we can go to. To take care of it," Bob said.

"An abortion," Linda said.

"Yeah," Bob said. "I mean, it's the sensible thing to do. We're in college. Who wants to bring a person into this world when there's a war going on?"

"Yes, it is the sensible thing," Linda said.

Bob sighed. "I don't think I have enough bread for the operation. Maybe I could borrow some. Say, you don't have any stashed away, do you?"

"I want to keep it," Linda said.

"The money?"

"The baby."

"You do?"

"Yes."

"Uh…then I guess we should get married, then," Bob mumbled. His impromptu proposal became family lore, an anecdote to trot out for friends and family.

The roles that neither Bob nor Linda ever wanted became their identities. Linda felt regret as she became a stay-at-home mom, or in her moments of self-loathing, "a housewife." Bob accepted an administrative position at Boston University in their department of Foreign Studies.

Being a stay-at-home wife and mother was exhausting. Bob had taken off exactly three days from work after little Jimmy was born. Linda had taken on the brunt of care for the infant, since it was what was *expected*. She had decided to breastfeed Jim, which had given Bob the excuse to extract himself from participating in the midnight feedings that were more like every two hour feedings.

Linda had struggled all that day getting Jim down. He had finally taken a nap, so she collapsed into the armchair by the TV and blissfully fell asleep.

"Linda," a voice called out to her, as if from a long distance. Faint and muffled through the ether.

"Linda." A bit louder now. Curious, she thought, Bob's not due home for…

"LINDA!" So loud now it shocked her out of her sleep. Linda looked around, bewildered. She put her hand to her face, it was wet. She had been drooling.

"You awake?" Bob asked, looming over her.

"I am now." Linda muttered groggily as she pushed herself up on her elbows.

"Is dinner ready?" Bob asked. Linda shot him a dirty look "Ok, ok." Bob conceded "I understand, it's just..."

"What is it, hon?" Linda asked, forcing a weak smile.

"I hate my job. I just hate it," Bob said.

"I *wish* I could work," Linda said. She walked to the little kitchen. She knew there was a box of Shake n' Bake in the cabinet. She could quickly throw together a little meal.

"Adams is an asshole, who wouldn't understand a good idea if it bit him in his pale white ass," Bob said. This was not the first time Bob had complained about his boss. Bob was restless at heart, and found himself looking for something more, something different. It was hard for him to stay at a job position for long. There would always be reasons to leave.

"Try to make it work this time, hon." Linda called from the kitchen, unwrapping the quartered chicken she had bought at Stop and Shop.

"I'm going to quit tomorrow." Bob called back.

"Don't." Linda walked from the kitchen, holding the Shake n' Bake bag in her hands, complete with the chicken and the herb and spice dredge. "Please, not again. I can't go back on food stamps, it's humiliating."

"Working in that office is humiliating!" Bob shouted. "I'm smarter than anyone there. It's a waste of my intellect and my time.

Linda absentmindedly shook the bag of chicken. "I'm begging you, Bob. Don't do this. Think of me. Think of Jimmy."

"I'm always thinking of Jim," Bob said. "I've got no choice do I?"

"What does *that* mean?" Linda shook the bag.

"Nothing. It means nothing." Bob slunk into the chair where Linda had just sat, he pulled his arm up. "What the?" It was wet from drool where Linda had slept earlier.

"Bob." Linda still shook the bag.

"I'm not going to quit," Bob said, sulking as he looked out the window.

"Thank you," Linda said, still shaking the bag. She turned to walk back to the kitchen.

"I can't," Bob mumbled.

Bob's eye wandered. Affairs started, affairs discovered, excuses and apologies were made. Then the cycle would begin anew. Linda had bought into this life. She was pot committed so Linda turned to her kids. Two years after Jim was born, Bob and Linda decided that little slim-Jim would benefit from having a little sister. This time, getting pregnant was not so easy a proposition, it had taken them the better part of a year to get pregnant. After many tries, three years later little Lyndsey Anne was born.

Bob styled himself as the *pater-familis*. Bob Sutton needed the world to see him as the great dad. He craved the validation and became churlish and sullen when he thought he was not appreciated. The kids, Jim and Lyndsey, could not predict what might send their father into a silent sulk. It might be the lack of a thank you over his magnanimous decision to stop on the side of the road for fresh-squeezed orange juice. It might build over the miles of a road trip to visit her parents until it exploded in a long tirade about the selfish nature of his kids, his wife, his boss, and the general misery of his so-called life.

When Bob came home from work, excited and happy for once, Linda could hardly be blamed for getting caught up in his excitement. While Bob could be selfish and petulant, he was very charming. Bob had a way of sweeping everyone up in his passions. The family rode this ride in queasy solidarity, the highs exhilarating and the lows terrifying. Bob Sutton left home one day, just a seed of a thought germinating in his mind, and by the time the commute was over, that seed had grown into a fully formed idea. When he stepped through the door, it was set in stone. He was utterly convinced that he was right. Bob had been presented with the business opportunity of a lifetime, and he was hell-bent to sell it to his family.

*   *   *

"Good news everybody! Family meeting time!" Bob Sutton announced as he strode through the door on June 14, 1977. Even at age eight, Jim could understand his father's joy was tinged with a dangerous mania. Everybody in the Sutton family knew that "family meeting time" really meant Bob Sutton grievance hour. Linda prepared herself for his latest passive aggressive reproach, but she was curious about his upbeat mood. Family meeting time and giddiness did not usually go hand in hand.

Bob liked to fashion himself the head of the household in most matters. Linda had made the decision to stay at home for the kids. She was surprised how much she enjoyed being a mom, but it came with its own price. Every day as Bob left their apartment to go to work, Linda would watch the door close behind him, slamming like the bars of her own personal prison. They couldn't afford daycare, not on one salary. Even though it had been her choice to stay at home, having a career wasn't really an option for Linda.

Nevertheless, despite her sacrifice, Bob was unrelenting in his dissatisfaction with her homemaking. Bob he railed against clothes on the floor, messy bathrooms, dirty dishes, and most of all when he wasn't greeted as the conquering hero upon coming home from a job he loathed. Bob proposed family meeting time under the pretense of a democratic debate but, for all intents and purposes, it was just a forum for dictating terms.

"We're moving to Vermont!" Bob crowed. Linda stared at him skeptically, Jim was dumbfounded, and little Lyndsey just played with her stuffed bear. "Well…" Bob stammered, "we're *thinking* of moving to Vermont. It's going to be SO great. It will be the adventure of a lifetime!" Bob punctuated the adventure by moving his arm in an enthusiastic fist-pump type movement that was meant to convey excitement but to Jim it looked like he was trying to punch his mother in the face.

"Um, why Vermont?" Asked Linda cautiously. She knew this Bob quite well. This was manic Bob. Happy Bob. *Determined* Bob.

Bob looked out at his family and began his hard sell. He had rehearsed it on the ride from work in the family's road-worn red Volkswagen station wagon. "You're gonna love it, Linda, kids…fresh air, mountains, swimming in the summer, skiing in the winter." Bob had imagined that by this point in his speech, his family would be rapt with anticipation. Instead, they just looked confused. "OK, here's the best part: We get to be our own bosses. We get to own our own business, just us. Team Sutton."

Linda half mockingly raised her hand. "Bob, what on earth are you talking about?" She tried to keep emotion from her voice. She didn't want this to escalate in front of the kids. "What business?"

Bob swung from Linda to Jim and Lyndsey. "Kids, here's the best part. You get to have Christmas. All. Year. Long." He spread his hands, palms out, for effect. Lyndsey smiled a broad grin, excited, but unsure of what her daddy was saying.

"Linda, babe, it's perfect for us. I met a guy last week who was at the university with his son, down from Vermont. We got to talking. This guy owns his own park up there. It's called Christmas Town." Bob turned to the kids "It's like *Disney World.*" He figured the kids would salivate at this tidbit. Disney World had opened in 1971, and the ads were everywhere that summer. *Now* Jim and Lindsey were jumping around, practically vibrating with excitement. Bob knew he had them hooked. So did Linda. It would be that much harder to be the voice of reason.

Bob launched into the history of the island and the resort. It was a full assault on Linda's common sense. They'd be buying the concession stand to operate and run. They'd live in a house purchased from Christmas Town. Bob had crunched the numbers. They had managed to save up money for what was earmarked to be a down payment on a house.

Currently, they lived in a cramped apartment in Malden. Bob and Linda had their eyes on a real "fixa-uppah" as they called it in Cambridge. Linda had always dreamed that Bob would get a job at Harvard one day and maybe, just maybe, the kids could go there…free. It wasn't a cheap zip code, so they had saved as much as they could. What they scrimped already could have bought them a perfectly serviceable starter home in Melrose. Bob explained that their money could buy the business *and* a house. "Job, home, done!" He said with a flourish. As relentless as the tide, Bob Sutton wore down Linda's resistance.

*　　*　　*

Upending a life is hard. There are countless little pieces that you don't realize you've got until you have to box them up. Over time, a home becomes incrementally smaller as the number of objects coming in does not equal what is leaving. Papers get filed away, books get placed on shelves, trophies for all to see, never to be read again. Attics and crawl spaces gradually become packed with lawn decorations, holiday lights, and old clothes that have outlived their usefulness. The arteries of the house become more and more congested with the plaque of everyday living until… it's time to move. Suddenly, that broken bike that Bob wanted to fix up became fodder for the tried-and-true all-American yard sale.

The day of the yard sale came. After fending off the "early-birds" typical of the yard sale ecosystem, it was a long day of "ooky-loos and dickerers. When all was said and done Linda looked down at what had been sold and how much was made. Enough for a couple of meals. She realized. She looked over to Bob, who was asleep on the couch they had failed to sell. She put the money in her pocket. Mad money is what she called it. What Bob doesn't know, won't hurt him. She though ruefully. It would go in the rainy day fund she kept secret from Bob.

Linda's parents drove up from Delaware to help pack up the apartment. Her mother had insisted on a Christmas sendoff spectacular blowout for the family when they were done. Essentially, a mini-Christmas for the family.

Her father was not as enthusiastic.

"Elaine, this is ridiculous," he grumbled. He took a drag off of his unfiltered cigarette that he refused to smoke outside, despite Linda's polite requests.

"Hush, Joe," Grandma Elaine said. "We're going to miss Christmas with the kids, besides, it's really just a preview of what every day is going to be from now on."

Christmas Day was the next day and it was a simulacrum of the cherished event. Grandma Elaine had gone all out. She brought the fake aluminum tree from Delaware, lights and all. The kids woke up confused, but as any child would do when presented with unanticipated gifts, they acclimated quickly to the situation.

Grandma Elaine sat under the metallic arboreal acid trip of a Christmas tree and handed out presents to the kids.

"Great, didn't we just have a yard sale to get rid of things?" Bob muttered to Linda. The two of them were at the back of the apartment.

"Let them have their fun" Linda relied.

"Who, the kids or your parents?" Bob grumbled.

The pile of presents grew, along with a mound of crumpled brightly colored wrapping paper. Linda began to notice a disturbing (to her) trend developing. Jim's pile was decidedly male: guns, action figures, and a baseball glove. Lyndsey's was a pink nightmare of dolls, dresses, and teddy bears.

"That's it!" She exploded. Linda grabbed the doll Lyndsey had just opened a switched it with a Tonka truck from Jim's pile.

"Lyndsey can be anything she wants to be and play with what she wants to." She glared at her parents, who looked on in shock.

"Do you want to turn the boy *funny?*" Grandpa Joe said, gesturing to the doll that Jim held in his hands. "Do you want him to grow up to be a *faggot?*" Bob recoiled, Grandma Elaine put her hand over her mouth dumbfounded.

Linda looked at Jim and saw it was too late. He had heard his grandfather.

"Dad, who cares? I don't. He can play with a doll, and it's not going to turn him into a girl. Just like Lyndsey's not going to become a dyke by playing with a truck."

"How did you raise such a cunt?" Grandpa Joe said, turning to Jim's sweet little shell-shocked grandmother.

Linda slapped her father. Grandpa Joe's head reeled to the side.

"Oh my!" Grandma Elaine said. A moment of silence passed between them all. Grandpa Joe glared at Linda, while rubbing his cheek.

"We're leaving. Now," Grandpa Joe said. He stalked to the door. Without a word, Grandma Sarah followed him. The door slammed.

Nothing more was said, and the kids were put to bed early.

The yellow Mayflower truck arrived on August 12, 1977. Jim watched in amazement at the efficiency of the men who moved as if they were one organism. A line of movers cleared out the third-floor apartment at Rainey Street in under an hour. Bob tried to assist the movers but just seemed to annoy them. After getting in the way for a third time, the foreman of the crew politely asked Bob stand down, lest they go into overtime charges. Bob stepped aside and fumed for a while until he declared it was time for him to pack up the fragile and precious items, such as the china and the Zenith Television. Those would go with the family in the station wagon, not the moving van.

The family Volkswagen was packed to the gills with boxes, so much so that Bob could not see out of his rear-view mirror. Sticking his head out the window to look behind him, Bob got one last look at the apartment that they had called home for six years. Bob was struck by how small it looked, with its fading green and white paint, overflowing gutters and uneven sidewalks. So long, old life Bob thought as he pulled out. Jim looked out the window to see the only world he knew recede faster and faster, blurring into memory until they made the turn onto Maple. They would never see that street or that home again.

* * *

To be a New Englander is an assignation and an identity. It is not a stretch at all to say that New Englanders look down at the rest of the United States with some degree of pity and disdain. They view their five states as the cradle of democracy and home to all true and good American values. That they think they have a monopoly on these traits and values is of course, ridiculous. Every region of the United States holds another in some degree of contempt. The south hates the north, the flyover states of the Midwest hate the coastal states, and *everybody* hates Florida. What makes New England unique is that, while they hold themselves above others as a region, they have within that region perpetual arguments over which is the better, the true religion, so-to-speak, the "best" New England state.

Vermonters bristle at the audacity of New Hampshire's claims of superior maple syrup. Robert Frost famously said, "good fences make good neighbors." This has been happily adopted by many New Englanders and especially taken to heart by Vermonters. Drill down deeper, you'll find the typical rural versus urban rivalries that exist in every state in the union. However, in Vermont there is a subculture that resides in the islands of Lake Champlain that elevates that sentiment to another stratus.

Lake Champlain is a point of pride for the Green Mountain State. Nestled in the Appalachian Valley, it is the jewel in the crown of Vermont. Curiously enough, even though both New York and Vermont lay claim to this lake, it is Vermont who has come out on top as the home to this placid body of water. The lake holds a special place in Vermont history. Discovered by Samuel De Champlain in 1609, Lake Champlain became a vital part of the region and its economy, linking the St. Lawrence Seaway and the Hudson Valley. It was De Champlain that first sighted a creature that would later be nicknamed Champ—America's home-grown version of the Loch Ness monster. Champ is a legend that is still nurtured by locals to this day. All refuse to admit the possibility that Champ may not exist and, in fact, be nothing more than a clever tourism marketing scheme.

Although not the most trafficked commercial waterway today, in colonial times Lake Champlain was an economic center of trade and commerce. During the Revolutionary War, local hero and proto-guerrilla Ethan Allen and his Green Mountain Boys paddled across the waters of Lake Champlain and captured Fort Ticonderoga in 1775. Most Vermonters hold Ethan Allen in high esteem to this day. There is a current of independence that still runs through this sparsest populated of the New England States. Vermonters look to the west at their neighbor across the lake and shake their heads at their lack of stewardship on the New York side. Sitting in the middle of the lake are what locals affectionately call the Islands and within those islands is the most exclusive, exclusionary culture in the state of Vermont.

There are twenty named islands in Lake Champlain: Isle La Motte, Valcour Island, Crab Island, Juniper Island, North Hero Island, South Hero Island, Stave Island, Knight Island, Carlton's Prize, Dameas Island, Cloak Island, Savage Island, Young Island, Four Brothers, Burton Island, Garden Island, Providence Island, Hen Island, Three Sisters, and Christmas Island. Perhaps it is because of their isolation from the mainland, or even each other, residents of the islands do not trust non-Islanders, even those with whom they share state ship. Any xenophobia that is a natural phenomenon of region or state is exacerbated by being an Islander. Some of the islands remained isolated for generations until bridges and ferries were built in the

1800s. There are locals that still bemoan the decision to join the mainland with great regret. One cannot simply move to the islands and hope in a generation or two to become an Islander. Families that can trace their residence back to before the Revolutionary War are true Islanders. All others are suspect.

In 1910, William Henry Sloat relocated his family from New York City to Vermont. William Sloat was a shipping magnate. His family built their fortune producing textiles for the Grand Army of the Republic. William's Grandfather, Howard Sloat acquired the lucrative contract to fabricate the uniforms for the Union Army. During the years of the Civil War, it is estimated that his company made millions. Howard Sloat purchased a home in what was at the time considered the wilds of New York, located near what would become Central Park. William Sloat, sensing the encroachment of New York City's manifest destiny, looked further northward. He bought an unnamed island in Lake Champlain on December 25th, 1910 and named it Christmas Island to mark the day it was purchased.

The Sloats spent a great deal of their fortune on infrastructure and steam-powered ferries to connect the islands to the mainland. William's wife, Mary, disliked the Vermont climate greatly, especially the harsh winters, in which the island would become completely ice bound as the lake froze over. Mary's melancholia and the name of the island inspired William Sloat to construct Christmas Town, a Christmas-themed park, little more than a botanical garden, complete with papier-mâché elves and reindeer.

Christmas Town became popular with both Vermonters and New Yorkers alike and attendance steadily grew. William Sloat added a train ride, a fake North Pole, and Santa's Workshop. Mr. Sloat employed real elves for Christmas Town. Posting notices for dwarfs in major papers of the day, Sloat lured over 50 little people to work and live at The North Pole in Christmas Town. The North Pole was designed to be an exhibit and a home. The little folk employed at Christmas Town were encouraged to live on property in scaled-down versions of real homes. Tourists would walk by and gawk at as a real-life Elf Village. For 50 cents, they could have their photo taken with an elf. For $3, the rubes could spend the night in a real elf house and sleep in comically small beds

Unfortunately for the park, and the Sloats, William Sloat met one Charles Ponzi by chance, on a cruise to Europe. After a day at sea, Ponzi convinced William to invest all his money in a can't miss money-making venture. The outcome for the Sloats was the same as everyone else who had the misfortune of being in business with Mr. Ponzi. Ruin.

The Sloats lost everything and were forced to sell the island to the state of Vermont. Christmas Town became one of only a handful of state-run amusement parks in the country. In the aftermath of the Stock Market collapse in 1929, Vermont looked to divest itself of the property. There were no buyers. As a result, the property laid fallow until 1945, when a returning GI named Glenn Murray purchased Christmas Town, and he gradually nurtured the park back to life.

Christmas Town prospered for a time, capitalizing on the craze of the road trip popularized during the 1950's. Americans were looking for anything to distract them from the memory of World War II and the nuclear sword of Damocles that dangled above their heads. Gradually, the novelty of Christmas Town faded and lost its luster. There were fewer and fewer tourists every year. Disneyland had opened in 1955 and made little Christmas Town look rinky-dink by comparison. Murray let most of the elves go and began to sell off different operations of his park.

The summer of love came and went. Americana was a tough sell after the Vietnam war. Glenn Murray looked into the future, and he could see the path of decline the park was headed down. He needed a way out before he too became a sad footnote in the history of Christmas Island.

*   *   *

Linda studied the map in the passenger seat of the Sutton's overloaded Volkswagen. Looking like something out of the great depression, almost every space was filled to the brim with the items Bob had determined too fragile or too valuable to risk being handled by the movers. They had even lashed several cardboard boxes to the roof with clothesline. Linda looked at the taut line above her head and plucked it. It made a deep THRUMMM.

"Careful" Bob admonished Linda. "That's holding up the..."

"I know what it's holding up, Bob." To her chagrin, in the boxes above their heads were all their important papers. Including both their degrees and diplomas from their college years. Linda had argued they should go inside the car, but Bob said there was simply no room. So up they went. Linda silently prayed the forecast stayed true and it did not rain.

Bob insisted on driving 30 miles out of their way to see the Bicentennial Giant Chair in Gardner. When it came time to stop for lunch in the wilds of rural Massachusetts, Bob groused at the lack of any kind of rest stop or scenic view in which the family could stop and stretch their legs. This lament began to grow into a complaint, a complaint that started sounding to Linda an awful lot like one of Bob's rants. Linda knew the patter well, and she knew that it would consume Bob until they were all miserable.

"There Bob, pull over. That's the perfect place," Linda said, knowing that they were all hungry and tired.

The red Volkswagen pulled off the highway. Jim and Lyndsey were in the backseat, Jim reading a book while lying on his back with his feet against the peeling vinyl ceiling.

She said to Jim, "You're going to get car sick." Linda had warned Jim more times than he could remember. He loved to read and had rescued several Hardy Boys mystery books from the garage sale. He sat in this position, until the car came to halt, presumably in the parking lot of the rest stop or road-side attraction his parents had picked out.

Jim sat up and as his eyes peered outside the window, he could scarcely believe what he saw.

"Get out of the car, scoot," Linda said. Lyndsey popped out of the car. Jim looked around nervously. Could his mother be serious? The place they were at—it was a *cemetery*. As far as the eye could see, it was row upon row of neatly arranged granite headstones.

Jim stood, mouth agape, as he watched their mother prepare the picnic lunch with calm precision. She took a patchwork quilt out of the back, walked a row or two into the cemetery, and spread it across the grass atop the final resting place of *Charles Harry Clarke and Family*.

"Come on," Linda called to her children. "They won't bite. It's just so nice, isn't it? I mean they take such good care of these places, it's really almost a shame not to use them." Jim managed a few bites of his ham sandwich just to make his mother happy.

Linda picked at a piece of grass. The kids were eating (albeit warily), Bob reclined against a headstone. The look on his face. *Content?*

"You know what Bob?" Linda said, scooting over towards her husband "I really do think Vermont can be a fresh start for us."

"Uh huh." Bob smiled, taking out a map. "I do too, honey."

A woman and a man walked by—they stared at the Suttons as they navigated the granite monuments. The man was so distracted he walked into a headstone, almost falling over.

"What's *wrong* with people?" The woman said, looking Linda's way.

"What's wrong with *you*, lady?" Linda countered.

"You're sick. Where's your respect?"

"We're not hurting anybody," Linda said. "Who's to say we're not relatives?"

"Are you?" The man said.

"Are *you?*" Linda said.

"No," the man said. "But I could be"

"I pray for your children."

Linda stood up and walked toward the couple. "I pray you and your friend mind your own business, or I'll take that wig off your head right now."

"I don't wear a *wig!*" Unbidden, the woman's hand moved up to her hairline. As she touched it, Jim could see it move.

"Ok then…" Linda reached out towards the woman.

"Harold, let's go!" The woman cried as she clamped her hands on her head. Harold followed after her.

"We're halfway there, kids!" Announced Bob. He had missed the whole affair, engrossed in the maps sprawled across the well-manicured grass.

Lunch was consumed with no further interruptions. As they got back in the car and continued their exodus, Lyndsey spoke up. "Do they speak English in Vermont, Daddy?" This was a concern for Jim as well so he listened carefully to his father's response.

"Yes, Lindz, everybody speaks English in Vermont." Bob chuckled, then paused for a second before saying, "Well, they *do* speak French up north, I suppose, near the border with Canada. I mean, they'd have to, it's so close."

Seeing the concerned looks flickering across her children's faces, Linda interrupted Bob, who had launched into the retelling of the story of French and English colonization of New England and Canada. "Bob, tell them that those are a few people and that they speak both English and French."

"No worries, kids. Everybody speaks English, even the Indians," Bob said.

Indians, thought Jim, worriedly.

Bob spotted a sign, it was the Border to Vermont. "There it is kiddos. We're home now!" Bob said, honking the horn as they passed over the border.

As the Suttons crossed from Massachusetts into Vermont, Jim expected something spectacular to happen. He wasn't sure what. Maybe he expected border guards, or a gate, but it was just a line…not even a line, just a sign welcoming them to "The Green Mountain State." It didn't feel like home to him. It felt like nothing.

"Do you see that?" Asked Bob, gesturing out the window at the vista, devoid of billboards, something that the state of Vermont had abolished.

"I don't see anything, dad," Jim replied, confused.

"That's right Slim-Jim," Dad said with a smile. "Nothing. Isn't it beautiful?"

* * *

Christmas Island sits right on the edge of the Vermont side of Lake Champlain, just south of South Hero Island. One of the smaller islands of the lake, it can be accessed only by ferry from Colchester Point. The Christmas Island Ferry is one of the older ferries operating on Lake Champlain, and it only runs seasonally, until the lake freezes, making passage impossible. The year-round residents cross in winter with snowmobiles or 4x4 trucks, but the average tourist isn't deterred by the risk of trusting the ice to hold. They just don't come - a fact the previous owners of Christmas Town conveniently forgot to tell the Suttons before they bought the concession stand license.

The Suttons arrived at Colchester Point, tired from their long journey from Boston, on August 14th, 1977. They could have made the trip in one day, but Bob's insistence on making a vacation of it had dragged the trip out to almost three.

Bob's enthusiasm was only slightly tarnished from the long trip. The same could not be said for Linda and the kids. As the Suttons drove up to the ferry gate, Linda felt a sense of relief to be close to the end of their journey. As the car pulled through the gate, Linda reflexively clenched her hands. She felt a sense of foreboding, not necessarily dread, but something like guarded anxiety over the unknown. The owners had mailed them photos of Christmas Town, along with the financials for the stand none of them had actually viewed in person. Linda chewed her thumb nervously, buying a home sight unseen was in Bob's character, not hers. After the down payment and closing costs, they had enough for the move and that was just about it. Linda had examined the pictures of the stand and the house that arrived in the mail in a stained manila envelope. The house looked utterly charming, a two-story Victorian-style home, complete with gingerbread fretwork. It was exactly the kind of home Linda had dreamed they would move into. In Cambridge. In *Massachusetts*. Not on a remote island in a small backwater state. She begrudgingly admitted it looked nice. Like Bob said, "You can't beat the commute!"

As the ferry pulled into port, Linda called the kids back to the car. Bob's eyes were wide, sparkling with anticipation as he drummed his fingers on the steering wheel. The metal gangplank came down with a loud slam, and the boat began to disgorge its passengers.

Next to the dock, by a beat-up pick-up truck painted in red and green Christmas colors stood an older gentleman. Fat and balding, the man chose to wear a thin mustache that did nothing to help his weak chin. In the corner of his mouth clung a toothpick that rolled from one side of his mouth to the other as he spoke.

"Hey, there's Glenn Murray," Bob said, waving to the man.

Glenn nodded, got in his truck, making a three-point turn, he began driving away. The Suttons followed him down the paved road, voyaging into the interior of the island.

The Sutton children pressed their faces against the windows as they drove into Christmas Town for the first time. Pine trees lined the road on the way up to the front gate. Painted signs with fanciful elves told visitors to "Come see the home of Santa" and "Feed Santa's Reindeer!" As they approached the gate covered with garland and Christmas lights, Bob noted that some of the bulbs were missing. He made a mental note to tell Mr. Murray. *Pride in your work...* Bob told himself, *...is a virtue.* As they passed through the gates though, the Suttons finally got a clear look at the state of Christmas Town.

The theme park had seen better days. The gravel roads were patchy and uneven from frost heaves. There were weeds in the grass, from infrequent mowing. Most of buildings had faded, peeling paint, and all the cement Christmas figurines were chipped. One concrete elf was missing a hand, though judging by its broad smiling face, he didn't seem to mind as he waved his stump genially in their direction. The pictures they had been sent, in retrospect, had been carefully curated to showcase the best parts of the park. It was admittedly charming but in need of TLC, a *lot* of TLC.

"Isn't this fun? This place has potential, doesn't it?" Bob said, reading the general mood of reticence in the overladed station wagon. The three of them sat mutely, taking in the lay of the land. "Yes, lots of potential." Bob answered his own question rather than letting it hang. "Now, let's see the house."

To Linda's relief, the house was like the photos Mr. Murray had sent, a charming Victorian-style home, nicely constructed with a beautiful lawn and a delightful white picket fence around it. Only one detail was different: it was small. Not in the sense that it lacked rooms, but in the sense that this house was made for someone small. Dwarfs. What Mr. Murray had not included in the photos of their home was anything that could give the Suttons an idea of scale. Just like the rest of the houses in Christmas Town, it was custom built for dwarfs, all the furniture, everything to scale. Linda jaw hung slack in shock.

She opened the door and ducked into the foyer. *This can't be*, she thought. *This, simply can't be.* The incongruity and absurdity of the situation took a while for her brain to reconcile. A dwarf would have strolled into the house and felt immediately at home, Linda being a "normal" person, felt like Gulliver. She half expected a gaggle of Lilliputians to come bounding around the corner. Bob would have more trouble navigating the house than Linda. His head often scraped the ceiling. Bob would grow accustomed to living in this house and would, as a matter of habit, walk around with his head tilted slightly to the right to avoid the low door heights, a habit he would sometimes take to work with him. Sometimes, as people talked to Bob with his head cocked slightly askew, they would subconsciously tilt their heads to match his angle.

Ever the optimist or, perhaps trying to put the best face on a disaster that was entirely his doing, Bob said, "Be it ever so humble, right gang?"

The kids loved it. Linda was too shocked to say anything. It was too late. They had signed the papers and the money was gone. Like it or not, this house was the Suttons' new home.

"Bad news, honey," Bob said walking into the foyer.

"Do you mean more bad news, or the obvious bad news?" Linda said.

"What do you mean?" Said Bob.

"The house...I mean...It's so...so," spluttered Linda, hardly able to get the words out as they all bumped around in her head.

"So charming?" Bob offered.

Linda glared at him.

"Ok, ok. I know," Bob said, taking her hand. "It's not the ideal situation, but we have to make the best of it."

"I'm going to give Mr. Murray the talking-to of his life. He lied, Bob, he intentionally mislead us." Linda wrenched her hand from Bob. "How are we going to live in this...in this...doll's house??"

"I agree. I'll be right at your side. But let's make lemons out of lemonade. Try to make the best of it. Once we unpack, this place will start feeling more like home, ok?" Bob brushed the hair from Linda's face and smiled at her. She gave in a little. She would have words with the Murrays, oh yes she would, but tonight, she could give this one little concession to Bob, let him have his small victory.

"Ok," Linda said. "I love you," she offered to Bob as a laurel.

"Love you too, Babe." He put his arms around her and bent in for a kiss. Just then a phone rang. Bob ran to the phone.

Linda looked outside. The sun was beginning to set. There was no sign of the movers. She walked around the house. The initial shock had worn off a bit, she had to admit it was a beautiful home. Just so very small. She heard Bob's voice raising in volume form the next room. Maybe he was giving it to Mr. Murray, she hoped so.

"Was that creep calling you to gloat?" Linda asked.

"Who?" Bob asked, his brow furrowing.

"Mr. Murray, did he call you? Was that who you were yelling at?"

"Uh. No. It was the movers," Bob said.

Linda felt that knot tighten in her stomach. Why were the movers calling?

"And?"

"Well, honey. It seems like they missed the last ferry of the day." Bob smiled, trying desperately to force jocularity into this awkward situation.

"So, none of our stuff is here," Linda said.

"Only what we brought in the car."

"Wonderful. Just perfect." Linda sat against the wall and slumped down to the floor, emotionally and physically exhausted. She could hear the kids thumping around merrily upstairs. It just made her want to cry. She struggled to hold it back. She didn't want to break down in front of Bob.

"They'll be here on the first ferry tomorrow. I promise." Bob slid down the wall next to Linda. She leaned her head against his shoulder. This was her life now, like it or not.

"Bob?" Linda asked, a thought had suddenly come to her.

"Yes."

"Earlier, when you said there was bad news, how could you have known the movers were late when they just called you?"

"Oh, that wasn't the bad news."

"It wasn't?"

"No."

"Then what was the bad news, Bob?"

"I came from the kitchen. There's no Maple Syrup."

Linda had spent the night tossing and turning on the miniature bed in the master bedroom. It was so small, they had to sleep on it diagonally, with their feet hanging over the edge. It wasn't the discomfort that had kept her awake, rather it wasn't only the discomfort that kept her awake, it was everything. The house, the move, the movers, they had all conspired to rob her of her peace. Crazily enough it was the absence of some stimuli that caused her the most distress. Having lived in a big city, Linda was used to the sounds of cars and people to lull her to sleep, kind of a big city version of white noise. Out here on the island, everything was eerily quiet. She could hear everything in agonizing detail—the creaks and moans of the house settling seemed a cacophony.

She had finally drifted off to sleep when the warm, sweet smells of breakfast woke her from her reverie. The call of "Breakfast! Come and get it while it's hot!" rang through the house. Linda staggered out of bed.

Linda knew that for Bob, scratch breakfast meant opening a box of Bisquick. She walked into the kitchen and it looked like a winter storm had hit. Every counter was covered with a fine dusting of baking mix.

With all of their cooking implements sitting in a truck on the other side of the lake, Bob had been forced to improvise. Bob had re-purposed Lindsey's plastic bucket she used at the beach as a mixing bowl, the little plastic shovel that came with it he further used to beat the ingredients. Again, they had no pans, so after searching and searching, Bob finally struck upon what he seemed proud to tell Linda was his most ingenious improvisation. He had discovered an old snow shovel in the basement. After scrubbing it clean, he held it over the flames as an ersatz griddle. It was this Rube Goldbergian scene that greeted Linda as she walked into the kitchen.

"Take a seat." Bob gestured to the tiny table using the shovel to direct her.

The Suttons enjoyed their first "real Vermont" meal in their real Vermont home eating Bisquick pancakes with something named *Old Cabin Syrup* with margarine, along with orange juice from a concentrate Bob had found in the freezer.

"Yuck," Jim said, spitting out a bit of pancake.

"What's the matter, Sweetie?" Linda leaned over with concern.

"I don't like it," Jim replied.

"What do you mean you don't like it?" Bob said.

"It's too sweet," Jim said, looking down. In fact, the syrup was old, thick and artificial. Bob had discovered the bottle in the pantry, god knows how long it had sat there. Jim was like any kid, he enjoyed sweets, but he never had a sweet tooth.

"*Too* sweet?" Bob stared at Jim. The whole table stood silent. Lyndsey was frozen, mouth full of pancake. Everyone seemed to sense that the mood balanced on the edge of a knife, which way would it fall? "This kid!" Bob proclaimed, grabbing Jim around the neck and tousling his hair. Linda inwardly let out a long sigh of relief.

After the dishes were cleaned Bob announced he was going down to the office. Linda rolled her eyes and said she would stay behind to unpack. The kids followed Bob to see the family business. The three Suttons walked around the bend of the road and the stand slowly came into view. Bob was pleased at what he found.

The pictures of the stand Mr. Murray had sent were exactly what he could see so far. For one it was full-sized. The stand was a charming 60's-style building with a slanted a-frame roof, reminiscent of an International House of Pancakes. The building had red roof shingles and the walls were painted a cornflower blue. There was a covered eating area with benches. Beyond the tables there was a small playground. A layer of fresh red cedar mulch had been recently laid down; the scent pleasantly greeted their noses. Bob removed the keys from a ring attached his belt and unlocked the door. The door protested and creaked as it swung on its hinges. As they stepped into what was to become both work and a home, all three Suttons stopped on the threshold to look around.

It was nicely maintained. Clean. There was counter service, complete with shiny chrome stools that were bolted to the floor. All tables had Formica counter tops. In the corner sat a rotating case for pies if the impulse should strike a customer's fancy

"Not bad," Bob said. "Not bad at all."

There was a souvenir stand in the back that sold bric-a-brac, stuffed animals, and Christmas decorations. As the kids poked around in the gift-shop and the lost-and found bin, Bob walked to the kitchen and flicked on the lights. To his relief, the kitchen was spotless.

"Finally, something going our way," Bob said. He walked into the storeroom to get an idea of the state of supplies. Bob opened the pantry door and looked inside. He grabbed a bag from one of the shelves. Bob reached down into the bag and pulled out a large white onion.

"Hey, Slim-Jim. Let me show you how to make onion rings."

READING THE SIGNS

2000

BORDER TO VERMONT 15

"Jim had told his mother of his summer project months ago, and she had said nothing at the time. As the date grew closer, he was sure she would bring it up, but she had remained silent. He wanted to talk to her about it, to get her blessing.

The week before he was to leave, Jim's mother had called him up and asked him to come help her assemble some new furniture. The request wasn't so unusual, Linda had taken to ask her son from time to time to help her out with the odd job¬—especially, when her arthritis acted up. But the timing was auspicious. He was sure it was because she wanted to talk to him about his trip.

Linda handed Jim an allen wrench. Jim took the tool from his mother and studied the pictogram IKEA instructions she had shoved at him. Linda looked at him impatiently.

She had long ago eschewed the idea dating. She was a striking woman for her age. Jim's mother had never been vain, allowing herself age gracefully and fearlessly. These days her hair was more gray than brown. She wore it in a single braid she swept over her shoulder. She didn't use makeup but one would hardly know it. She still possessed what people called natural beauty, perhaps because she had stopped caring.

Linda had struggled mightily to keep Jim in college. He was not a model student. His grades in high school were average a best, to his mother's continual frustration. The councilors at his high school told her he had the intellect to be a top-tier student but lacked the drive. When Jim's admission letter from Rutgers arrived, Linda breathed a sigh of relief. It wasn't Ivy League, but it was in-state and close to home in Hoboken. He had always had a love of literature and the written word, so he majored in English Literature, with a minor in Education. Linda had threatened to withhold her meager contribution to Jim's education unless he dropped his idea to minor in Philosophy. Linda thought that Jim should have something to fall back upon, as she told him over one particularly contentious Thanksgiving break. Ultimately, she had been right. Jim went on to get his master's in education and found a teaching job at a public school in Brooklyn.

"It's been a long time, Mom." Jim looked from the pile of Ektorp™ pieces of wood and particle board to his Mother's spartan apartment. Ever since his mother had relocated to her Highlands condo in New Jersey it had been more difficult for Jim to make the trip across the river from Brooklyn. His mother had never been sentimental as far as Jim could remember and the apartment reflected that ethos. The walls were white, maybe eggshell, unadorned, save a few store-bought pieces of mass-produced art. There was not one family photo in the condo, not on the walls or the mantle above her gas-fueled fireplace.

"Not long enough, for you apparently." Linda grunted and rubbed her hands. Jim, perhaps in solidarity with his mother's arthritis unconsciously rubbed a faded scar on the palm of his right hand. His mother was stubbornly independent, but increasingly she found it harder to do certain things on her own. She would occasionally ask Jim to do minor jobs, like the furniture he was assembling today open the odd jar of pickles, if he were in the neighborhood.. As Jim sat on the taupe-colored carpet of her floor sorting through the pieces, his mother stood above him, hands on her hips.

"Here's the problem, Mom." Jim gestured to the instructions. The people in the generic drawings always looked so happy to be assembling their IKEA furniture. Just for once, Jim would like to see them arguing with each other after realizing they assembled side A, instead of part B.

"What?"

"We assembled this side *backwards*. See these two little holes in the drawing, they're supposed to be on the back side." Jim gestured to the paper.

"This isn't the back side?"

"No."

"Well, they should have told us then." The microwave dinged to signal the tea had finished heating, and she walked into the kitchen.

"They did mom, we just didn't do it right."

"Maybe they didn't tell it right," she shouted from the other room.

"Maybe," Jim muttered. He stood up and walked into the kitchen. "Mom, about the trip..."

"We're just going to have to start over. Or maybe just return the junk." His mother went to the refrigerator, holding her tea in both hands so she would not drop it.

"I don't want you to worry." Jim put his hand on her shoulder.

"Where is that cream?" His mom placed her tea on the counter and reached into the refrigerator with her right hand, these days it had started looking more like a claw from the arthritis. Her knuckles seemed huge.

"Mom," Jim said firmly. "The trip. I'm going." He tried to hug her but she shrugged him off.

"There it is." She grasped the slender box of creamer with the palms of both her hands, bringing it up to her nose for a sniff before pouring it into her tea. The silence hung in the air. She brought the tea to her lips and took a sip.

"You can go. I'm returning this pile of crap."

"I can finish it, Mom," Jim said.

"Just go." Linda turned to the sink and poured the tea down the drain. "Cream's gone bad."

Jim reached for his keys on the counter and walked to his car He grabbed the handle and started to turn it when he felt a gentle pressure on his shoulder. Jim turned around. His mother stood there. She opened her mouth for a moment as if to say something, then closed it again. Jim nodded and opened the door. His mother leaned into the car.

"Just be careful. You dig around in the past, all you get is dirty," Linda said. She shut the car door and walked back to her apartment without another word.

*   *   *

WELCOME TO THE STATE OF VERMONT

Jim watched the sign grow larger as his rusty maroon Ford Festiva puttered ever closer to the border. It had been 22 years since his family uprooted and resettled in Vermont. Jim had resigned himself to feeling the great weight of the years as he crossed that invisible line. He felt numb, maybe a little disappointed. Jim looked down at the seat next to him and fished through a stack of Map Quest printouts, each labeled with a town name, held together with a black metal binder clip. The car smelled like fast food, crumpled bags on the passenger side, grease-stained and stale, memories of bad choices. He reached down without thinking into one of the bags. He grabbed a Hershey bar and unwrapped it. He put the candy under his nose and breathed deeply. The scent was bio-chemical to him, like pheromones. He devoured the chocolate. It tasted so good, he immediately had another.

Jim Sutton had grown into a young man in the years since he had first crossed that border. He was tall, with brown hair and green eyes. Jim had been naturally thin his whole life, but age and metabolism seemed to be catching up to him. He had noticed his stomach was starting to grow juuust a bit rounder these days, a bill overdue with his terrible diet.

Jim had occasional relationships over the years but none that blossomed into anything serious. In fact, he had just broken up with his most recent girlfriend, which was just the push out the door he needed.

Inspiration had struck while he was in the school cafeteria of all places. It was Friday, pizza day. Jim moved his tray down the line, bypassing the greens and choosing, the pizza. And the tots, and the…there they were: Onion rings. They were hack rings, frozen rings, *corporate rings*, nothing like the ones his father taught him to make. This. Was. It. He would finally write his book, about *these*, about *onion rings*.

Jim planned out the trip for the summer when he'd be off from teaching. He would start at the bottom of the state, crossing into Vermont from New York at Hoosic Falls. He would criss-cross the state, make his way north, skirt the border with Canada then make his way down Lake Champlain, finishing at Christmas Island. Jim would write reviews of the places he visited and the onion rings from the restaurants he would find along the way. It would all be very hip, trendy. He planned a wry tongue-firmly-in-cheek writing style. Vermont was not particularly known for its onion rings, but he planned to use the food as a platform to outline the history and culture of Vermont. Like his current trip, it was about onion rings, but also not. *The Onion Ring Lover's Guide to Vermont* was the title he had finally settled on.

The Festiva creaked and groaned in protest as it strained up a steep hill. *This doesn't bode well*, thought Jim. It would only get hillier and more mountainous from this point. The gears ground loudly as he tried to get the clutch to catch, but the car shuddered and stalled. A pickup truck veered around Jim as he attempted to restart the car. Gravel spun up from the tires of the beat-up Chevy as it used the breakdown lane to swerve around the little maroon car.

"Go back to *New York!*" a voice shouted from the pickup as it sped away. Jim looked at the truck, it had Vermont plates with several faded bumper stickers. A faded SNELLING 90 sticker was stuck fast to the bumper, next to a newer one that read "TAKE BACK VERMONT."

Finally, the clutch popped in place, and the car shuddered its way up the hill.

The Ford Festiva was Jim's rickety, temperamental traveling companion. The gas gauge had stopped working years ago so Jim had to guess how much was in the tank. As a rule of thumb, Jim gave himself about 200 miles between fill-ups. It was a round number—easy to remember. He glanced at the odometer. Time to fill up.

Jim pulled off at the next exit, finding a gas station/store/yoga studio. Underneath a faded 7-Up advertisement hung a hand lettered sign: *Gas, Food & Enlightenment. Drishti Yoga Studio.*

The store was that silver-gray color wood weathers to after being exposed to the elements for too many years without a fresh coat of paint. There were two old-style pumps out in front with a hand-painted corrugated cardboard sign that read "self-serve." The word "leaded" had been scratched out next to the rotating number-style gauge. Another hand-lettered sign on each pump read "CASH ONLY, NO EXCIPTONS PLEASE PAY INSIDE."

The screen door slammed behind Jim. The store was pretty much what Jim had come to expect. Bored teen worker behind desk, check. Beer cooler, check. Overpriced dry goods, check. Freaky yoga mats and paraphernalia, check.

"Jackpot" Jim muttered to himself as his eyes spied the rack he had been searching for. Every gas station has its array of junk food for the discriminating traveler. Truth be told, Jim's trip had been as much fueled by Zingers and Cheetos as it had been by onion rings and his desire to hit the open road. The rack in front of him had chips and candy, with questionable provenance, but Jim was not particular. He passed over the Ever-present Slim Jim section. He had been called "slim-Jim" as a nickname for as long as he could remember. He hated that nickname. He loved beef jerky, but by that name, he could never allow himself to purchase one. It felt like a betrayal.

Jim walked to the counter with his snacks. There was an ice cream freezer in front of the register stocked with Ben & Jerry's. A faded "Factory Seconds, try at your own risk," sign was taped to the inside of the sliding glass door. Jim peered into the frosty case, indeed there were pints of Ben & Jerry's ice cream, and a stack of cookie ice cream sandwiches, with the curious name: Chessters.

Residents of Vermont are privileged to be able to buy cast-offs from the factory. These pints are rejected for various reasons, such as too much air in the ice cream, too little air, or even too many mix-ins. The sign on the freezer was warranted though, because for every Chunky Monkey with extra chocolate, there was a Georgia Peach missing flavor altogether. It was a crap shoot, the Vermonter's version of Russian Roulette.

"Ten on two outside and the snacks as well," Jim said.

The teen looked up from his wrestling magazine. Another handwritten sign on the cash register read, *"CASH, GRASS, OR ASANA, NOTHING IN THE UNIVERSE IS FREE. (INCLUDING KARMA, SO TIP WELL)."* There was a stack of Chakra stickers by the register for sale.

"Yoga?" Jim asked.

He shrugged. "Whatever floats your boat. Or walks your downward dog."

Jim laughed.

"You're not from here, are you?"

"How did you know?"

"New York plates." The teen cocked his head toward the window. The register popped open with a ring, and the boy took out the change and placed it on the counter. He looked back at his magazine.

"Ah, yeah. Just seeing the sights," Jim said,.

"Sights?" The boy put the magazine down. "Nothing to see around here. You're too early for leaf season."

"Actually, I'm doing research for my book." Jim stiffened slightly with pride. "I'm a writer."

"Writer, huh?" The teen replied with a drawl. "Watcher write?"

Jim felt a twinge of excitement mixed with trepidation. He considered himself a writer. He knew he was one, but deep down, the fact that Jim was writing a quirky travel guide with food reviews was kind of embarrassing. For a moment he considered lying. Bracing for disappointment, Jim replied, "I'm writing a book about onion rings."

"You know you're in *Vermont*, right? Why not do a book about maple syrup, or ice cream, or creemees, or somethin'?"

"Because that would be *too* obvious."

"No kidding?" He said. "I love onion rings. Every year at the fair."

Jim smiled. He knew the fair the teen was referring to. *The Champlain Valley Fair and Exposition* is held every year in Essex Junction Vermont, right before Labor Day, marking the end to summer.

"Listen," he said. "What's with all the sauces these days? Nothing beats ketchup as far as I'm concerned."

Jim opened his mouth to explain.

"Hey, you been to Luly's yet?"

"Luly's? No, I've never heard of it." Jim was piqued. This name was not on his list.

"It's a bit off the beaten," he said. "It's so great. Best onion rings I've ever had!" The boy's face became serious. "You gotta go. You just gotta."

"Where is it? I'll definitely put it on my to-do list." He was already writing it in his head: *...I pulled up to the old country store. Little did I know that inside I'd find directions to the best onion rings in Vermont..."*

"It's worth it. Our family stops at Luly's at least once a month." The boy grinned as he gave Jim the directions, his hands moving in concert and contour to the roads he was describing. "Oh man, you're gonna love it!"

Jim grabbed his purchases and walked to the door.

"Good luck!" the teen called. "Oh yeah, and Namaste. I'm sposed' to say that to everyone."

"Namaste to you too."

Jim was energized by the prospect of a hot tip. A few fat raindrops hit his head. He craned his neck, as a gentle rain started to fall. It was that particular sort precipitation that happens on those rare summer days when the sky appears so blue, so bright, and yet it still rains. The delightful incongruity delighted him. He whistled as he filled up the car. Jim sat in the driver's seat as he reached into the glove compartment.

"Where is it" Jim mumbled to himself. Aha! As he pulled his hand out, he could see he found the pen he was looking for.

"What the..." Jim looked at his fingers, apparently the pen had exploded at some point. Sticky black ink now stained his fingers.

"Fuck me." He immediately regretted cleaning the car of its trash. Right now, one of those old greasy napkins, or even an Arby's bag would have been useful. Looking around, all he saw he could use was his maps. Jim reached over to tear off a corner. He tried not to get ink on the rest of the map but still managed to leave some tell-tale smudges. He made a mental note to clean those when he could.

He spied a stub of a pencil. By some miracle, it didn't have ink on it. There was hardly any lead visible, so he used his fingers to pick enough wood away to be able to use it. Jim grabbed the ripped map and wrote in the margin in big block letters:

LULY'S

The summer rain had disappeared as quickly as it came. The roads were wet, but not slick from the brief interlude. He turned on the radio, he was in the mood to sing. Jim was generally a rock aficionado, but he had a dark secret he didn't often share with people. Jim couldn't resist a perfect pop song. So when Britney Spears pop opus *Hit Me Baby, One More Time* came on the radio, Jim found himself singing along with it at the top of his lungs. Jim really got into the first chorus and caterwauled as he drove down the road. He was about to launch into an epic rendition of the second chorus when his car crested the top of a hill. The sight in front of him literally took his breath away. He stopped to pull the car over. Setting the parking brake, he stepped out of the car to get a better look.

From his vantage point on the hill Jim looked over the green valley. A light mist hung in the air. Golden light caught the droplets, illuminating them as if a million lightning bugs had taken wing during the day. The sun was setting, and it was that particular time of day that they call magic hour. The valley shimmered in the golden light. A breeze swept through the clearing. He closed his eyes and listened to the leaves rustling in the breeze. Jim filled his lungs with the fresh earthy smell that comes after a summer rain. He let the moment wash over him. Everything seemed to be lining up just so. The unforeseen tip, the valley below him, this moment. They were signs. He had his doubts about this trip, he had occasionally wondered if it was folly, but as that feeling of contentment and happiness washed over him, he could not help but feel optimistic.

Someone once said, "If you don't like the weather in New England, just wait a few minutes." Rolling across the valley, like a curtain was a wall of water. The blue sky turned gray and ominous in a matter of minutes. It came upon Jim so fast that he was already soaked by the time he ran back to his car.

Jim started the car. The wipers beat back and forth, seemingly doing little to clear the torrent of water pouring over the windshield. Fearing running into another car, he rode the brakes—they whined and squealed in protest. Visibility dropped to only a few feet. Jim slowed the car to a crawl, crossing his fingers that he would not be hit. The car forded the crest of another hill.

Suddenly the rain. Just. Stopped. It was gone, like it never even happened. The valley was sunny and bright, as if a curtain had been drawn back. He glanced in the rear-view mirror. A dark wet wall hung behind him. He had passed through the storm. Jim smiled to himself, and the little car groaned in protest as it climbed over the hill then started down the steep slope to the bottom.

Jim had only taken his eyes off the road for what he thought was a moment, so it was a surprise when he looked through his rain-streaked windshield and standing placidly in the middle of the road was a genuine, 100% Vermont black & white Holstein dairy cow, chewing her cud.

"FUCK!" Jim shouted.

Jim pressed the pedal to engage the brakes and felt almost no resistance. He stomped his foot to the floor and the pedal went down with far too much ease. The brakes were gone. The cow stood in the road, as cows are wont to do, not moving at all, for anyone.

He yanked the wheel, the car fishtailed, hydroplaned, losing control. The cow turned its head as Jim and the Festiva skidded by. They regarded each other cow and man, man and cow—both frozen—as the world seemed to rotate in slow motion. Jim turned the wheel to no avail. He was unable to keep control, and he went skidding off the road, slamming into a roadside sign.

Jim pried his hands from the steering wheel. The car was a mess of notes and papers and trash. Fingers trembling, he found a crushed package of Twinkies. Jim ripped open the wrapper with his teeth and squeezed them into his mouth. He closed his eyes, swallowed, then sighed. Better, he thought.

Jim assessed the damage. The car had come to a rest on the shoulder. He fell to his knees and peered under the car. Jim was no mechanic, but there were parts sticking out that he was sure shouldn't be sticking out. Jim rose from his crouch, took a deep breath and walked to the front of the car. He was relieved to see that only the bumper and part of the front grille were damaged. Cosmetically, the car didn't seem so bad after the collision. However, Jim noted that the same could not be said for what he had collided into. In front of his car lay a broken gilded wooden sign. Jim leaned over and pulled it up, reading the ornate, gilded raised carved letters.

WELCOME TO STRAWBERRY FALLS

(UN)SETTLING IN

1977

Living in a little people house had its fair share of challenges. It was a lovely home. It was, in every way, the house Linda had dreamed that she would one day buy... only it was made for dwarfs. The house was fashioned in the Victorian style. The entryway drew visitors into a beautiful marble foyer that led to the main stairs to the right and a sitting room to the left. It had beautiful hardwood floors with precise maple inlays. There were pocket doors that Linda half-adored, because they were half-sized. In the bathroom, Linda had to lean down under the shower fixture as it came up to her forehead. The house had three fireplaces, all tiny. None of the fireboxes accommodated wood greater than a foot in length. Both Bob and Linda marveled at the kitchen. Where had the builders of this home found fully functional miniature stoves and ovens? Bob and Linda were faced with the unenviable task of fitting their full-sized lives into a half-sized house.

The Sutton children, Jim and Lyndsey, loved the house from the moment they set foot in it. Adults forget what it is like to be small. When you are a child, the world is a constant reminder of what you can and cannot do. In the new Sutton homestead, the children found a world seemingly made just for them. Stairs were no longer a task to labor up. They scaled them while their parents would opt to take them two or four at a stride. At the dinner table, where their legs would once dangle, the children found themselves sitting, feet on the ground, while their parents sat with their knees up in their chests. Everything about this home felt warm and inviting to the kids. While for their parents, it felt cramped and claustrophobic. Bob and Linda had spent a large amount of money on the new business and the move. For the time being, they had to live with it, and in it.

Something else the Suttons hadn't considered was that even though this was Vermont, one of the most northern states, home to ski lodges, sugar shacks, and ice boating, summers could be unbearably hot. These hot spells don't last long, but they happen. Compounding the heat is the humidity... muggy, sweaty, dripping humidity that at times makes Burlington feel more like Tampa. The Suttons had sold *all* of their fans in the garage sale. Bob was convinced they would not need them, a decision he regretted by the second night in their new home.

"Why am I wet?" Bob exclaimed as he woke up, the sheets sticking to his tee shirt. He staggered to the bathroom and filled a glass of water.

"What's the matter?" Linda groaned.

"It's too hot," Bob complained.

"Crack a window."

Bob opened the window but there was no perceptual change to be felt. Living on a small island, it might not be unreasonable to assume the breezes off the water might keep it temperate. Sadly, the surrounding woods insulated the house from any cooling lake effect. Bob staggered back to bed, banging his shins on the diminutive bed frame. He fell back into bed with a thud. That night, the Suttons would be introduced to another one of Vermont's charming amenities not found in any tourist pamphlet or guidebook.

Linda was the first to be struck. She had been unable to fall back asleep after Bob had opened the window. She lay on her back, staring at the ceiling when she first heard them. These creatures had the innate ability to seek out their prey. Guided by the very breath of their victims, seeking out blood. She heard a high-pitched whine in her ear. Linda sat straight up in bed. *Mosquito!* Linda found that a squadron of them had reconnoitered their way in through a hole in the screen. The Suttons spent the next few nights in agony until he patched all the holes.

Linda scratched at bug bites as she started unpacking the boxes that had finally arrived from the movers. Bob had informed Linda that the house came fully furnished, so they wouldn't need their beds or chairs. Inwardly cursing the stupidity of buying a furnished house sight-unseen, Linda found their plates and began to put what she could of her life back in order.

Looking around the kitchen, she saw the remnants of their first breakfast in their new home and their new life. There was a stack of dishes in and beside the sink. The syrup and pancake residue had begun to harden aggressively after a day in the sink. Everything Linda touched seemed to be sticky. Once again, Linda wondered how she had let herself fall into the role of housekeeper. Linda resolved that she'd clean up the worst of the mess, she would leave *some* dishes soaking in the sink.

"What am I the fucking maid?" Linda said. The whole ordeal was exacerbated by the half-size design of the kitchen. By the time she had finished working, all of the dishes were clean. *Sometimes it's best to just get it done,* Linda thought wearily. She would let Bob skate *this* time, but next time he'd pull his weight.

Even though it was 1977, the Sutton's home had not had one of its appliances upgraded, which meant no dishwasher or garbage disposal. By the time she was done, Linda wasn't sure if she was dripping from the water in the sink or from the humidity of the house, which was almost tropical. Linda leaned on the top of the fridge, opened the freezer door and stuck her head inside.

"Great," Linda grumbled. "It's taking on frost."

Linda had it with cleaning up Bob's messes for the day. The movers were due to arrive. What's the point really? All their furniture was full sized. It would never fit into their current home. If they put their queen-sized bed into their bedroom, it would literally just be that a bedroom, no room for anything but bed. They did have a garage, any pieces that were too big would go there for now, until she figured out something better. She resolved to put away some of the boxes they had already brought via the Volkswagen. They were sitting in the foyer. She had tripped over them twice already,

She walked back to the stack of boxes, found one marked LINDA and opened it. Inside she found her diploma from Boston University. Linda held her diploma in hands pruned from hours of dish washing and scrubbing. She stared at the name on the diploma. *Linda Elizabeth Boyd.* That was the name of a person that didn't exist anymore. Who was she? What had happened to her? What would that Linda think of Linda Sutton? Would she be disappointed? Happy? Disgusted? Linda had no answer.

Linda walked upstairs to the room that she and Bob had designated as the study. Linda found a hammer and a nail and hung her diploma on the wall. She stood there for a while and looked. It was only after she brushed the hair from her face that she realized she was crying.

*   *   *

After Bob and the kids had taken in the lay of the snack-shack that was to become their business, Bob set about getting it up and running. It was late in the summer season, but the park was still open, and people began to trickle in with the first ferries. Bob had grand visions of this being a family affair. One day he'd be in the kitchen with teenage Jim while Linda and Lyndsey worked the front as servers and hosts. Those dreams would have to wait until they grew older. For now, Bob would have to get along with employees. It would eat into his profits to be sure, but there was just no way around it.

"Daaad…" Bob felt a tug on his apron. Jim and Lyndsey stood by his feet.

"What is it?"

"We're bored. What is there to do?"

"Bored? In *Christmas Town?*"

Jim and Lyndsey silently nodded in unison.

Suddenly, the bell on the screen door clanked—a young woman entered the shop.

"Go play." Bob said. He watched the newcomer.

"Where, Dad?" Lyndsey asked

"I don't know. Go to one of that booth in the back. I'll be with you in a bit."

The young woman stared at Bob.

"And do what?" Jim asked.

"I don't know. Color?" Bob said. He grabbed a couple packs of crayons and butcher paper and shoved them into Jim's hands. "Now go. And watch your sister."

The young woman was starting at him, arms crossed defiantly.

"What?" Bob said to her.

"Me and Paco, we've got jobs here. Mr. Murray said so."

"Oh yeah, of course you do." Bob smiled and held out his hand to her. "We need all the help we can get." Bob thought that he would relish the day when he fired this one. Bob had never been the boss. But deep down inside there was a part of him that yearned to have power over people. "My name's Mr. Sutton, but you can call me Bob."

She took off her jacket, revealing a fading candy-striped uniform. She pointed to her name tag. "Audrey," she said. "I don't work the grill, that's Paco." Audrey reached behind the counter and pulled out an apron and check pad. "I don't work weekends. We get paid every two weeks, okay?" She walked away.

The door rang out again. Bob assumed the shirtless man in the doorway was Paco. He was in his late twenties, had long hair, mutton-chop sideburns, and rose-colored sunglasses perched on the nose of his face.

The man stood there without a stitch of clothing on his tan, muscular torso, balancing what was certainly a red rolled joint behind his left ear. "Hey man," the young man said with a smile. "They call me Paco. I'm your grill man." Bob stared at the outstretched hand for a moment before shaking it. "Did Audrey give you the drill, man? Whoa, 'grill man, drill man' heh." Paco gestured toward the server. "We're strictly weekdays and we get paid, like, every other." Paco leaned against the counter. "And, like, if we don't get paid, we don't show. Ass, grass, or cash, I don't work for free, man." He grabbed an apron and strolled into the kitchen.

Bob "You will be wearing a hairnet, won't you?"

"I feel you, man, I feel you." Paco looked out of the order window, smiled and laughed then went back to readying the grill, still sans hairnet.

The bell on the shack door rang out again. A short man in a sweater with a bad toupee walked in. "Where's the bathroom?" he asked.

Audrey looked up from doodling on her pad. "Oh, yeah. I don't do bathrooms either. You're gonna have to clean them yourself."

The bell rang out again. To Bob's relief, it was a customer. He filled the cup of coffee and came back *twice* to refill. The gentleman finished and left a 12-cent tip. Bob scooped the money off the counter and moved toward the register.

"Hey!" cried Audrey, watching from across the counter. "We pool tips here, Bob!"

"I'm the boss, Audrey. You've got to stop telling me what to do.". He took the change and dropped it into a glass jar marked, "Tipping is not a city in China."

It was slow for the rest of the morning, and Bob started watching the clock.

Things got busier toward noon. Park staff, as well as patrons, came in with the lunch rush. Things were finally settling into a nice groove.

Then Bob felt a tug again on his apron. "We're bored." Jim and Lyndsey were back.

"Again?".

"I wanna go home." Lyndsey said.

"I know Lyndz," Bob said. "But daddy's got to work."

"Wanna go home." Lyndsey said.

"I know sweetheart, but daddy's got to make money."

"WANNA GO HOME!" Lyndsey shouted. The stand grew quiet as every eye fell upon the Suttons. Bob grinned.

"I wish we could, darling," Bob said, conscious of the fact that this was now a performance.

"I WANT MOMMY!" Lyndsey shouted. Tears flooded her eyes. Jim looked down at the floor.

"Please honey, not now." Bob said.

"NOW!!" Lyndsey shouted, punctuating it with a stamped foot, tears rolling down her cheeks.

"It's all right," Bob cooed. "You're okay. You're just tired."

"I'm NOT tired!" Lyndsey sobbed "I want mommy!"

"Jim!" Bob hissed. "Do something about your sister."

Jim had no idea what to do. Jim was eight years old.

"*Please!*" Lyndsey implored.

Bob stroked his daughters hair and looked around the stand for some sort of sympathy. A woman sitting at the counter shook her head.

"Ok, how about this: I'll make you guys some food, would that be better?"

"No" Lyndsey sobbed.

"What can I do. Do you want a toy, how about a toy?"

"Two?"

Her red eyes looked up at Bob, hopefully.

"Two?" Bob asked, "I don't know…" Lyndsey squeezed her eyes again, tears started to come Fine, yes. Two, just please stop."

Lyndsey sniffled, smiled and wiped her runny nose on the sleeve of her jumper.

"What about me?" Jim asked.

"What about you?" Bob yelled. Jim took his sister's hand and walked back to the back booth.

"It's ok, everybody!" Bob said merrily. "Everything's ok." He stood up, grabbed a rag and began to wipe off the counter, eager to avoid the stares of his customers and employees. Bob scanned the counter as he wiped it, and that's when the dwarf walked in and took one the red vinyl stools at the counter.

He had striking ice-blue eyes and brownish-blonde hair. His hands were stubby and rough, from a life of hard work. He looked to be in his 30s.

"Hey, you must be one of the elves here at Christmas Town." Bob held out his hand to greet his presumed fellow employee.

The man looked up from the menu. Bob could see there was a burning anger behind those piercing eyes. "And you must be the fool who bought this ridiculous money pit. I'm not an elf. I'm not a gnome or a piece of scenery." He placed the menu on the counter. "I am the maintenance man here. If you wonder what that is, I am the man who makes things run. I am the one who keeps this broken-down place from falling apart. That's who I am. *You* are the guy who calls me when your traps clog, your pipes freeze, and your roof leaks."

Audrey walked by, laughing, and slapped the dwarf on his back.

"I'm Nick. Nick Summers." Nick held out his stubby hand toward Bob. "It's okay, I don't bite."

"Bob Sutton. I'm sorry for the—" Bob couldn't figure out what to say next.

"You have no idea how difficult it is to work here, with people who look the way *you* do." said Nick. "Sometimes, the children point, you know? Ham sandwich."

"What?" Bob said.

"I'll take the ham sandwich, Bob."

"God, yes. Ham sandwich, right away. You want cheese on that?"

"Swiss, with mustard. Rye."

"Right away," Bob said.

Jim had watched the exchange between his father and the dwarf. Now, he couldn't stop looking. Suddenly, Nick's blue eyes met Jim's. Jim quickly looked down. After a while he dared to lock up. To his horror, Nick was still looking right at him.

Nick smiled. He held up one of his fingers, then gestured to a saltshaker. Jim leaned forward. What is he doing? Jim thought. Nick gestured to each of his arms and made a show of pulling one cuff of his sleeves, then the other. He picked up a napkin, placed it over the saltshaker. Using a knife as a wand, he tapped the top of the napkin. Then he pulled it away and the salt shaker was gone. Jim clapped. Nick nodded and gestured for Jim to look down. Jim looked down. Sitting in front of him was a saltshaker.

Jim looked up from the trick with a smile on his face only to find Nick had himself disappeared from the diner.

OE

2000

The tires seemed to be in good shape, and the engine didn't appear to be damaged. The majority of the destruction seemed to be limited to the bottom of the car.

Unbidden, a conversation entered Jim's head. "Why don't you bring a cell phone, Jim," his mother said. "I'd just feel so much better knowing you had one in case of emergency."

Jim had scoffed at her. Cell phones were a nuisance. They interrupted in his classes. What kind of kid could afford a cell phone? What kind of parents got their kids a cell phone? But now he needed one.

"What to do?" Jim said. Again, talking to himself. He looked back up the hill. "When's the last time I saw another car? Never."

He had two choices: Wait for someone to drive by or strike out on his own. The benefits of staying put was definitely attractive. The only thing was taking the risk of no-one happening upon him, then he'd have to spend the night in the woods *and* set out to find help.

"I'm such a fool." Jim said. "And an ass. I'm a foolish ass. Why did I ever think that anyone would want to read a book about onion rings? Onion rings? Seriously??"

Suddenly he heard honking. To his surprise he saw an old beat-up tow truck rattling up the road. It looked like it was about to break down. Jim's car looked more road-worthy than the clanking assemblage of rust and shaking metal that approached him.

The driver looked to be in his late teens to early twenties. His shoulder-length brown hair was swept back from his face in locks that seemed to be either greased or gelled.

"Did you do that to the sign?" he yelled out the window.

Jim sheepishly nodded. This made the young man laugh out loud.

"They are gonna have a shit-fit over that, man!" he said. "They met for months on that fucker. Committees. All that bullshit. Well, come on stranger, get in. You're in luck, I've got the only garage for twenty miles. We'll swing back and get your car, see what we can do to get her up and running."

Jim climbed into the cab of the truck. The inside looked as nice as the outside. The dusty upholstery appeared to be vintage to the Eisenhower administration. The springs squeaked as he sat in the bench seat. The windshield had a crack that meandered in a lackadaisical journey across the whole of the glass pane. Fuzzy dice and a set of metal dog-tags hung from the rear-view mirror.

The man hoisted Jim's car. "Alright then. Off we go!" The truck shuddered and rattled under the new weight of the Festiva. "Come on sweetheart." The mechanic spoke sweetly to the truck. The clutch caught and the truck stalled. "It's ok, don't hold out on me" the mechanic cooed, stroking the dashboard, almost sensually. "Come on, give it up…"

Jim was revulsed. To his shock the truck seemed to respond to his ministrations. The engine settled and puttered merrily.

"That's my girl." The mechanic winked at him.

Jim clutched the door handle.

"Where were you headed, stranger? I'm Dodge, by the way," said the man, extending a hand.

Jim took the stranger's grease-stained hand, shook it and heard himself saying, "James, Jim Sutton at your service."

"Yeah," said Dodge, with a snort. "Your service, HA!" and glanced back at the road. "Not too far now."

"New Yorker, huh?" Dodge said.

"Yes, Brooklyn," Jim said.

"I won't hold that against you."

"Uh, thanks."

"So what's wrong with her?"

"A cow," he said. "A cow jumped out across the road, I swerved to avoid it. I don't know what happened, the brakes didn't work, and I lost control trying to stop the car."

Dodge nodded sagely. "Cow. Jumped. Ok, they'll do that. Could be brake fluid's gone." Then he smiled at Jim. "Could be something else, could just be *OE*." He shifted the truck expertly. "Seen a lot of OE in these parts. Must be the weather. It can cause the OE to really act up."

"Can it be fixed?" asked Jim nervously.

"Anything can be fixed, bro." Dodge stood up and smiled, "for a price."

Jim looked out the window at the trees speeding by, wondering how much it was going to cost. When people asked him what kind of car he drove, Jim liked to change the subject. It had been a graduation gift from his mother. And he was embarrassed by it. It was ugly. And small, so small. Too small, like a half-car. He felt like a giant in it. The steering wheel practically brushed his knees when he turned.

"What brings you round here, anyway?" asked Dodge. "Leaf season's a-ways off yet."

"I'm a writer," Jim said.

"Writer? What kind?" There was a slight waver in Dodge's smile, he gripped the wheel just a little tighter.

"I'm writing a tour book on Vermont. It's about onion rings."

Jim expected the usual follow up questions. None came. In fact, no other conversation between the two occurred for the remainder of the ride. The tow truck crossed into the town proper of Strawberry Falls.

Jim had visited many small towns in the green mountain state. Strawberry Falls was like many of them in most aspects, with the exception of its exceptionalism. Everything was perfect. No detail was overlooked. From the red barn on the hill, to the black and white Holsteins that grazed on a hillside, to the brand new tractor that puttered by them on the way into town. Jim would have imagined it unbelievable , if it were not in front of his very own eyes to witness. It was the very model of a picturesque New England Village. All the street signs were custom, wrought iron with white enamel letters. A QUINN STREET sign directed them, with a fanciful arrow, toward a bridge leading into the town proper.

There had been a Quinn in Strawberry Falls as long as there had been a Strawberry Falls. And Strawberry Falls was founded before there even was a state of Vermont.

In 1760, Ethan Allen journeyed through the region looking to profit off of the New Hampshire Land Grants issued by the Governor of New Hampshire. It had once been Abenaki territory, but being on the losing side of the French and Indian war had its consequences. It was now up to England to parcel out the land.

Ezekiel Quinn, a member of Allen's surveying party, fell in love with a parcel of land south of Chittenden county tucked in between the valley of two ridges of hills. He elected to stay behind, establishing the town of Strawberry Falls. The town got its fanciful name from the falls of the Willoughby River, which ran through a green valley full of wild strawberries. Ironically, strawberries, as a cash crop, never worked in Strawberry Falls.

Years later, Ethan Allen returned to Strawberry Falls, seeking out his old friend Ezekiel. Allen was organizing a group of fellow patriots he dubbed with the sobriquet the "Green Mountain Boys" to fight for the independence of a new state that was to become Vermont. Quinn answered the call of his future country and left to fight the British. Ezekiel died during the capture of Fort Ticonderoga, but he left behind a son, Johnathan, in Strawberry Falls.

From the years of 1771 through 1791, Vermont was its own republic with its own government and even its own currency, locally called Vermont Coppers. Today many Vermonters look back at this time fondly. Nonetheless, in 1791, Vermont became the 14th state, the first outside of the original thirteen colonies.

In 1838, Jonathan Quinn commissioned the construction of a textile mill astride the Willoughby River. When the Quinn Mill was sold in 1902 the new owner renamed the factory The Mary Tapplan Sloat Textile Mill, after his wife. The little town of Strawberry Falls thrived as the Sloat Mill grew to employ over two hundred people.

Dodge's ramshackle tow-truck chugged and rumbled over covered bridge that crossed the Willoughby river. It was the kind of covered bridge one would find in a Vermont calendar. On the left the river tumbled over a fall. Below the falls, the river continued down to a valley. On the right, the river snaked its way around a bend. Some local had tied a rope to one of the numerous maple trees that lined the river. Perfect for swingin.'

The Sloat mill sat at the bend of the river. The red brick edifice jutted out into the river, an interloper into the natural flow of the water. The mill was designed to capture the energy of the water that rushed by it on its journey towards the southern border of Vermont (and ultimately the state of Massachusetts).

Dodge drove through the town, past a mix of colonial buildings and Victorian manors. The streets were lined with maple trees that regally towered across the lane, their green leaves reaching toward heaven. This was no town in decline. Strawberry Falls appeared to have escaped the blight that decimated so many rural communities in the 1970s. To the contrary, the town was charming and seemed to be thriving. All the houses were pretty and just as neat as pins, no peeling paint or a cracked window to be seen.

Everyone's lawn was emerald green, maybe too perfect.

Finally they reached Norman Auto Body. There were neat stacks of tires in front two bays. Inside, up on one of the lifts was a green Subaru Forester. A mechanic brandishing an angle grinder worked below the car, shielded by a welder's mask. Sparks showered down, dangerous angry lightning bugs in search of an explosion. There were various nondescript puddles on the floor, including the one the mechanic was standing in. Jim mused it *could* be water, or it might be gasoline. He did not want to hazard a guess. Jim could see beyond the building, to the high chain link fences that encircled the auto body shop. Inside the penned in lot were scrap cars, old motorcycles and other various items in different states of rust and decay. Behind that green fields of *something*? Jim couldn't tell from his vantage point.

The fence bore a weather worn "BEWARE OF DOG" sign. Jim looked closer. Indeed, there was a sleeping German shepherd lying against the chain link. At first Jim thought it was dead. He stared at it for what seemed an age. *It's not moving. I haven't seen that dog move in a minute. That is a dead dog.* Suddenly, the beast snorted, waking itself. From what? Sleep, coma, the underworld? The dog sniffed the air, eyes still closed. It groggily rose to its feet and shambled up to the fence.

"Hey'a Kaiser Bill, you a good boy?" Dodge reached into his pocket. He fished out a Baby Ruth bar and fed it through the holes in the chain link fence, wrapper and all.

"Hey!" said Jim, "You can't feed that to a dog! It's got chocolate, it will kill him!"

Dodge turned back to look at Jim. "You don't know nothing," then turned back to the dog. "Nothing can kill old Bill here."

Kaiser Bill would have perplexed scientists, as he would eat almost *anything*. One time Bill ate a whole box of chocolate bars that Dodge ordered to refill the garage candy machine. The only side effects were an upset stomach and a wicked case of the trots.

Jim thought that maybe Dodge was right. This was a hulking mass of a dog, and as Bill swallowed the candy bar, wrapper and all, Jim could see the badges of a long life as a scrapper. The dog bore a lifetime of scars all over his body. Including one peculiar scar that traversed his face across one of his eyes, an eye that now had a pearlescent quality, pale and milky white. Jim had a feeling that whatever conflict resulted in those scars probably left Kaiser Bill's opponent in *worse* shape. The moth-bitten and worn dog, having finished his treat, laid back down on the ground with a hearty thump.

"Bill don't look like much," Dodge said. "But he's got spark when it counts." Dodge kicked the fence, smacking the dog it its face. Kaiser Bill growled at

Dodge and bared his fangs as he turned his good right eye to face Jim.

"Fucking dumb ass dog." Dodge said and lurched at Bill, who recoiled slightly. "That's right." Dodge said with a smirk.

"Um, nice dog," said Jim warily. Kaiser Bill did not growl but instead looked away from Jim, closed his eyes, and tucked his head down for a nap. Jim wasn't sure whether to be relieved or insulted that Bill did not regard him a threat. *Could dogs play mind games?* He wondered.

"Alright pal, let's get her up, then we'll figure out the damage." Dodge shot Jim a wicked smile. "Wait inside. There's coffee if you want it."

Jim glanced around to the waiting room. The term "waiting room" may have been too generous. The front room included the register and the desk. There were a couple of old plastic chairs sitting next to some end-tables with some predictably old magazines. Against the wall, there was a coffee pot brewing what Jim hoped was fresh coffee. The only TAB-branded soda machine Jim had ever seen sat in the corner as pink as Pepto. It had been stocked with both Coke *and* Pepsi products in defiant disregard to brand loyalty.

An ancient candy machine caught Jim's eye. It was the kind that had pull knobs. Aha. He stared at the front. There was an AbaZaba bar! Jim was pleasantly surprised to see the candy, as it was largely unknown outside the western part of the United States. He fished around his pocket for change. Finding the correct amount, he plunked the coins in the machine. Jim felt a satisfying thud as he pulled the knob. KA-CHUNK. The yellow and black checkered AbaZaba bar came flinging down. Jim looked at his change again. Yes! He had enough to buy another.

Dodge stuck his head around the corner. "Ok, Buddy, ass is in the air. We got a few questions for you. Come on back."

Jim followed Dodge into the garage. The Festiva was up on the lift as promised. The front tires seemed to be hanging at angles more askew than they should.

The other mechanic stood under a green Subaru Forester, looking up at the undercarriage, the visor of the welding mask pushed back on their head.

"Who taught you to drive, sport?" the mechanic said in a voice that was higher than what Jim expected. The incongruity bounced around Jim's head, an answer in search of a question. Meanwhile, the mechanic turned around, and she said to Jim, "Because whomever it was, they should be *shot*, or at least imprisoned." Jim stood there struck dumb, face-to-face with the most striking blue eyes he had ever seen, certainly the most attractive mechanic he had ever met.

ROUTINE MAINTENANCE

1977

The Suttons found themselves living in two worlds. During the day, Christmas Island buzzed with people and activity, but after hours, they had the island to themselves. Few people live year-round on Christmas Island and for good reason. The bungalows on the north side, while charming, were built for summer tourists, not to withstand the long Vermont winters. More importantly, the only way to the island is by boat. Sure, some locals would attempt to swim to it from time to time, more often than not under the influence of a sixer or two. Over the years more than one teenager met their fate in the cool clear waters of Lake Champlain misjudging how challenging a swim it truly was.

Deep in the winter, when Lake Champlain ices over, the ferry stops operation until the spring thaw. Then the only ways on and off the island are iceboat, ice skates, driving, or walking across the ice—all dangerous.

Nevertheless, Christmas Town stays open *all* year to take advantage of any tourists around the winter holidays. If one is determined enough to venture to Christmas Town after the lake has iced up, privately owned iceboats and trucks shuttle those brave souls to the island for a small fee. There is no postal service to the island. Christmas Town, and those who live on the island, got their mail via a post office box on the Burlington side of the lake. There is also no school on the island, which meant that the Sutton children had to take a ferry. The Suttons were aware of this before they moved. What was not disclosed was that the ice would inevitably shut down the operation of the ferry, a fact that spurred just one of the many arguments the Suttons had with the Murrays.

The Murrays didn't live on the island. Mr. Murray hardly set foot on the island any more than he needed. He subcontracted a large portion of the operations of Christmas Town to various parties. A shrewd businessman, Murray required a franchise fee from every vendor. Each month on the first, Mr. Murray would take the ferry or in ice-bound times he'd drive his pickup truck and demand his cut of the profits. It did not matter whether it was a fat or lean season, Murray never missed a month.

Every morning during the school year, when the lake was ice free, Linda Sutton would wake up at 5:30am to get her children ready to take the ferry to school on the mainland in Burlington. Jim was old enough to enroll in grade school. Jim and Lyndsey would climb into their mother's red Volkswagen station wagon drive onto the ferry. In the first weeks living on the island, they would all get out of the car to look around as the ferry puttered across the lake. Eventually the novelty wore off. More often than not, they sat in the car. On more than one occasion, they all fell asleep, the loud toot of the ferry horn waking them when they reached the other side.

Lyndsey was still one year away from Kindergarten, but Linda found a pre-school in Burlington that would take her for half the day. Linda had become friends with Jane Sprague, another mother at the pre-school, who picked Lyndsey up in the morning at the dock in exchange for some passes to Christmas Town.

Jane stood beside her metallic green Gremlin, waving to Linda and family as the ferry pulled into dock. She held her son Jack, who was also waving. Not as happily as his mother but dutifully waving.

As Linda walked toward Jane, she spied Mr. Murray leaning on his truck. He was scowling. Was it the first already? thought Linda. Linda and Mr. Murray did not like each other. After the discovery of their miniature home on the island, Linda had let Murray how she felt. Mr. Murray said that he had given as much information as he was ethically and legally required. "A contract's a contract" Mr. Murray grumbled. In the time she had been on the island, Linda had heard "a contract's a contract" so many times that she swore she would sock the next person who said it.

Bob asked Linda if she could "let it go."

"Let it *go*, Bob? This man cheated us. He lied to us. We sunk all of our savings into this." She gestured to all of the house. "*This*." After the confrontation, Mr. Murray refused to acknowledge her presence, except when collecting his franchise fee.

Bob spent most of his time at the stand, unable to afford additional help. Weekends were the worst for the Suttons, especially Linda. The care of the children fell on her shoulders. Bob dared not dream of taking time off during the busiest time of the week. Bob worked all day, every weekend, so Linda was obligated to entertain the kids during those hours.

It was not the life that was promised when they moved. Bob and Linda hardly saw each other anymore. Their sex life had dwindled to almost nothing. They would tumble into bed exhausted, sometimes not saying one word to each other as they drifted off into unconsciousness.

Linda handed Lyndsey off to Jane and turned to face Mr. Murray. She noted how his body language changed as she approached. Calm, she told herself. Don't sink to his level, his low, rotten, scummy, way, way down deep level. She forced her face into what she hoped was a bright smile. "Good Morning!"

"Mornin', Mrs. Sutton," Mr. Murray said. This was another thing that drove Linda mad. Mr. Murray insisted on addressing her as Mrs. Sutton, never Linda. He had no problem calling Bob, "Bob," because Bob was a man.

"You got the fee for me here an' now, or do I have to take the trip?"

Anger grew in Linda's stomach as she felt her head get hot. Calm down Linda, don't give him the satisfaction.

"Bob's got your fee at the stand."

Bob had sold the family on being masters of their own fate, but franchisees at Christmas Town were masters of worthless plots.

"Next time maybe bring it. Save us both some time," Mr. Murray said, and he turned to walk back to his truck. Linda opened her mouth to argue, but she caught herself. He wasn't worth the fight. She just wanted to get back home.

The house required far more repairs than either Bob or Linda had anticipated before they bought it. Linda had taken to frequenting the public library in Burlington. She immersed herself in the home improvement section. Hiring a contractor was out of the question, and Bob was tied up in the business. So, the maintenance had fallen on her. She had diagnosed several major problems already. The brick in the foundation needed to be pointed. There was dry rot setting into the woodwork, including most of the porch. The paint was peeling. It easily came off in ribbons of brittle chips when she ran her finger along the clapboard. Linda was certain that the paint contained lead. Thinking about the lead paint her kids might be inhaling had kept her up for two straight nights.

Linda pulled the family car back onto the ferry to make the return trip to Christmas Island. She had no intention of staying in the car, since it was right next to Mr. Murray. She got out, making sure to avoid eye contact. But she could feel his eyes on her, boring into the back of her head. She would not look at him, she would not give him the satisfaction.

As she plunked change into the coffee machine, she felt a pang of guilt. There was a pot of coffee back at the house. With their money troubles, this small indulgence felt extravagant. She drank her coffee, consoling herself with the knowledge that she had paid for it with her money, not Bob's. Linda made a little extra cash on the side babysitting or taking in laundry for the other vendors on the island. She never told Bob about her mad money. It gave her some consolation that she had a rainy-day fund, small as it was.

Bob, Linda thought. Even though she was frustrated by this new and complicated life, she did feel sorry for him. Bob was a virtual prisoner to his job. Owning his own business and being the boss had proven to be harder than Bob anticipated. He spent too much of his time working the tables and grill, which left almost no time for clean-up and bookkeeping. Since it was the end of the summer season at Christmas Town, visitor attendance was slowing. Mr. Murray had assured him that it would pick up around November. That was little solace to Bob now. Under normal circumstances Bob would have the profits from a full summer to get through the leaner times.

Mr. Murray had sold Bob the concession right after the plum time of year, pocketing most of the money that would have gone to the bottom line. Compounding the pain, was the fact that the other islanders who worked at the park were not friendly. A comparison of last year's snack stand numbers showed a significant gap. As hard as Linda tried to ingratiate herself and the family to her fellow Vermonters, she felt that they were failing some inexplicable Vermonter test. Linda hoped they'd pass it soon or it meant food stamps.

Linda pulled off the ferry and watched Mr. Murray's truck head toward the snack stand.

Leaf season had arrived on Christmas Island. They didn't get many leaf-peepers traveling to Christmas Town. There were maples on the island but pine trees dominated. But when families grew tired of the pretty colors and the kids started complaining, Christmas Town would see some spill-over.

That night Bob informed Linda that there were more people at the snack stand than ever.

"That's great news Bob," Linda exhaustedly replied. "You can hire some more help now, right?"

"I wouldn't go that far. I'm stretched thin, but we can manage."

"Bob, I'm stretched, and no we can't," Linda said, "manage."

"Okay, I might be overstating profits a bit." Bob nervously smiled. "By my figures, we'll just have to shine on a bit longer, live off the profits until we hit the Christmas Surge. If all goes well, yeah, I think we can hire a hand. Maybe two."

Linda felt her spirit deflate. She had held onto hope for so long that hope itself was what kept her going. The only thing that made her feel worse was when Bob had mentioned the Christmas Surge. My god, Linda thought, Christmas is coming.

Linda knew their precarious financial situation would not afford them to buy many presents for Jim and Lyndsey this year. Lyndsey was too little to know what was normal for Christmas morning, but Jim was eight. He'd notice the dearth of presents. The thought of her little boy asking why Santa gave so few presents this year filled her with dread and made her stomach hurt. So long rainy-day fund, Linda thought. That little voice in her head had an answer. But isn't that what the fund is for? She could accept this logic, but it seemed like she was stealing from herself. Linda had become increasingly impatient with Bob and their new life. Although she had agreed to come here, it felt like it was Bob's deal, Bob's debacle. She was paying the price for his folly. They all were.

Linda had become industrious under the mantle of handyman (handy*woman*). In the 1970s, the idea of purchasing a brand new starter-home in the suburbs lost its luster. The new generation established their claim to the present by reclaiming the past. The genesis of this renovation revolution was mostly financial. It was cheaper to find a fixer-upper and bring it back to life. The future would be built on the bones of the past. Even with the boomers valiantly fighting to restore these pieces of Americana, many fell to the wrecking ball. It was here that Linda scavenged for parts to fix up her home after dropping Lyndsey off at daycare during the weekday.

Linda became a fixture around the salvage yards. She could sort through the waste like a miner and come out with gems. She not only found rails and clapboard but also a hand-turned post that was *perfect* to replace the rotten one on the porch. Linda found glass doorknobs, gilded hinges, and fancy dust corners for the stairs (a luxury upgrade of the era that allowed for easier sweeping).

Linda found she had an eye for sorting gems from junk. She became a connoisseur of restoration and brought her own hammer and pliers to pry hand forged nails from old useless wood. Even though these little touches were unnecessary, no one would really notice the nails, Linda would. It made her feel useful. The junk dealers and salvage yards were glad to be rid of what they saw as garbage. Linda hardly knew it, but she was a trailblazer. Junk yards had yet to catch up to her vision. They didn't see they were casting aside gold. She had an affinity for the work. It kept her mind off her life. Junk therapy.

Linda looked longingly at the pile by the garage. The best stuff she would bring inside to clean up and prepare for immediate installation. Linda didn't need to replace the knobs and hinges it their house. Bob never noticed her projects, but Linda did, and it pleased her. The rest of her treasure she covered with a tarp to keep out the elements. The pile grew with each trip. Linda realized that she had more projects than she could do on her own. It didn't matter, because having the materials made her feel better. She was making sure she had something to do, making sure she always had an escape.

AUTO BODY

2000

"So, you had one hell of a tumble, eh sport?"

The mechanic was in her mid-twenties. Jim couldn't stop looking at her blue eyes. Suddenly he was acutely ware that he was staring.

"Looks like you might have gotten a bit of sun as well," she said.

Jim gulped. Any sort of answer got caught by his misfiring brain. If his mother could see him now, she would be furious. From as long as he could remember, Jim's mother had insisted in instilling progressive values in her children.

"Exactly how attached are you to this car?" she asked Jim.

"Freckles," Jim said.

"What?" replied 'Freckles', genuinely taken aback

"Uh, acutely attached to it." Jim stammered, feeling blood rush to his cheeks.

"Are you sure?"

"I need it for my trip. I need it to get back to New York."

"A New Yorker, eh? Well, you're screwed. Were you and the car close?"

Jim felt his panic rising. The book was tumbling out of his grasp. I'll never finish it if I leave now, Jim thought bitterly. "But Dodge said it was something he'd seen lots of times. He said it was OE."

Freckles looked at Dodge with a scornful look. "OE? Really, Dodge, *operator error*?" She threw her dirty gloves at Dodge, who laughed and ducked. They hit him in the side of the face, leaving a greasy black smudge.

"Owww…Fuck you, Cammy!" Dodge shouted.

"*Cammy.*" Her name's Cammy.

Cammy turned to Jim. "Don't mind my little brother. I think he was adopted or maybe dropped on his head. Like, a lot. Let's look at this car. I'll show you."

Cammy grabbed a flashlight. She walked under the car, and Jim noticed for the first time that she had a slight limp. Shining the light under the car, Cammy motioned to Jim. "First things, first. Your axle's broken, clean through. You probably heard a nasty scraping sound. That was your axle dragging on the road. You'd only be pretty screwed if that was the only thing wrong. Brakes are gone as well. So you're not just pretty screwed, you're royally screwed. If I had to guess, the parking brake was engaged. You forgot it was on, right?"

He did not know what to say.

She put her hand on Jim's shoulder. "It happens a lot more than you think. Believe me, you're not the only one."

Jim was distracted by the hand on his shoulder. A voice in Jim's head told him to snap out of it.

"So, we're looking at a snapped axle, brakes and a new spindle for the right front."

Stupid, Jim thought bitterly. Jim had opted out of collision insurance. But he had no choice. He heard himself say, "Ok, let's do it."

Cammy shrugged. "Dodge, get the paperwork."

Cammy faced Jim. "I have to be up front with you on this." She winced. "We don't have the parts. Your car, it's old. I can't just pull a new part off the shelf and I know we don't have these out back in the junk pile." A crestfallen look slid down Jim's face "Wait, wait, wait. This is okay." Cammy interjected. "I do this all the time. Dodge will call around. *Someone* will have it." She smiled at Jim. "It just means that you're stuck here for a while."

Jim swallowed. It was fixable. "How long is 'a while'?"

. "Hard to say, really." She looked at Jim apologetically. "A day at the least, maybe two. It's no problem. I can set you up a nice place to stay! I'll even get you a friends and family rate. I'm really close with the owner."

"That," Jim said, "would be great."

"Dodge!" Cammy shouted. Her brother was writing up the invoice. "Make some calls on the parts and make a run to Rutland or White River Junction, I'm thinking. Take the pickup."

"Aww, can't I just take the tow?"

"No. I might need the tow to move the car from the lift if another job comes in."

"I might be back in time, Cammy. I'm the only one who understands how to run Maisey."

"I understand how to run the truck just fine. Besides, where are you going to put the parts we need?"

"I'll find room."

"*Dodge.*"

"Fine. I'll take the pickup," Dodge said. "Don't blame me if she don't take to someone else driving her."

"The truck will be fine. It's a car, Dodge." Cammy stood in front of her brother with her arms folded. Dodge looked over at Jim. "What's he going to do meanwhile?" Cammy looked at her brother and said, "I'm taking him up to the hotel."

Dodge cocked his head toward his sister, "You're takin' him to the hotel? She's not gonna like it."

"I don't particularly care what she thinks. I think she'd be happy to have a customer, any customer this time of year." Cammy replied.

Dodge's brow furrowed. "If you take him up to the hotel and I have to go on a parts run, there'll be no-one here at the shop. He looks capable of walkin.'"

Cammy put her hands on her hips. "Look around, Dodge. It's not like we're super busy, or even busy at all." She gestured to the Subaru on the lift. "I just finished the oil job. That's it. It's slow. It's rude not to offer him a ride."

"I was just sayin' it's a nice walk, that's all," Dodge sulked. "Are you gonna be a while?" Dodge asked his sister. "I don't think we should be closed."

"The sooner you go, the sooner you'll be back," chided Cammy.

"Alright, *alright*. I'll go. I'll take the stupid pickup." Dodge stalked out of the garage. Jim heard the screech of an engine starting up. A clattering of gravel from wheels starting up fast hit the sides of the garage, making a ruckus as the pickup peeled out of the lot, kicking up dust in its wake.

"Dumbass," she said. She turned to Jim. "Well, you've had quite a day, haven't you? We're not exactly showing you our best side here in Strawberry Falls, are we?"

"It's ok," said. It had indeed been a long day. He just wanted to find a room, any room, and fall asleep.

"C'mon," said Cammy ."I'll drive you up." Cammy stopped to say goodbye to Kaiser Bill. The was a scrap of wrapper dangling from the dog's mouth. "Hey! Who gave Bill a candy bar?"

"Uh, I think it was your brother," said Jim nervously.

"That asshole. He's going to *kill* that dog." She bent down reaching through the chain link with her fingers to scratch Bill's scarred shout. "Bill's one of the last things left I have of my Dad. He's nigh indestructible, Bill is. But he's not immortal." The dog leaned into the scratching. Jim saw his tail slowly gain speed into a full wag. "Yes, who's a good boy?" Cammy looked up at Jim "Don't let him fool you with his appearance. He may look like a dog, but he's a pussycat. Well, to me at least. My dad and I trained this guy from when he was a puppy, I think he would *kill* for me. Wouldn't you Bill?" Cammy looked back at Kaiser Bill "Be good to this one, he seems nice." Jim felt a flush of excitement at her endorsement. "But if he sets one foot in the junkyard, bite his nuts off." She walked away, leaving Jim in shock. Cammy glanced over her shoulder. "Coming?"

Jim followed Cammy to the truck. She kicked the passenger side door open. It missed him by inches. "Whoa, heads up, sport," she said. Cammy rubbed her hands together, like she was warming them, then turned the key in the ignition. The old truck creaked to life. Jim could hear the gears grind as she aggressively threw the clutch into first.

"There you GO!" she said to Jim. "S-u-c-c-e-s-s…That's the way you spell success!" she sang in triumph. She turned to Jim. "See, I told you I could handle the tow. There's not a car or an engine I can't run or fix."

Jim was faced again with having to make small talk. "Cammy's a pretty name," he blurted out.

Cammy scrunched her nose as they drove out of the lot. "Yeah right, I hate it. It's short for 'Camaro,' of all things."

"Camaro, like the car?"

"Camaro, exactly like the car," said Cammy, her head askew in disgust. "My Dad was a really big gear-head. Loved cars."

"Well, that would also explain Dodge, huh?" said Jim.

Cammy laughed. "Yep, but he's got the good one. I still don't understand why my Dad couldn't have chosen a better name for me, especially when the name Portia is already out there." She shook her head. "Dad was the one who started this shop. He's the one who made sure my brother and I knew how to put together a car engine before we could put together a sentence." She looked over at Jim. "Well, maybe not that early. He wanted us to be able to take care of ourselves. He dreamed of passing on the business to Dodge one day."

"Dodge runs this place, then?" Jim asked.

"And you are…" Cammy asked Jim, sidestepping the question.

"Oh! Uh, yeah," Jim said. He had forgotten to introduce himself.

Another thing his mother would chide him about if she were here. "My name is Sutton, James Sutton."

"What are you some kind of secret agent?" Cammy laughed.

"What...Oh. No." Jim fumbled. "You can call me Jim"

"Ok, Slim-Jim" Cammy laughed. Jim inwardly winced at the unwitting mention of his childhood nickname.

Cammy turned the truck down Main Street and pulled up in front of the hotel. On the left side of the hotel stood an Art Deco movie house replete with ornate façade and flashing marquee. The theater was having a film festival of some kind. Jim couldn't figure out what it could possibly be, a sign read: *Strawberry Falls Festival: Casablanca, Weekend at Bernie s, The Wedding Singer, Ashes & Diamonds, Shakespeare in Love, Mathilda, Grand Canyon, Everyone Says I Love You, Mr. Bean, Rockadoodle, The Rocketeer and The Godfather II & III.* If there was any kind of theme it was lost on Jim.

The right side of the hotel backed up a building that seemed to be residential apartments, judging by the faded *"Firemen, save my child/cat first"* stickers in the windows. Below the apartments was a Chinese restaurant. In yellow letters on many layers of brown paint, were Chinese characters. In English below them, *"The Ho-Hum Restaurant."*

Le Grand Hotel Vermont. The sign read in large gilded letters above the hunter green awning. The building itself was constructed in 1897. Quarried from granite shipped straight from Barre. The Quinn Family envisioned the hotel to be the crown jewel of a bustling city nestled in the hills of Vermont. The textile mill had proven a solid money-making venture. The Civil War had been costly in human lives as well as uniforms. The Quinns found themselves flush with money, so they resigned themselves to elevate their little town into a major city to rival Rutland or even Burlington. These hopes were grand but that did not stop the investment of copious amounts of money into building the foundation of an urban center— a foundation that never had a house built on it.

The influenza epidemic of 1918 hit the town of Strawberry Falls hard. One quarter of the town died from the Spanish flu. The Quinn family was not exempt. Jacob Quinn, the owner of the Mill succumbed in March. Elizabeth Quinn, Jacob's wife was named as his heir, as he had no surviving children. Elizabeth, upon advice from her financial advisors, invested heavily in the stock market of the 1920s. When the crash came in 1929, the Quinn fortune was wiped clean, as if it had never happened. Properties held by the Quinns, including the Mill and the Hotel were seized by the bank. Elizabeth Quinn uncomfortably settled into the middle class. Never again would the Quinn family hold such wealth and power as it did before October 1929, but there was always a Quinn in Strawberry Falls. As close to royalty as the town would ever see.

When the textile mill closed down, the town began its slow decline. Townspeople moved where the jobs took them, that meant away from Strawberry Falls. The hotel fell into disuse and disrepair and was seized by the bank (again). In 1969, a mysterious young couple moved into town. They bought the hotel on the cheap. The curious couple encouraged the town to buy the mill property and convert it to retail space. The town's fortunes turned on the surprising rise in popularity of foliage viewing. Strawberry Falls transformed itself into an autumn destination. More people came, year after year, to view the leaves. And the town evolved to accommodate those tastes. The mill converted to an antiques mall. Unexpectedly, after the arrival of the mysterious couple, the town not only survived but began to thrive.

Le Grand Hotel Vermont was a mixture of the rustic and the refined. The centerpiece of the lobby was an enormous granite fireplace. Large enough for a grown man to walk into comfortably without stooping. In front of the fireplace sat two green high-back chairs, richly upholstered, next to side tables—perfect for brandy after a long day hunting or taking in the seasonal colors. Dark wood paneling lined the walls, which were adorned photos of all the past the owners. A history, if you will, of the Quinn's and their hotel up through the new ownership. A genuine Currier and Ives print of a moose trudging its way through a marshland hung over the mantle.

The high ceilings and tasteful decorations lent itself to a sense of majesty of bygone days. A grand staircase, the effect somewhat altered by a motorized lift, rolled its way down from a second story mezzanine. Rich, dark mahogany wood, railings replete with honey maple risers. A red-carpet runner ran down the middle of the stairs like a tongue lolling out of the mouth of the hotel. At the bottom of the staircase, on the post, perched a gilded light fixture, almost a chandelier, surrounding a gilded bird cage in which there were two finches who flitted around, chirping pleasantly.

The staircase terminated next to the front desk, which was topped with white marble that matched the floors. The desk was adorned with gilded lamps with green velvet shades and gold fringe. Sitting on the green and gold desk blotter lay a beautiful brass bell next to a rubber tipped hammer. There was a hand-drawn calligraphy card in a miniature frame on an easel that stated plainly, "Ring for service." Behind the desk were cubby boxes, each with a brass hook on the front. From each hook hung a matching brass and green enamel room key. Up above, a crystal chandelier was suspended from the pressed tin ceiling.

"This is really something," Jim said. He walked over to a wall covered with pictures to get a closer look. The biggest framed painting was of Ezekiel Quinn, the founder of the town. The man looked down upon the lobby with a fierce expression of disdain. Other Quinn's were represented and noted in various photos and tintypes. A newer photo caught Jim's attention. In the photo a man and woman smiled from the lobby of the hotel. The hotel was gutted in the picture. The man had brown hair and a mustache. The girl in the photo was smiling and held her hand over the swell of her belly. The placard below the picture read "*The Normans – 1971.*"

Below the picture there was a small marble table with clawed feet.

A lamp identical to the one at the front desk illuminated what Jim took to be a makeshift shrine. There were several photos of the man from the most recent picture on the wall, even more with the woman. There was one Jim assumed to be of the man as a very young boy. On a lace doily rested a pair of wire-rim spectacles. As he looked closer at the pictures on the table and saw another photo of the man and his family, Mother, father, sister, and brother.

Jim picked up the photo. There was something familiar about that woman.

"That's my dad," Cammy said. Her voice made him jump and almost drop the photo. Jim turned to see Cammy standing uncomfortably close to him. She took the picture from Jim and reverently placed it back into the shrine. "He died a few years back."

"I'm so…sorry," Jim said.

"Don't be," Cammy said. She took her finger and ran it along the gilded frame. "Dodge found him. He went out to drop off a customer. When he came back, he saw Dad—" She stopped for a moment, lost in thought as she gazed at the frame. "Dad was under a car. The lift broke. He just died there. Alone."

"Cammy!" a woman's voice rang from atop the grand staircase. She rode the motorized lift down the stairs. Jim immediately recognized the woman from the photo on the wall and table. She looked to be in her fifties. She had brown hair with one white streak. There could be no doubt whose mother she was. She had the same eyes as Cammy, the same shaped face, the same pointy chin. They could have been sisters, if not for the age difference.

"Telling tales out of school and to a *stranger*, no less. I raised you better."

"I'm sorry, Mom," Cammy said. Then she turned to Jim. "This is my Mother. She owns this place."

"Forgive my daughter," she said. She slid into a wheelchair that was at the bottom of the stairs. "She takes after her father." She held out her hand to shake Jim's. She gave him a tight, practiced smile. "I am the proprietor of this historic hotel. My name is Evelyn Norman."

"Jim Sutton," he said shaking her hand.

"Mr. Sutton," Mrs. Norman said looking directly at Cammy. "What can I do for you?"

Cammy answered before Jim had a chance to speak. "His car's broken. I said he could stay here."

"Did you?" said Mrs. Norman still looking at her daughter. She finally turned to Jim. "Well, I am afraid my daughter may have made you promises that we just can't fulfill. Let's see if there are any rooms available."

"Any rooms available?" Cammy replied, incredulous. "Mother, there's nothing but rooms available. It's not peak season, the hotel's empty."

"Mr. Sutton," she continued, let's look in the reservations book. What my daughter doesn't realize is that it is precisely because it is off season that we are short of ready rooms." Mrs. Norman took out a black ledger, making a show of running her finger down the list. She shook her head. "I just don't see it."

"Mother! This is crazy. You're running below capacity. Dodge told me that there was only one other lodger this week."

M "I suppose you talked to your brother then before this morning. Dodge stopped by a few minutes ago. Before you and your guest arrived. Things have changed. I had a call for a room just this afternoon. I just don't have the room ready."

"Look, it's not a problem," said Jim. "I can stay somewhere else."

Cammy turned to Jim. "No, you can't. Not in Strawberry Falls. The nearest place to stay is twenty miles away."

"I'd be more than happy to make a call and find you another hotel," Mrs. Norman said.

"No, you won't. This is insane. He's got no car. He's only in town for a day—two at the most." She glared at her mother. "If you can't find a way to squeeze him in..." Cammy smiled at her mother, then turned to Jim.

"If she can't find a room for you, you'll stay with me. You can crash on my couch."

Jim started to protest. "Listen, I don't know…"

"No," said Cammy. "I insist."

"Fine!" Mrs. Norman sighed exasperatedly, "I'll just have Renate make up another room." She shot her daughter a wicked look. "I'll have to get the spare linen from storage." Pushing the registration book toward Jim with one finger, Mrs. Norman brusquely said, "Sign in, please." She plucked his keys from a cubby using a mahogany stick with a brass hook on the end. "Room 126."

"Let me help you up to your room," Cammy said.

"You will do no such thing," said Mrs. Norman. "I still run this hotel, and I will run it as I see fit." She rang the bell on the counter three times. Nothing happened. Mrs. Norman rolled her eyes."Buckley" she muttered under her breath and wheeled out the door into the depths of the hotel.

Jim heard footsteps on the stairs. He looked up. Descending the exquisite staircase was an African American man. One would not have called him *middle aged*, the salt and pepper of his beard and hair would not have suggested that. Nor would you have called him *elderly*. The air in which he held himself did not suggest that either. There was a vigor to his walk, and yet something else. Sadness?

"Checking out Anton?" Cammy asked the man. He smiled at Cammy as he doffed his tweed Mackintosh hat, which stylishly matched his jacket.

"I'm afraid so, darling. I'm just waiting for my wife, she will be along shortly." He smiled as he tucked the days *Burlington Free Press* that he had picked up from the front desk under his arm and walked into the parlor next to the fireplace.

"Doesn't' he need to check out?" Jim asked confused.

"Anton is one of Mother's long-term residents here at the hotel." Cammy replied. "He's sweet."

"If he and his wife stay here year round, then why is he checking out?" Jim queried.

"It's just Anton who lives here." Cammy looked wistfully at Anton, who presently had the paper out and was reading it with great intent. "Every day he comes downstairs, reads the paper, does the crossword and waits for his wife."

Jim looked at Cammy expectedly.

"His wife never comes." Cammy answered his wordless question. "He reads his paper, then has a meal then goes back up. It's the same routine day after day."

"That's sad." Jim said.

"I think its romantic..." Cammy replied "..to love someone with such devotion."

Mrs. Norman burst through the door. The woman's face bore the unmistakable lines of unchecked frustration. Only for a moment. She regained her composure, calmly wheeled back into her usual comfortable post and rang the desk bell once again. Scarcely a moment had passed when the door behind the desk flew open with a bang. A sweaty young man appeared in a green and gold bellhop uniform.

"You rang, ma'am!" wheezed the young man, discreetly wiping sweat from his brow. His black hair was slicked back under a matching green and gold pillbox hat.

"Yes, Buckley," Mrs. Norman glared at the bellhop. "Take Mr. Sutton's bags up to room 126 for him, would you dear?"

"Right away, Ma'am." Buckley turned to Jim. "Sir?" Jim stood there holding his bags, if you could call them that. A beat-up wheeled travel suitcase, a duffel bag, and a satchel with all his notes.

"Oh! Yeah," mumbled Jim. He handed him the suitcase and duffel bag, opting to carry his satchel himself. Jim started up the stairs and glanced back at Cammy, who smiled, then waved.

"See ya, Jim. Stop by the shop tomorrow morning after breakfast, I'll give you an update on your car."

"Breakfast?" asked Jim

"Sure!" said Cammy. "I know my mother would be more than happy to place your order for tomorrow." She smiled at her mother. "Wouldn't you?"

Mrs. Norman talked through her teeth. "Certainly, Mr. Sutton, just fill out the card in your room with what you want. I'll make sure you get it bright and early."

Jim continued up the stairs to his room. Buckley inquired what brought him to town, Jim gave the usual spiel.

"Hey, we serve those here!" said Buckley brightly. "At the hotel. You think you'd like to review our onion rings?"

"I don't see why not," Jim said. Finally, a bit of luck. "Could you put in an order for me?"

"Sure thing!" Buckley said.

There was a single queen bed, a dresser, lamps, and a window. Jim pulled back the lace curtains and saw Cammy driving away. The furniture could have been mahogany but most likely were just stained look-alikes. On the wall hung was a Currier & Ives lithograph of an American Bald Eagle in mid-flight, red, white and blue bunting wrapping around it. Jim noted there was no television. It was one of those hotels, he thought.

Jim unpacked his notes and set up at the desk by the window. He preferred to use natural light, but it was growing dark outside. *Is it that late already?* Jim wondered when the onion rings would arrive. He didn't feel like calling the front desk. Mrs. Norman had acted oddly during check in, but this was Vermont. What he needed was a hot shower. Then he could put this whole horrible day behind him.

Jim stepped into the shower. The water hit his skin and he let out a long-protracted sigh. He washed the road-grime off his body. He turned the hot water up, then again, and again, his body acclimating to the heat until he realized the bathroom was filled with steam. Skin pink and flushed, Jim stepped out of the shower. Grabbing a towel, he dried off and walked over to the mirror on the wall. It was of course, fogged up. Jim wiped away the condensation on the glass. He had a few days growth of beard on his face. He looked closer and saw amongst the dark brown were flecks of white. Jim sighed. *Great.*

Jim was half awake, half asleep when he heard a noise, the bolt on the door slowly turning. Was there even a chain on the door, did I put it on? Jim wondered groggily. He heard the door open. In the dim light from his window, Jim saw a figure walk across the room. His heart skipped a beat. His worst fear, alone in the dark with an unknown assailant. Jim sat up in bed, his heart racing. He looked around. What could he use as a weapon? *Paperback book, keys, socks?* The figure moved closer, holding something in their hands. What was it? Jim squinted in the dim light. Was it? Yes. He could smell them even before he could see them. It was a plate of *onion rings*.

"I brought these for you," the figure said. It was Cammy Norman. Jim was speechless. He opened his mouth. "No, quiet," Cammy replied.

Jim's eyes adjusted to the darkness. Cammy stood at the foot of his bed. She was wearing her work clothes, her hair still pulled back into a bun. She held out the plate of onion rings. "I made these myself," she said, placing them on the desk. Cammy reached up and with both hands pulled the rubber band out of her hair. The hair, now freed from its constraints, sprang forth, wild, unkempt and untamed in all its curly glory. Putting her index finger on her lips as if to say *shhhhh*, as Cammy walked toward the bed, she unbuttoned her work overalls, stepping out of them. Jim sat dumbfounded at what was transpiring. Cammy was down to her underwear. He could see the grime and dirt on her skin, like a tan. She kicked off her underwear and paused there, naked, eyes shining brightly in the dark. As she walked towards the bed, her limp seemed more pronounced. Cammy pulled back the covers and slid into bed with him. Jim could feel the coolness of her body against his hot skin, it did not bother him. Cammy's naked body pressed against him as she leaned in to kiss him. Jim could smell and taste gasoline as he felt her tongue dart past his own. He felt her hands move down, tugging off his boxer shorts. Jim started to move Cammy onto her back when she resisted him. Confused, Jim stopped. She pushed him forcefully onto his back while she sat astride him. Jim looked up at Cammy. She closed her eyes as she started moving in rhythm.

LONELY ISLAND

1977

"Shoot milk in Santa's mouth, win a prize!"

Jim glanced over at the carnival barker. An apathetic teenager leaned listlessly against his stall, megaphone in hand, held in front of his bored face. The midway section of the park seemed to exclusively employ this species of teenager. The midway was like any other you could find in any average park or carnival. The only distinction was the Christmasification of the games. In this case, it was the classic shoot-the-clown-in-the-mouth-game. But instead of a clown it was Santa and instead of water the guns shot "milk," which was water with a white, milky additive. At one time the sight of rows of Santa faces, mouths agape, waiting to receive a jet of water would have caused Jim pause, but today it was just another day in Christmas Town.

Jim and Lyndsey Sutton were given free rein to explore Christmas Island. This is not to say their parents were reckless. On the contrary, Bob and Linda had stressed to their children the importance of staying safe, avoiding strangers, and staying far away from the water.

"Well, kiddos?" The teen had spotted them. Jim knew that avoiding eye contact was key to deflecting this kind of attention. This day he was dragging Lyndsey in tow, and she had stared the teen right in the face, opening them up to his hard-sell approach.

"Uh, not today, thank you" Jim said, pulling Lyndsey along.

"Come on, one try one dollar," the barker pressed.

"No, thank you," Jim firmly replied, casting his eyes to the ground.

The teen got the message. "Merry Christmas Eve," he tonelessly replied.

It was not Christmas Eve or even the Christmas season, but one of the "charming quirks" of Christmas Town was that by decree of management, every day was to be treated as Christmas Eve, be it the day before Christmas, the fourth of July, or arbor day. The only day that was not Christmas Eve was Christmas Day itself. Normally, one would expect on that solitary day, Santa would have the day off, but Christmas Town of course, had a role for him to play. Santa was in residence in Christmas Town that special day, taking a rest from the long night and any child could deliver him a thank you note in exchange for a miniature candy cane.

Jim and Lyndsey made their quick exit from the Ice Palace section of the park where the midway lived to continue on their circumnavigation of the island.

Christmas Town was divided into quadrants surrounding a central core. *The Ice Palace,* the quadrant located in the lower right side of the park, was the amusement style area of Christmas Town. There was a small ice rink where visitors could rent skates by the hour. A merry-go-round was redecorated to look like Santa and his reindeer. A calliope played Christmas tunes such as "Santa Claus is Coming to Town" and "Rudolph the Red Nosed Reindeer" year-round. There was a boardwalk that extended into the pine tree forest. It seemed charming enough until dusk, when the mosquitoes would feast on anyone who dared to venture into the woods.

In the lower left quadrant of Christmas Town lived *Reindeer Woods,* a wooded area that largely contained live animals. Visitors wound their way through real woods, stopping along a trail punctuated by candy canes and gingerbread men to observe each animal in its enclosure. Even in its glory days, Christmas Town's animal attractions were not impressive. There had always been a handful of charismatic mega-fauna, but the real attraction was a real reindeer herd—a herd that, over the years, had dwindled to two solitary specimens.

Jim and Lyndsey ran along the trail through Reindeer Woods, they passed the sugar shack. Christmas Island did not have a robust population of Maple trees. Certainly, not enough to tap and render sap into syrup. Nonetheless, Christmas Town boasted of a *genuine* working sugar shack. Glenn Murray imported raw sap from a maple grove on the mainland. It was a small operation, but the best part was the sugar on snow. A beloved Vermont tradition, sugar on snow is a delicacy not to be passed up. Maple syrup is heated to a blistering two hundred and thirty-five degrees, it is then poured in strips over snow (when the sugar shack could manage it would use fresh fallen snow, other times, a snow cone machine provided the shaved ice). When the hot sugar meets the snow, magic happens, the syrup hardens into a sticky, chewy, taffy-like substance. Most shacks have a jar of pickles on hand. One would think the combination unlikely, but the sweet and sour go together magnificently.

"Lyndy!" The voice called out. Jim and his sister stopped at the sound. Out of the Sugar shack a middle-aged woman waved at them from the doorway.

Jim waved back. "Hello Mrs. Lakeland." Reindeer Woods was maintained by the Lakelands, a family out of Essex Junction. Tom and Kathleen Lakeland had retired from the nine to five world. They traveled on the ferry each morning to take care of the animals and attraction.

"Hi Jimmy," Kathleen replied, walking up to his sister. Kathleen liked the Sutton children, but she loved Lyndsey by far the most. "Hello darling," Kathleen purred as she hugged Lyndsey. Kathleen held both of her closed hands in front of her. "Pick a hand."

"That one," Lyndsey said, pointing to her left hand after careful consideration.

"Good choice!" Kathleen said. She opened her hand to reveal a maple candy treat on her palm. Lyndsey squealed with delight, grabbing the candy and popped it in her mouth. Kathleen laughed and gave Jim a wink. She opened her left hand, revealing an identical candy. Jim smiled and took it and put it in his pocket for later.

"Now you kids scoot!" Kathleen said. "Get on with your adventures."

In the upper right quadrant of the park sat *Winter Wonderland*, the next stop on Jim and his sister's travels. This part of the park consisted of a path that wound through oversized Christmas figurines, giant ornaments that reflected visitors faces like fun-house mirrors and oversized presents. There were candy cane slides and gingerbread playhouses. Winter Wonderland was designed to look like it was eternally a "winter wonderland" complete with fake concrete snowbanks and plaster snow men. Jim could tell which trees were fake and which were not, especially in the summer months, when real green leaves made the fake pine trees look pathetic and faded.

For special occasions, Mr. Murray would authorize the use of two kinds of snow machines. One was no more than a soap bubbler. The other machine was a remnant of Christmas Town's glory days. In its prime Christmas Town had ten snow machines that ran even in the summer months. Over time, the machines broke down one by one. Of the ten machines, only two still worked.

Winter Wonderland's most popular ride was a miniature train called Winter Express.

There was no snow today, fake or otherwise. Jim and Lyndsey would not be stopping in Winter Wonderland. They were headed to Elf Village this day. *Elf Village* was the Sutton children's favorite part of the park. Like their home, it was comfortably scaled for their size, or more specifically, for little people or dwarfs. There were no longer any real live elves employed by Christmas Town. It wasn't cost-effective to hire and house whole clans of dwarfs on site. Elf Village at one time was a real dwarf colony with homes for the actors to live in, a walk-through attraction for "normal" people to gawk at. The elf homes were still there, but crude animatronic elves had replaced the living scenery of the past. Jim and Lyndsey loved playing in the little houses, they each had their favorite. To get to Elf Village, they chose to cut through The North Pole.

In the middle of Christmas Town, like the hub of a wheel, stood the centerpiece of the park, *The North Pole*. This was where Bob Sutton's snack stand was located. More importantly, this was where Santa Claus lived. Santa Claus was the super-star of Christmas Town. Nestled amongst fake icebergs, visitors to Christmas Town could wait in line to see Santa and sit on his lap. As children queued, they shuffled past chipped cement elves, polar bears, and penguins. It has been reported many times to the park the inconsistency of having polar bears and penguins together, since penguins are never found at the North Pole. The park staff took to saying: "Penguins want to see Santa too!" or, "they're on vacation!"

The kids knew a shortcut that would bypass Santa so they could go straight to Elf Village. It took them through the back room of The North Pole. An area exclusively for the use of Santa and Santa's helpers.

Jim pushed the large metal door open. The first thing that greeted any outside visitor was the smell. Forty years of Santa sweat permeated the walls of the locker room. The second thing one noticed was impressive collection of Santa Claus outfits. Organized by size, the Santa costumes circumnavigated the room in a sea of red velvet and ermine. There was a locker of padding for actors not possessing the natural girth to pull off the requisite belly like a bowl full of jelly. It was like something you might see in the basement of the world's most specific and disturbing serial killer.

The current actor cast in the starring role of Santa at The North Pole did not require padding or a fake beard. Mr. John Roebling of Colchester, Vermont had spent his whole adult career at the post office as a mailman. Although he was round enough, John Roebling was strong. Strapping, after years lugging mailbags, John delighted the Sutton children by letting them swing on his biceps. He took immense pleasure in playing Santa. While there have been many wonderful people who played Santa at The North Pole, they'd had their fair share of miserable human beings, drunks and reprobates as well, Mr. Roebling was none of these. Jim received the news of kind Mr. Roebling's death in 1994 with great sadness. John Roebling died in Naples, Florida of a heart attack while, of all things, retrieving the mail at the end of his driveway.

"Stinky," Lyndsey said. Jim grabbed her hand, they rushed by a large mail sack stuffed with letters, next to the door leaded out the other side. Visitors came year after year for Letters from Santa. Any child (or adult) could drop a letter to Santa in the blue and white mailbox and receive a genuine letter right from Santa himself. Every month, Mr. Murray would stop by to pick up the letters from Santa and send them to a re-mailing outfit in the nearby town of North Pole, New York so that, when "Santa" sent back his form letter reply to the children, it would bear a genuine "North Pole" cancellation stamp on it.

Blinking in the sunlight and glad to be out of the funky locker room. Jim glanced over towards his father's snack stand. His dad was outside. He was talking to a man holding a clipboard.

Christmas Town had a compliment of outside vendors that did business with the employees of the park. Some of these vendors had children who would occasionally accompany their parents to the island on errands. Occasionally Jim would muster the courage to say hello, but these days any outside children sighting were few and far between. This particular day, Jim saw one of these rare creatures had chosen to make a visit. A young boy milled about by the snack stand. He kicked at rocks with a bored abandon.

"Lyndsey, go play by the tree over there." Jim pointed at a stand of maple trees by the side of the path.

Lyndsey looked at her brother with confusion. "I want to go to Elf Village."

"I'll take you later. Just go," Jim hissed, pushing his sister over towards the trees. The turned his attention to the boy. Jim swallowed and quickened his pace.

"Uh, hi," said Jim, walking up to the boy.

"Hello," the boy replied cautiously. He was seven, maybe eight. He had piercing blue eyes and sandy blonde hair that was parted just so—something that neither Jim nor his mother could ever hope to achieve.

Jim regarded the boy's manner of dress. He wore a crisp shirt that looked almost new. Maybe it was. On the breast of the shirt was a little embroidered green alligator. The boy was still kicking rocks as Jim looked down and saw that he was wearing beautifully brilliant white Nike tennis shoes. Jim's own shoes were Keds that his mom had bought in the supermarket of all places.

"My name is Jim Sutton. I live here. What's your name?" Jim blurted.

"I'm Brandon Bowles. My dad sells supplies." Brandon puffed out his chest. "He says he's the only one keeping this place running, you know."

"Oh! I bet he knows my dad!" Jim said. "We run the stand."

"My dad says half the people here are deadbeats," Brandon replied.

"Not my dad!" Jim said defensively. Brandon shrugged.

"You really live here?" Brandon asked Jim.

"Oh yeah!" Jim said. "We live down the road." Jim paused for what he was sure was the coup de grace. "It was built for *dwarfs!*"

Brandon's eyes bugged wide. "Really? That is so cool!"

"You wanna see?" asked Jim.

"Yeah!!" said Brandon.

"Let's go!"

Brandon started down the road, then stopped. "Wait, I better ask my dad if it's okay."

Brandon's dad was with Bob. He was dressed in blue jeans and a chambray shirt. He looked tan—tanner than anyone who lived in Vermont should have the right to be. He had the same sandy blonde hair and bright blue eyes as Brandon. When he spoke, his teeth looked impossibly white.

"I can hold off on the canned goods if you like," said Brandon's father, looking over his clipboard. "I just hate having to take stuff back with me. You *did* order this, you know?"

"Ron, I know what I ordered," Bob said. "Can't you put it on the tab?"

Ron Bowles looked down skeptically at the clipboard and turned a page. "I don't know. You're extended pretty far already."

"Ron, I looked at the prices you charged Glenn, they're nowhere near what I'm getting from you."

"Glenn?" Ron smirked. "Those were my 'friends and family' rates."

"So, we're not friends, then?" Bob said.

"Bob, we only really just met. Maybe down the line." Glenn clapped his hand on Bob's back. "Ok, buddy?"

There seemed to be two prices and two attitudes for "islanders" and non-islanders, and especially "New Yorkers," which the Suttons inexplicably seemed to have been labeled.

"I run a snack stand. If I don't have food, I don't have anything to sell." As Bob spoke, he saw Jim and Brandon out of the corner of his eye. "Hey buddy, what's up?" Bob said. He saw that Jim was with another child. "Who's your friend, slim-Jim?"

Jim gritted his teeth. He hated that nickname. "This is Brandon Bowles. I met him outside. Can I take him to see the house?"

"Brandon *Bowles?*" Bob turned to Ron Bowles. "This your boy, Ron?"

"Yes."

"You know, I saw him around a couple of times before. We never formally met." Bob turned to the boy. "Nice to meet you, Brandon. I'm so glad you and Jimmy are going to be friends," he said.

"Daaad…" Jim was mortified. "I just wanna show him the house."

"Well, I don't see why not, do you Ron?"

Ron wore a blank expression bordering on mild annoyance. "I don't know, Bran—"

"Please, Dad, *please*," pleaded Brandon. "He says they live in a house made for *dwarfs!*"

Ron Bowles looked from Brandon's hopeful face to Bob's. He looked at Jim, paused for a second, but knew he really had no good reason to say no, even though he wanted to.

"Alright Bran, but I want you back here soon. We're not sticking around any longer than we have to." He looked over at Bob. "End of summer, you know, have to drag the kids everywhere. Can't wait for school to begin, am I right?"

Jim and Brandon tore out of the stand, screen door slamming behind them. Brandon was impressed with the Sutton's home. Jim took him on a tour of the house, much to the surprise of Linda who was stripping layers of built-up paint from the fireplace in the living room.

Jim looked forward to Tuesdays and Fridays when the ferry would arrive with Brandon and his father. Jim and Brandon had many adventures and took full advantage of the quirks of Christmas Island. Brandon was a welcome fixture at the Sutton home, but Mr. Bowles did not permit Brandon to ever spend the night. Jim dreaded the knock on the door that meant it was time for Brandon to leave for the mainland.

September came, and it was time to go to school. Normally, like most kids his age, Jim would have seen the end of summer as the death of fun. Not so for Jim Sutton. He looked forward to starting at his new school, especially when he found out that Brandon would not only be at the same school but in the same class.

Linda got up early that first day to wake her kids only to find Jim sitting on the edge of his bed already dressed and ready to go.

"Jesus, James! How long have you been up?"

"I couldn't sleep, Mom! Too excited."

"You have to be rested for your first day," she said. "You're going to crash." She straightened Jim's clothes and tried to get his hair to stay flat. After several attempts, she exhaled loudly. "Fine, stay that way…I'm getting your sister. Go downstairs. Eat breakfast." Jim slid off the edge of the bed and ran. He heard his mother's disembodied voice call out to him, "Make some for your sister too. I don't want to be late to the ferry!"

Jim flew down the stairs and jumped over an orbital sander that was currently residing at the bottom. His mother was stripping the floors on the first level in order to refinish them. He burst through the swinging door to the kitchen. His father was there, sitting with a cup of coffee in one hand and yesterday's paper the other. No paperboy would ever deliver the day's paper to the island. The ferry route made it impractical. Bob would bring home newspapers his customers abandoned at the snack stand.

"Hey sport, first day of school!" Bob said. "Big day!"

Jim looked around. He had expected his father to have prepared food for him and his sister. Bob had only prepared his own breakfast. Jim grabbed a box of Cap'n Crunch.

"I DON'T WANNA WEAR THAT." Although Lyndsey was a whole floor above them, her piercing crying could be heard throughout the house. Jim looked at his dad, who glanced at him over the paper. Jim rolled his eyes; Bob raised an eyebrow. They both shook their heads and went back to their breakfast.

Linda came running down the stairs dragging Lyndsey behind her. "Jimmy!" she barked at him, "come on—we have to go now."

Jim made a move to put his dish in the sink. His mother grabbed his hand. *"Now!"* she sternly stated. Jim looked back and saw his father, still absorbed in his paper. Jim was dragged out of the house to the station wagon. Lyndsey climbed into the front seat.

"Aw, no fair!" cried Jim. "Why does she get to sit in the front?"

"I here first," Lyndsey said.

"But Mom," protested Jim, "she got to sit there last time, when we went to the store."

Linda had little patience this morning for the very real and important arguments of preferential seating that seemed to dominate her children's day to day lives. "Figure it out on your own," she said, making sure that Lyndsey's diaper bag and Jim's backpack were in the car and not on the counter.

"Mom, it's my first day at school!" Jim said.

"My first day, too," Lyndsey said.

"You're not going to school!" yelled Jim. "You're going to daycare."

Lyndsey started to cry.

Linda had had enough. She picked Lyndsey up out of the front and plopped her in the back seat, kicking and screaming the whole time.

"You'll ride with Mommy when we drop off your brother." Lyndsey turned beet red and started shrieking. Jim climbed into the front seat, satisfied with how things had panned out. Linda gripped the steering wheel, threw the car into gear, and pulled around the circular driveway toward the ferry dock. Her nerves were jangled enough, then she saw people walking up from the dock. Great, she thought, the ferry is already unloaded. Linda pulled up to the ferry just as the gate was closing down.

She got out of the car, leaving it idling, and ran to the man lowering the boom. "Please!" she pleaded with the man at the gate, clasping her hands in front of her, as if in prayer or supplication. "*Please* let me on the ferry. It's my kid's first day."

The ferryman started to object.

Linda burst into tears.

Feeling sorry for her, the ferry operator relented and let them on the boat.

Linda floored it when they docked on the other side, skidding out of the gravel parking lot. When they pulled up in front of the school, Jim was relieved to see there were other kids still being dropped off. Running out of the car, he looked back at his mother. To his horror, she was out of the car and waving madly at him.

"Have a great day, Slim-Jim!" she shouted.

Jim prayed no one heard. Jim gave a small wave, as he walked away, head down.

Jim was relieved when he finally saw Brandon talking to a group of other boys. This is great, thought Jim. I can make new friends! Jim walked up to the group and said, "Hey Brandon!"

Brandon turned around to face Jim. The expression on his face bore no recognition. Brandon said nothing. All the boys stared at Jim.

Maybe Brandon didn't hear him? "Hi, Brandon. It's me." He looked around at the boys. "It's me, Jim. Jim Sutton."

A boy said, "Do you know this kid?"

"Yeah, he's just some poor kid from New York my dad says I have to be friends with."

Jim's head felt hot. Tears welled up in his eyes.

"Look! He's starting to cry," the boy said, laughing.

"B-but..." Jim spluttered.

A third boy joined in. "Awww, poor Slim-Jim going to cry? You need your mommy? Why don't you go back to New York, *flatlander.*" Jim's ears felt hot.

The rest of the day went equally as badly for Jim. He was a new student at a school where most of the kids had been together since kindergarten. It was impossible for Jim to find a foothold in any social group. New wasn't exotic in this school, it was different. Different was odd. Different was bad. Jim found himself as alone in this new school as he ever was on Christmas Island. He sat by himself in the cafeteria with his brown bag lunch. A folded piece of notepaper fell out. Jim opened it and in his mother's handwriting it read, "Have a wonderful first day, I love you." Somehow, this just made him feel worse.

When the day was finally over, Jim grabbed his bag and ran out the door. The old red Volkswagen station wagon was parked outside of the school. Linda leaned against the car, smiling. He could see Lyndsey sitting in the front seat.

"How was your first day?" asked Linda.

"Great Mom!" Jim said, forcing a smile on his face. He couldn't bear to tell her the truth. He didn't want to say it out loud, because then it would become real.

"That's wonderful," Linda said. "See, I told you it would be alright!" Jim got into the back seat and remained quiet on the ride back to the ferry.

It was the same story for the rest of the week. The kids largely shunned him as an outsider. Brandon refused to acknowledge his existence. Jim was relieved when the bell rang on Friday. He would have the weekend to relax... and then it hit him. A knot tightened in his stomach. Brandon's dad made a Saturday delivery to Christmas Town.

Saturday morning came. Jim lay in bed, staring at the ceiling.

"Wakeup, sleepyhead! Gotta get the day going," his mother said, pulling off his covers. "Besides, the morning ferry's coming in, and you know who will be on it. Get up, I'll make you some eggs!"

Jim trudged downstairs. He saw his sister sitting at the kitchen table.

"Move it!" Jim said, shoving his sister out of her seat. "I want to sit there."

Lyndsey looked hurt and surprised. "Mooommmy!" she shouted.

"James! Leave you sister alone right now!"

Jim was only half-heartedly antagonizing his sister. Glaring, he sat in across from her and stared at the plate of eggs.

"Eat your eggs, sweetie," his mother ordered. "Then you can go see your dad at the stand. I'm sure Brandon will be there by the time you're done."

Jim picked at the eggs until Linda saw him playing with his food. "Enough! Now scoot. Go see your friend. Honestly, what's with you?"

Jim slowly sulked his way out the door.

"Take your sister with you."

"Really mom?" Jim slumped.

"Really Jim. Just take her."

Right then Jim would have wanted anybody else for company. Almost anybody. The thought of seeing Brandon, gnawed at him. Lyndsey seemed unaware of Jim's discomfort as she happily skipped a few steps behind him. As they turned the corner, Jim saw John Roebling sitting on a tree stump, smoking what appeared to be a red cigarette. Santa quickly put out his cigarette on the ground as he saw Jim approaching.

"Mrs. Claus doesn't like me to smoke, but I sneak a few from time to time," Mr. Roebling said his deep voice rumbling, adding a "Ho, Ho, Ho!" to punctuate his point.

"I know you're not Santa, Mr. Roebling," Jim said.

"How do you know?"

"My dad told me the truth."

"He did?"

"Yes," Jim said. "He told me that you're just one of Santa's helpers, that the real Santa is too busy to be here year-round."

"Oh!" John Roebling said, relief visible on his face. "Well, you're a smart boy, I'm sure you would have figured that out on your own."

"You smell funny," Lyndsey said to Santa, scrunching up her nose. Jim was embarrassed, but to tell the truth, there was a strange smell in the air.

"Oh, little one, that's one of Santa's special cigarettes," Santa replied jovially.

"Grandpa smokes cigarettes. You don't smell like grandpa," Lyndsey replied. She was right. Jim sat on his grandpa's lap many times. The smell of burning tobacco was quite familiar to him.

"Sure, I was, gumdrop." Santa poked her on the nose, then he pulled out the pack of cigarettes and tapped one out. It was long and white, with a yellow filter. He put one to his lips, took out a lighter and lit up. A puff of smoke rose from his mouth, a more familiar smell wafted with the white-blue smoke.

"You still shouldn't smoke these, Sonny-Jim," John said. "Filthy habit— one I picked up in the service."

"You were in the army?" Jim said.

"Oh yeah. Signed up the day after Pearl Harbor."

"What was it like?" Jim moved closer.

John's face grew dark. "You don't want to know, Jim."

"Please tell me," Jim implored.

"I know your dad wouldn't want me to do that, Jimmy." John tousled Jim's hair, making him resemble a hedgehog even more than he usually did. "Speaking of him, are you two on your way to your dad's?"

"Yeah," Jim sullenly replied.

"What's the matter kiddo?" John said. He put his arm around Jim.

"Nothing. I'm just late." Jim replied pulling away.

"Well, let me walk you," John said.

Together the three of them followed the path that led to Santa's house. John opened the back door.

"Remember Sonny-Jim, Santa's always watching so be good for goodness sake." He winked. "And Merry Christmas Eve to you both!"

Jim forced a smile on his face. "I will."

As Jim walked around Santa's house, he spied Brandon Bowles outside of the snack stand.

"Come on Lyndz, let's go." Jim reached for his sister's hand an turned to go back to the house when Brandon spied them. He called them over. Jim stood frozen in place, unable to comprehend. Was this some kind of trick?

"Go to dad's stand," Jim whispered to his sister.

"I don't wanna," she replied.

"Get lost!" Jim hissed. "I'll let you have my desert." That was all the motivation Lyndsey needed and she bounced down the path, away from the approaching Brandon Bowles.

"Hey Jim!" Brandon called in a friendly voice.

Jim cautiously walked over.

"Did you see what Mr. Gilbert was wearing on Friday? Bell bottoms!" Brandon laughed.

Jim was shocked. Brandon was acting like nothing had happened. Like he hadn't ignored Jim all week. Like he hadn't called him poor.

"Mr. G is stupid," continued Brandon. "Hey, you wanna go play in Winter Wonderland while my dad makes his drop offs?"

Jim wanted to believe. "Yeah, sure!"

And they ran towards Winter Wonderland. It was as if nothing had happened. Brandon was laughing about school and making jokes.

But as they turned the corner, Jim saw Reid LeClaire, one of Brandon's friends.

"It's okay," Brandon told Jim. "I told Reid to come with me today. We feel really bad about what happened at school."

Reid moved toward Jim. He glanced over at his parents who were walking farther down the path. "Yeah, I wanted to see where you live. Bran said you live in a house made for dwarfs? That's cool!"

"Oh, yeah!" Jim said. "Our house has little furniture and everything. You want to see?"

Jim glanced over at Brandon, happy to have his friend back. But then the face that looked back was the face he saw in school. *Cold.*

"You really are *dumb*, aren't you?" asked Brandon. Reid walked over and pushed Jim hard, into the bushes where he landed on his back, scraping his arms and legs while tearing a jagged hole in his shirt.

Brandon laughed and pointed at Jim's torn tee shirt. "Wanna bet his mommy fixes his shirt and he wears it tomorrow?" Jim struggled to get up.

"You like living in dwarf houses? Do you, *freak?*" barked Reid, looming above him. "Dwarf lover."

"Why?" Jim asked plaintively. "Why are you doing this?"

Brandon looked down at Jim. "Because." He bent down to pick up a rock. He cocked his arm back. Jim looked away in awful anticipation.

Jim didn't see him. None of them did. He was on one of the roofs of the gingerbread houses watching the whole exchange.

Jim heard a soft thump, and then he heard his voice. "Stay away from him." Jim opened his eyes to see Nick. The dwarf handyman appeared, as if out of nowhere. Nick had carried a miniature toolbox, he seemed to be wearing some kind of box around his neck. As Nick stood there, even with Brandon and Reid being eight-year-olds, he still had to look up to see eye to eye with them.

"Who are you, his *dad-dy?*" Reid replied in singsong.

"I would say pick on someone your own size," said Nick. "I'll let you make an exception for me." Nick walked forward, curling his stubby fingers into a fist. Jim could see the well-defined muscles of Nick's diminutive arms, twitching under his white tee shirt and overalls.

Brandon looked at Nick. "You can't touch us, you're a grown up." Then he looked at Nick and sneered, "Sort of a grown up."

Nick reared back and punched Brandon in the stomach. Brandon slumped to the ground, gasping for air. Nick glared over at Reid. "Try me," he said as Brandon lay on the ground below him wheezing. "I know who you are, I saw what you did. Now go. Get out of here."

Brandon got up, his eyes burning with tears. Reid stood beside him.

"I'm going to tell my father about this," Brandon wheezed.

"I don't think you will," Nick said. He offered Jim his hand to help him up.

"Yes I will," Brandon sneered. "You're going to be in so much trouble. Grown-ups can't hurt kids."

"Ah yes, but it will be my word. The word of an adult, and a pitiable one at that," Nick said.

"The word of an *elf*." Reid laughed.

"Elf?" Nick growled; his eyes narrowed. "I'd watch yourself boy, don't you know elves are magic?"

Nick held out his small hand to the side, palm to the kids. It was empty. Brandon looked to Reid as if to say, "this is crazy." Nick smiled. He quickly made a motion with his hand and suddenly at the tips of his fingertips was a photo. Brandon and Reid stood silent, their jaws slack in disbelief.

"Ah, yes," Nick said, as he held the square picture in his hands, turning it over and over.

"What is that?" Reid sputtered.

"This?" Nick cocked his head. "This is a Polaroid picture. You know it's really an amazing bit of technology. You take a picture with one of these." He tapped the black box around his neck. "And out comes one of those." He showed them the square picture. "It's magic."

Nick held the picture out in front of him, Brandon made a grab for it. "Ah, ah!" Nick scolded him. "Not for your grubby little hands." Nick grabbed Brandon's shoulder firmly with his hand. "Let me make this clear to you. I expect you'll go to your daddy and tell him the 'mean little man' beat me up. I tell you this, if you do that, if you tell anybody, your daddy or even your friends, I will find you. If you bother this young man here, I will find you. If you tease or hurt or even look at this young man again, I will send this picture of you hitting Jim here, to your daddy."

"You wouldn't" Brandon replied.

"I would," Nick said. "And I'll also tell him how you tried to beat me up as well."

"That's a lie!" Brandon said.

"My word against yours, kid." Nick said. "Now go, or I'll tell him this afternoon." Brandon and Reid backed away and ran down the path, out of sight.

"Do you think they'll tell on you?" asked Jim.

"Who knows? Who cares?" Nick slid the Polaroid into his pocket. He examined Jim's shirt, which was ripped. "You should come with me. I'll get you something to put on." Nick turned to walk down the path. Jim just stood there. "Come on," said Nick. "We can't have your parents seeing you like that."

"Thank you, Nick."

"It's nothing, Jim. I ran into Santa who told me to keep an eye on you."

Jim looked up in surprise

"I'm glad I did."

The two walked along the path to the maintenance shed. It was a bit outside the perimeter of Christmas Town, not far up the road from the Sutton's house. Nick pushed open the door. What greeted Jim was something of a disappointment. The inside of Nick's shed looked exactly like the inside of any shed. The counters were the usual heights. The chairs were "normal" sized. There was not one thing that was dwarf sized to be seen.

Nick walked over to a workbench. He pulled out a cardboard box, looked inside, and brought it over. "Lost and found. Look inside. You might find a shirt that will fit you." Jim rummaged through the box, opting for the yellow *I saw the Mystery Spot* t-shirt. It came down almost to his knees.

Nick surveyed the new ensemble. "Well, that will do, at least until you can get home. When you do, switch shirts. Throw away, burn or bury the torn one, or else your mother may ask questions."

"Why are you doing this?" asked Jim.

"I know what it's like to be alone," Nick said. "I've been different all my life, and I know a bully when I see one. There's only one thing a bully understands, and that's fear."

"Oh, yeah, you scared him alright," said Jim.

"For a little while, maybe," Nick said. "He'll stay away for a bit. He'll be back when he feels braver. Once you've found a bully, it's hard to lose him."

Jim's heart sank at these words. The idea of having to face this again, or over and over, knotted his stomach.

"My dad says that if I get bullied I should fight back," Jim said. "All bullies respect is strength. If I don't stand up for myself, I'll be pushed around my whole life."

"I'm not going to lie to you," he said gently. "I've been hurt and bullied too much in my life not to know what happens in these situations. There is no solution. Violence is never the best way. My advice: stay out of his way. Try to find some other friends if you can. Find something that can occupy your time. What do you like to do, draw?"

"I like reading."

"There you go! I know your school has an excellent library. Check out books, get lost in those worlds," Nick said. "But I have an even better idea for you."

"What is it?" asked Jim, his curiosity piqued.

"Why just read? Why not write? Make up your own stories and fairy tales or swashbuckling adventures."

"I can do that?"

"Absolutely," Nick said. "Just tell stories and write them down. Even stories where the bully loses." Nick winked at him. "I think we missed a bit of dirt, right here..." Nick reached his little hand toward Jim's head. "...In your ear. Ah yes, I'm right. This was in there." As Nick pulled it back, sitting in the palm of his hand was a silver Hershey Kiss. Jim exclaimed in delight at the trick and grabbed it from Nick's hand.

"Now, you're all cleaned up. I bet I know what would make you feel better."

"What?" asked Jim.

"Well, go home and get changed, and when you come back, let's go to your dad's stand. I have a feeling that if I order you a plate of Christmas Town's world-famous onion rings, that will do the trick."

Jim ran out of the shed. He smiled all the way home.

MEET THE LOCALS

2000

Jim Sutton stared at the ceiling. *Did yesterday really happen?* Gentle morning light suffused the room. He turned to his right, expecting a warm body beside him only to find the bed cold and empty. Cammy's absence only added to Jim's confusion about everything that had happened the day before. Jim looked to see if there was a note on the bed or dresser but found nothing. He stared at the empty plate on the side table. There were only a few crumbs of onion ring batter left on the white china. The only evidence of his late-night rendezvous. Thoughts of the night before came to his mind. After their surprise encounter, Cammy had rolled onto her back, putting her arms behind her head. She stared up at the ceiling. Jim had opened his mouth to say something.

"Don't," Cammy said. "I'm hungry. You hungry?" she asked. Jim reached to pull at a curl of her hair. Cammy slapped his hand away playfully. "Don't!"

Cammy got up and walked over to the dresser, still with the pronounced limp. She picked up the plate of onion rings and brought them back to the bed. After Cammy had downed two of them, she turned to Jim and said, "Aren't you going to have one? I brought them for you, after all."

The onion ring was lukewarm as Jim popped it into his mouth, nevertheless it was the sweetest thing he had ever tasted. The two of them sat in the dark until the plate was empty. Cammy placed the dish on the side table. She curled up beside Jim, pulling the covers up over her body. Jim wished he could stretch out this moment forever.

Now, Jim held the empty plate in his hands. The time was 7:30am. Jim sighed. Why couldn't I just let myself sleep in? Suddenly, he remembered that he had ordered breakfast the night before. He walked to the door, almost tripping over his open suitcase. He opened the door and looked down. There it was, sitting on a bamboo tray: two fried eggs, bacon, rye toast and a coke, with a side of pancakes. Jim was never a big coffee drinker. His father had forced him to drink some once, when he was a child. It tasted so bitter, he spat it out, much to his father's chagrin.

Jim set the breakfast tray on the desk by the window, shoving aside his satchel with all his notes. The first thing Jim noticed was that the eggs were cold…not even lukewarm, cold. The same went for the bacon, which was now brittle. It crumbled when he took a bite. Jim checked the toast. Stale. Breakfast had probably been there for hours. Jim took a sip of the soda; it was flat and watery. *Well played, Mrs. Norman*, thought Jim.

He picked at his cold breakfast, but he was thinking about Cammy. He was glad that he would have an excuse to see her again when he stopped by the auto body shop to check in on his car. Maybe he could use the time to get to know Cammy better. Maybe he could ask her to a dinner and a movie.

His mind still on Cammy, he nearly forgot his satchel as he headed for the door. At least he could get some writing done. Perhaps this little sidetrack wasn't such a bad thing after all, he thought as he walked down the stairs. Passing Anton on the stairs, Jim clapped him on the shoulder.

"Morning Anon." Jim said merrily.

Anton flinched at Jim's touch, recoiling.

"Hmmph" Anton replied, increasing the speed of his descent.

The finches in the cage on the staircase chirped merrily, Jim made a mental note to include them in the review he would write about the hotel—a little bit of local color. As he looked for the birds, he saw Mrs. Norman, who sat at the bottom of the staircase observing him as he descended.

"Good morning, Mr. Sutton. I hope you found my hotel to your satisfaction."

"Oh yes," said Jim. If she only knew. "Breakfast was particularly good." He smiled, not wanting to give her the satisfaction.

"I am *so* glad," Mrs. Norman said. "I'll make sure, then, you get it just the same way tomorrow."

"Oh, please do." He turned towards the lobby door.

"Leaving so soon Mr. Sutton?" Mrs. Norman purred.

"Yes, I'm headed over to the garage."

Mrs. Norman's jaw clenched ever so slightly. "You don't want to be leaving now, relax for a while. I have the morning papers if you like." Mrs. Norman inserted herself between Jim and the door.

"That's ok, I just want to see about my car." Jim waited for her to move out of his way. Mrs. Norman remained motionless.

"Mr. Sutton, I don't think you've fully experienced our hotel. Did you know the marble was imported all the way from Italy? The first owners of this hotel, the Quinns, had it shipped here through Canada, down the St. Lawrence Seaway to Lake Champlain—"

"That is very interesting, I'd *love* to hear all about it. Later." Jim interrupted as he brusquely moved toward the door.

Jim walked to the garage. The idea of seeing Cammy again got him walking fast, taking big strides past the fence where Kaiser Bill rested against the rusting chain-link. Bill sniffed the air, his one good eye popped open. Jim kept on walking, doing his best to avoid "eye" contact. Bill rose to his feet slowly. Then he heard a low growl as the dog shook his head, his dog tags jingling.

"I come in peace," Jim assured the dog, putting his hands in the air. Kaiser Bill cocked his head and growled again, this time a throatier rumble. Jim picked up his pace.

The front desk was empty. Jim rang the corroded bell that sat on the counter. Craning his neck to look back into the garage, he saw Dodge talking with Cammy. Dodge glanced over at the sound of the bell. He saw Jim and frowned. Dodge nudged Cammy. She turned to walk to the desk, Dodge following closely after.

"Can I help you?" Cammy said, her face blank.

"You sure can." Jim smiled as he laughed.

"Yes?" Cammy looked at him quizzically.

"Uh, yeah, I wanted to check on my car," Jim mumbled, taken off guard.

Cammy picked up a clipboard. "Ah, yes," she said, turning a page. "Mr.... Sutton? Yes. It's right here. Dodge was able to find one of the parts. I'll install that today. Unfortunately, he'll have go out on another run for the other. Is there anything else?"

"What?"

"Is there anything else you need, Mr. Sutton?"

"Uh...um...I guess not," Jim stammered.

"Well then, we'll be in touch." Cammy left. Dodge, who had been watching the whole time, laughed.

Was he crazy? She acted like she didn't even know him. Did he just dream last night? As he stood at the desk, collecting his thoughts, a police car careened into the parking lot, spraying gravel. Through the garage window Jim saw a wild-eyed, young police officer stumbled out of the car. He ran into the office. "Are you, you?" the policeman asked Jim. A silver badge that read "Deputy" was pinned to his chest. His name tag said AVERY. He looked to be 20, maybe 22. He was skinny with pale, almost translucent skin that came factory installed with his bright red hair. The insubstantial red wisp of a mustache on his lip quivered as he reiterated his point. "Are you him?"

"I don't know."

"Sutton," wheezed Deputy Avery, his hands on his knees. "You Sutton?"

"Yes," said Jim cautiously.

Cammy and Dodge entered the office.

"Alright, you need to come with me, sir," Deputy Avery said.

"Am I under arrest? What did I do?"

"Just come with me sir. I've been sent to retrieve you," said the deputy, gesturing to his car.

"Is he under arrest, Dwayne?" asked Cammy. "He deserves an answer."

The deputy glared at Cammy; his shoulders slumped. "No, you're not under arrest." He looked back at Cammy. "Happy?" Turning back to Jim he said, "I've been sent to bring you to the town hall meeting."

"Town hall meeting?" Jim asked. "I'm confused."

"Oh, yeah!" crowed Dodge, laughing. "This is gonna be good! I can't wait to see this."

Cammy pushed Dodge back into the garage. "You're not going anywhere, Dodge. You're fixing that axle, asshole. Then you're going on a parts run."

"Just go," Cammy said to Jim. "It's not that bad." For the first time since last night, she smiled at him.

Jim walked in a daze to the deputy's car. Avery opened the back door and put his hand on Jim's head.

"Hey! He doesn't need the perp ride treatment, does he Dwayne?" Cammy shouted. Deputy Avery looked back at Cammy with a withering glare, then hung his head.

"Would you like to ride up front, sir?" he said, clearly annoyed.

Relieved, Jim walked around to the passenger side of the car. Avery got in and shook his head at Jim before putting on his aviator-style sunglasses. He shifted the car into reverse and started to pull out of the parking lot. Jim looked back at Cammy who was standing in the doorway, her arms crossed, a funny look on her face. Cammy's eyes met Jim's then flicked away.

"Hey! Hey, remember, their bark's worse than their bite!" Cammy called out to him.

Jim watched her in the passenger side mirror as the police cruiser pulled away. Jim resolved to keep his mouth shut, especially since he had no idea what he had done or why he was being called to this town hall meeting. How did they even know he was there, or who he was?

The cruiser idled down Main Street, past *Le Grand Hotel Vermont* and then turned onto Maple Street. There were more buildings, including a red brick firehouse and City Hall.

Strawberry Fall's City Hall was an impressive edifice. Three stories tall, constructed from genuine Vermont Barre granite, in the neo-classical revival style of architecture. Judging by the crowds of people walking up the steps, it seemed to Jim that the whole town had shown up. Deputy Avery pulled up in front and parked his cruiser.

"Mr. Sutton, if you would follow me, I am to escort you in." Avery opened the car door.

Jim stepped out of the cruiser and tried to get his bearings. The crowd of people looked him coldly. Jim couldn't determine if this was the typical New England stoniness or something different. It felt different, like it was directed at him. He shook it off, looking to avoid their glaring faces. Facing the parking lot now something struck him. All the cars are brand new. Almost. Every car in the parking lot was from this year, or the last few. Jim might not know how to operate cars, but he could still tell a new one. He looked the other way down the street to the oncoming traffic. I'll be damned, brand new—does everyone in this town have a new car? He looked back again to the lot, well, almost everyone. The tow truck from the garage would have stuck out in most situations, but it its current position, was all the more obvious a rusty plebeian amongst its more upscale perfect sisters and brothers.

"I bet Dodge came to see the show," Jim muttered.

"What did you say?" Deputy Avery said, yanking his arm.

"Nothing."

"Enough sightseeing, buddy." Deputy Avery grabbed Jim tightly by the arm and pulled him toward the stairs. "Town meeting time."

Most towns in Vermont have a town meeting day on the first Tuesday in March. Strawberry Falls took the idea of the town hall and ran with it. Locals found the idea of elected officials so objectionable, that they made it their only form of government. Strawberry Falls' unusual civic arrangement came after a distasteful political scandal.

In 1962, the town had staked its fortune on a Visitor's Center that would capitalize on tourist dollars from those traveling through to ski in places north, such as Stowe or Smuggler's Notch. The town proved too obscure to attract those tourists and facing a fiscal crisis, taxes began to be levied to make up the shortfall.

An emergency town meeting was called in March of 1963 and a motion was brought to the floor to abolish the City Council and the Mayor. The proposal called for all town business to be held via Town Hall meetings—everything from the budget to the painting of streetlamps would be decided by consensus. The town of Strawberry Falls got used to this form of citizen government and never again elected a mayor or town council. From then on, the town could call a meeting at any time to discuss any matter. And Strawberry Falls had called a meeting that day, one with a specific item on the agenda. Jim had no idea that it was him.

Jim Sutton walked into the main room of Strawberry Fall's town hall. The room had ample seating, arranged in rows like pews. On the stage, in front of a green curtain, stood a wood podium. A glass and pitcher of water sat next to the podium, along with a small gavel. Soaring above everyone on the white plaster ceiling was a gilded bas relief medallion of an American Bald Eagle in flight, holding a cluster of maple branches in one foot and an American flag in the other.

Deputy Avery walked Jim down the center aisle toward the front benches. As he was escorted, Jim could see people glaring at him. What on earth did I do? thought Jim, as he was plunked unceremoniously down on an empty bench near the front. Avery looked at him with a self-satisfied smirk. He retreated to the back of the room where he crossed his arms, never taking his eyes off Jim.

The crowd of people in the room murmured to each other. It sounded like a flock of geese talking and squawking, a general unidentifiable din. Unexpectedly, the noise level dropped off, leaving one voice audible over the others.

"…well I don't know, the doctor says the rash will go away in a week or so." The voice trailed off as people craned their necks and stood up.

Jim heard a mechanical whir and stretched his neck to look. He could not see what or who people were looking at through crowd. He could track the progression of this person or thing as it journeyed down the aisle by watching the heads turning as it passed.

"It can't be…" Jim said, as he got his first good look. As the figure made the turn onto the ramp, Jim saw her in full: Mrs. Norman. She drove up to the podium, primly parked herself there and adjusted the microphone on the lectern.

"Ahem," her voice echoed through the hall, "I believe we can bring this meeting to order." She picked up the gavel and banged it on the table. "Old business?"

A tall man with long gray hair and a beard stood up, took out his glasses and unfolded a piece of paper. The man wore a gray suit, white button up shirt and tie-dye tie. He looked like the kind of guy who was a high-school guidance counselor by day, a past-his-prime rocker by night.

"Yes, Ma'am," he said, looking over the paper. "Last meeting, Randy Spangler applied for a variance on his barn expansion. It was pending approval from the architectural committee, headed up by Ralph."

"Ralph?" asked Mrs. Norman, looking over at a thin balding man in khaki pants and half-moon glasses. Ralph stood up and as he began to speak, Jim heard Cammy speaking to him, hardly above a whisper, right next to his left ear.

"That's Ralph Ahern, he's an architect. Moved here from New York City seven years ago. The tall, weird looking guy, he's Mike Ziter. He runs the video store." Jim started to turn his head.

"Don't turn your head!" hissed Cammy.

"What are you doing here?" whispered Jim.

"I can't let you face this by yourself," said Cammy said. "I know the ringleader that orchestrated this. I feel responsible in a way. She can be a busy body. Sorry." Jim looked up at Mrs. Norman, engaged in reviewing the various bits of old business.

"I don't understand what's going on here, why am I—"

"Shhhhhh...your part's coming up," she said.

"Thank you, Mr. Ziter," Mrs. Norman said. She turned her gaze ever so slightly in Jim's direction. "New business?" she said curtly.

"I have some, Abby." A middle-aged woman stood up. She wore her brown hair a no-nonsense bob. She adjusted the hem of her plain work shirt nervously.

"Chair, please. Ms. Stein," Mrs. Norman said.

"Uh yeah. So 'Chair,' me and my partner..." Ms. Stein gestured to another woman, sitting to her left, she bore a similar no-nonsense haircut, but wore a simple black frock. They could have been sisters, but clearly were not. "We would like to apply for a zoning variance to add a shed to our property."

"Granted," Mrs. Norman said. "Unless there are any objections. Any opposed?" she asked. Jim craned his neck, not a hand was raised. "Good. Approved then. Thank you, Miriam and Edna. Moving on then. More new business?"

A ropy Native American man, wearing a red baseball cap stood up, scowling. "If it pleases the chair?"

"The chair recognizes Charles St. Onge" Mrs. Norman replied.

"I submit my petition to repatriate the land that was stolen from the Abenaki Nation." He looked around the room. Audible groans could be heard form some of the townspeople in attendance. "All the land from here to Swanton is the legal and lawful property of the Abenaki peoples!" He gestured to the room at large.

"*Mister* St. Onge." Mrs. Norman replied with a note of exasperation. "This is *old* business. We all are well aware of your claims, and those of your compatriots such as Homer up north. There is nothing that would please our town than to assuage your concerns, but as you know, this is a complicated issue. Not as pressing as other business." She stared the man down.

"Noted." Charles grumbled, and began to sit down.

"Charles?"

"Yes?" Charles replied, frozen in mid-sit.

"Is there anything *else* you would like to address?" Mrs. Norman smiled through clenched teeth. "Something more *pressing?*"

"Oh!" Charles sprang up "Yes." His face grew serious again.

"I would like to address the issue of vandalism to town property, reckless driving, and leaving the scene of a crime without notifying the proper authorities." Charles St. Onge seethed as he spat the words out. Jim shifted uncomfortably in his seat as all eyes turned to him.

"Deputy Avery, you have a report?" asked Mrs. Norman.

"Yes, Ma'am," said the deputy. He took out his notepad as he walked towards the podium. "I received a complaint last night that the town sign had been run over and damaged. I went out to survey said damage and saw there were indications of a vehicular involvement in this particular incidental occurrence presently that I was currently faced with."

A satisfied look passed over Deputy Avery's face. "After assessing the damage and taking forensic samples of paint chips from the sign, I returned to town to process the evidence." Avery flipped to the next page. "This morning I received an anonymous tip pertaining to the identity of the particular individual involved in the crime." He glared at Jim. "I had information that he was a flight risk and was attempting to flee the scene of the crime. Upon receiving this information, I moved to apprehend the perpetrator and bring him to justice, which I did. And he is here now. Right here. Now." Deputy Avery flipped the book shut but quickly added, "Oh, yes. I would like to petition the Town Hall for funds to process the samples of paint I took from the damaged sign to link them to the car currently at the Norman Auto Body."

"I'm sure that won't be necessary," said Mrs. Norman looking at Deputy Avery. "There must be ample evidence, perhaps an eyewitness or someone who overheard a confession." She looked around the room. "Where is Dodge Norman. I don't see him." At this point, Cammy stood up.

"Dodge is at the garage, mom. I told him to stay there."

"You will address me as Mrs. Norman or The Chair, Camaro, in this venue," said Mrs. Norman icily. "Dodge was called upon to give testimony. His presence was specifically requested."

"I told him this was a waste of time, *mother*," Cammy spat. "I'm ending this pointless exercise." She turned to Jim. "Did you crash into the sign?"

"Y-yes," Jim stammered.

"Good," Cammy said. She then turned to Charles St. Onge. "How much will it cost to repair the sign?"

"I guess with repairs and paint, two new posts, maybe Seven hundred... Seven fifty."

"Seven hundred and fifty dollars," Cammy repeated. She then turned to Jim. "You'll pay it, right?"

Jim stared at her.

She nodded as if to say, *Say yes dummy.*

"Yes, yes of course," Jim said.

"Good," Cammy said. She turned to her mother and Deputy Avery. "It's settled. He'll pay. The sign will get fixed."

"There's still the matter of fleeing the scene of the crime," interjected Deputy Avery.

"Come on Dwayne," said Cammy. "Fleeing the scene of the crime? The guy is staying in our town. He's having his car fixed here. He's hardly fleeing."

"Still," said Deputy Avery in a wounded voice.

"Still what? He's paying. It's done," Cammy said. She addressed her mother. "It's *done*, right?"

Mrs. Norman stared at her daughter, her left eye twitching. "I think Miss Norman is correct in this matter, but it's not up to me. I am not a judge. It should be up to the town." She gestured to the room. "Let's open it up to a vote, shall we?" She straightened in her chair, adjusting her jacket. "All those in favor of Mr. Sutton paying the fine and closing the matter, vote aye now."

Jim looked around the room as hands shot up, and he heard a multitude of voices say "Aye," not quite in unison.

"All those opposed who would like to seek legal means against Mr.

Sutton, vote aye now," said Mrs. Norman, looking around the room. This time, arms again were raised, and "ayes" could be heard, but not as many as the previous vote.

"It appears that the fine stands. As long as Mr. Sutton pays it, he is free to go," said Mrs. Norman. "Is there any other new business?" No hands were raised so she took her gavel and banged it on the table. "Then I call this special Town Hall meeting closed." She pointed at Jim "I suggest you pay your fine as soon as possible, then leave."

Jim stood up and turned around, half expecting Cammy to have disappeared. He was pleasantly surprised to see her still there.

"Thanks," Jim said to Cammy. "You really saved me back there."

"Nah, you were fine," replied Cammy. "They would have come to this conclusion on their own. I just sped up the bullshit."

"Well, thanks anyway. It was nice to have a friend in here."

"Awww...aren't you just so sweet," teased Cammy. "Speaking of friends... ugh, here comes Mary LaPointe." A woman about Cammy's age approached them. She dragged two young boys behind her with a baby perched on her hip. She looked to be six or seven months pregnant. A bored man in a Von Dutch trucker hat trailed behind her. The man seemed oblivious to the pack of children she was herding or more likely did not care. Jim couldn't discern. What Jim could tell was, Mary had locked her gaze on Cammy and was making a beeline straight toward her.

"Camaro Norman! I thought that was you. I told Judd here it was you, and you know what he said? He said I just had to come over and say hello. So here I am, and...hello!" Mary said this with a bright smile on her face. Jim looked at Jed and seriously doubted that Jed was aware of who Cammy even was.

"Hello, Mary," Cammy said.

"Say hello, Jed!" Mary prodded her husband with her elbow.

"Hey," Jed grunted.

"Well, I said to Jed is it Camaro? Who can tell under all that dirt? It could be a boy as much as it could be a girl," she said, laughing. "Scratch a surface, and I'm sure that it's you. How have you been?" She didn't wait for an answer. "I am pregnant again; can you believe it? Of course, you can, look at me," Mary said, looking down at her belly. "Doctor says it's twins. Boys. Again. I am just swamped with boys." She rolled her eyes crazily. "I keep on saying it's Jed's fault on account of he's such a big. Strong. Man." She turned her gaze to Jim. "Speaking of men, who's this fella?"

"This is Jim. And we're leaving," said Cammy, turning to go.

"Wait, don't go," implored Mary, temporarily letting go of the hands of her two boys who then immediately disappeared into the hall. "I think what you did was nice for this young man, but poor Dwayne."

"Dwayne can get over it," Cammy said. "I did. It was *high school*."

"All I'm saying, Camaro, is that…"

"*Cammy*, please."

"All I'm saying, Cammy, is that Dwayne never got over you. He's a good man. He comes around the house, you know? To talk to Jed. Well, not talk, mostly drink beers on the porch. But he talks about you all the time."

"He can talk all he wants, I'm not interested," Cammy said. She grabbed Jim's hand. "You can tell him that for me next time he's over for beers." She started to walk away, gently pulling Jim with her. "C'mon, let's go." Jim looked back at Mary and Jed standing with their brood. She slapped Judd on his shoulder and then proceeded to look for her errant children.

"I truly hate her," Cammy said. She let go of his hand as soon as they were out of view of Mary. Jim felt all the eyes of the town hall on him as the two of them walked through the hall. Seven hundred dollars. The trip kept getting more and more expensive.

As Cammy lead Jim through the crowd, he noticed that Mrs. Norman was starting at him. Her eyes burned through him. He tripped and stumbled into Cammy.

"Whoa, what's going on?" Cammy said.

"Nothing," Jim mumbled. His eyes flicked to Mrs. Norman. Cammy tracked them and craned her neck.

"What? My mom, you want to see her? You know what? I think we should. What she did was really over the line."

"Uh, no." Jim said, pushing forward.

"I'll back you up," Cammy said.

"Honestly, I just want to get back to my room and write."

"Oh, Ok." Cammy nodded to Jim. "Come on, I'll give you a ride. My truck is parked around the corner. I'll take you anywhere you want to go."

"I don't have anywhere to go, except my room," Jim said. He was relieved he had avoided a dramatic confrontation.

"Oh, yeah right," Cammy said. "The car. Well, hop in. I'll take you somewhere." She walked up to the truck, opened the driver-side door, got in then kicked open the passenger side. "Get in, I won't bite."

"I don't know…" Jim hesitated.

"Get in. I owe you an explanation."

FIXING A HOLE

1977

Linda was feeling particularly melancholy. A mysterious package had arrived at their P.O. Box in Burlington. Heavy, wrapped with twine and packing tape, the box bore no return address. The canceled stamps said Dover, Delaware, so Linda had an idea whom the box may be from.

She had waited to open the box until she returned home. It sat on the passenger seat of the station wagon, an unwelcome presence. When she pulled into the driveway, she used her keys to cut open the tape. Linda looked inside the box. It was a jumbled mess from the long journey to Vermont, but Linda could easily see what made the box so heavy. It was filled to the brim with photos. Of her. Of Linda, her family. She shuffled through them, picture after picture of her, of the kids—it seemed like every picture she ever had taken of her as a child. Then she found the note:

"*We have no daughter now.*" It was in her mother's distinctive, flowing handwriting.

Linda closed the box, brought it inside and pushed it into the back of the hallway closet. Closing the door, she looked at her tools sitting next to the closet. *The roof.* It was as good a day as any and work would hopefully settle her troubled mind.

She perched on the roof of her house on Christmas Island, Vermont and took a moment to take in the view. Really take it in. After all the time on the island, and all of the chaos and stress, she had become inured to the beauty that was Vermont. Her pressing project of the moment was to replace the damaged slate roof shingles. While she was up there, she would clean out the Yankee gutters. When a Yankee gutter starts to leak, it's not as simple as a patch or replacement as it is built into the house *itself*. Many homeowners would tar the metal gutters when they developed the inevitable leak. This solution was adequate to the job, but over time, even tar cracks and water can find its way into the house.

From this vantage point, Linda could see above the tree line and got lost in the vista. It was November, most of Vermont was past prime leaf season. But, on the west side of Christmas Island, there was a clutch of maple trees in full color, standing in contrast against the pine trees that dominated this part of the island. Here and there, streaks of fire red and gold color shot up the pine trees as well. Linda never thought poison ivy could be beautiful, but there it was. Maybe it was the toxins. She couldn't say, but they were flame red, bright and bold against the green of their host trees.

Beyond the pines from this height, Linda could see the dappled light reflecting off of Lake Champlain, thousands of jewels shining and winking as if they shone just for her. She sat there, lost in the moment until a voice broke her reverie.

"I'm going back to the stand!"

It was Bob. He had stopped by the house for a break from a lunch rush that never came.

Once upon a time, with the kids out of the house and both of them home, it would have been cause to fool around. Linda could hardly remember the last time they had sex. Most of the time Bob staggered home, turned on the TV, and camped there for the rest of the night. Most nights Linda just wanted to sleep as well. These days sex seemed like a long-forgotten notion, something that Linda knew people did, just not her. Bob strolled down the path to the snack stand. Linda stood up and stretched. She walked across the roof toward the chimney.

Linda heard the crack of a slate shingle under her boot and felt a slight give to the roof. Before she knew it, she was falling through rotted shingles and underlayment right into the spare attic bedroom the kids used as a playroom. As she tumbled ass over teakettle, she thought about what she might be falling on. She hoped a moth-eaten bed mattress was below. No such luck. Linda slammed into the hard wooden floor, landing on her side. She lay there gulping for breath, holding her arms over her face to shield it against falling debris.

Linda couldn't say how long she was on the floor before she dared to move. She wiggled her toes and other extremities. *So far so good*, she thought. Linda counted her blessings and realized that she was, in fact all right. Not to say there wasn't any damage.

Linda gingerly changed out of her work clothes and found a large, angry blue-black bruise that went from her armpit to mid-thigh. Her heavy work clothes, which consisted of an old shirt, gloves and overalls had taken the brunt of the impact, though she did find a nasty scratch that went the length of her arm. Linda went to the tiny cabinet. She found a bottle of hydrogen peroxide. Linda looked around the small bathroom for a place to sit, the only option was the toilet, which was of course dwarf-sized. Sitting on the toilet, knees up to her chin, Linda contorted her body and poured hydrogen peroxide on the cut to clean it. She winced as it foamed and bubbled. After cleaning herself up, Linda limped up to the attic to survey the damage.

As Linda stared up through the gaping hole in the ceiling, she could see clouds drifting by in the perma-gray sky. This is the worst possible time, she winced. Winter's almost here, and the snow is coming.

Living in a house this old meant it was drafty in the best of conditions. Linda stared at the hole in the roof, envisioning of all their money flying out of it, flapping away like all the other migratory birds on the island, never to be seen again. Doing the mental arithmetic, she could see what already was shaping up to be a lean Christmas becoming downright Dickensian. After cursing her bad luck, the pragmatist kicked in. There was no sense wallowing in misery. They needed to fix this roof, and quickly. First, she had to break the bad news to Bob.

"What did you do?" Linda heard from the other side of the phone. Linda had called Bob at work after staring at the rotary in the kitchen for two minutes. Not so much in fear of telling her husband about the damage that had been inflicted to her and the roof, but to gain her composure, to have a moment of peace, of nothingness. It was what some might call a Zen moment.

"I'm fine, Bob," Linda said, annoyed at his tone.

"Oh, of course…are you okay?" he said his voice strained. "There's a hole in the roof?"

"Yes, I made it when I fell through it."

"Were you careful?"

"Of course, I was careful. I didn't make the roof rotten, Bob. I just stepped on it." Linda doodled angrily on the little pad of paper they kept by the phone for messages. A 3-D cube, a house, and the word *ASSHOLE*.

"If you hadn't been up there messing around, this wouldn't have happened."

"Are you blaming *me*, Bob?" retorted Linda incredulously. "This is not my fault."

"Well, you were up there. If you were not, the roof wouldn't be broken, would it?" Bob said. "You'll have to find a way to fix it."

"Of course, I will find a way. I always find a way."

"The house is your responsibility, Linda. I work, you know?"

"I work too, Bob. I work my ass off cleaning and fixing up the ridiculous excuse for a house while you play big shot." She clenched her fist so tightly, it drew blood. She could have broken her neck falling through that roof. Part of her wished that she had died in the fall. Then Bob would have been forced to find her. That would have shown him. Then Linda thought about her kids. The vision of them finding her cold lifeless body gave her chills.

"Just do your job," Bob said, "and I'll do mine. Remember, my job makes actual money. Money we now have to spend on your accident." The harsh words spat out of the receiver.

Linda recoiled from it as if she were holding a snake. "Fuck you." She didn't even scream it like she wanted to. It came out as a sigh of exasperation, more or an exhalation than exclamation. She hung up the phone. So hard that the bell in the receiver rang out.

Linda stalked over to the cabinet and flung it open. She grabbed the yellow pages from the stack of books, next to the cooking books. At least the accident caused some excitement in their worn-out, repetitive lives. She furiously thumbed through the pages. M...P...R...Roofing. Linda spent the next few hours calling roofing contractors.

Of the roofers that actually picked up; two told her it was out of roofing season for them and to call back in the spring; three refused to come out to Christmas Island at all because of the remoteness of the house. The two that would come informed her that they were booked until the new year. The last contractor suggested that she wait for her husband to come home.

Linda hung up the phone. As usual, she was on her own. She would have to figure out a way to fix this by herself. A thought popped into her mind: the kids. She would have to pick up the kids in two hours. Great, just peachy keen. Maybe if she hurried up and caught the early ferry, she could stop by the library in Burlington. Do they even have books on how fix roofs? After she picked up the kids, she planned to stop by the hardware store and buy some plastic sheeting to cover the hole the best she could.

Linda started up the Volkswagen and set off to the ferry landing. From time to time, Linda would see Christmas Town's handyman, Nick Summers, walking, or waddling as it were, down the road on his way to his service shed. Pleasantries were occasionally exchanged in passing—never anything longer than a brief conversation. Nick waved at Linda as she slowed down to pass him.

"Afternoon Mrs. Sutton. Headed out early today?"

Normally, she would have responded with a platitude. Today Linda's guard was down. Her patience thin, she spoke frankly, more truthfully than she normally would have.

"Well, Nick, I'm headed out to figure out a way to fix a hole in my roof."

"Hole in your roof? What happened? Branch?"

"Me, I happened," said Linda. "I was cleaning the gutters, and I fell through it, right into the attic."

"Are you okay? Were you hurt?"

"I'm fine," said Linda said. "The only thing hurt was my pride."

"Is there anything I can do to help?" said Nick, looking genuinely concerned.

"Not unless you know how to fix roofs—"

"As a matter of fact, Mrs. Sutton, I do. I'd be happy to help you," Nick said.

Linda looked at him, her mouth agape. She was spent from the day, spent from the fight with Bob, from the frustrating calls to the roofing men. She was touched by this act of kindness. But she couldn't possibly accept Nick's help, even if she had unintentionally asked him for it.

"Oh no, I really couldn't," she said, feeling embarrassed.

"Winter is coming, and so will the snow. You'll have a hell of a time getting a roofer out here on such short notice. It would be my pleasure," Nick said.

"I can't put you out, take you away from your job," protested Linda.

"Nonsense. Plastic elves and gingerbread houses can wait. I insist. Final word. I'll stop by later and take a look. Tomorrow we can start."

"But—"

"Final word," Nick said gently. He turned away from the car and started walking to the maintenance shed. Linda was not sure what had transpired. Linda glanced at her watch. She had better hurry if she was to make the early ferry. Putting the car in gear, she drove away.

Her schedule was spiraling out of her grasp with each diversion. She had barely enough time to find the books she needed in the library before picking up the kids and making the ferry back home.

There was not enough time to make the dinner she had originally planned. She had planned on a roasted rosemary chicken with potatoes, but because of the accident, she went to Plan B. Linda grabbed four frozen pot pies, two turkey, two chicken, from the freezer. She didn't have time to preheat the oven, so it would just have to do going from cold. Bob arrived home from the stand and sat down at the kitchen table. There was a turkey pot pie cooling on his plate.

"Pot pie?" asked Bob, with just enough disdain in his voice to irritate Linda.

"Bob, after the day I've had—"

"It's okay, pot pie is fine," Bob said. "Isn't it, kids?" Bob said, leaning over to Jim and Lyndsey, who were quietly waiting for their mother to sit at the table before they dug into their own pot pies. For the kids, pot pies were a treat. They had little appreciation for homemade food, much to Linda's frustration. Bob started to sing to the kids.

"Chicken pot pie and I don't care! Chicken pot pie and I don't care! Chicken pot pie and I don't caaaaaare!" This song delighted the kids. To Linda's dismay, they proceeded to sing it over and over and over.

The repeated choruses of "Chicken Pot Pie" ringing in her ears, Linda set about clearing the table and tackling the dishes. The small sink was unmanageable. Bob sidled up to her and dumped a new stack of dishes in the soapy water. They disappeared into the murky water like a sinking boat meeting its demise, a trail of bubbles in their wake.

Bob watched Linda stubbornly trying to scrub encrusted food from a plate she had been soaking since before dinner. "You okay?"

"Yes, I am fine," Linda said.

"I'm sorry about earlier. You just caught me at a bad time."

"It's okay, Bob. I forgive you."

"Don't you want to hear about my day?" asked Bob.

Linda heard the wounded tone in his voice. "Sure, Bob. Let's hear about your day."

Bob chose to ignore this tone, because he continued. He had a planned speech in his mind and was going through the prewritten text.

"I was going over the books. We're doing okay, but I definitely see an uptick coming with Thanksgiving and Christmas. I think we have enough to hire a seasonal worker."

"Really Bob?" Linda said, turning toward him. "Do you think that's wise with the gaping hole in our roof?"

"I think it's a good idea. You know how hard I've been working? It's that, or you come and work a shift."

"You know that I can't, not now with the roof and the kids."

"All the more reason, then," said Bob, walking behind Linda and massaging her neck. "I'll put an ad in the paper."

"Fine."

Later, Linda listened to Bob making a big show of putting the kids to sleep. Bob decided to play monster with the kids, chasing them around the house. As a result, a twenty-minute process took two hours. When Bob finally got the kids to sleep, he triumphantly came into their bedroom. Linda was still awake, her mind full of restless thoughts of home repair and money woe. Bob felt slighted by her indifference and told her so. Linda, exhausted from the day, just let it go and turned on her side. It wasn't long until she heard Bob's light snores from the other side of the bed.

Linda woke up the next morning to find Bob gone. Rousing the kids from bed was especially difficult. They had gone to bed so much later than their normal bedtime that Linda had to practically dynamite them from under the covers. It didn't help that the house was freezing cold.

After a grumpy breakfast, in which her children complained about everything, including the cold cereal, Linda packed them into the car. She cranked the heat to as high as it would go. Volkswagens took a while to get warm, so cold air blew out of the vents. Of course, the kids slept the whole ferry ride to the mainland while Linda stared ahead blankly. She dropped off the kids at their respective destinations then made the return trip to Christmas Island.

Linda was so inured to the spectacle of Christmas Town that she hardly noticed it anymore. The bright lights and fanciful decorations just blended into the background as she drove by them. As she turned onto the bypass road toward home, she saw Nick. He was sitting on a pile of asphalt shingles . Linda had completely forgotten her conversation with him the day before. Was it only a day? So much had happened. She certainly did not expect Nick to keep his word. He smiled as she approached him.

"I'm sorry if I gave you the wrong idea. I can't let you do this." Linda gestured at the pile of construction materials that Nick had brought with him. In his red pickup there were electric saws, miter boxes, roofing hammers, and tar paper—nothing extravagant or particularly exotic, but beyond her means to obtain.

"I know your family is struggling here," Nick said.

"It's too much. I want to pay you for this."

"Nonsense. I won't hear it," Nick said.

Linda noticed that Nick had already set up his own ladder in addition to hers in preparation for work. "Now, I have some ideas of what we should do, but it is your home, so…" He made a gesture toward Linda. Linda took out her bag and pulled out a library book on roofing.

"Do you learn everything from books?" asked Nick.

"Yes," Linda said.

"There are a great many things that can be learned from books, but woodworking is not one of them." Nick took the book from Linda. "You should have come to me sooner."

"I don't need any help. I can do it fine on my own," she said. She grabbed the book back from Nick.

"I'm sure you've done amazing work. I only suggest that sometimes an apprentice needs a master."

"Oh," said Linda uncomfortably. "Well, ok then."

Nick stood up and looked around, craning his neck to look up at the roof. "You've done a nice job. I am particularly impressed with the Yankee gutter you replaced on the front porch. Very tricky business."

"But..."

"I recommend we replace the whole roof. Slate roofs last forever. If you've got rot from leaks in one place, you've got it everywhere most likely."

Linda looked up at the roof—her mouth a drawn line of concentration. "So, we take it down to the rafters then?"

"Exactly."

"What are we waiting for then?" She walked away toward the ladder.

"Indeed," laughed Nick as he bent down to pick up his tool belt.

The two of them started the process of stripping the roof. It killed Linda to trash all the beautiful slate. She knew there was no way to remove the thin brittle rock without shattering it. Linda was amazed at how agile Nick was on the roof. The man worked without a safety line, unlike Linda, who had been rigged up with a harness and rope. Nick bounded across the roof nimbly. He was fearless. By afternoon the two of them had created a mound of debris.

"I think we can call it a day," Nick said as he tacked the last edge of the plastic tarp to the roof beams. Linda stood on the inside of the attic, checking to make sure that there were no obvious holes in which rain or, God forbid, snow could get in. The sun was setting, its light cast through the plastic sheeting, illuminating the whole attic in an ethereal golden glow. As Linda turned her head from the bright light of the setting sun, her eye caught Nick's shadow, dancing across the wall.

The next day, Linda knew Nick would be waiting for her after she made her morning journey to drop off the kids. The chill felt sharper than the day before. Nick was holding a thermos in addition to his tool belt. As Linda got out of the car, she waved to Nick. He nodded, removed the plastic cup from the top of the thermos, unscrewed the cap, and poured steaming liquid into the cup. He held out the cup for her.

"Coffee? You shouldn't have," said Linda.

"I didn't." Nick winked mischievously. Linda, curious, brought the cup to her lips

"Hot chocolate!" She exclaimed with delight.

"There's nothing better on a cold morning than hot chocolate my father always said."

Nick and Linda both decided that they would take advantage of working from the inside attic as long as possible. The process of dragging the plywood sheets up the stairs was tedious. Once they started nailing them in place, the work went quickly. When Nick mentioned his parents, a thought started that stayed with Linda all day. To her shame, she had never really thought about Nick's parents or asked where he came from.

Linda was curious. It took a while for her to get up the courage to ask Nick the question that had been bouncing around her brain since that morning. "Nick, you mentioned your parents this morning. What were they like?" She immediately regretted the question.

"What were they like?" responded Nick. "Do you mean, were they like me?"

Linda reddened and felt horrible.

"I'm sorry, I shouldn't have—"

"It's okay. I don't mind."

"My parents were both little people. They were hired to be a part of the scenery of Christmas Town. You may or may not be aware of the history of the attraction. At one time there was a 'real live elf village.'" He punctuated with air quotes showing his disdain. "There were over fifty 'elves' living here on Christmas Island. As the fortunes of the attraction waned, the population dwindled until there was only one family left on the island, my family." Nick's eyes grew sad. "My parents didn't mind staying on the island but refused to be displayed as a living attraction. They were housed for free in another home on the island, one that the owners assumed would be more suited for their stature."

"This. This is your house? We took this from you?"

"No, no. The house was never theirs. It always belonged to the owners of Christmas Town," Nick said. "Well, it was owned by Christmas Town until your family bought it."

"We evicted you to come here?" Linda said, feeling sick.

"Not at all. My parents died when I was seventeen. Did you know they're buried here on the island? There's a small cemetery overlooking the north shore. It's actually nice." He stopped for a moment, lost in thought. "The owners offered me a position as an 'elf' because of my history with the park. I turned them down. I said I would stay on if I could apprentice the island handyman and one day take over when he retired."

"What history?" asked Linda.

She could see genuine pain in his eyes. She felt terrible.

"You are looking at the only 'real live elf 'ever born in Christmas Town." He gestured to his whole body.

"You were born here?" Linda said, her jaw slack.

"When my mother became pregnant, the owners of Christmas Town were elated. It became a marketing angle that they could exploit. My parents were put on display full-time in Elf Village. People came to see the pregnant elf. There were advertisements in the paper and even a radio ad. There was some concern and curiosity over whether I would be 'normal' or like them. Yes, little people can have 'normal-sized' children. You can imagine management's delight when it was revealed that I would be a dwarf like my parents. The owners seized upon another promotion opportunity. They announced a contest to name the baby elf. They convinced my parents to participate by offering them an extra wages. The owners got to choose the name. I was named Nicholas Claus Summers. I was named after jolly old Saint Nick himself."

"I...I..." stammered Linda. She wanted very much to be out of this conversation.

"Don't worry, it's okay," Nick said. "After I was born, my parents had a change of heart about Christmas Town exploiting their child. The owners had plastered my newborn face all over New England. People came to see me. They would have their picture taken for a dollar. They lined up three deep to see me paraded out in a baby buggy that was drawn by two miniature ponies. Christmas Town made a lot of money. My parents never saw a dime other than the pittance they got for my name. The owners begged my parents to reconsider. They were firm. I was not to be a part of the spectacle anymore."

"I am so sorry. I feel terrible that we got you kicked out your home," said Linda. She placed her hand on his.

"Oh, you didn't. No one has lived here for years." Nick smiled at Linda. "My parents both died of pneumonia, I moved out. I wanted to be free of anything that reminded me of them, of that time. I was glad to hear that it was sold and a family would be moving in. I was surprised to hear it was a normal sized family, but it pleased me nonetheless. I was even happier to see you restore the old lady. You're doing a great job."

"Really? I work so much on this house. It never feels like I get anywhere."

"I've noticed," Nick said. "When I make my rounds, I pass here. I can see the difference."

"I'm glad someone notices. Bob never says anything." She realized that she was perhaps sharing too much. "I mean, Bob's so busy with the stand. He comes home tired from working on his feet all day. He just wants to have dinner and sleep. I feel sorry for him."

"Well, I think it's time we put down our first course of shingles, don't you?" interjected Nick, mercifully changing the subject.

Linda had never found manual labor to be stultifying. To the contrary, she found some degree of pleasure in the more repetitive tasks. Linda discovered that when they achieved a rhythm in the placement and nailing of the new shingles, it was relaxing, almost hypnotic. Before she knew it, they had covered the whole roof. Linda took a moment and looked around. It was new, fresh, and perfect. Linda felt a great swelling of satisfaction as she surveyed her handiwork.

Linda sank to her knees on the top of the roof. She leaned against the brick chimney and started crying. Nick bounded across the roof to her.

"Linda, what's the matter?" he asked, trying to comfort her.

"I don't know," sobbed Linda, but she knew. Linda had enjoyed having another person to talk to. Tomorrow would be a day like all the ones before the accident, alone in the house. She would continue her projects, filling the time until she retrieved the kids and Bob came home. She would be alone again— alone with nothing but her doubts to keep her company.

GETTING HIGH

2000

"Where are we going?" Jim asked. He had only gotten into the car because Cammy said she would give him some answers. Such as: Why did you sleep with me, then ignore me?

"I'm taking you somewhere special. It's not much farther." As she made a turn, the massive brick building came into sight as they drove beyond the map and aspen trees. What once had been a mill, the living heart of the town, now re-purposed for selling overpriced furniture, and bric-a-brac, a glorified flea market.

"Antiques," Jim replied dryly.

"Yes and no."

The rusty tow truck shuddered and stopped at the cracked blacktop parking lot where it wheezed and ticked angrily. Jim got out of the truck and started to walk toward the entrance to the mill.

"Where do you think you're going?" asked Cammy.

"We're not going inside?"

"Inside? No." Cammy had a huge smile. "Outside…and maybe upside."

"Upside?"

Cammy extended her index finger and pointed to the sky. Jim looked up. All he could see was the side of the factory and the massive twin brick smokestacks.

"Up there?"

"What, don't you trust me?"

"I trust you fine." Jim really didn't, but what else could he say? "Can we even be here? Isn't this private property?"

Cammy laughed. "Yeah, it is. But trust me, they won't mind."

Cammy turned and walked under a metal fire escape. The ladder was retracted. Cammy stood under it for a moment, searching the ground for something. She bent over and picked up a fist-sized rock. Taking careful aim, Cammy threw the rock and hit a release lever. The ladder came loose and clattered down with a loud clang, accompanied by a shower of rust. Cammy put one foot on the ladder and looked back at Jim. "Come on now..." She started climbing.

Jim gulped. Placing his right foot gingerly on the first rung, he tested it with his weight. When it held, Jim began climbing.

"Stop looking at my ass," Cammy shouted down at him. Jim, averted his gaze, not daring to glance up. He gingerly pulled himself over the top, stretched and looked around. They were at the top of the mill. Cammy began to walk toward the immense brick smokestacks.

"Halfway there!" she said brightly. "Don't worry, they haven't used those stacks in fifty years."

"Who's worried?"

"You want to go first?" she asked.

"Why don't you?" asked Jim. "This is your thing, remember?" He looked up.

"*Such* a gentleman," Cammy said. Jim made a move to start climbing.

"Kidding, kidding!" Cammy said, stopping him. Cammy started her ascent. Jim followed behind. This climb was different than the first one, just a straight shot but...Right. Up. The. Smokestack.

After a minute or two Jim's arms and legs started to feel leaden, but he kept climbing. Up and up they went, it seemed like there was no end in sight until his hand reached for a rung and grasped empty air. *At last*, Jim thought as he pulled himself up.

The opening of the smokestack had been covered with what looked to be two by fours and beams. In the middle of the deck sat two folding beach chairs. Cammy already up, leaned against the questionable wrought iron railing looking out over the valley. Jim tentatively tested the deck with his foot, trying to sense any rot or give. It seemed solid enough, so he chanced it. He stood next to Cammy at the rail. What he saw took his breath away.

Strawberry Falls is nestled between two valleys in the foothills of the Green Mountains. From their vantage point on the top of the smokestack Cammy and Jim could see the whole valley in three hundred and sixty degrees. The effect gave the impression of being surrounded by an endless sea of trees. The village below looked like a picturesque miniature. The Willoughby River snaked lazily through the vista. Jim could see the whole town, including Norman Auto Body and its junkyard backed up to what looked to be rows and rows of corn fields.

"Wow," Jim said, stunned at the sight.

"Right?" asked Cammy. She looked out over the valley.

Jim peeked over the edge. Whenever he was near a ledge, he always wondered what it would be like to hurl himself over the edge. Swallowing the impulse Jim stepped back.

"You're sure we're allowed up here. I feel like maybe I'm being set up again. Is that cop around the corner?"

"Relax. I know the owner," Cammy said.

"You do?" Jim said, "And they don't m—"

Cammy gave him a knowing look.

"Oh…Is there something she doesn't own here?"

"Mother doesn't own everything. Just some things." Cammy's smile faded slightly. "This building is important though. More than you would think."

"How so?" Jim asked, his writer sense kicking in.

"When this town was founded, the Sloat Textile Mill provided uniforms for the union army during the civil war. Most of the town could trace their fortunes to this mill. Cammy leaned down and picked up a rock from the roof.

"Strawberry Falls prospered for a while. Then like life itself, time and progress passed the town by. When World War Two came, the mill lost its government contract, and it simply just could not sustain the cost of staying open. So, it shut down."

"The town must have struggled."

"It would have, but a savior showed up in the form of the Color-Brite Paint Company." A note of disdain colored Cammy's words. "The mill was perfect for them. You see, they were a Canadian company out of Montreal. The prospect of a factory across the border, so close was too good to pass up. So, they set up shop, converted the mill to a paint factory and re-employed those workers who had lost their jobs. It seemed the perfect fit. They even created a special color just to mark the opening of the new factory: Strawberry Falls Red. The whole town got behind Color-Brite. Someone had the brilliant idea of a town wide promotion. They would literally paint the town red."

"The whole town?" Jim said incredulously.

"The. Whole. Town," Cammy replied. "Red. It was promoted as Paint the Town Red. Every house bought into it. But they didn't think it through.

It was the nineteen fifties, and when people started saying 'better dead than red about the communism...' within a year there was not one single red house left in Strawberry Falls."

Jim started to laugh, but there was a look in Cammy's eyes that gave him pause.

"The mill was good for the town, for the jobs, but bad for other things. The production of latex paint stunk up the town, an acrid, chemical smell hung to almost everything around here. These were the days before the EPA and the clean water act. Do you know they nicknamed the Willoughby River the 'Rainbow River' on account that it would literally change color depending on what shade of paint they were manufacturing?"

"No," Jim said lamely.

"Of course, you wouldn't," Cammy scolded playfully. "But that wasn't the worst. Like most companies, Color-Brite was concerned with worker productivity. There had been numerous reports of workers sneaking off the line for cigarette breaks. Their solution was to chain the doors shut. After which, productivity rates began to climb along with profits."

"That's bad, I mean it couldn't possibly be safe."

"No. It was not. It was the fourth of July weekend of nineteen fifty-seven. It was unseasonably hot. No one knows how the fire started. It took hold on the first floor and by the time anyone realized what was happening it had spread out of control. The line workers ran to the exits, but the doors were chained. From the outside."

"My god."

"Yeah," Cammy continued. "Those workers were trapped. By the time the fire department came it was too late. They cut the chains and the door was blocked with charred bodies. Three deep. One hundred and fifty people died that day."

"That's terrible..."

"Color-Brite swore they would rebuild and help the town. When the grieving families asked for help, they lawyered up. So, people sued, people fought, and Color-Brite hid behind their international status. An agreement for restitution was made. The mill would be rebuilt, and a fund would be set up for the surviving families. I bet you can guess what happened."

"They never paid," Jim said.

Cammy nodded. "They rebuilt the mill. People were excited to get the town back to business, but on midnight, January first nineteen fifty-seven, eight Mayflower vans silently drove into town, packed up the mill and drove over the border, never to be seen again. No fund, no jobs. The mill shut down and the town shut down with it. It wasn't until someone had the bright idea to market the town as a foliage destination that it was able to recover."

"Your mother," Jim said.

"My mother." A silence then fell between them.

Jim looked out again at the valley. He pointed at the corn fields. "That's a clever way to grow corn. I can't say I've ever seen it before." Corn fields were terraced in neat rows that creeped up the side of the hills.

"Actually, that was my father's idea," Cammy said. "When my parents got here, Strawberry Falls was almost a ghost town. When the Mill work left, almost everyone moved with it, but my parents saw something in this little town."

"Your dad, the mechanic?" Jim asked looking over the valley.

"It's not a big deal, really," Cammy replied. "Dad read an article in the National Geographic. He just pointed people in the right direction."

"Is it profitable?" Jim asked.

"We're a foliage town, but that's for only one short window during the year."

"I mean, the amount of effort it takes to harvest, it can't be cost effective to…" Jim continued, incredulous.

"I told you that I owed you an explanation," Cammy interrupted. "I wanted to take you somewhere we could talk away from prying eyes." Cammy lowered her head in embarrassment.

"You know, usually people do this the other way around, get to know each other first, then sleep together," Cammy began. "Strawberry Falls is a small town. I've lived here since I was born. I grew up going to first-runs at the movie theater on Main Street on Fridays, double feature matinees on Saturdays. All my life, the eyes of the community have been on me. It's worse because of the position my mother holds. I've dated people here, mostly in high school. When I left to go to college, I thought I had left this place behind. I got dragged back, but I never intended to get stuck. If I get involved with someone here, I'll never leave."

Cammy's face turned serious. "What I did was wrong. You're not from here. I saw my opportunity, and I pounced on it, so to speak. I'm sorry. You seem like a nice enough guy. I guess what I'm saying is, maybe if it's okay, I'd like to get to know you." She looked away from Jim and quickly added, "I understand if you don't want to. That's perfectly okay."

"No," Jim said. "I think I'd like that…to get to know you." Cammy smiled at him. "But I don't understand what happened at the garage."

"Oh yeah," replied Cammy. "My brother has always been...close to me. Closer to me that I am to him. I mean, I love him of course. He's my brother. Sometimes he can get protective. He's always been weird about anyone I date. He's good friends with Dwayne Avery now, but in high school they got into a fist fight. It was pretty bad. It wasn't until after I broke up with Dwayne that Dodge warmed up to him."

Cammy kicked a loose piece of mortar from the ledge, watching it fall. Dropping in and out of beams of sunlight on its journey towards the roof, so far away that they didn't even hear the impact when it bounced out of view. She leaned in toward Jim.

"Your turn," she said. "Dodge told me you are a writer. That's pretty cool."

"I don't know how cool it is," Jim said. "It's not like I'm writing the great American novel."

"What are you writing then?" asked Cammy.

"I feel silly, telling you," Jim said.

"Come on, I want to know." Her elbow rubbed against Jim's.

"I'm writing a travel book about onion rings. Well, not just onion rings—Vermont, too. It's going to be called *The Onion Ring Lover's Guide to Vermont*," Jim said, averting his gaze.

"Onion rings, eh?" she said with a sly smile. "Are you going to write a chapter about me, then?" Jim felt the heat rise in his face.

"Uh...no... Of...of course not," he began.

"Why not?" teased Cammy. "It might add some spice."

Jim froze.

Cammy saw him flailing and rescued him. "Seriously though, I think that writing any book takes a lot of courage. I'm impressed. Really. I've always loved reading. In school. I wanted to be a doctor, so I did plenty of reading."

"A doctor?" asked Jim. "Now I'm impressed."

"Yeah, my dad said I had a talent for fixing things." Her voice grew excited. "You know, fixing a car, in a way, is a lot like fixing a person. You find out what's wrong, and there's a way to fix it. It's simple and kind of reassuring that most of the time there's an answer."

"You wanted to be a doctor, what happened?"

"Life happened. My dad had the accident. Mother had her fall. I got the call at school from my mother. She was inconsolable. My parents were high school sweethearts. They were inseparable. When she lost him, it threw her into deep despair. It crushed my brother." She winced at her poor choice of words. "It devastated my brother. I came home to help, and I got stuck."

"You can't leave?"

"It's not that simple," said Cammy. "I want to go, but I think about my mother and brother here by themselves…It's just not the right time."

Jim could see how uncomfortable Cammy was. "I used to live here as a child. Well, not here, but in Vermont. I lived up in The Islands."

"Really?" Cammy said. "Where, Grand Isle?" Although Jim had brought up the topic, he immediately regretted it.

"Christmas Island."

"No *WAY!* You lived there? I didn't think *anyone* lived there, just that creepy old Santa Land."

"Christmas Town."

"Yeah, that's right. Christmas Town. We went there a couple of times when I was little. It was rundown and there were like, only two reindeer." She smiled at him. "You lived on the island?"

"Yes."

"Oh my God! What was that like?"

"You might think that living in a year-round fantasy land would be nonstop fun. My father moved us all there to run the snack stand. It was supposed to be an adventure. It turned out to be the worst year of my life."

Jim stared into the valley. "When we left Vermont, I never wanted to come back."

"Then why did you?"

"I always wanted to write something. The idea came to me in a lunch line in a cafeteria of all places. Despite that terrible year, I have a few nice memories of the state itself." Jim gestured to the valley below them. "It's truly magical here, one of the most beautiful places I've ever known. It's special. I can see that. I also know I need to face my past. There's a person at Christmas Town I haven't seen since I left. I owe it to him to come back and thank him for what he did for me."

"Wow, what happened?" asked Cammy.

The thought about where the conversation was heading made his stomach hurt, and any words he might have said died on his lips, leaving an awkward silence between them.

Cammy moved along the railing towards him. He had a moment of realization that she was leaning in toward his face. He could smell the gas on her skin, feel the heat from her. A sharp intake of air, a rush of adrenaline, he felt her soft warm lips against his. He surrendered to the moment.

Jim opened his eyes to see Cammy looking back at him.

"Now that's a memory worth keeping," she said.

She took hold of his hand. On the inside of Jim's hand, crisscrossing his palm, were faded white scars. "What's this?" Cammy asked.

Jim pulled his hand back.

"Nothing," he said and put his hand in his pocket.

Cammy didn't press any further. They both stared out at the leaves.

"When my dad died, I blamed myself," Cammy said.

"Why? Weren't you away at school?" asked Jim.

"Yes. I know it doesn't make sense. Dad taught Dodge and me the business. Dodge was always going to take over. 'He's a good mechanic,' Dad would say. 'You're a great one.'

Dad always said that I was like him. I could diagnose a problem just looking at a car. He was proud of me. He wanted me to stay and take over the business, both of his kids. But when I got a scholarship I took the letter and showed it to him. He said nothing. I told him I never wanted to be like him and stormed away.

That summer I was terrible. I refused to work at the shop. I threw away the tools he gave me. Dad offered to drive me to school, I turned him down. I buried myself into my studies. Never thought about cars or home. Instead of coming home, I told my parents I got a summer job and found an apartment off-campus with my roommate. I informed them I would not be coming home. Not then, maybe never."

"Just because you weren't there doesn't mean it's your fault," Jim said.

"They would come and visit me, all three of them. Did I tell you what school I went to? Princeton. Yeah. Small town girl makes good at Ivy League school."

"Princeton? I went to school in New Jersey, too," Jim said. "But just Rutgers."

"Really?" replied Cammy. "Rutgers. No shame there, it's a good school."

"It's no Princeton," Jim kidded.

"Yeah, sometimes when dealing with all those trust fund twits with their silver spoons shoved up their asses, I wish I had gone to a school like Rutgers." Cammy laughed. "Like I said, my parents would come to visit me. I'd make excuses. I'd make sure I would only see my them for half an hour, maybe less."

"I'm sure you had your reasons," Jim said.

"I was furious with them. Well with her." Cammy shook her head. "My first day of college, after unpacking, my mother took me aside. Dodge and Dad had gone to check out the cafeteria—Dad wanted a beer. My mother sat down on the bed—this was before her accident, before she needed the chair. I sat down next to her. And I will never forget what she said."

"'Camaro,' she said, 'I look around this campus and I see the best of the best. These boys and girls are all going places. They're meant for big things. I look around this room and what do you think I see?'" Cammy stopped; her jaw clenched. "'What mom?' I asked her, I couldn't believe it, she had never spoken like that about me. She said, 'I see an impostor.'"

"No."

"Yep." Cammy nodded. "I couldn't believe it. I didn't say anything. I couldn't. She got up, straightened the wrinkles in her dress and walked to the door. She then said to me, 'You don't belong here, and you know it. You belong with your *family*. Your brother needs you. Your Father needs you. *That* is your destiny, your purpose, the sooner you realize it, the happier you will be.'"

"Wow," was all that Jim could muster.

"I almost didn't go home at the end of that school year. I went back to help out Dad and avoided my mother. My sophomore year, they drove down again for parent's weekend. I was a real bitch to them. My dad came over to give me a hug. I turned away. I could see the hurt on his face as they left. I didn't care. They drove back to Strawberry Falls. A month later I got the call from my mother that my father was dead."

"It's not your fault. You know it was an accident."

"Don't you see? He was alone in the shop. Dodge was out on a service call. Dad was crushed under a car when the jack failed. If I was there, I could have gotten that car off his chest. It pressed down on him, pushed all the air out of him until he passed out. I could have saved him if I had stayed. If I just became what he wanted me to be." Cammy had tears running down her face, the wind whipped at her curly hair as it fluttered in the breeze.

"You'll never know," Jim said, "it could have happened even with you there."

"It's the not knowing that is the worst. I made a decision and because of it, someone I loved is gone. Some first date," Cammy said, wiping away tears.

Jim kissed her. "Best one I've ever had."

The two of them descended the rusty ladder. Jim was more than a little relieved when he felt terra firma under his feet. As they walked to the tow truck, Cammy informed Jim that she had to go back to the shop.

"I had a really nice time getting to know you," she said as they pulled up to *Le Grand Hotel Vermont.*

"I did too," Jim said. He was desperate to prolong the moment. He struggled to think of something, anything.

"I'll keep you updated on the progress of your car, Mr. Sutton," she shouted as he climbed out of the car. Jim watched the truck drive away and walked into the lobby of the hotel. He made a beeline towards the lobby the stairs, hoping to avoid a confrontation with Mrs. Norman.

Jim heard chirping. He looked down at his feet and was surprised to see birds hopping around on the carpet. Somehow, the finches had gotten out of their cage on the stairs. As Jim walked toward them, he expected them to fly away. Instead, they hopped away from his approach.

"Good evening, Mr. Sutton," said the voice that Jim least wanted to hear.

"Yes, it is Mrs. Norman," he said. She drove herself over. Jim wondered if she had been waiting for him the whole time. *That's crazy. Get over yourself.*

"Have you been taking in the sights?" she inquired. Jim felt a tinge of panic. Could she possibly know?

"Yes, I have. Your town is lovely," Jim replied. "You know, it is so lovely that I'm thinking of staying *longer.*"

"Are you?" she said, betraying no emotion. "How *nice.* I assume you'll find other accommodations then?"

"Can't I just extend my stay?"

"Oh, I'm afraid we simply cannot do that," she said and wheeled her way over to the front desk. She took out a sheet of paper. "Reservation," she said, holding it up, but not so Jim could see what was written on it. "Just came in today. What a shame. We did so love having you stay at *Le Grand Hotel Vermont.*"

"Oh, too bad."

"Please do come back again," Mrs. Norman said, wheeling away from the desk.

Jim shook his head and started up the stairs.

"A moment, Mr. Sutton?" Jim turned back to her. She sat there smiling at him, her hands folded in her lap.

"Yes?" Jim said.

"Would you mind helping me with my birds? I would try myself, but you know..." She gestured at her chair and her legs.

"Of course." He had been taught to be polite even in the face of such a hateful, spite filled woman. Jim crouched and began chasing the birds around the floor of the lobby. They hopped away from him until he corralled them near the stairs. He took a soft fluttering mass of feathers in his hand and walked to the cage. The bird felt warm and fragile, as if the slightest strain might crush it. It was this feeling perhaps that led Jim to hold the bird too lightly, and it popped out of his grasp. It did not fly away but plummeted toward the floor. Fortunately, God watches over not only fools and drunks, but apparently little birds as well. The finch bounced once, then immediately began to hop around. Jim recaptured it, the small bird fluttering softly in his hands, chirping in protest.

"Why don't they just fly away?" he muttered to himself.

"Because they *can't* fly away." In her lap, she held the other finch.

"What?"

"They can't fly, Mr. Sutton." Mrs. Norman wheeled up to Jim. She reached up to the cage. The wire doors opened with a squeak of metal on metal as she placed the bird inside. "Their wings have been clipped."

"Cut?" Jim replied in disbelief.

"Certainly, Mr. Sutton. It's called pinioning, a relatively simple procedure, really."

"Who would do such a thing?"

"I would, Mr. Sutton. A person in my state certainly can't chase birds all over the house, especially if they try to fly away or up high where I cannot reach them." Mrs. Norman took the bird from Jim's hands, placing it in her lap.

"That's cruel. What about cats or predators?"

"Predators?" Mrs. Sutton snorted. "I provide all the protection they need. Besides, they don't want to go. They're perfectly happy where they are."

"Their actions would suggest otherwise," Jim said.

"Sheer ignorance. They don't have the intelligence to decide. I know what's best for them. I keep them safe."

"By having a vet mutilate them?"

"We spay and neuter dogs, Mr. Sutton. A neutered dog is more docile, less likely to wander. It's a kindness I do for them." She looked lovingly at the bird cradled in her hand. Jim could see it twitching and resisting gently against her grasp.

"*You* do this to them?" Jim said in astonishment.

"Yes, it's easy. I've done it many times in the past, and I'll do it in the future. You simply cut the pinion joint, here." Mrs. Norman took the fluttering bird and pulled the wing back. The bird fluttered and struggled, clearly in discomfort. "There, there," she cooed at the bird. "I'd show you myself, but it's a shame you'll be moving on. Maybe you'd learn something."

"I…I need to go to my room."

"Very well, Mr. Sutton." She took the bird in her hands, opened up the wire cage and placed it inside, to join its companion. She took a piece of wire and twisted it around the bars to secure the door. "Remember, check out is at ten am. Sharp."

Jim had only made it up a flight before he stopped. He wanted to go out. He wanted to be out of the hotel. He quickly turned and made a beeline for the exit. As he walked by the parlor, he glanced inside. In one of the high-back chairs sat Anton reading his newspaper. Anton's eyes peered at Jim from above the newsprint. With the Mackintosh hat and his big round brown eyes, Anton bore more than a passing resemblance to some kind of cartoon owl. Jim smiled at him. Anton's eyes narrowed. He shook his head, made a show of adjusting his paper and deliberately looked down averting his eyes.

"Ok then," Jim mumbled to himself as he walked out the door.

He turned arbitrarily to the right, passing the movie theatre. He made a face as he passed the poster for *Weekend at Bernie's*. Next to that poster in a frame that said COMING SOON was a silk-screened poster that read BREAD AND PUPPET THEATER. The art on the billet showed one of several reaching hands towards the word BREAD above them.

As he walked down Main Street, Jim passed the video store, a travel agency and a place named *Gene's Greens*. A head shop based on the marijuana leaves painted on the front windows. A woman walked out of the store, holding a milk crate full of various paraphernalia. Jim recognized her from the town meeting. It was Miriam Stein. Jim waved at her and smiled, which stopped Ms. Stein in her tracks. Slack-jawed she stared at him. As he approached, her eyes narrowed. Shaking her head, Miriam continued walking to her car. Their paths crossed.

THUD, Jim felt the impact of her shoulder into his.

"Ugh." He exhaled, taken off-guard from the contact. "I'm sorry lady."

"That's right you are," Miriam said. She continued walking to the curb, where a green Subaru Forester was parked. The back of the car was plastered with bumper stickers. Amongst the selections that could be discerned, there was a BERNIE FOR SENATE sticker, a peace symbol, THINK GLOBALLY ACT LOCALLY, 2 MOMS ARE BETTER THAN ONE, a PHISH band sticker, and one of those COEXIST bumper stickers made up of all the world's religious symbols. Edna, also from the meeting sat inside the car in the front passenger seat. She stared at Jim.

"Don't call me '*lady*,'" Miriam said.

"What should I call you?"

"Don't call me at all," Miriam offered. "Better yet, don't call anyone, just go back from where you came from, New Yorker." She placed her crate into the back seat, glared at Jim, sat in her car, and slammed the door.

Jim was a little shaken but continued walking down the street. He then saw something that piqued his interest—a peculiar store. Stacks of books were piled in the windows. Not as window decorations, more like storage. *Turn a New Leaf Books – New & Used*, the sign read. A cardboard sign was taped under it that stated, *& Internet Café*. The interior of the bookstore was much like what he saw in the window. Every possible space was taken up with stacks and stacks of books. In the back of the bookstore sat an orange iMac next to a coffeemaker. A sign above the computer read, Internet sign up: first come, first served. Another sign above the coffeemaker read Fifty cents a cup. On your honor, with an arrow pointing down to a rusty coffee can.

Handwritten signs hung from the ceiling by kite string and paper clips with names like TRAVEL (GOOD), TRAVEL (BAD), HELP YOURSELF, TRUE and MADE-UP. He could not hazard an actual number, but it seemed to him there must have been at least five cats in the store, some lounging on the stacks, one overweight tabby taking a nap on the counter.

As Jim walked through the door, the few people browsing glanced up. A tall man with khaki pants and a blue button-up oxford shirt walked Jim's way. He was trim. His thinning blonde hair was perfectly coiffed and moussed. His clothes were crisp and neat. Jim presumed he was an employee.

"Can I help you?" the man asked.

"No, I'm just browsing."

"Good luck with that, stranger," retorted the man. "This is not your average bookstore." He gently touched Jim's arm as a sign of friendship.

"I can see that," Jim said. "I was curious about TRAVEL (BAD) myself."

The man rolled his eyes. "Oh, that—that's Tate's doing." He walked over to the section. There did not seem to be any discernible pattern to why they were categorized as such. He saw travel books for Texas, Washington D.C., Japan, Disneyworld (not Disneyland) and Martha's Vineyard.

"Mystified?" the man asked.

"Uh, yeah," said Jim, picking up a copy of *Travel Guide to New Hampshire*.

"It's all places that Tate hates. Honestly, I told him that's what it should be called, 'Tate hates,' but he didn't find that funny." The man looked closer at Jim, narrowing his eyes.

"Wait a…I know you," he said, trying to place Jim. "I remember now! You're the one from the Town Hall. You're the sign guy!"

"Uh, yeah," Jim said.

"Don't be scared. I voted to just give you the fine. Accidents happen, right?" He turned with a flourish, picking up a stack of books and deftly putting them in what Jim presumed were their correct places. Turn a New Leaf didn't seem to be operating under the Dewey Decimal System or any other system he could discern.

"I bet you're staying at the Hotel, right?"

"Yes, up the block," answered Jim.

"Well, *that's* got to be awkward, what with Mrs. Norman taking you to task and all. Especially since Cammy stepped up to defend you."

"You have no idea," Jim said.

"Oh, you'd be surprised what I know. My name is Evan by the way." They shook hands. "Enchanté, my good man." Evan laughed. "That's an odd family, the Normans." He glanced around the store. "I could tell you more, just not right here, you know?"

"It's alright. I think I'll just look around for a while," Jim said.

"Well, make yourself at home. If you need anything, just ring." Evan gestured to a silver bell on a tray on the counter next to the sleeping tabby cat.

Jim walked around the store breathing in the scent of aging paper, the smell of foxing and mildewed paper was as intoxicating as any perfume.

Stopping over at the wall of used paperbacks, he looked along the cracked and lined spines. Some of them were so worn he could not tell what the title was. He picked up one and turned it over. It was V.C. Andrews' *Flowers in the Attic*. He put the book back and settled on a collection of Phillip K. Dick stories. He had read *Do Androids Dream of Electric Sheep?* in high school. A thought popped into his head and he scanned to see if they had it…yes! He found a copy of *Slaughterhouse Five* by Kurt Vonnegut. To his delight, they had *Cat's Cradle* as well. Jim gathered up his choices and brought them to the front desk and rang the bell.

"Ready to check out? Wonderful." Evan got behind the register and started tallying up Jim's choices. "Oh, this book, it's my favorite," he said, holding up the copy of *Cat's Cradle*.

"I like Vonnegut," Jim said.

"Oh, so do I," said the man. "So does Tate," he said. Evan picked up another book from under the desk and dropped it in the bag.

"I threw in a book I thought you'd like," said Evan. "Don't worry, it's on the house. No charge. Not everyone in Strawberry Falls is rude."

"Thank you," said Jim. He took out his wallet to pay for the books with the little cash he still had. He took his bag and exited the store. When he had walked out of sight of the bookstore, he opened his bag to see what the shopkeeper had added. *One Hundred Years of Solitude*, by Gabriel Garcia Marquez. He had already read that one. He opened the book and a slip of paper fell out. Jim opened the folded paper and it read. "Call me. *802-879-0077 – Evan.*" Flattered but uninterested, Jim shook his head, re-folded the paper and put it in his pocket.

The sun was readying itself to set. It was not fully light, yet not quite the twilight before sunset. Jim thought about grabbing a bite to eat at the Ho Hum Chinese food restaurant. He looked at the menu that was taped to the front window. He wanted to try the pizza egg rolls and was very curious to find out what exactly a "redneck egg roll" was. Jim decided he'd surprise Cammy with some takeout. Bag in hand, he walked down Main Street towards Norman Auto Body.

When Jim arrived, there was something taped to the front door. BE BACK SOON, was written in sharpie on a scrap of cardboard with a smiley face underneath it. Jim tried the door, it was locked. Maybe she was out back, Jim thought as he walked around the building. Jim could see the junkyard, with its rusting ghosts of cars. On the ground by the fence was a heavy chain with a padlock. The door looked to be ajar. *Maybe she went back there*, Jim wondered as he walked to get a closer look.

As he approached, Jim spied movement. It was Kaiser Bill. The ancient dog rose unsteadily to his feet. His tail wagged AND he growled at the same time. *Is that a good sign?* Jim wondered. Sniffing the air, Kaiser Bill pushed his nose up to the fence. Jim looked down at his bag of takeout.

"You hungry, boy?" Jim looked at Bill, who wagged his tail again, this time with more vigor. Jim looked in his bag.

Why not? he thought and pulled out a redneck egg roll. He held it warily in front of Kaiser Bill's nose. The dog sniffed the egg roll and recoiled, his tail down. Jim shrugged and took a bite.

"Ugh, I don't blame you," Jim replied. The redneck egg roll seemed to consist of pieces of Slim Jims swimming in cheese wiz. He spat it out. Kaiser Bill looked up at him with a wounded look on his face.

"I'm sorry boy, if it's any consolation, I hated it too." Then he had a thought. He reached into his pocket. He felt the two AbaZaba bars and pulled one out.

"There's no chocolate in it, so in theory it's good, right?" Jim asked Kaiser Bill, who sniffed, tail wagging one more. Gingerly he fed the candy bar through the fence, Kaiser Bill took it from him and began wolfing it down, tearing at the wrapper to get at the taffy.

Jim shrugged and cautiously tried the door, pushing it open a bit. Kaiser Bill stopped eating, his head swinging around on a swivel. Jim froze. Kaiser Bill regarded Jim for a moment, then wagged his tail and set back on devouring the taffy, which had proven more of a challenge. Jim opened the door further. No reaction from Kaiser Bill. He tested the dog again, putting his foot in the door. Still no reaction from Kaiser Bill.

Exhaling, Jim walked through the gate. He looked around for Cammy, but it was hard to see anything around the piles of cars and junk. The junkyard was thankfully laid out in rows. Jim walked past a rusted-out Buick, following a well-worn path through the junk. Still no sight of Cammy, or her brother for that matter.

The path terminated at the edge of the junkyard, where it backed up to a corn field. The corn was high. As Jim walked closer, he was surprised at how tall it was. He had thought the trail ended at the rows, but he could now see he was mistaken. The worn stretch of dirt continued down rows of towering stalks. Jim had never been in a corn maze.

Jim spread his arms to touch each row of corn. Wincing, he drew his hand back after cutting it on a sharp leaf. As he looked around, he felt as if he were in another world. The stalks rustled as they swayed in the wind. There was a powerful smell in the air. Not sweet or earthy strangely enough, more pungent, almost skunk like.

Jim peered into the next row. It appeared darker green, like a shadow. Intrigued, Jim pushed through the corn stalks. He swore as another long green leaf cut his cheek. Smarting, he pushed on, the funky smell growing *stronger*. Finally, Jim stepped into a row, blinking as he stared in disbelief.

Swaying in the same gentle breeze as their neighbors, almost as tall as the corn surrounding it were rows of cannabis plants. Marijuana. Jim stood in slack-jawed disbelief at the sheer number of plants around him. They were robust and in full bloom, bees happily pollinating the heavy buds of the mature cannabis.

What have I gotten myself into? Jim thought. He could see that the pot was interspersed at regular intervals in the corn field, too precise for some random stoners personal stash. This was someone's crop. Jim knew he had to leave. Now.

Jim froze. *What was that?* As far as he knew, he was alone in the corn field. He heard rustling from a few rows over. Was it the wind?

Not daring to breathe, Jim stood rooted to the spot. He cursed his bad luck as he thought about running. The rational part of his mind stopped him, that was a good way to get lost. Best if he kept his wits and retraced his steps.

The rustling grew closer. It was headed right toward him. Jim closed his eyes and prayed. Maybe if he stayed especially still they might not see him. The rustling was almost to his row of corn/pot.

He felt something wet on his hand. Jim recoiled and fell back into the corn. Eyes open now, on his back, Jim looked up. He felt hot muggy breath on his nose as the junkyard dog, Kaiser Bill loomed over him. The dog licked his face.

"Jesus Christ, boy, you scared the shit out of me," Jim whispered. He rubbed Kaiser Bill's chin, who wagged his tail happily.

Getting to his feet, Jim dusted himself off. He looked around; his worst fears realized. He was lost.

"How am I going to get out of here?" Jim said to himself. Kaiser Bill's ears cocked, and the dog lurched down one of the rows. Kaiser Bill turned back towards Jim, almost expectantly. Jim followed him. He was glad he did as the dog led him back to the junkyard.

Any thoughts of finding Cammy were dispelled. Jim just wanted to leave the junkyard.

I'll just pretend nothing happened. I was never here, Jim thought. He was relieved to see no-one had returned to the garage, the note still taped to the door. Jim threw the bag of cold Chinese food on a rubbish heap and resolved to head straight back to the hotel.

Thoughts swirled through Jim's head as he struggled up the hill. Whose pot was that? Is it Dodge's? Is it Cammy's? Jim looked behind him. No one was following as far as he could tell. IF it was Cammy's, so what? It was none of his business. If he just stuck to his plan and pretended like it never happened, everything would be fine. Besides, it could be anyone's pot. Who was to say it was Cammy's? It just didn't seem like it would be something she'd be involved in.

Jim turned up the street to *Le Grand Hotel Vermont*. He heard a siren and a bright light shone in his eyes, blinding him. *My god*, he thought. *They found me.*

"We have laws for loitering, sir." A voice came from a police cruiser, its floodlight pointed right at him. Jim had to admit, he was relieved it was the police. He could just make out a figure standing by the door, half in, half out of the car.

"Sir, please move on, sir." Jim shielded his eyes from the bright light burning his eyes. He could barely make out the face. Unfortunately, it was one he recognized.

"Deputy Avery?"

"Sir, if you don't move on, I will have to take you into custody," Deputy Avery spoke, moving the light as Jim moved, ensuring it was always pointed squarely in Jim's face.

"I'm just walking down the sidewalk. Come on!"

"Sir, please move on," Deputy Avery repeated. Jim staggered his way to the car, spots still swimming in his eyes.

"This is harassment," Jim snapped.

"Step back, sir." Deputy Avery put his hand on his holstered gun. Astonished, Jim put his hands up and slowly backed away.

"I can't believe this."

"You better believe it," Deputy Avery responded. "I'd arrest you right now, but I don't want you to have to stay in town any longer than necessary."

"This is crazy."

"I'd advise you to shut your smart mouth before I shut it for you," Avery said. "I'm telling you to leave. Once your car is fixed, I want you to drive away from this town and never come back. If you do come back, you even think of coming back, you will be sorry. I cannot be held responsible for what happens to you."

"W-what?"

"You've been warned." Deputy Avery got into his car. He shut off the light and pulled away. As he drove off, he rolled down his window and shouted, "Fuck off and go back to *New York!*"

Jim was dumbfounded, then frustrated. The only thing keeping him here, at least for the time being, was Cammy and his broken-down car. *Small town, small mind*, thought Jim. He was looking forward to relaxing in his room with his new (old) books. To his relief Mrs. Norman was not in the lobby. However, Anton was still there at his post.

"Hello Anton." Jim waved at the middle/old aged man.

"Harumpf" Anton snorted derisively. Not the sound, *actual* onomatopoeia.

Who actually says the word "harumpf" Jim thought as he shook his head in amazement as he turned to the staircase that lead to the rooms upstairs.

At his room, he reached into his pocket for the room key. He pulled the keys out and went to put them in the lock, only to discover the door was unlocked.

He was not expecting what greeted him on the other side of that door. Cammy sat with her legs crossed in the comfy chair wearing nothing, save her smile. Her untamable curly hair was down, or more specifically, out. Her freckled skin shone like she had just walked out of the shower. In her hands, she held a plate of golden-brown onion rings. Cammy picked up a ring and flirtatiously bit into it.

"Hungry?"

THE MOST WONDERFUL TIME OF THE YEAR

1977

"Keep on cranking!" Bob shouted.

Jim dutifully turned the crank of an old-fashioned ice cream maker while sitting on the floor.

"How much longer?" Jim whined, looking at his dad plaintively.

Bob peered into the barrel.

"Still a ways to go," Bob said.

Linda had discovered the old ice cream maker on one of her trips to the junkyard. It was frozen with rust, but after some TLC and a few hours of sanding, she had brought the old beauty back to life.

"Perfect," Bob declared after she had shown him how it worked. "Just what I need for the Christmas rush!" He gave her a hug, then disappeared into the kitchen to experiment.

Everyone at Christmas Town felt the pressure to step up their act for the *actual* holiday. Attendance spiked during the months of November and December. Since Thanksgiving was right around the corner, that meant the rush was on its way. The theme park tried its best to provide added value during those peak months.

Seasonal staff were hired to be elves and Santa's Helpers. Mrs. Claus appeared during Christmas Time to handle overflow from the kids who came to see Santa. Elves were instructed to direct children, whether they wanted it or not, into two lines: one for Santa, one for Mrs. Claus. It was not until the children reached the front of the line, where it forked left or right, that they realized they were not in the "Santa" line. This predictably caused some meltdowns. If the parents made a big enough stink about it, they got to go to the front of their preferred line. Most parents were so exhausted by the time they reached the front that they just went along with whatever lap they were designated.

Bob had brought his kids to work with him that weekend. And he had found success in formulating a darn good sweet cream ice cream. Bob intended to use the ice cream as a base for some holiday flavors. Jim was sill turning the crank, albeit more slowly now, while Lyndsey was sitting on the counter busy with her own chore. Bob had heard one time that the smell of baking chocolate chip cookies can make people buy and eat more food. To test this hypothesis, Bob planned on baking cookies during the day. He'd be able to sell the cookies as well—a win-win.

Lyndsey couldn't read the recipe or measure the ingredients, but what she could do was stir. Bob had helped her at each stage and to his surprise, Lyndsey really seemed to enjoy it. He had just added the chocolate chips to the huge metal bowl sitting in front of his daughter when the doorbell rang out. Customers. Two college aged men walked through the door. They stamped their feet in an attempt to warm up from the cold outside.

"Come on in!" Bob said, happily waving them to come to the counter. The two young man accepted his invitation and sat down on the swivel chairs.

"What can I get for you?" Bob asked pushing two menus in front of the young men.

"Coffee?" One of the young men said to his compatriot, who nodded to the affirmative. "Two Coffees please."

"You got it. Two cups of Joe coming right up. Take a look at our menu. Today's special is a patty melt with fries." Bob walked away to fill the order.

"Hey there young lady," one of the men said to Lyndsey. He wore glasses and had long curly hair and a bushy beard. Lyndsey turned her head down but kept mixing.

"What's your name?" the other young man said. He too had glasses, but his long hair showed signs of thinning. "I'm Ben." He smiled at her. Lyndsey stopped mixing altogether.

"Lyndsey." Jim's disembodied voice came from the other side of the counter. Ben and his friend leaned over to see who had answered them.

"What are you doing down there?" Ben said.

"Making ice cream," Jim grumbled.

"Really?" Ben said. "That's cool, man. I love ice cream. What kind?"

"Sweet cream. I think it's almost done," Jim replied.

"I'll have to try some."

"Sure, let me…" Bob had grabbed his scoop when the bell on the door rang out loudly, looking up to Bob's chagrin, he saw the visage of Mr. Murray. He was carrying hundreds of Christmas lights around his shoulders. Bob knew Mr. Murray did not like any of Bob's improvements. In Mr. Murray's mind, the stand was perfect the way it was, and Bob was just mucking it up. Staring at the ice-cream maker, Mr Murray shook his head.

"Sutton!" Mr. Murray barked as lurched up to the counter. "I need a drink, these goddamn lights are going to be the end of me."

Right after Halloween Mr. Murray embarked on the tedious task of stringing up the miles of Christmas lights. A process that involved methodically testing each bulb.

"Want some Holiday wassail?" Bob suggested "I had it made special for the season."

Mr. Murray glared at Bob. "Beer," he said.

"Sure, what kind do you want? I've got some Bud—"

"That piss water can go screw." Mr. Murray scowled. Bob nervously looked over at his kids. Jim stood there frozen, eyes wide, Lyndsey was still on the counter a huge spoon of cookie dough in her chubby little hand.

"Pee-pee" Lyndsey giggled.

"Lyndsey!" Bob admonished her. "Um, what would you like then?"

"I drink Blue," Mr. Murray stated flatly. "Don't they have Blue in New York?

"Yes. I've got that. Once again, Glenn, we're not *from* New York, and you know it." Bob walked over to the fridge and prayed he had some LaBatt's Blue.

"Don't need a glass," Mr. Murray called out. "Just bring the bottle."

"No bottles. I have a can, though." Bob held up the silver blue can.

Mr. Murray scowled.

Bob set the can in front of Mr. Murray. He grabbed the cold can, pulled the pop top and proceeded to down the frosty beer in one long pull. Wiping his mouth, he threw the pop-top on the counter.

"Put it on my tab," Mr. Murray said.

Bob knew that meant give it to him for free.

"Whatever you say. Hey, I hope you have a good Thanksgiving next week."

"I will Sutton, once I get these son-of-a bitch lights up. Thanks for the brew." He stomped out the door.

"Son-of-a bitch!" Lyndsey said brightly with a smile.

*   *   *

With Halloween over, Bob Sutton began preparing for the holiday rush he had long been warned about. The loss of the prime summertime profits had hurt his family. Bob was banking on a great holiday to ease the pain on their bank account. In the storage space behind the stand, Bob found some unused Christmas decorations. Whenever Bob tried to find time to put up decorations, some issue would take him away. So they sat there, a constant reminder of tasks undone.

Bob had ingeniously developed a system of selling ad space on the paper place mats the diner used every day. He personally went door to door around Burlington businesses and convinced them to buy little squares monthly at the snack stand. It wasn't much money but enough so he could consider hiring a seasonal worker. The faster he got tables served and turned over, the more money he'd make.

A man walked through the door of Bob's snack stand and looked around the place. Rail thin and ropy, he stood there impassively chewing gum, eyes moving slowly around the joint.

"Carl?" Bob called out to the man standing in the doorway.

"Bob," Carl said. It was more of a statement than a salutation.

Carl Donovan answered Bob's advertisement in the *Burlington Free Press* he'd placed for a short order cook. Carl's skin seemed too translucent, too taut, the veins a little too close to the surface. Carl was in his fifties and had served in Korea, as he would tell anyone who came into his orbit. He displayed the eagle and anchor tattoo proudly on his right forearm as evidence of his stint with the Marines. On his left arm, Carl bore a tattoo of a hula girl. The lines that had once presumably been black were now bluish and fuzzy. He was a journeyman, going from job to job. Carl was a good short-order cook but had a short-order fuse.

"Nice to meet you," Bob said.

"Yes," Carl grunted. "Where's my kitchen?"

"Well, like I said, Paco's the head cook. The kitchen is back this way." Bob walked towards the kitchen door; Carl followed close.

"So how was the ride on the ferry?" Bob asked.

"Fine."

"So nice this time of year, but cold, right?" Bob offered.

"Yes."

Bob gulped as he pushed open the door. Paco was in rare form. He had tied a transistor radio to one of the shelves and was getting down as he cooked. Stevie Wonder's *Boogie on Reggae Woman* played out tinnily from the radio. As usual, he was shirtless and not wearing a hairnet over his long hair which hung down to the ass-crack of his tight bell-bottomed jeans.

"Paco, how many times do I have to tell you, please wear a hairnet."

"I get it boss. I get it man." Paco flipped a hamburger expertly in the air, catching it in a bun.

"Hairnet!" Bob shouted as Paco ran back to the walk-in freezer. Paco laughed and saluted him. Paco grabbed a bag of frozen French fries and sauntered his way back to the grill hairnet-less. Flipping a sizzling burger on a bun, Paco slid it on the window ledge to the inside of the stand.

"Order up!" Paco shouted. Audrey came to the window and grabbed it from his hands.

"Paco." Bob tried to get his cook's attention. Carl stood at Bob's side, rigidly silent. Paco reached over to the fryer, dumping frozen potatoes into the roiling oil..

"Paco," Bob yelled.

"What?" Paco replied, confused. "Oh yeah, hairnet. yeah man…"

"I *told* you I was bringing the new cook in today," Bob said.

"Oh yeah, where is he?"

"This is him," Bob said. He gestured to the stern man standing next to him.

"Ohhhh," Paco said. Grinning, he wiped his hand on the back of his tight jeans and held it out to Carl. "Pleased to meet another grill man."

Carl stared at Paco's outstretched hand.

"Carl, Paco. Paco, Carl."

"Boss man says you're good. Where you flip em' before?"

Carl stared at Paco.

"Carl?" Bob implored.

"Okinawa."

"Oh, is that the Japanese place on 22? I love Japanese food," Paco said. "Heck, I even love the Japanese if you get my meaning." He winked at Carl.

"Listen junior, I don't know who your parents are, but if you were my son, I'd take you out back and whoop some respect into you," Carl growled.

"Whoa, man I didn't think—"

"No, man, you didn't think. I doubt you can think. I can smell the reefer on you from over here." Carl wrinkled his nose in disgust. "Okinawa ain't a restaurant. It's an island. I cooked for real men, in a real war. Something you wouldn't know anything about."

"Hey now!" Paco raised his voice, the smile vanishing from his face. "I'm just trying to be friendly, that's just rude man."

Carl stepped towards Paco. "You going to teach me a lesson, dirty hippie?"

"Maybe I will."

"Try it junior," Carl spat out.

"Hey!" Bob shouted "Let's just take it down, let's all get along." He stepped in between the two men.

"I'm trying here, man," Paco said.

"Try harder," Bob replied. He turned to Carl. "Are you going to be cool with this? We can end this now and I can find another cook."

"I'm good." Carl said. "I'm fine if he stays on his side of the kitchen."

Bob turned to Paco. "Are you good with that?"

"Yeah, I'm cool with that," Paco said.

"Good. Now let's start over. You two shake," Bob ordered.

Paco held out his hand, this time Carl took it. "Paco."

"Carl."

"Nice to meet you, let me show you the kitchen," Paco said.

"That would be fine," Carl replied. Bob supervised Paco's tour of the kitchen. To his relief the tension seemed to be broken. Over the next few days, the two of them were working like a well-oiled machine, any grievances seemed to be forgotten or at least put aside for the sake of work.

Bob was on the lookout for a new waitress. Angie had suddenly quit. "Family issues," she said. On a rare trip off island, Bob brought fliers to post around downtown Burlington. They read as follows:

HO HO HO
WANTED: Waitress for holiday work at snack stand at Christmas Town
on Christmas Island. Experience appreciated, but not a must.
Lunch provided, salary plus tips.

Bob drove the creaky station wagon up the hill to the main campus of the University of Vermont. Bob watched all the young coeds going to their classes and felt a pang of nostalgia. The students looked so tantalizingly youthful. Bob posted his notice on a few bulletin boards until he arrived at the main building. A group of students brushed by him without a second look or thought. I suppose I'm just an old man to them, Bob thought ruefully.

Bob pried off a thumbtack to post his billet to find there was no room on the board. He tore off an offer for "BABYSITTING: EXPERIENCED GIRLS ONLY WANTED." Bob posted his advert. He stood back and saw that it just blended into the general chaos of the board. As Bob was leaving, he saw a pair of pretty girls walking toward him. They were smiling and talking to each other, their hair bouncing as they walked. These girls had life in them, so much possibility and potential. They breezed by him; he might as well have been invisible.

Bob walked back to his car, deep in thought about his time in school. He wondered what it would be like if he applied to be a student now.

Bob had missed out on the summer of free love, going straight to marriage and kids. Part of him resented passing on partaking in that seminal time. Bob shook off his daydreaming. He looked across the University quad with longing as the Volkswagen ground into gear and puttered back down the hill toward the road that would bring him back to the ferry. To home.

Over the next couple of days Bob expected a flood of calls. He stared at the phone, as if by just looking it would ring by the force of his will. Throughout the day Bob would walk over to the avocado green phone on the wall and pick it up, just to make sure the line was still working.

Eventually, Bob's vigilance waned. When the phone rang during the lunch rush, Bob had no expectations when he picked it up. Carl and Paco had been at it in the kitchen. Carl had called Paco "a dirty hippie." Paco threatened to use his frying pan on Carl's face. Such altercations were becoming more frequent. Bob found himself acting more like a referee than a boss. After separating the cooks and ordering them to opposite sides of the kitchen, the phone rang.

"Why do I got to wash dishes, when Mary over there gets off scott-free?" Carl blustered, glaring at Paco, who flipped Carl the bird.

"Because I don't have money for a dishwasher," Bob explained again to Carl. It was hard enough getting Paco to wash a dish during slow times. The phone stubbornly kept ringing. Bob stalked over to the wall to answer it.

"What?" he growled, forgetting his manners. There was silence for a second, then a young woman's voice spoke through the receiver.

"Uh...hello...I think I may have reached a wrong number."

"This is the Snack Shack," Bob said, trying to sound friendly.

"Oh, yeah…I was calling about the job, the waitress job."

Bob cursed himself for how rudely he had answered.

"Has it been filled yet?"

"Oh no!" Bob said. "Are you looking to apply?" There was a moment's hesitation on the end of the line. Bob felt her slipping away.

"Yes," the voice said. "But…" Bob's heart sank at 'but.'

"I don't have much experience as a waitress."

"Well, how much experience do you have," asked Bob.

"Uh, none," came the voice. "But I'm a real hard worker."

"That's okay. When can you get here for an interview?"

"Tonight…uh…today!" came the voice excitedly from the other end. "You won't regret it. Bye!"

"Wait, wait!" Bob shouted into the phone

"Oh! Yeah?" came the voice over the phone.

"What's your name?"

A sweet laugh came lilting from the other end of the line. "Jenn. Jennifer DuPree."

Jenn DuPree made the trip across the ferry for her interview. Bob had resolved to hire her if she was half normal.

Bob wiped the remains of a candy cane milkshake from the counter top. A customer and his two rambunctious kids had left behind a mess that boggled and frustrated Bob to no end. Spilled milkshakes, overturned salt and pepper shakers, and food crumbs were evidence of the finished lunch long after they left. The 2% tip certainly did not make Bob feel any better. The bell at the door jingled merrily. Bob glanced up.

A young woman stood in the doorway. She was barely out of her teens, if that. She was slim, her shoulder length brown hair, styled in a flip. She wore a peasant's blouse embroidered with flowers accessorized with a pooka shell necklace. Her eyes met Bob's and she smiled. Bob stopped wiping up milkshake, assessing this new variable.

"You must be Bob," she said d. "I'm Jenn DuPree."

"Bob," he said taking her hand. "But you knew that. Let's sit over there. We can start the interview." He gestured to a booth in the back. Bob sat down across from Jenn as she slid a sheet of paper in front of him.

"Here's my resume. Like I said, I don't have any waiting experience, but I did have jobs. You see, I worked as a cashier at the Grand Union in Essex Junction." Bob looked over the sheet of paper. Under jobs, she even listed babysitting. He glanced at the education section.

"It says here you're attending the University of Vermont. What year are you?" asked Bob, glancing up over the top of the paper.

"I'm a sophomore," she said. Nineteen, thought Bob. So young.

"Major? I don't see it listed."

"Well, I'm majoring in Botanical Science."

"I'm impressed." Bob replied.

"I want to go into research. There are a lot of exciting things happening in Biotechnology," she said.

Bob noticed that her lipstick was the exact shade of pink of the salmon he had for the special tonight. Shaking off this distraction, he refocused.

"Like I said, I'm impressed. Why a job here? I'm sure a girl with your smarts could find a desk job somewhere less, um…remote."

"Oh, I'm just looking for a fun job. I have my whole life to have a serious one," Jenn replied.

"This job's not fun. It's a lot of hard work," countered Bob.

"That's exactly what I'm looking for. I want to experience this kind of hard work. I want to experience everything in life, you know?"

"I do," said Bob. He thought about how he had felt when he was her age. It wasn't so long ago, but it felt like a lifetime.

"I don't want to be on the other side of forty, thinking that I missed out. I want to collect as many adventures as I can." Bob would have expected the same from himself.

"Well, okay, I can promise you that much. You'll get some experience, but I'm not sure if it's as romantic as you think. You've got the job. You can start tomorrow or Monday if you like."

"Really?" asked Jenn. "I'll start tomorrow, if that's ok."

She shook Bob's hand vigorously. "As for it being romantic, *I'll* be the judge of that," she said with a look of determination. Bob watched her leave and then glanced away, aware he was staring.

*   *   *

Thanksgiving came to Christmas Island with its usual mix of excitement and trepidation in anticipation for what was around the corner. The night of Thanksgiving all staff of Christmas Town were expected to attend a private lighting ceremony that was held annually by the Murrays. Bob had circled the date in red pen long ago on his calendar. Under the pre-printed "THANKSGIVING DAY" he had written the following:

Lighting ceremony. Make good impression.

Bob and Linda agreed on an early "Thanksgiving Dinner" so he could enjoy the meal before he went to the snack stand. Christmas Island was open every day of the year, including Thanksgiving and Christmas Day. Their Thanksgiving lunch or "Lunchsgiving" as Linda had called it had gone off with several hitches and not at all as he had expected, but there was little Bob could do now. He was almost grateful that his job required him to go and leave behind the disaster that was their first Thanksgiving on the island.

Bob came home the night of the lighting hoping to find his family excited and ready to go. His expectations were quickly dashed. Linda had gotten a late start to "dinner." The kids were running around the house screaming and shrieking.

"Linda, I thought we agreed to have dinner ready," said Bob, walking into the kitchen, dodging the kids. Linda tended the miniature stove, every burner occupied.

"It's not easy getting dinner done. No one's eaten yet," she said, stirring frantically.

"I don't understand what's so hard about this. I told you we had an event to go to," Bob protested. He looked into a pot. In the boiling water he could make out thin strands of dancing noodles. "Spaghetti? On *Thanksgiving*? We couldn't have leftovers?" Bob picked up an empty wine bottle from the counter and stared at it incredulously.

"You know why leftovers are out of the question. I was busy and lost track of time." She went back to stirring. The sauce had boiled over and splattered molten projectiles all over the stove and kitchen counter.

"Busy? What, your *projects?*" asked Bob, annoyance in his voice.

"Yes, busy. It's not easy, you know."

"Linda, it's nice you have a hobby, but Mr. Murray is expecting us there."

"Hobby? *Hobby?*" spewed Linda, her voice rising. "I'm working so we don't live in filth. I literally made sure we had a roof over our heads."

"A roof you broke," countered Bob.

"You know, I cook, I clean, I try to make our life better. A life you wanted Bob. All you do is shit on everything." Jim and Lyndsey, who had been running around, stopped in the doorway at the swear word. They stared at their mother.

"That's not fair," Bob said.

"No, it's not. It's not fair that you did this to our family—that you did this to me." She grabbed the boiling pot of spaghetti off the burner and dumped it into the sink. She turned off all the burners, picked up the saucepan and to her children's surprise, poured the still spattering sauce into the trash.

"Come on kids," said Linda. "We're going out." She grabbed Jim and Lyndsey, dragging them to the front hall. Leaning down as she picked up Jim's boots.

Suddenly, Linda felt light-headed and wobbly, her feet leaden. How much did I drink today? She thought. Steadying herself in the cramped hallway, she shook her head in an attempt to clear the cobwebs. Linda struggled with the kids as they squirmed while she pulled on their winter jackets and boots.

The Suttons walked to Christmas Town. Linda glanced down the road leading to the maintenance shed where Nick worked. Since fixing the roof Nick stopped by almost every day to say hello to Linda and check-in on the progress on the house. Sometimes he'd stay for a cup of coffee. Most times he'd politely decline. Linda looked forward to his visits. It was nice to have a friend. The Suttons trudged down the road in silence, the glow from the park growing brighter.

Mr. Murray stood on a wooden platform in the center of Christmas Town, and the Suttons were one of the last families to arrive. Mr. Murray had already started addressing the crowd. Bob caught only a snippet of the last thing he said. He strategically moved his family closer to the stage where they could be seen by the owner.

"...better year than last year," spoke Mr. Murray, eliciting a loud cheer from the crowd. "Now, it's that time. Time to light 'em up! Who wants to do the honor this year?" shouted Mr. Murray. Bob's arm shot up. He saw that he was the only adult. Realizing that this was a kids only request, Bob awkwardly pawed at Jim's hand to raise it up, only to have Jim pull it away. Frantically, Bob grabbed Lyndsey and held her up for all to see.

"There we go," said Mr. Murray, gesturing to Lyndsey. "Come on up, sweetie."

Bob weaved through the crowd, Lyndsey still over his head. He navigated the sea of people in front of the dais. He placed her on the stage next to Mr. Murray.

"It's ok. This is *fun*," Bob assured her.

Lyndsey was stiff as a board. She looked terrified at the idea of having to do something, *anything*, in front of all these people. Mr. Murray held in his hand a wooden box, in the middle of the box was a big red button. Mr. Murray shoved the box into Lyndsey's hands.

"Okay, everybody?" he prompted the crowd. "Ten...!" Mr. Murray began. People took up the chant

"NINE!"

"EIGHT!"

"SEVEN!"

"SIX!"

"FIVE!"

"FOUR!"

"THREE!"

"TWO!"

"ONE!"

At "zero," it was obvious to everybody but the terrified little girl on the stage that she was supposed to push the button. She stood there, frozen in the glare of the klieg lights that had been set up to illuminate the dais. Bob, who had been standing off to the side, whispered to her.

"Lyndz...sweetie, push the *button*."

She stood rooted to the spot.

"Push it!" Bob said loudly. Nothing. Bob creeped out on stage and attempted to take the box from his daughter. Lyndsey chose that moment to shake from her paralysis. She jerked the box away.

"NO. MINE!" she screamed. She backed away from her father, unwilling to part with the gift. Bob lunged. She ran to the other side, trailing the cords from the box. She tripped over the cables, fell flat on her face and split her lip. Lyndsey screamed in pain and confusion as Bob yanked the box from her. By this time, Linda had made her way to the stage. She cradled her crying daughter, shooting daggers at her husband. Bob was mortified and tried to remedy the situation. He looked at Mr. Murray who scowled at him disapprovingly. Bob held the box in his hands and realized he could only do one thing. He reached down and pressed the big red button.

Nothing.

Bob pressed again. Nothing. Panic set in. He saw that when Lyndsey tripped, she'd disconnected the wires attached to the box. Bob reconnected the wire. Triumphantly he held it up, looking out on the crowd. All he saw were confused disappointed faces. The best idea he could think of was to start the countdown again.

"FIVE!" Bob said, no one taking up his chant.

"FOUR!"

"THREE!"

"TWO!"

"ONE!" Bob continued without anyone joining in. At "one," he pressed the button.

The sight was enough to make even Bob forget what had just transpired. Bob had grown tired of the charms of Christmas Town over the course of the few short months they'd lived here. In that moment, by the light of all the decorations, it all seemed truly *magical* to him. Whole trees were wrapped with bulbs such that you could see every limb and branch. It was as if starlight had been trapped and suspended in mid-air. Bob heard the "oohs" and "aahs" from the gathered crowd. The illumination cast a warm friendly glow around the park. Bob looked around, swept up in the moment. This is what it's about. This is why we moved here. Bob looked to his family to share the moment.

Linda sat on her knees rocking Lyndsey in her arms. Lyndsey was sucking on her fingers, eyes red from crying, bloody from the lip. Jim was bored. The kids were a mess. Linda looked even worse. Her eyes were dark and ringed, a shadow of the radiant woman he had fallen in love with all those years ago. Bob felt embarrassed and ashamed.

Dejected, Bob turned to leave.

He felt a hand on his shoulder. It was Mr. Murray. "That should have gone better, Bob."

"I know, sir."

"I expect *more* from my employees. This is an important time of year. Don't make me regret selling to you, Bob," he said, frowning.

"I know, sir," Bob said. He hated eating crow. Bob excused himself to gather his family, the evening was ruined. "Come on, let's go home,"

"Already? We just got here," Linda said.

"Let's get the kids and just go. It's already past their bedtime." The Suttons walked home in the same silence in which they had arrived. Bob listened to the crunch of the snow under his feet change to the crunch of gravel as they exited the park. When they arrived home, he walked upstairs and lay down on the bed. Before he knew it, he was asleep.

*   *   *

Bob elected to come to work early the next morning to meet the anticipated holiday rush. As Bob left the house, he could see Nick walking his way. It relieved him that Linda had found a friend. He knew if she had her way, the whole family would pack it up and leave Christmas Island tomorrow. He nodded to Nick, who gave him a salute back. Bob assumed that Nick was on his way to see Linda. Good, he thought. Let him deal with her craziness today. Bob had other things to worry about than his domestic problems. This holiday season was literally going to make or break his family. Didn't Linda realize how much pressure he was under?

Bob arrived at the snack stand only to see that someone had beaten him there. Jenn was standing by the door, bundled up in a brown jacket with a scarf around her head. She was stomping her feet to keep warm.

"You're here early," said Bob.

"I couldn't go home for Thanksgiving this year," said Jenn, waiting eagerly for Bob to open the door so she could go inside. "I figured you might need the help, so I took the early ferry."

Bob unlocked the door and they both walked in. He flipped on the light switches and watched the interior of the diner slowly flicker to life.

"Besides," she said, "I wanted to do a little project."

"Project?" asked Bob. Jenn walked over to the register and picked up the box of ornaments Bob had long ago taken out of storage.

"I thought I'd decorate. I saw these, and I figured I'd take the initiative."

Bob smiled. She was a girl after his own heart.

"There's nothing sadder than a box of un-hung ornaments at Christmastime. It's like they're not fulfilling their purpose, their Christmas destiny," she said as she strung up a fake plastic garland on the counter.

Bob set about preparations for the day as the others arrived at the snack stand. Soon the merry sounds of spatulas and clanging plates rang out from the kitchen. Bob smiled, his first for the day.

Tom Lakeland bellied up to the counter. Jenn walked over with a cup of coffee at the ready.

"Thanks darlin'" Tom winked at her. "Some night, eh' Bob?"

"Oh, yes. those lights were quite a sight," Bob said.

"That they were. That they were." Tom laughed. "When they were lit, that is."

"I didn't mean to—"

"I mean, the look on old Glenn's face. His head was so red, for a minute, I thought you lit him up" Tom laughed.

"Kids will be kids," Bob replied weakly.

"That they will. That they will. How is that little peanut, not too scared, is she?" Tom's face grew more serious.

"She's fine."

"I'm so glad. Kathy was worried sick."

"Well, give her my best." Bob said. He turned his back. He had to endure variations of the same conversation all day. And it wore on him. He just wanted to move on from the incident.

The doorbell rang again, and in strode Santa Claus. Normally, John Roebling would not be dressed as Santa when he came to eat at Bob's snack stand, but today was different. The day after Thanksgiving, the Santa hours were extended for the remainder of the holiday season. This meant there was less time to get ready. As a result, John would put on his suit at home and wear it over to work. Mr. Murray insisted that Santa only be seen in Christmas Town, so John wore a long overcoat over his Santa suit as he took the ferry. People rarely questioned his patent leather boots. Sometimes John would catch looks from passengers. If it was a child who spotted the boots, John would look over at the child conspiratorially then wink and put one finger up to his lips as if to say, "Shhhhh…"

Today, John was in full costume as he walked in, red suit, black patent leather boots and belt, red hat, and wire rim half-moon glasses. John had a full, naturally white beard that was irresistible to children. They just couldn't help but pull on it. He bellied up to the counter and perched himself on top of one of the stools.

"Morning, Bob," John said, picking up the menu out of habit. He had been there so many times he certainly did not need to read it anymore.

"What'll you have Joh…I mean 'Santa'?" winked Bob. Jenn already had a cup of coffee ready and set it in front of John. The coffee spilled over the lip and pooled in the saucer underneath it.

"Hmmm," said John, putting a finger aside his nose. "I think I'll have the Ho, Ho, Hotcakes, with a side of bacon, if you please."

"What, no reindeer sausage?" ribbed Bob.

John winked at Bob. "Ask me *after* Christmas. Vixen has been vexing me."

"I'll be sure to do that," said Bob, scribbling down the order.

A loud crash came from the kitchen, cutting through the din. The stand grew silent, Bob could hear shouting. Bob looked through the window and froze.

Paco stood still shirtless, still no hairnet, with his back to the store room. He was edging backwards, away from Carl, who was steadily approaching him, frying pan in one hand. Paco swung wildly at him with a meat cleaver, breathing heavily, it glanced off of a metal shelf with a CLANG!

Bob ran to the kitchen door. I have to stop this, he thought. But he had no idea how he would do it. Someone's going to die, and it might be you if you go in there.

"Stop it!" Bob shouted, horrified. He couldn't afford a bad day, not in the prime of the Christmas rush.

As Bob raced to the kitchen, Jenn and all the customers craned their necks to see the commotion. By this time, shouting could easily be heard emanating from the grill. Even Santa stood up in his seat trying to catch a glimpse.

Five minutes earlier Paco had arrived late to work. Carl was manning the grill, flipping flapjacks. He growled as Paco walked into the kitchen, a still-lit joint dangling from his lips. Paco immediately stripped off his shirt. He walked past Carl.

"In my day, only assholes smoked reefer," Carl said.

"Fuck you old man," Paco retorted. He flipped Carl the bird, then walked to the sink to wash up.

Carl picked up a frying pan, walked over to the prep station, and bashed Paco across the back of his head. Paco went down, hitting his head on the sink as he headed to the floor. Carl loomed over him and raised his arm to inflict another blow. Instinctively, Paco kicked at Carl, shoving him across the kitchen where he slammed into the butcher-block island. Paco pulled himself up and reached for the nearest object that he could use to defend himself—a large meat cleaver. Paco swung it in the air in an attempt to keep Carl at bay.

The door burst open, and Bob ran in.

"What the *fuck* is happening in here?"

They both paused to stare at him.

"This old creep is trying to kill me!" shouted Paco, still waving the cleaver in Carl's direction. Carl spoke nothing as he continued approaching toward Paco, pan in hand.

"Quiet! Carl, back off!" warned Bob. As Bob stood paralyzed by indecision, the crowd moved to the door.

John Roebling loomed behind Bob in the doorway.

"My God, someone do something," Santa implored in a general sense, but mostly to Bob who was in the nearest position to act.

Before Bob could spring into action, Carl lunged at Paco. "I'll kill you," he shouted, swinging the cast iron frying pan. Paco swung the cleaver wildly. Midair, the immovable object met the irresistible force. In Bob's kitchen there were many lax rules, but both Carl and Paco made sure all the knives were sharpened and honed to a fine edge. The blade cut through flesh and bone with almost no resistance. Paco's wild swing had made its purchase on the hand swinging the pan. The digits were cut right below the knuckle, sparing the thumb. They fell to the floor with the frying pan and lay there—curiously fake-looking.

Carl stared at his hand in shock as did Paco, who was frozen in terror. For a moment, no one in the kitchen moved or said anything. But then an inhuman bellowing emanated from Carl's lungs, a deep, primal sound that broke the détente.

Carl lunged at Paco with his good hand. With impressive strength, he pushed Paco over to the grill. Flush with adrenaline, Carl grabbed Paco's head with both hands (what remained of his right hand) and pressed down as hard as he could, holding Paco's face to the grill. All this happened in an instant. Bob stood slack-jawed in shock. Suddenly, he felt John Roebling pushing by him.

Santa sprang into action, running to the grill where Paco's screams and the smell of burning flesh filled the kitchen. Santa's fist connected with Carl's face with such force that he drove a tooth up into his jaw that later had to be surgically extracted. Carl was knocked backward onto the floor, laid out cold with one blow. Santa stood over the motionless body, fists clenched, ready for more.

Bob snapped out of his inaction and ran over to Paco, who was screaming in pain, holding his burned face. He could see Paco's skin blistering and bubbling.

"Jenn, call the mainland for an ambulance!" he shouted.

"And the cops," Santa said, looming over Carl's motionless body.

Word about the altercation quickly spread over Christmas Town. A crowd began to grow. Bob wanted nothing more than to get back to a normal workday, but no-one was in the mood to eat. Mr. Murray, the last person Bob wanted to see, walked in, his face red and flushed, as if he had run the whole way. He probably did.

"Bob! What on earth is going on here?" Mr. Murray shouted angrily.

"There was a fight, Mr. Murray," said Bob. He looked down at his hands, they were shaking, he quickly shoved them in his pockets. He felt nauseous, the adrenaline was still coursing through his system. Bob clenched his jaw tightly to stop it from quivering uncontrollably.

"I can see that. On the *opening day of Christmas?* Are you crazy, stupid, or just incompetent?" Mr. Murray was a barely contained coil of anger. Spittle flew from his lips. "You and your trash family are in so much trouble…" He was so upset he was unable to finish his sentence. Mr. Murray's face had gone from red to eggplant in his apoplexy.

The paramedics arrived on the scene at the same time as the police. Christmas Island has no local police force and fell under the jurisdiction of the Burlington Police Department. The police and paramedics raced through Christmas Town to the snack stand, where they pushed Bob and Mr. Murray aside.

"Where are they?" demanded the paramedic. Bob gestured to his office. Paco was lying on an old couch, moaning softly and holding his face. Bob had wrapped it with a towel filled with ice to try to slow the damage. Carl was tied to a chair with rope and aprons. He was awake now, glaring and struggling against his bonds. John had wrapped up Carl's right hand in a kitchen apron, and it was soaked through with blood. The paramedics ran into the room and immediately began to administer first aid to both the men. The police took Bob aside to get his statement.

"We're not done here," Mr. Murray growled at Bob through gritted teeth.

Bob felt his interrogation with the police like an eternity, during which Bob seemed to have to answer the same questions over and over.

"Good thing Santa was here, eh?" the officer said, flipping his notebook closed.

"Yeah," Bob said. He was drained of all energy.

"Come on, you must be used to this kind of stuff, being from New York," the cop replied.

"Not from New York."

The paramedics wheeled an unconscious Paco out on a stretcher. The medics had sedated him. Jenn sat in the corner by the fake tree she had put up, looking shocked. The police led Carl out the door in handcuffs, one hand now expertly bandaged. Bob stood up and watched his two cooks exit the restaurant. Only after the ambulance pulled away with sirens flashing, did Bob sit down. He slid into the booth, looking at nothing in particular. The phone rang. Bob stared at it on the wall, as it rang and rang.

Jenn held out the phone to him. "Bob, um…I think it's your wife." Bob shuffled over to the phone in a daze. As he spoke to Linda, his mind was like a sieve, he couldn't hold one thought or the next. She might have said something important, or she might not have. It didn't matter. As soon as he hung up the conversation drifted out of his mind, lost forever. He retreated to an empty booth and put his head down on the table, it was cool and felt good on his forehead.

Bob became aware of someone sitting in the booth, he looked up to see Jenn sitting across from him.

"I told everyone to go home and locked the doors," she said looking across the table. "I thought that would be for the best."

"Yes, that would be for the best," Bob repeated weakly. He looked around the stand for the first time. It was empty. There were still half-eaten meals on some tables, abandoned by customers. Chairs lay on the ground, overturned. As Bob stood, he could see a trail of blood leading from the kitchen to his office then back out through the front door. Many feet had tracked it around the floor. Bob walked into his office to the sight of a pool of blood. The rope and aprons they had used to constrain Carl, now lying in a crumpled red mess. Bob sank into his chair. Jenn walked through the door and leaned against it, not daring to say anything.

After a few more minutes of silence, Bob walked over to the coat rack, picking up a clean apron. He tied it behind his back.

"I guess I better clean up," he said to Jenn, exhausted. "You don't have to stay, go home."

"No," Jenn said. She put on an apron. "I'm staying."

"You don't have to."

"I *want* to," Jenn said, walking to the closet where Bob kept his cleaning supplies.

The first task was cleaning up the blood. Even after a vigorous mopping, there were still dried patches that required Bob and Jenn to get on their hands and knees to scrub with a stiff bristled brush. Bob's arm grew sore from repetitive motion.

As he replayed the incident over and over, he grew more and more depressed. Why had he waited so long to act? Maybe if he had stepped in, Carl would still have his fingers and Paco wouldn't be horribly disfigured.

Bob and Jenn finished cleaning up. By what would have been closing time, the stand and diner bore no evidence of the events that had unfolded.

"Thanks for your help," Bob said.

"It's not a problem. You looked like you needed it." She smiled at him.

"You can take the day off tomorrow," Bob said to her. "I don't expect it will be busy after…" he trailed off.

"No, I'll be here. I think it will be a better day. It has to be, right?"

Bob leaned over. The kiss was brief. Bob felt his lips press against hers. He pulled back and looked at her face. Jenn wore a shocked expression. She turned around, put on her jacket and left the restaurant without a word.

Bob sat in a booth for a long while before he locked up and went home.

DIGGING AROUND

2000

Jim opened his eyes. He stared at the ceiling, not daring to look over. Cammy Norman had visited him again in his room for the second night in a row. They had sex again, but this time it felt different, closer. Jim genuinely liked this girl despite the fact that it seemed the whole town, including her mother, had some kind of personal vendetta against him. Jim thought about the night before. After they had sex, Cammy curled up beside him, fitting into the crook of his arm. Jim understood on a certain level why Cammy wanted to keep their affair secret.

When he had wrecked his car, the idea of spending two to three days stuck in this town seemed like an eternity. Now Jim felt time slipping through his fingers like sand.

She had her back to him, the covers draped over her lovely form. Jim watched her breathing for a while, the swell of her chest moving in and out.

Finally, Cammy stirred and turned to face Jim. "Morning, lover," she said, making his heart skip.

"Morning, yourself," Jim said. "I can't believe you're still here. I mean, I want you here. I'm glad you're here," he stammered. She smiled back at him, brushing her wild hair from her eyes.

"I'm glad I'm here too," Cammy said, pulling the covers up. "I'm a little surprised myself."

"Your mother...She—"

"I can deal with my mother," Cammy said. "I know this hotel better than anyone. I grew up in this hotel. I know its secrets. Don't worry."

"Who's worried about her when I have the police out for me?"

"How do you mean?" inquired Cammy, furrowing her brow.

"Well, Deputy Avery had a few words with me on the street last night. He pretty much told me to leave town or there would be consequences."

"Did he?" Cammy said, propping herself up on one elbow. "That little shit. He and Dodge are thick as thieves. This is exactly the kind of thing I have to deal with all the time. My brother is so protective. Sometimes it borders on obsession. Ever since Dad died, he's gotten worse. I'll take care of it."

"No, please don't," Jim said. "I want us to enjoy our last day together." Jim immediately regretted what he'd said.

Cammy frowned. "Last day?"

"Yes. I mean, the car will be fixed today, right? After that, I have to move on." They had never discussed the future.

"I guess you're right," said Cammy, getting up. Her limp was more pronounced as she rummaged around the room for her clothes. "I better get to work then."

"Cammy, please don't be upset," Jim said, getting out of bed, tripping over the comforter.

"Why would I be upset? You had your fun, right? I'll fix your car, and you can get back to writing your book."

"It's not like that, Cammy. These two days have been two of the best in my life," Jim said.

She stood in front of him, in her underwear, arms crossed.

"There's not a reason for me to stay after the car is fixed. Is there?"

"You tell me," she said.

"Do you want me to stay?'

Cammy struggled to pull up her jeans. "No. Yes. I don't know."

"I don't know what this is. I don't know what it could be. What I do know is I've never felt like this before. It's so fresh, so new I don't want to mess it up. But I think I might have." Suddenly he had an idea. It was crazy, but...What the hell, he thought.

"You could come with me," Jim said.

Cammy looked perplexed. "You mean, move away with you? Move in with you? You're crazy. I hardly know you. You definitely don't know me."

"No. Well, not exactly," Jim replied. "Hear me out. I like you a lot. I think you like me."

Cammy stared at him, eyes wild.

He continued: "I already have a whole trip planned out. It takes me all around Vermont." Jim walked over to the desk and picked up the stack of Map Quest printouts.

"Come with me," he said, brandishing the papers. "We can discover Vermont together, get to know each other on the way. Look." He showed her the map with the highlighted route. "See, it loops back around. I'd be heading back this way after…" He stopped for a moment as his finger passed over Christmas Island. "Come with me. Let's have an adventure."

"What about the shop, my brother?"

Jim could see in her eyes, the battle waging in her head. "I can't leave him again."

"Your brother's older now. He can handle it. You said it was the slow season. I imagine he can fend for himself the rest of the summer."

"I don't know." Cammy said reticently.

"You don't want to?"

"No, I do *want* to. I just don't know if I can."

"You said you never wanted to be trapped. I'm setting you free," Jim replied.

"I don't need you to set me free," Cammy said. "I'll think about it." She finished getting dressed "You're right, let's enjoy the moment. Think about the future later." She walked over, limping slightly now, and grabbed Jim by the collar of his button up shirt and kissed him. "I'll see you later, after I fix up your shitty car," she smiled. "I promise."

"When?"

"Soon," Cammy said. "Stop by the shop later." She opened the door, making sure no one was watching. She picked up the tray in front of the door and brought it in.

She handed the tray to Jim. "Here's your breakfast."

"Ice cold as usual, I imagine," Jim said.

"Ughhhh, mother," she said, rolling her eyes. "Sorry, I'll make it up to you. We'll have lunch!" With that, she drifted out the door.

Jim had a terrible feeling she was slipping away. He'd pushed her too far too soon. He sat in contemplation as he chomped on his stale toast.

Jim got dressed and walked down to the lobby. Again, he was greeted by Cammy's mother. She waited at the bottom of the stairs in her wheelchair. She had abandoned any pretense of politeness. She scowled at him as he walked across the lobby to the front door.

"Headed out for the day, Mr. Sutton?"

"Yes," Jim replied, smiling. He reminded himself that he ultimately wanted this woman to like him. "I just love your hotel. I'll make sure to give it its own chapter." Jim knew that innkeepers lived for placement in travel books and magazines. Especially books. Word-of-mouth reviews were one thing, books were evergreen. "I'll have to order the house onion rings and give them a test-drive."

"That would be nice," Mrs. Norman said. "But I believe you've already tasted what we have here at *Le Grand Hotel Vermont*."

"Really?" asked Jim. Could she know?

"I think you have," Cammy's mother intoned. "There is very little that I do not know about in my hotel." Jim felt his stomach tighten. God, she does know. Is she bluffing? Flustered, Jim tried his best to extricate himself.

"Well, anyway, I'd love to try them again," he replied.

Mrs. Norman held up her hand. "Mr. Sutton, you have a message," she said. "Would you like me to retrieve it for you?"

"Yes, of course," Jim replied, wondering who would possibly send him a message here.

Mrs. Norman wheeled herself behind the desk. Picking up an attenuated claw device, she plucked an envelope from the cubby marked with his room number. She dropped it in his hand.

"Have a nice day, Mr. Sutton." She drove herself out of sight.

Jim had hoped that the message was from Cammy. But she wouldn't risk it, not with her mother, he thought. Turning the envelope over in his hands he saw it wasn't sealed. He opened it. Inside was a card the same color as the cream-colored envelope. Embossed at the top was a gold maple leaf. On the card said the following:

Mr. Sutton.
The book you requested is in. Stop by the store and pick up at your earliest convenience.
– Evan

Jim was confused. He hadn't ordered a book. As he stepped out of *Le Grand Hotel Vermont*, Jim could see that today was not one of those wonderfully idyllic Vermont days. It was typical of Vermont for those who lived there. Vermont can be stunningly beautiful, but two thirds of the year it snowed while the rest of the year was a toss-up of sun and rain. The sky was gray, and clouds hung over the valley in a blanket of languid sodden dullness. Jim decided he'd head back to the bookstore.

There were only a few people milling about the store, perusing the canyons of books. A Persian cat with a pushed-in face rubbed against Jim's leg. He tried to shoo it away but was unable to shake it. The cat stuck to Jim as if glued to him, moving in tandem, even as he tried to walk away. Jim looked down, worried he might step on it, increasingly annoyed at its persistence.

"Mr. Sutton, so glad you came by," Evan said. "I take it you got my note."

"About that—"

"Oh, that's perfectly okay," Evan interrupted. "We are more than happy to fill orders for our customers." Evan grabbed Jim's arm surprisingly hard and guided him around the desk. "I have it in the back, if you would just come with me."

Evan led Jim around the monoliths of books to the back of the store.

"Look, I'm flattered, I am, but..." His voice trailed off as he realized how crazy he sounded.

Evan bore a wry smile, as if he were stifling a laugh. "Oh, you're cute. I see what Cammy likes about you, but you're not my type," Evan said, sitting down at his desk. He folded his hands and looked up at Jim. "Didn't you get my note *yesterday?*"

"I did, but—"

"Ah, yes 'flattered.'" Evan cleared his throat. "I needed to talk to you. Alone. Strawberry Falls is a small town, a very small town. As you've probably noticed, there is very little that goes unobserved. Look, we all know that Cammy likes you. Cammy's lived here her whole life. All of us have seen her and Dodge grow up. Like a lot of the kids here, they feel a certain attachment to the town. 'It takes a village' kind of thing, you know? It's a little different with the Normans."

"What do you mean?" asked Jim.

"You know, being a bookstore owner is like being a hairdresser or a priest. Everyone wants to talk and everyone wants to confess something. They just need a friendly face. People come in here and tell me the most interesting things. I keep their secrets. I mean if I didn't, what kind of friend would I be?

"What are you trying to tell me?"

"When the Normans arrived here, Strawberry Falls was a different place. Piece by piece, person by person, it seemed as if the community had been disintegrating a little each year. This town was in danger of just blowing away." Evan held out his hands for effect, waving his fingers dramatically. "Strawberry Falls was a town without a purpose. One day a young couple came to town. He was young and brash. She was smart, barefoot, and pregnant. They had a lot of cash. This couple was met with the usual suspicion. When they bought the old hotel and announced plans to fix it up, everybody thought they were crazy. It was the Normans who pushed for Strawberry Falls to become a leaf destination. It was Abigail Norman who proposed transforming the old mill into an antique mall and financed it out of their own pockets. To this town, it was as if the Normans dropped out of heaven. This town owes them a lot. You wouldn't ever tell by how they look, or where they live but the Normans are the wealthiest family in town. And they share their wealth. It's not unheard of for bags of groceries or cash to be delivered to a family in need. I don't think there is any business that hasn't been the beneficiary of their generosity, including mine. The Norman family is beloved here. Because of this, we are protective of their children and their secrets. It was a real tragedy when Mike died. This town feels such an enormous debt to this family. It is probably why most questions about them went away. There are those who still wonder, though."

"What? Wonder what?" asked Jim.

"When I say the Normans dropped out of heaven, I'm not kidding. It was like they dropped out of nowhere. They had nothing but their names and their money. They have never talked about their past. They have never, not once had anyone visit them. Not one relative, one friend. Anyone. In a small town, it is impossible to keep secrets. Strawberry Falls' biggest secret is the Normans. They have protected their privacy and their children fiercely. There are those in town who would let the Normans do whatever they like. Strawberry Falls has installed the Normans as the town's royal family with Abigail as their queen. The only reason anybody in town wants you gone is because she does."

"But why? I haven't done anything," Jim said.

"Haven't you?" Evan looked at Jim skeptically. "Cammy likes you. That's enough. Anyone who knows her can see it. When she stood up for you at town hall, it sent the tongues a wagging. But your greatest sin is that you're an outsider."

"This is crazy."

"Yes," Evan said. "Abigail is the queen here. I'm warning you to tread lightly. She's got you in her sights. I'd advise you to pack up and leave as soon as you can."

"You, too?" Jim looked at Evan sourly. "Another threat. I've already gotten one from the deputy."

"Have you?" Evan replied. "Well, that's not a surprise. Dodge is as protective of his sister as he is his mother, but that is unsettling."

Jim looked at Evan in disbelief.

"Please don't take my warning as a threat. I love Cammy as if she were my own daughter. She's endured a lot of pain. What with her disfigurement."

"What disfigurement? She's perfect as far as I'm concerned."

"You're sweet, not to notice" Evan smiled. "Cammy was born with one leg shorter than the other."

"Her parents put her in leg braces some quack doctor recommended she wear as an infant." Evan continued. "Every night as a child her mother would turn the mechanism in an attempt to even out her legs. The pain must have been unimaginable, especially for a little girl. Watching that girl hobble around town in those braces, always a smile on her face…" Evan shook his head.

"We were so proud of her when she left for school, and so sad when she was forced to come back. I'm glad she's having some fun with you around. But I can see the writing on the wall, as they say. What it says is 'Don't cross the Normans.' They've dealt with 'problem people' before. Let's just say they don't live in Strawberry Falls anymore."

Jim stood rooted to the spot overwhelmed by the flood of information.

"I do love secrets," Evan said. "I wish I could tell you more, but some secrets are best kept hidden. It's for your own good."

Evan walked over to the desk and picked up a book. He pushed it into Jim's hands. It was a worn copy of Anna Karenina. Evan led him out of the back room.

"Here's your book. I hope you like it."

The bell to the door jingled merrily. Jim turned around. To his surprise, Dodge Norman was standing in the doorway twirling a set of keys on his fingers, grinning.

"They said you'd be here," he said.

"Who said? How would they know where I was? Ah, yes…your

mother."

"Whatever," Dodge spat. "Anyway, your car's done. I was sent to get you."

"Cammy sent you?"

"That's right," Dodge answered. "You ready?" Jim made a motion to reach into his wallet to pay for the book he never wanted.

"No charge. On the house," Evan said.

The sidewalk was slick and dark with water. It had started raining. A few random drops spattered on Jim's neck, cold and startling. The rusty old tow truck from the garage sat in front of the bookstore. Dodge walked around to the driver side and got in. He leaned back and kicked the passenger-side door open. Smiling, Dodge held out his hand to help Jim into the cab. Jim took it hesitantly and climbed into the car. Dodge started up the truck, pumping the gas and grinding the gears.

"It's okay, girl…" he cooed to the truck, rubbing the dashboard as if to reassure it. The car shuddered. Jim could feel the gears catching. "See, just like a woman. You gotta' know how to caress 'em."

Jim managed a faint smile, but he felt uncomfortable. He was relieved to be finally retrieving his car. He was familiar with the streets to the garage, so it surprised Jim when he watched as Norman's Garage came into view, and then out of it.

"Uh, didn't we miss a turn back there, man?" Jim asked, attempting to sound calm.

"Yep," Dodge said. The rain grew heavier. Dodge turned on the windshield wipers. The glass was so dirty Jim wasn't sure if it made things better or worse. The rain was too light to wash the dirt off the windshield, so it smeared across in twin arcs, muddy, creating a hazy, dream-like effect.

"Where are we going?".

"We've got a couple of errands to run first. I hope you don't mind, buddy."

As they stopped at a red light, Jim thought about opening the door and jumping out. Then he remembered that the passenger-side door was broken. Only a swift kick would dislodge it. He wouldn't have the room to stomp it open with Dodge still in the car. Dodge reached over to the glove compartment in front of Jim and unhooked the latch. The door swung down. On top of a faded and tattered owner's manual from god knows what year, sat a revolver and a box of bullets. Jim stared at in shock, he looked closer, the gun sat on an old worn manual and a tattered AbaZaba wrapper. Dodge reached into the glove compartment and fished around.

He grabbed something red from behind the revolver then slammed the door shut. He locked the glove box and took the key.

The something in Dodge's hand was a joint—red from the color of the rolling paper. The metallic click of a zippo lighter rang out as Dodge coaxed life from the joint in his mouth. He took a long drag. Holding it in, he held the joint to Jim.

"You want a drag?" Dodge asked, smoke shooting from his mouth.

"No thanks," Jim said.

"Your funeral."

The wipers beat a staccato rhythm.

Oh, my god, it must be his pot I found. Does he know? It was too late. Jim missed his chance to get out of the truck. The light turned green; the truck lurched forward.

Dodge drove the truck to the edge of town. Then he turned down a tree-lined, dirt road that was muddy from the rain. As the two of them ventured deeper down the road, Jim became aware that they were traveling farther and farther into the woods and farther and farther from civilization. Jim glanced around the cab of the car for something to defend himself with. That's when he realized that the truck had been recently cleaned. There was nothing that Jim could see that he could fashion into an instrument of defense.

"Is it much longer?" Jim said. His mouth was dry, the words barely coming out as a croak.

"Nope," Dodge said.

Dodge made a turn down a side road. Jim had tried to keep a mental map of every turn. Panic and fear settled into his mind. He knew he had lost any semblance of knowing where he was or how to get back. The truck pulled into a clearing. Through the smeared windshield, Jim could see another car there. Jim could make out the shadow of a figure as well. It was standing next to the car. Dodge put the truck in park and shut down the engine.

"We're here," he said turning to Jim. He leaned back and kicked over Jim to open the door. "Get out."

Jim sat in the truck, frozen. His mind was racing, thinking about what he should do. Although it was mid-day, the overcast skies cast a dark pall over the valley. The shadowy figure walked toward the truck, illuminated for a second in the headlights. With the wipers off, the rain made a constellation of sparkling stars on the glass that refracted thousands of raindrops, making it impossible to see…him or her? As he/she approached the truck. The figure walked around the corner.

He wore a rain poncho with the words "STRAWBERRY FALLS PD" stenciled on it. Over his hat, he had a clear plastic baggie, designed to keep the fine felt brim protected from the rain. Deputy Avery stood in the doorway of the truck glaring at Jim, rain dripping down from his hat in rivulets. "Get out of the car," he ordered.

"Is there something wrong, officer?" Jim asked.

"No. Just get out of the car," Deputy Avery said. He put his hands on his hips in such a way that the poncho moved back to reveal his service revolver.

"It's okay, man. You can come out," said Dodge. He had walked up behind Deputy Avery. Dodge didn't seem to mind the rain. "This is what we came to do."

Jim climbed out of the truck, feeling a little faint. What's going on? Jim glanced at the clearing; the trees were a ways off. *If things get weird, can I make a run for it?* He followed Dodge and Deputy Avery to the rear of the truck. Dodge reached into the back by the winch and pulled out a shovel.

"Come with me," Dodge said, gesturing for Jim to follow him. They walked to the middle of the clearing. Dodge looked at Deputy Avery, who gave him a slight nod of approval. Dodge handed the shovel to Jim.

"Dig," he said.

"W-what?" stammered Jim.

"Dig, Jim," Dodge said, nodding to the ground. He still had the shovel in his outstretched hand. Jim looked over at Deputy Avery in a desperate plea for help. After all, he was an officer of the law.

"You heard him. Dig," Deputy Avery said, again putting his hand on his hip, near the gun.

Jim took the shovel from Dodge, his hands shaking. He put the blade in the ground and pulled up the first shovelful. Jim looked up at Dodge.

"How deep? How much do you want me to dig?" Jim asked, trying to stall. His mind was racing. Could he use the shovel as a weapon? Deputy Avery was too far away now. He'd get shot before he ever got to him.

Dodge took another joint from his breast pocket. "I'll tell you when," said Dodge. He turned to Deputy Avery. "Want one? I have to sneak em'. Cammy and Mom hate it when I smoke."

"Sure, I'll take one," Deputy Avery said.

"None for you until you finish your chores," Dodge scolded Jim, laughing. "Keep digging. The sooner you finish, the sooner you'll be done."

The rain made the digging difficult. The deeper he got, the more the bottom of the hole filled with dark muddy water. The hole grew deeper per Dodge's and Deputy Avery's instructions. They supervised, leaning against the truck. Watching them smoke their joints, Jim became keenly aware of the shape and depth of the hole. The longer he went, the more certain Jim became that he was digging his own grave. He had excavated the hole to the depth of his shoulders. He threw shovelful after shovelful of mud over the top, arms and back aching from exertion.

"That's enough," came Dodge's voice from above.

You sure?" Jim said Beyond the edge of the hole above him, he watched Dodge and Deputy Avery. The rain had not relented. Jim was soaked. The way he was feeling the water could easily be sweat or tears. But he'd show nothing. He didn't want to give them the satisfaction. He wouldn't beg for his life. If this was it, he'd meet it. He thought of his sister, then his mother.

"Get out," Deputy Avery said.

Jim flopped out of the hole, staggering to his feet. Deputy Avery and Dodge stared at him. Dodge looked at Avery and smiled.

"You ready?' he said to his friend.

"As ready as I'll ever be," said Officer Avery.

"You don't have to do this," Jim said. Dodge smiled placing his arm around Jim's shoulders. Dodge took the shovel from Jim and handed it to Avery. They walked Jim to the back of truck. Jim could feel the panic scream through his body. He closed his eyes and tried to calm himself. In that moment, Jim became preternaturally aware of his surroundings. The sound of the raindrops on the leaves was deafening. The feeling of water on his skin, the beads of sweat that ran down his neck in between his shoulder blades, the smell of the rain and the earth. These sensations cried out, each demanding to be recognized before it all ended.

He opened his eyes. A sense of calm washed over him. The panic was gone. It was no use fighting it. He was outnumbered and out gunned. If it ended here, so be it. His last thought was that he wished he could tell his mother. The idea that he'd just disappear without leaving a trace would crush her. Jim laughed at the absurdity of his dying in the state where his family had gone through hell. It was strangely appropriate. The thought of his mother not knowing what had happened to him, or where he was buried made him even sadder, if that was possible.

"You can open your eyes," said Dodge.

Wiping rain away from his face, Jim looked from Dodge to Deputy Avery, and back again.

"Help me get these down." Dodge gestured to two black metal drums on the back of the truck. Jim walked over to the edge of the truck and grabbed the top of one of the drums. Am I going in these barrels? In how many Pieces?

"Careful!" Dodge said as Jim began to tip one over. "They're real heavy." Indeed, Jim thought as he tested the weight. Very heavy. He wouldn't be able to move them by himself.

What's in here?" Jim asked, confused.

"Oil," Dodge answered as he positioned himself to lift the barrel.

"What?"

"Old oil. When we do an oil change, fix an engine, the old oil goes in the barrels," Dodge said, knocking on the drum, which emitted a dull clang.

"And you bury it? Is that legal?" Jim asked.

"No." Dodge laughed, looking at Deputy Avery. "You gonna report me?"

"I think I'll let you off with a warning, this time," Avery said.

The three of them rolled the barrels to the hole. Dodge made Jim push them in, then fill the hole. When the hole was covered and the dirt mounded up over the barrels, Jim stood back to look at his handiwork. It indeed looked like a grave. The thought of it sent a chill down his spine. Jim turned around to see Dodge and Deputy Avery watching him, their faces grim.

"We done here?" Deputy Avery asked Dodge, not looking at him, instead staring at Jim. The knots in Jim's stomach returned.

"I dunno," Dodge drawled, fingering the shovel. He walked back to the truck and threw it in. He opened the driver side door and got in. After shutting the door, Dodge looked at Jim who was standing there, not daring to move. "You coming or are you walking back?" Jim somehow got to his feet to work and staggered back to the truck. He climbed in and said nothing.

"Home again, home again, jiggedy jig, eh little piggy?" Dodge said, turning the wheel to pull out of the clearing and back onto the road. He looked Jim over. "I think you might have gotten some dirt on you, dude." This amused him to no end as he laughed and turned onto the road back to town. Jim, still reeling from (what he thought was) his near-death experience, was silent the whole ride back. The tow truck made the turn onto the main road back into town.

"Tell you what—I'll drop you off at the hotel so you can change. Then you're picking up your car, right?"

Jim nodded. They passed the garage heading the other way. Jim looked out the window. Cammy was in the parking lot. She saw them passing by. Cammy raised her hand to smile and wave at them. Her expression changed as the truck drove by. Jim wondered if she could see the look on his face.

He leaned over to look in the passenger-side rear view mirror. Above the OBJECTS MAY BE CLOSER THAN THEY APPEAR letters on the mirror, Jim watched Cammy walk out into the street as they drove away. The truck pulled onto Main Street. Dodge made a wide U-turn to pull up in front of *Le Grand Hotel Vermont*.

"Scuse me, buddy," Dodge said. Leaning back, he kicked the door open. Jim got out, dazed.

"Don't forget your bags!" Dodge called after Jim. "I'll be waiting here."

Jim didn't look back. All he wanted was go up to his room and figure out what to do. Part of him wanted nothing more than to take Dodge's advice and clear out of town. He really liked Cammy, maybe more. He didn't want to be another chapter in her sad story. If only he could tell her goodbye, but he was sure Dodge would make sure he never saw her again, one way or another.

Jim's shoes squished with each step as he walked through the lobby of the hotel. Not only was he still soaking wet, he was covered in mud that left a trail on the floor behind him. Good, Let her deal with it, he thought. To Jim's disappointment, for once, Mrs. Norman was nowhere to be seen. He would have loved to have faced her as he looked now. Jim walked up the stairs, soiling the beautiful runner with each step. He unlocked his door. For one crazy moment, he thought that maybe Cammy would be there waiting for him. This of course would be impossible.

As Jim opened the door, he was not greeted by Cammy, but by a rather shocking tableau: To Jim's surprise, someone had come in and packed him up. His suitcase lay on the bed with all his clothes he had put in the chest of drawers. Jim looked in every drawer just to make sure that they were, in fact, all empty. Not only had someone packed up his clothes, someone had laid out a fresh change of clothes for him. As if they knew. Jim grimaced. Mrs. Norman. Jim opened his suitcase. Everything he owned was there, folded. Neater than he could possibly manage.

Wait. Panic gripped him. Where is it?

He looked for the satchel with his notes, but it was gone. He searched the whole room, looking under the bed, in the closet. Jim turned over every inch of the room searching for his satchel to no avail. He sat on the bed, uncaring as mud dripped off him and onto the bright white bedspread, Jim's mind came to a horrible conclusion. He was done. It was all over. The book, the trip, both gone forever.

He had been defeated.

LOSING FAITH

1977

For Linda the disastrous Thanksgiving of 1977 was not about a failed lighting ceremony or a bloody fight at the snack shack—It was about the loss of faith, in anything. It began at 5:00 am. She reached out, groping in the darkness at the alarm clock in an attempt to stop it ringing before it woke Bob. Careful not to wake her children, Linda groped her way downstairs in the enveloping darkness of the house, expertly avoiding low ceilings. She was so familiar with her home she could have walked through blindfolded.

A house is a living organism. During the day, it hums along with all its pieces and parts and people. At night, with the outside world still and retired, the inside of an island home becomes quieter than you could believe. Sounds become amplified. Linda became distinctly aware of the slap-slapping noise her bare feet made on the floor. As she turned on the kitchen light, she heard the small electric pop, then the dull buzz of the incandescent bulb as it flickered to life.

She was too tired to think. As she waited for the oven to preheat, she opened the refrigerator to take out the turkey. The turkey that she had purchased was smaller than she would have preferred, but the size requirements to fit in their tiny oven precluded a bigger bird. It would do, but she lamented the loss of leftovers, one of the evergreen joys of the holiday. As she picked up the bird, Linda cursed inwardly. She could feel the crunch of frozen meat as she poked the plastic bag with her finger. The Sutton's refrigerator was notoriously inconsistent. Milk would go bad in only a few days, but sometimes she'd take lettuce out of the crisper only to find it frozen and ruined. One time when she had been careless where she placed them, a dozen eggs froze solid. There seemed to be distinct temperate zones inside of the icebox that Linda could not navigate.

She ran the bird under the tap for a while to try to warm it up. She hacked out the giblets with an ice pick. I'll just have to use the meat thermometer, she thought, pulling it out of the utensil drawer. Taking the sharp pointy probe, she plunged it into the deepest part of the breast. It seemed her efforts to thaw it under the tap were successful as it slid in with little effort. Elbow deep in the turkey Linda filled the cavity with her special sausage stuffing. Bob always complained that it wasn't like his mother's but Linda didn't care. If he wants his mother's he can make it himself, she thought. Besides, she hated apples in stuffing.

Linda was a sourdough fan. She had baked a loaf specifically for this meal. The bird barely fit as she pushed it into the oven. She double checked the temperature, then lurched back to bed to try to get a little sleep.

It seemed like only a moment after she closed her eyes Bob was shaking her awake.

"Happy Thanksgiving!" Bob said. Linda sat up in bed, her eyes still crusted with sleep.

"What time is it?"

"It's seven," answered Bob.

"*Seven?*" asked Linda in disbelief. She picked up the alarm clock at the side of her bed in hopes that she might have heard him wrong. To her dismay, it indeed said 7:03. She stared at Bob

"I'm headed into work," said Bob

"Isn't the stand closed? It is Thanksgiving."

"No" Bob said. "I told you; we are always open."

"Right."

"Right!" Bob said. "Don't worry," he said and kissed her on the forehead. "I'll be back in time for dinner. When is it, 2:00?"

"2:30."

"Even better!" Bob cheerfully walked out of the room, leaving Linda fully awake and unable to formulate what to do next.

I guess I'll get up and start working, she thought.

Linda peeled and cut away until 8:00 when the kids woke up. They had the week off for Thanksgiving, so she had let them sleep in. Linda placed two bowls of cereal in front of them.

"I don't want Cheerios," sulked Lyndsey. "I want scrambled eggs."

"I'm sorry sweeties, Mommy doesn't have time to make you eggs. Mommy has to clean and prepare for Thanksgiving dinner."

"I don't want it!" Lyndsey screamed. She flung the bowl of Cheerios as hard as she could. It struck the wall and the ceramic bowl shattered. Milk dribbled down the wall. A few soggy "Os" stuck where they had impacted.

"Lyndsey Anne Sutton!" shouted Linda. "That was BAD. Very Bad." She angrily stomped to the broom closet to grab the sweeper and dustpan. Best behavior, my ass. "Fine, you don't get breakfast then."

Lyndsey started crying.

Linda dumped the shards and milky remains of breakfast into the garbage can. She tried to tune out the shouting. Truth be told, she felt like joining in. Linda walked from kitchen into the living room. She picked up a decorative throw pillow and screamed into it as loud as she could until her vocal cords hurt. Gathering her composure, she returned to the kitchen.

Jim sat at the table eating his cereal, not daring to speak. Lyndsey's wailing had subsided. She sniffed and wiped tears from her eyes. Linda cleaned up breakfast and plunked her children in front of the black and white TV in the living room.

With the children occupied, Linda continued down the checklist for the feast. Turkey, check. Rolls ready to go, check. Next up, potatoes. She had bought a bottle of cheap wine for the meal. It sat on the counter. After Linda finally finished peeling the potatoes, she thought, What the hell? and opened it. As she swirled the red wine (she knew damn well that turkey went with white, but she didn't care, thank you) around in her glass, she luxuriated in the scents of the day. The turkey was languidly roasting in the oven. The rich delicious smell permeated the room. Linda took a moment to baste the bird and check the thermometer. Still a ways to go, she noted. Typically, it would be almost done by now. Maybe the turkey was more frozen than she thought. She sat down, tipped the glass back, poured another, then closed her eyes for a well-earned moment of peace.

Linda woke to Bob announcing his arrival back in the house. She looked up at the clock on the wall, a garage sale gem Linda had acquired. The black cat eyes moved back and forth. 2:00. *Could it be 2:00 already?* She must have dozed off. A mild panic set in. Her first thought was the food on the stove. She checked. To her dismay, the cranberry sauce boiled over in the pot, running over the sides creating an angry bubbling black tar on the burner. The potatoes did not fare much better. Instead of being light and fluffy like she wanted, they were pasty and glue-like, too starchy. *It's okay*, she told herself. *I can fix this. First check the bird.* She opened the oven. It looked beautiful. The turkey was golden brown, the skin perfect. Picking up the baster, Linda took a syringe-worth of turkey juice and bathed the turkey in rich juices. She looked at the thermometer again. It had barely budged from the last time she checked. That was okay. She would need time to salvage the side-dishes anyway.

Linda reached into the back of one of the cupboards, searching for that brown and yellow box. At first, she couldn't find it, and it frustrated her. She *knew* it was there. Success! She pulled out a box of instant potato flakes. It was at this point that Bob walked into the kitchen.

"*Instant* potatoes?" Bob remarked, his voice dripping with disappointment. Linda turned to face him, so very tempted to lose it.

"No. I just need them to fix something," she said, turning to the pots.

"Fix something? Is the meal okay?"

"Yes. It will be fine. Just check on the kids, please," Linda said.

Bob rolled his eyes and walked out of the kitchen.

She went to the refrigerator and pulled out a carton of milk. Sniffing the top to make sure it hadn't curdled, Linda mixed the potato flakes and milk in small amounts to try to fix the consistency of the mashed potatoes. Like an alchemist, she transmuted the gluey mess into something that was relatively good. Pleased with her results, Linda scooped out the mash into a ceramic dish to keep them warm for dinner. She put a big pat of yellow Cabot butter on the top.

Turning her attention back to the turkey, Linda opened the oven again. She stared at the thermometer. It hadn't moved, not at all. This can't be right, she thought. Grabbing a pair of oven mitts, she pulled open the oven door to get a closer look. She pulled the thermometer out and examined it. To Linda's horror, it was melted. The tiny oven was barely big enough for their turkey and the thermometer she used had been too close to the heating element. The plastic had melted preventing the needle from moving up.

"I used the wrong thermometer. How could this happen?" Linda must have grabbed the wrong one in the early morning hours. She looked in the drawer, sitting there was her metal thermometer with the glass top. Almost in tears, but too tired and frustrated to let herself cry, she composed herself. It would just have to do. She poured herself another glass of wine.

"Dinner!" she called to her family. She entered the dining room to see the table empty. Bob walked in with the kids. "You couldn't have set the table?" she asked him.

"You didn't ask," came Bob's lame reply.

"Do I have to?" she said, setting the bird on a carving tray, the one with the metal spikes to hold the bird in place and a little wooden moat to catch the juices. Linda walked over to the glass cabinets where the good dishes were. She grabbed the settings and haughtily set them down. Bob got out his electric carving knife, ready to do his part. Bob reveled in the typical male honorific of carving the bird.

Linda sunk into her miniature seat, once again aware of the ridiculousness of fitting a half-sized home in a full-sized life. She thought for a minute about Nick. Maybe she should have invited him. He was probably alone today. It was better that she had not. She would have been embarrassed to have a guest in this chaos.

The moment she took a bite of the turkey, she knew she had failed. The white meat wasn't moist and juicy as she hoped, but dry. Really dry. Almost chewy. Bob, to his credit, had nothing but praises for the meal, but Linda could tell he was disappointed. Jim and Lyndsey both hardly touched their food, partaking only in the rolls and mashed potatoes. Linda uncorked another bottle of red wine. She felt like a total failure. It was the only meal of the year that she looked forward to. It was the only meal of the year she could expect some gratitude. She felt like she had let herself down.

Dessert was mercifully uneventful. Both Bob and the kids raved about the pumpkin pie, which made Linda feel even worse. She had bought the pie from a bake shop in Burlington. It only underscored the spectacular failure of the main course. When it came time to clean up she turned to Bob, who informed her he was required to meet with Mr. Murray for a few minutes before the big lighting ceremony.

The lighting ceremony! Linda had completely forgotten about it in the chaos of dinner. She would have to get the kids ready and fed by then. It was scheduled to be at 9:00pm. Linda wondered how long it would take. She hated putting the kids to bed after 11. Bob strode out the door, announcing he'd be back before dinner. Linda knew he was desperate to make a good impression on Mr. Murray, and that it heralded the start of the much talked about holiday rush.

She was left on her own to clean up. The kids tired of watching TV and started chasing each other through the house, knocking over chairs, running into tables. Linda had to chase them down and carry them upstairs, one under each arm to change them for the event.

"I don't wanna go!" screamed Jim, wriggling away and slamming the door to his room in her face.

"Fine!" Linda snapped. "I don't care. Look like pigs, then!" She stalked back downstairs to clean up the mountains of plates and pots, the flotsam and jetsam of Thanksgiving. Linda picked up the bottle of wine and saw there was an inch or two still in the bottom. Linda tipped the bottle up to her lips, not bothering to even use a glass, and drank the remainder. She turned her efforts to finishing the massive pile of dishes. When she was almost done, she felt a tug on her kitchen apron. She looked down. Jim was standing there.

"I'm hungry," he said expectantly.

"You should have eaten when we did, then," Linda replied, annoyed. "I'll fix you a plate of leftovers."

"I don't want turkey." Jim made a face.

"You don't want turkey? What *do* you want?" she asked incredulously.

"Spaghetti," Jim replied with a big smile. "Please?" Under normal circumstances, Linda would have insisted on Jim and his sister eating what she had prepared, but Linda herself was not particularly looking forward to Thanksgiving leftovers this year. She acquiesced and grabbed a box of pasta and jar of Ragu from the pantry. She had the kids at the table and the meal cooking when Bob came home. *Damn it, where did the time go?* She looked up at the cat clock. Its sprightly eyes seemed to mock her. Bob made a stink over the kids not being ready. Linda couldn't take it, so she dumped the food and got them ready. She was sorry they'd be going out hungry, but she knew this event was important to Bob. She dutifully got everybody bundled up and ready to go.

Bob led the family to the center of Christmas Town, Jim followed behind him, looking at the ground, kicking rocks and stones. Lyndsey pulled at her mother's winter coat.

"Up", she said, holding her arms open, the universal sign for "pick me up."

"No, sweetie. You're a big girl now. Big girls walk." Linda said gently, rubbing her aching head.

Both Bob and Jim had continued walking, oblivious to the fact that the girls had stopped.

"Up!" Lyndsey said, standing firm. Linda caved and leaned down. She was really too big to be carried for long. Linda eventually had Lyndsey climb on her back and hold on. It was not the best decision Linda could have made, still woozy from the effects of day drinking. As soon as Linda hiked Lyndsey on her back, they tumbled forward into one of the park's artificial snowbanks. The cold and wet snow on her face was bracing and gave her a jolt, enough to regain her composure. Linda staggered to her feet, pulling Lyndsey up with her, dragging her the whole way, just catching up Bob and Jim as they arrived at the ceremony.

Bob had been oblivious to Linda's ordeal, as he was too focused on locating Mr. Murray. There was already a huge crowd gathered but Bob insisted on moving towards the front. *To be seen by his boss*, Linda thought to herself. Mr. Murray was giving a speech that Linda couldn't hear when, suddenly, Bob yanked Lyndsey out of her arms and pushed his way to the stage.

Before she knew it, Lyndsey was up on that stage. It came as no surprise to Linda what happened next. Lyndsey was hungry, tired and scared. What did Bob expect? After the incident to Linda's great relief, the family went home.

As Linda could not stop thinking about what a debacle the day had been. A wave of nausea overtook her. She ran to the bathroom, hitting her shoulder on the small frame of the doorway as she careened towards the toilet. In between vomiting up wine and the failure of Thanksgiving, Linda sobbed and hung onto the tiny porcelain toilet, cradling it in her arms. It was cool against her skin, the only relief she had all day.

Linda woke up with a hangover. She regretted so much from the night before, including much of the things she had said and done. She resolved to try to do something nice for Bob once she woke up and shook off the dull thudding in her head. Wincing in the morning light, she creakily got out of bed. Bob had already left for work. Last night, he had tossed and turned, keeping Linda in a constant state of semi-consciousness. She knew that this was a day he had fretted and worried about for weeks. She recalled him even mentioning this "Christmas rush" time on the move up. Thinking about the move gave Linda pause. It seemed like a lifetime ago. *It seemed like a whole different person ago.* They all had changed over these short few months. *Short* she thought, *but at the same time, oh so long.*

Linda went to check on the kids in their bedroom. Both beds were empty. Hanging her head and sighing, Linda walked down the stairs. She would have preferred a little time on her own before she had to "go to work." As she entered the kitchen, what she saw made her feel like a terrible mother. Jim had prepared breakfast on his own this morning. Both children were sitting at the kitchen table quietly eating cereal.

"Mommy, I made breakfast!" Jim said, smiling.

"Yeah, Jimmy made breakfast," said Lyndsey. "I eat the Cheerios this time," she said, holding up her bowl. *That's just great. My son is a better parent than I am*, Linda thought bitterly.

"That's *wonderful*, sweetie. I am so proud of you!" Linda said, tousling Jim's hair. She smiled, despite the shame she felt at sleeping off a hangover while her kids fended for themselves.

No wonder Lyndsey loved it, Linda observed. There was enough sugar at the bottom of Lyndsey's bowl that it literally could not be absorbed into the milk. *I'll pay for that later at nap time*, she thought wryly.

Linda held out little hope for working on any of her projects that day. With the children home from school, it would be difficult to find time in between lunches, naps and toy pick-up duty. She sighed as she looked out the window, the tarp on her treasures flapping gently with the breeze. Later, she told herself. She stopped to check on the kids. They were happily zoned out in front of the television. Linda had just finished putting the dishes away when there was a loud knock at the door.

Linda smiled at the thought of a visitor and hoped that maybe Nick did decide to stop by, just to say hello. She didn't have any coffee brewed, but she did have instant crystals in the metal tin in the cabinet ready for just such an occasion. She was surprised as she opened the door to see Kathleen Lakeland, the animal caretaker, her face ashen.

"Kathy, what's wrong?" Linda asked, forgoing the usual small talk.

"Is your phone not working?" Kathleen asked worriedly. "I tried calling and calling and there was no answer."

Linda looked back to the phone in the kitchen. To her surprise, it was off the hook.

"One sec." Linda said, turning away from Kathleen.

"Wait..." Kathleen called after Linda, but it was too late. Linda trotted to the kitchen, the receiver of the phone was on the ground, under a stuffed animal, its long curly cord stretched out. Linda picked it up. She could now her the familiar, "phone off" warning, repeating its annoying tone over and over and over. Shaking her head, she put the phone back on the wall.

"Kids." Linda laughed, running back to Kathleen, who stood at the door, her face remained curiously serious.

"Has Bob called you yet?' Kathleen asked nervously.

"No, what's the matter?" Linda replied, feeling her stomach cramp.

"There's been an accident at the snack stand, I tried calling," Kathleen blurted. Linda's breath caught in her throat.

"My God, is Bob okay?" Linda spat out, fighting against her paralysis.

"Yes, Bob's fine. There was a fight with Paco and some new cook. The police are there. I don't know much more. I thought you should know."

"Ok, thanks," Linda replied in a daze. Bob was okay. That was good. Police being involved? That was bad. All she wanted to do was call Bob, to hear his voice, reflexively, she started to close the door on Kathleen.

"Linda, wait!" Kathleen exclaimed, door closing on her. "If there's anything I can do. I can watch the kids for you if you need it. Please call."

"Oh yes. Thank you so much, Kathy," Linda said, falling back into normal pleasantries. She shut the door. Linda rushed to the phone. Stupid. What a time for it to be off the hook, she thought. As she dialed the digits on the rotary dial, Linda cursed the number for having so many nines and zeros. The phone rang and rang for what seemed like an eternity until it was picked up and an unfamiliar female voice answered.

"Hello?" She sounded exhausted.

"Who is this?" asked Linda, confused.

"I'm Jenn the waitress at the snack shack." Linda then remembered Bob saying something about a new hire. He hadn't mentioned her by name.

"Oh, hello Jenn. Could I please speak to Bob? This is his wife, Linda."

"Oh, Mrs. Sutton. Uh…hello…um…nice…" Linda could hear Jenn wince after the platitude. "…uh…to meet you. I'll get Bob." Linda heard the receiver placed on the counter. In the background, she could hear the muffled sounds of commotion and many different voices.

"Hello," came Bob's voice. Linda was shocked by how small and quiet it sounded. "Bob, what happened?" Linda said, cradling the phone as she talked to her husband. "Kathy said there was an accident. Are you alright?"

"I'm fine." His voice was toneless.

"Is everybody okay?" Linda probed.

"Paco's hurt. Carl is…" He stopped for a moment. "Carl's fired. He's under arrest."

"Oh my God…that's…that's just terrible. Do you need me to come there?" Linda was prepared to drop everything and run over to the snack stand, is he ok?

"What happened?"

"Carl attacked Paco. Look, the police are here. I need to go. I need to clean up. It's a mess. There's blood."

"Do you want me to come down and help?" Linda asked, thinking about taking Mrs. Lakeland up on her offer to watch the kids.

"No. It's okay. I'll be okay." Linda doubted very much that Bob was okay.

"Alright. I guess I'll see you later then?" Linda said, feeling helpless.

"Don't wait for me for dinner."

"I'll have a plate ready for you. I insist. I'll make sure we eat together," Linda said, trying to show solidarity with her husband.

"Okay, I guess. I gotta go."

"I love you," Linda said into the phone. She heard a click. She wondered if Bob heard her. She hung up the phone, her headache reasserting itself. Now, the reality of the situation sunk in. If Carl was under arrest and Paco was injured, how would Bob manage the stand? *Or at all?* She felt guilty for her petty complaints. He had said the police were there. All she wanted to do was go to him and help. She couldn't leave the kids alone, not during something like this.

She looked at one of the many numbers written in pencil on the wall next to the phone. She dialed. It rang three times before someone answered.

"Hello?" It was Kathleen Lakeland.

"Kathy, this is Linda."

"Oh, Linda, I just got back. I'm so glad you called. Do you have any news?" Kathleen asked.

"No, not much, that's why I wanted to call. I think I should go and help Bob. I just need someone to watch the kids for me." Linda twirled the phone cord around her fingers, a nervous habit.

"I'd be happy to. The only thing is, I have to stay here until probably 5:00, maybe 6:00." Linda winced. This meant she would have to wait hours until she could see her husband.

"That's okay. Can you feed them if you're here?" she asked Kathleen.

"I'd be happy to," came the reply from the other end. Relieved, Linda closed her eyes and put her head against the wall.

"Thank you, Kathy. I'll put out some food for the kids."

"It's not a problem. I'll call you when I'm on my way over."

"I can't tell you how much this means to me, Kathy. I'll find a way to make it up to you," Linda said. Linda hung up the phone, and immediately re-dialed Bob. Busy again. She felt like a failure, as if she were letting him down when he most needed her.

The next few hours went by tortuously slowly for Linda. Constantly checking her watch and the clock on the wall, Linda was a bundle of nervous energy. She paced around the kitchen like a caged animal.

"Everything okay, mommy?" Jim asked his mother.

"Everything is fine, sweetie." She smiled at him.

Linda tried to put on a happy face for the kids. Her thoughts were with Bob the whole time. She chewed her nails right to the quick. It felt good. The pain gave Linda some satisfaction, a sense of control. She would periodically get up to call Bob. Every time the cruel busy signal was all she heard crackling and cackling at her. She tried one more time. No luck. She placed the receiver back into the cradle and it rang in her hand. She withdrew it with a shock like she had been stung. Shocked, she answered.

"Bob?" she said hopefully.

"It's Kathy," came the voice from the other end. "I'm coming over. I'm so sorry it's so late."

Linda stood by the door in anticipation. It was dark already when Linda spotted the headlights of a car making the turn into the driveway. She opened the door and ran out to greet Kathleen as she got out of her car. After few words of instruction, Linda was off on foot to the snack stand. Linda wanted to run. Her heart was pounding in her chest, but she made herself walk. It would do Bob no good for her to be flustered and filled with anxiety.

After walking through Christmas Town, Linda spied the building that housed Santa. A sign hung on a nail on the closed door: Santa is feeding his reindeer and will be back soon.

As she turned the corner, she could see light coming from inside snack stand. Linda sighed with relief. Bob never left the lights on, always the last one to lock up. Thank God he's still there, and that the police didn't take him to the station. Linda was almost there, so she quickened her pace. She walked to the door. The "CLOSED" sign was in the window. Linda peered through the window. What she saw was forever burned into her brain.

There was no sign of the fight, save for a pile of red stained rags by the counter. A festive tree stood in the corner, lights twinkling merrily. Linda saw something that at first, her mind could simply not comprehend.

Linda stared in through the frosted window; Bob was standing by the counter with a young woman. Linda didn't recognize her. Perhaps it was the Jenn she had talked to over the phone. Linda smiled, she lifted her hand to knock on the glass when she saw her husband put his arm around this young woman's waist, pull her in close, and kiss her.

Linda froze in place, feeling heartbroken, furious, and a voyeur all at once. The woman did not pull away from the kiss. It seemed to go on forever. Suddenly, Linda did not want to be there, she didn't want him to see her. Her face flushed and hot, she backed away from the stand and wandered back into the center of Christmas Town.

Linda could not feel her feet, a lump sat in her throat. She was aware she was walking but didn't know where she was heading.

You're a fucking idiot, Linda, she thought. You should have never trusted that he would keep his word. There had been discretions before, back in Boston. Bob had gotten down on one knee and declared he would never hurt her again. Now here they were.

She felt angry, being *so worried* about her husband. She felt a fool. She was sure every person she passed could see her shame and embarrassment. How long had this gone on? How many people knew? Her legs, acting on muscle-memory, took her out of Christmas Town. She was not even conscious of how far she had walked until she stood before a door.

Linda stared blankly at the door of the maintenance shed. She felt her arm rising, unbidden. She heard the knock. She waited. She didn't know what else to do. I should turn around, she thought, but where would I go? The thought of going home brought her to tears. How could she hide this from her children? As soon as they looked at her face, she was sure they would know.

Linda shook her head and turned to walk away, not entirely sure where she would go. Just away. The door opened.

"Linda?"

Linda saw Nick standing in the doorway. The light coming from the interior of the maintenance shed formed a corona behind his head. What am I doing? she thought. This was stupid. She should just go home. But the thought of going home made her madder still. Her kids were there, their kids.

"Oh! Hi, Nick," she said, smiling through her pain. "I have to be going now." She turned to walk away, embarrassed.

"Wait, going? Is this about Bob?" Nick said.

"You know?" she asked, horror sinking in. She felt the betrayal anew, knowing her friend knew of Bob's infidelity.

"It's gone around. I think everybody knows," Nick said, his face concerned. This was too much for Linda, and she burst out in tears. "Oh dear, why don't you come in? I think I have some tea. We can talk about it."

The last thing Linda wanted to do now was talk to about this, but she felt bad refusing his hospitality. She gave him a nod, thinking her voice might crack or that she may start sobbing if she tried to talk.

Linda stepped into the maintenance shed. She had never seen the inside before. It was packed to the rafters with tools and boxes. There was a workbench with machines in various states of repair. There were chairs. In the corner there was a cot with a blanket and a few pillows.

"You don't live here, do you? You told me you had a house," she said. The bed looked well-worn and slept in.

"Sometimes I stay here if it's late," Nick said, putting a kettle on a portable heating element that was already glowing bright orange.

"In here? Doesn't it get cold?"

Linda examined the shed. It was definitely built for storage and not particularly insulated against the heat or cold. "I have a space heater," Nick said, jumping up on a chair. "Luckily, I don't take up much space." He winked at her. All it did was make Linda feel terrible for her imposition.

"I'm so embarrassed that you know about Bob," said Linda, looking down at the floor. The tea kettle began to whistle. Nick looked up at it. He jumped down and walked over to his workbench and found a ceramic cup.

"See, that didn't take long. I just had a cup a few minutes ago," he said. "Now, why would you be embarrassed?"

Linda felt her face redden. Did he really not care? Had she misjudged him? Nick finished pouring the boiling water. As he handed Linda the cup with a smile, it was only then she realized her hands were shaking. She took the mug. She cupped both hands around it, absorbing the heat. She raised it her lips and scalded her tongue. The pain felt good, strangely grounding her. The tea was watery, it hadn't had time to steep, but the warmth she felt as it trickled down her throat was calming. She took another sip.

"I don't know what to say. How long have you known?" Linda asked.

"I've known since this morning, right after it happened," Nick said sympathetically.

"Wait, what? It just happened this morning?" asked Linda, creasing her brow.

"What do you think we're talking about?" Nick probed.

"Bob's cheating on me," Linda said. They felt dirty coming across her lips. After she said them out loud, she felt angry.

"What?"

Her sadness eclipsed by her confusion. "Wait, what did you think we were talking about?"

"The assault at the snack stand," Nick said.

"Oh," she said, embarrassed.

"Why do you think Bob's cheating on you? With whom?" Nick asked, sitting on the bed next to Linda.

"With his new waitress, *Jenn.*" Venom dripped as she spoke the name. "Nick, I saw them in the stand. Holding each other. Kissing."

"What are you going to do?"

"I don't know," Linda said. "Honestly, I have no idea. I'm just so mad. I sacrificed *everything* for him. I moved here, away from my all my friends." She looked at Nick. "Well not *all* of my friends. It's been hard on the family. I thought I could hold us together through strength, by sheer will. I saw the signs, you know?"

"What do you mean?" Nick asked.

"He's cheated before. He told me he would never..." She started crying. Nick touched her shoulder. It felt warm and comforting.

"We've been drifting since we got here. He's been so busy with the stand. I probably should have tried harder to be more understanding."

"Why?" asked Nick, looking at her seriously.

"What?"

"Why should you have to be more understanding? Bob's a busy man. Maybe you did drift, but it takes two. Don't excuse him. It doesn't excuse you, but don't excuse him."

"I feel trapped, Nick You don't understand. I have nowhere to go. I have no job experience. I got pregnant in college and went right into being a full-time mom."

"There are many people who make nice livings as full-time moms. It's a difficult skill set."

She gazed down into the murky water in her cup. "What makes me so mad is that I did this to myself. I could have been a doctor or a teacher or a writer. What have I become? What did I do to myself?"

She began to sob.

"I hate my life," she spluttered through racking sobs. "I hate it. I'm trapped. Even if I wanted to go, take the kids away from this place Bob would never just give me the kids. I have nowhere to go."

"What about your parents?" Nick asked.

"My parents." She laughed through tears. "I burned that bridge. My parents told me 'they have no daughter' I'm dead to them." The tears ran down Linda's face. "He's broken me."

"Bob," Nick said quietly.

"Yes. There's no way out of this. I'm just going to have to be alone. Well, alone with my kids. I have no one. I spend so much of my day making sure everybody else is taken care of. Who's going to take care of me?" Linda covered her eyes. Nick placed his hand on hers. "Who would want to?"

"I would," he said. Linda saw him looking at her with such compassion that it made her happy and sad at the same time. An impulse took Linda as she gripped Nick's hand. This is crazy, she thought. As she leaned down, another thought popped into her head.

Bob deserves this.

She closed her eyes. When Nick's lips met hers. Linda abandoned any feelings of guilt and surrendered to her emotions. Longing, desire, revenge? To her relief, Nick reciprocated her advances. Another thought flitted across her mind as she pulled Nick down on the cot.

I deserve this, she thought.

Linda was surprised how gentle and tender Nick was. Nick's hands were strong and comforting. After it was over, Linda laid on her back staring at the ceiling, in contemplation of what she had done. Linda was surprised how little she felt at all. In some ways, she mused that this had been coming for a long time. Bob had betrayed her again. It felt good to be in charge of her life again. It felt good to be desired. It felt good to be treated like a woman. It just felt good.

FAMILY PHOTOS

2000

"Well, fuck me."

Jim sat himself on the bed of his hotel room. He didn't care that he was still soaking wet and caked in mud. He just plain didn't care anymore. Strawberry Falls had broken him.

He looked around the room at his handiwork. Every drawer was opened, the bed had been turned upside-down. The bed had been stripped to the frame, which sat in the room strangely naked, like a skeleton on display in a museum. There was not an inch of the room that Jim had not searched, then searched again.

Jim had turned over the room five times in vain, searching for his missing satchel. The satchel held every note and story that Jim had written for his book, every idea and every receipt. His whole purpose was in that bag. He was sure that Cammy's mother was responsible. She had stolen it or had ordered someone to do it.

Jim looked at the door, knowing he would have to walk out of it sooner or later. Dodge was waiting for him outside, presumably to take him to his now repaired car then escort him out of town…at least he hoped it was as simple as that.

Jim's brush with Dodge and Deputy Avery had shaken him. His fight-or-flight instinct screamed at him *LEAVE. NOW.* Jim knew that he couldn't stay. If he did, he'd probably end up in a hole next to the oil drums he had just buried. He would leave, get the fuck out of this town, and make Strawberry Falls a distantly fading memory in his rear-view mirror.

Jim stood up, his shoes squished and oozed water and mud. He looked at himself in the mirror. He was still covered from head to toe in mud. Caked in it. He looked like a survivor of a post-apocalyptic zombie war.

When he had come into the room, someone had gone through his suitcase and set out clean clothes on the made bed, presumably for him to change into. The first thing Jim had done was throw those clean clothes across the room in his unsuccessful search for his notes. He walked over to the crumpled pile. He looked down at the clean slacks and button-up chambray shirt.

"Fuck that, I'll walk out of here the way I came in," Jim muttered.

He shoved his belongings in his suitcase. Scooping the room key off the counter, he walked out the door, dropping the key in the hallway. Let them pick it up.

Jim knew that Dodge was waiting for him in front of the hotel. He had no plans to get in a car with Cammy's brother again. He thought for a moment about just sneaking out the back, but the idea of slinking out like a coward galled him.

Jim's shoes squished with each step he took down the hallway. Jim dragged his suitcase down the stairs letting it bump loudly on each riser. After the first flight, Jim heard a clunk. One of the wheels had broken. As Jim approached the foot of the staircase, he was disappointed to see that it was Buckley the bellhop who greeted him. Of course, when he wanted to see Mrs. Norman, she was nowhere to be found. Buckley gave Jim the once-over, and Jim saw the surprise on Buckley's face. Good.

There was no doubt that Jim was a sight to behold. His face was streaked and filthy. His hair slicked back, covered in mud. His blue jeans had taken on a dirty, almost greenish hue. Buckley stared at Jim as he squished down the stairs.

Jim walked over to the front desk and rang the bell.

"Uh...sir, can I help you?" Buckley asked, taken aback.

"Yes, you can get the proprietor. I want to thank her for the hospitality."

"You don't have to check out. You can just leave." Buckley gestured to the door.

"I know," Jim said. "I want to speak with her, please. I'll wait here." Jim leaned against the register, mud smearing the countertop where his arm rested, a pool of dirty water gathering at his feet.

"Just a minute, sir. I'm not sure if she's available." Buckley edged around Jim, giving him a wide berth.

THE ONION RING LOVERS (GUIDE TO VERMONT)

"Oh, I think she'll see me," Jim said as he strolled into the lobby. Buckley followed, staring at the trail of muddy footprints. Jim walked over to a sofa and made a big show of sitting down on the immaculate upholstery. Putting his arms behind his head, Jim let out a huge sigh and proceeded to place both of his muddy feet on the coffee table. Buckley's eyes widened in horror. "I can wait all day," Jim said.

Buckley scurried out of the room.

"You can tell Dodge that, too!" Jim shouted. Jim looked over to his left, sitting in his usual high-back chair, was Anton, keeping his daily vigil

"Anton." Jim said, nodding his muddy head towards the man.

Anton held the day's paper in his hands, but it had fallen to his lap along with his jaw, which hung slack in amazement? Confusion? Horror?

"You wanted to see me, Mr. Sutton?" Mr's Norman's voice rang out echoing through the lobby. Jim turned to see her wheeling herself around the corner.

"Yes, I did," Jim replied.

Mrs. Norman turned to her long-term resident, and put on her sweetest smile. "Mr. Williams, I do beg your pardon. I believe you left something in your room, perhaps your *wife* has it?"

Anton nodded and hastily got up "I believe she does, Ma'am." He rose, taking off his hat in deference, exposing a perfectly circular shiny bald spot on the top of his head. He quickly made his escape up the stairs.

"I believe you were checking out," said Mrs. Sutton, turning her attention once more to Jim, all sweetness drained from her words.

"I am, yes. Happily. But you have something of mine."

"Do I?" Mrs. Norman stared at Jim with steely resolve. "It is distressing when someone takes something they are not supposed to."

"You know what I'm asking for. I know you stole it," Jim said.

"Stole? That's quite a slanderous allegation."

"Care to make it libel?" Jim countered.

"Libel?" Mrs. Norman laughed at Jim. "How? I know you have nothing."

"So, you admit it."

"Yes, I admit it freely," she said, to Jim's shock. "It's just your word against mine. I'm a trusted member of this community. My husband and I ...we saved this town.... You. Who are you? You're just a transient. You're a moment in time. You're a memory at best."

"I'm a writer. I can tell the truth."

"As a writer, I think I would choose the next words you say to me very carefully," Mrs. Norman said.

"Are you threatening me?" Jim said.

"No. I don't threaten. I take care of my family."

The front door slammed open. It was Dodge.

"There's the fucker!" Dodge growled as he stalked towards Jim.

"Stop, Dodge," Mrs. Norman's said.

"Why? Let me teach him a lesson." Every muscle in Dodge's thin frame seemed to be twitching.

"Granted. He's a rude one, but I can handle this."

"I'm gonnna…" Dodge growled.

"Dodge. Sit. Down," Mrs. Norman ordered.

Dodge looked at her then slunk off to a high back chair and sat down, with a displeased thump. He clawed the arms of the chair with his hands.

"If you didn't look just like your daughter, I would find it hard to believe you were related at all," Jim said, trying to regain a foothold on suddenly rocky purchase. "She's nothing like you." Jim wondered if he could make it to the door before Dodge? If he did, what chance would he have without a car?

"You think you know her? After a few days?" She laughed out loud. "You think you can fuck my daughter and it gives you some insight into the person she is?" Jim was taken aback by Mrs. Norman's words. It must have shown. "You think I didn't know? You think I didn't know the first night you defiled her? You don't think I know everything that goes on in my hotel?"

Mrs. Norman wheeled herself behind the front desk. As she came back into view, Jim saw his satchel sitting on her lap. "I don't *have* to do this, but I will offer you a deal," she said.

"A deal? But you said—," snapped Dodge, jumping out of his chair.

"Sit!" she commanded her son.

He remained standing and started to pace like a captive animal.

"Like I said, I offer you a deal. Leave. Leave town, and these are yours." She gestured to the satchel on her lap. "I've read them, you know. Trash. You're a terrible writer. I don't know what you're really fighting for."

"Let Cammy go," Jim said, "and we have a deal."

Dodge sprung from his mother's side like some jungle animal, seething with barely contained rage.

Jim put his hands up in front of him.

Duck. The word bounced in Jim's brain. An intense pain came from the left side of Jim's head and overwhelmed his senses. His vision danced with white spots, and he heard a high-pitched whine. He became keenly aware that he was falling. He tasted metal, his mouth swimming in it. WHAM. He felt it again, this time on the right side of his face. The sound of shattering glass. Pain. Sharp pain. Suddenly he struggled for air. When his vision cleared of the spots, the whine started to subside. Jim looked up to see Dodge standing over him.

"She," he said. A punch made purchase with Jim's head.

"Will." A kick to his stomach.

"Never." Again, to his face.

"Leave!" This time a kick to his side. A sharp hot searing pain shot through him.

Dodge paused, then smiled. He swung back his foot as if he were getting ready to punt a football, then kicked Jim in the ribs. Jim heard an audible crack. Groaning, he grabbed Dodge by the ankle. Using all his strength, Jim cried out in agonizing pain as he twisted and pulled Dodge's leg. Off balance and taken unawares, Dodge fell on top of Jim. Wincing, Jim rolled on top of Dodge.

Jim punched Dodge as hard as he could. His knuckles cried out in agony as they met the bone and muscle of Dodge's chin. Dodge's head snapped to the side. Jim hit him again and again pummeling Dodge with his fists. Dad would be proud, he thought. Then Dodge pushed Jim across the floor.

Both men scrambled to get on their feet as fast as they could. Spitting out a mouthful of blood, Jim looked around for something to use to defend himself. The only thing within reach was one of the many family pictures on the wall. He smashed the frame and held out a broken piece of glass. "Don't make me use this." Jim croaked.

To his shock. Dodge froze in his tracks. He looked to his mother, then back to Jim. Jim looked at Mrs. Norman and for the first time he saw fear in her eyes. She was staring at the photo that had fallen out of the frame.

What's with this picture? Jim thought.

Jim picked up the photo which had been folded under itself to fit in the frame. It was an old black and white photo of Cammy's father as a child. He unfolded the part of the photo that was bent back, and what Jim saw shocked him.

As Jim looked down at the fifty-year-old photo, the face of Cammy Norman stared back at him. The photo showed two children in front of a barn by a corn field. The boy looked to be about eight, the girl younger, maybe five or six. Jim turned the old photo over in his hands. He could feel the brittleness of the paper, smell the foxing. The back was stained and yellowed. In pencil, almost completely rubbed away, Jim read the following inscription.

Michael and Abigail Norman – 1963
Ages nine and five.

A horrible realization set in; Jim looked up from the picture. Mrs. Norman sat in her chair. When their eyes met, understanding passed between them. *But how could this be true?* His mind reeled with the implications. Dodge reached under his shirt and pulled out a revolver.

"It's okay Dodge," Mrs. Norman said.. "Clever boy, such a *clever* boy," she said.

"How *could* you?" Jim stammered. He looked over at Dodge. "*Cammy?*"

"Yes, both of them," Mrs. Norman said, looking Jim straight in the eye. "I really wish that you had just left. It would have been so much easier." She looked at him with regret in her eyes. "Simpler."

"I don't understand," Jim said.

"No, I don't suppose you would." Mrs. Norman wheeled to Jim, and took the photo from Jim. She looked down at it lovingly. "You can't help who you love, you know?" she said smiling. "No one can understand, certainly not you…what it is like. Maybe Dodge can." She nodded toward her son, who was humorlessly staring down Jim.

"He *knows?*" asked Jim incredulously.

"I always loved my brother. We were inseparable. He was my first kiss, my first time, and my first and only love," said Mrs. Norman, smiling wistfully.

"It's wrong," Jim said.

"Is it?" She turned her face to Jim. "Is it sick to love someone? Have you ever loved a person so much it hurt you to be apart from them, that you felt they were a *part* of you? Have you ever had to hide your love?"

"Jim glared defiantly at Mrs. Norman.

"*You* have no idea," she scoffed. "We hid our love until I got pregnant. I never even considered any other option than having her. We made our decision. We would start our lives over in a new town. New town, new lives. Strawberry Falls was an ideal place. Little, sleepy, off the beaten path, a place we could start over and love in full view of God and everybody. We made our decision. It's surprisingly easy to change your identity. People are more than willing to help out a young couple who 'lost everything in the fire,' including birth certificates. Even the social security administration was eager to issue numbers to this 'poor rural couple.' The happiest day of my life was when I married Michael. When Cammy was born, I knew she was special. Too special for just any boy. I knew she would need someone made just for her." Mrs. Norman put her hand up to her shoulder to stroke the hand of Dodge.

"Dodge is...Cammy and Dodge?" Jim spluttered in disbelief.

"Yes. Dodge was made for her. They are meant to be together. They are royalty here; they are destined to be the King and Queen of this town. No one will get in the way of that, especially not you."

"He…you know about this?" Jim said, looking from Mrs. Norman to Dodge's face.

"Yes," said Dodge flatly.

"Does Cammy know?" Jim asked in disbelief.

"Yes, but she's somewhat… resistant. In fact, you're not going to tell anyone anything, not anymore." Mrs. Norman gestured to her son.

"Finally," Dodge said, raising the gun. Jim leaned on the counter, still woozy from the beating. Could he get to the door before the shot?

It happened so fast, at first Jim could not tell what had happened. Dodge suddenly cried out in pain.

"Let go!" Dodge bellowed as he waved his arm back and forth. Jim could see that something was latched onto it, tight. It was dark and brown, all teeth and fur. Its eyes were closed, but when they opened, Jim could see one was milky white. It was Kaiser Bill. The revolver dropped from Dodge's mauled hand.

"Bill!" Mrs. Norman scolded the dog. "Release!" The dog held fast. Dodge hollered and began to hit the dog on its snout. The growling grew louder. Jim slowly backed towards the door.

"No," Cammy yelled.

Jim turned around. She was standing in the doorway, tears welling in her eyes. Her hair was plastered to her face, wet from the rain. Water dripped off the ends of her curls onto her mother's once immaculate rugs, now covered with ground glass and Jim's blood.

"Cammy," Dodge pleaded, on his knees. Jim could see blood around Kaiser Bill's mouth.

"No," Cammy said, staring at her mother.

"Camaro!" Mrs. Norman scolded.

"Bill!" Cammy ordered. Kaiser Bill released his grip. Cammy whistled, Kaiser Bill calmly walked to her side and sat in obedience.

"Camaro, how much did you hear?" Mrs. Norman said.

"You're sick," Cammy said.

"You know, I wanted you to have the same experience as I did, falling in love, the closest love in the world."

"All this time, all these years, it's been about this?" Cammy said.

"I did it all for you, dear," Mrs. Norman said, her eyes glinting with tears.

"You did it for me? For me? You wanted me and…Dodge?" Cammy held up her hand to stop Dodge from moving closer. Kaiser Bill growled, and Dodge froze, cradling his wounded arm. "All the boyfriends you never approved of…. The curfews? College? Oh my God…*Daddy?*" The tears were rolling down her face.

"It was all for *you*," replied Mrs. Norman, all traces of tears now gone. "The town, the shop, the hotel…all for you and your brother." Jim watched it all unfolding, unable to move. Dodge was only feet away from his gun.

"The town would never tolerate that," said Cammy.

"We are *royalty* here Camaro. We make the rules." Mrs. Norman said, her eyes shining. "We *are* Strawberry Falls. The town will accept it because without the Normans, there is no town. There are no winter jobs, or goodwill checks."

"What?" Cammy said.

"This little town can't sustain itself on leaf peeping. Who do you think keeps everyone's bellies fed, who keeps them in new cars, who pays for the schools, the police, everything? Mrs. Norman laughed. "I've built a kingdom, an empire, all for you."

"Stop," Cammy said. "Stop talking!"

"Camaro, dear. I know this must be very…*overwhelming,*" Mrs. Norman said in a calm reassuring voice. "Look into your heart. Look at your brother. He loves you. He's dedicated his life to you. Can't you see him for the man he is?"

"What I see makes me sick," Cammy said wiping away tears and smearing motor oil across her face in the process. "You've been working to trap me here," she glared angrily at her mother. "My whole life all I've ever wanted to do was leave this crappy town. All this time it's been you. I stayed here because of you, to take care of you." She spat the words at her mother like bullets. "Fuck you!"

"Camaro! Language!" scolded her mother. "I have had enough of your attitude, young lady. You always thought you were too good for this town. You were the one who broke your father's heart. It was Dodge who had to suffer when you left us." Mrs. Norman's eyes darted towards Jim. "Do you think this one is worthy of you? A common writer, a flatlander?" scorn dripping from her words.

"I don't know. No. Maybe. Yes," Cammy replied to her mother.

"That's really a shame," Mrs. Norman said. She turned her chair to face Jim. "He's got to go. And not in his car." She looked over at Dodge, who looked at his gun, then warily to Kaiser Bill.

"Are you talking about killing him? This is madness," Cammy said, her voice rising.

"He knows too much, dear. We are pillars of the community. Our family secrets must remain secrets. He knows."

"Yeah, so do I mother," Cammy replied.

"No, he knows. Dodge caught him in the cornfield." Mrs. Norman looked to her son, who nodded.

Cammy's brow furrowed, she looked at Jim, then shook her head.

"So what?" Cammy replied. "*Everybody* in town knows, mother. It's the worst kept secret in Strawberry Falls. It's the worst kept secret in Vermont. They call it Strawberry Kush, you know? And not just because the bud is red. Let us go mother," Cammy said.

"There is no 'us' for you and Mr. Sutton. There is no future for you and him, at least there is no future for him. The sooner you come to understand this, the easier it will go."

"Easier? I'm not going to let you kill him," Cammy said.

"There's nothing you can do about this. What needs to be done will be done. It's gone on too long as it stands. Dodge!" Mrs. Norman called to her son. He slowly edged his good hand to the revolver on the floor.

"Stop," Cammy's voice was calm and quiet, so calm it made her mother and her brother stop in their tracks. "I'll stay."

"What do you mean?" asked Mrs. Norman.

"I'll stay. I'll stay in Strawberry Falls, but you have to let him go," Cammy said.

"I don't know, dear..." started Mrs. Norman.

"This is the only way I'm staying here. If you kill him, I will disappear from Strawberry Falls, and from your life. I know more secrets than he ever could. I could make life very hard for you, or easy. Let him go mother. He won't write anything about this." She nodded toward Jim. "Will you?"

"Not a word," Jim replied.

"Let him go. Tonight, he'll take his car and he'll leave Strawberry Falls behind him forever," Cammy told her mother, tears streaming down her face.

"And then you'll stay…willingly?" her mother asked cautiously.

"Yes," Cammy said, her eyes looking away from Jim to the floor.

"I think I can accept that," Mrs. Norman said. "But his notes stay. He leaves with his life. That is all."

"That's fine, mother." She reached into her pocket and pulled out the keys to the Ford Festiva and tossed them to Jim. "Here, it's parked outside."

Jim caught them and stood up. He started to walk toward Cammy.

"No," Cammy said, her voice cracking. "Get out. Leave and never come back." Cammy's eyes were red as tears ran down her face.

"You don't have to do this, Cammy," Jim said.

"Yes," Cammy said, wiping her face. "I do."

"I won't leave you here with them," Jim said, gesturing to her family.

Cammy gently laid a hand on his shoulder. "There's no other way this can end, Jim."

Jim saw the truth in her words. If he stayed, he'd end up in some random hole, deep in the woods. If he left, he'd leave with what he had on his back, but he'd have his life.

As he picked up his suitcase, Kaiser Bill nuzzled against his leg. Jim reached down and scratched him between his ears.

"At least you liked me, eh?" The dog closed its one good eye and leaned into the scratch. Jim turned for one last look. Dodge stood behind his mother, holding his bleeding arm, Mrs. Norman had her hands primly folded in her lap. Cammy stared blankly. Was it resignation, or defeat? Jim would not hazard a guess. She gave him a half-hearted wave.

"You're forgetting something, Mr. Sutton." Mrs. Norman broke the silence, her voice back to her sickly-sweet proprietress tone.

"What?" Jim responded, completely drained.

"The fee."

"What? For the room? Just charge my card on file."

"No, Mr. Sutton. The fee. The fine for your wanton destruction. The sign."

"Oh yeah." Jim sighed. "What was that? Seven hundred dollars?"

"Seven fifty" Mrs. Norman replied. "Payable to the town."

"Seven fifty," Jim repeated. "Do you take checks?"

"Of course."

Jim took out his wallet, found his emergency blank check and filled it as requested. He handed it over, and managed one last look towards Cammy, who could not meet his glance, as her gaze directed toward the floor.

The car was outside, as promised. Jim looked down at his clothes, still caked with mud. Scraping some of the muck off, Jim climbed into his car. He knew he had to get out of this town, and fast. Jim put the keys into the ignition and turned. The engine purred like he had never heard it before. He looked in his rear-view mirror at *Le Grand Hotel Vermont*, a figure silhouetted in the window. The loss of his notes was a bitter pill. *But fuck those notes, at least I'm alive.*

He made the turn down Main Street, to the road that led north out of town. He compulsively checked his mirrors to make sure no one was following him. To his relief, the road remained empty behind him. Still on edge, as he approached a bend in the road, he saw a sign.

NOW LEAVING STRAWBERRY FALLS. - COME BACK AND VISIT US NEXT YEAR!

Jim drove past the sign, disappearing into the dark of the night.

THE LEVEE BREAKS

1978

Christmas Town had a good holiday season, not great...but good. They rebounded from the altercation between the cooks at Bob's stand. In fact, an unexpected effect of the altercation was an increase in gawkers who had read about it in the *Burlington Free Press*. In the short term, Bob had been forced to man the grill while Paco recovered from his injuries. Carl's trial was scheduled for late February, and Bob was already dreading it, knowing he and Paco would be compelled to give testimony.

It was looking like the Suttons might have enough money to see them through winter. It did not hurt that luck finally seemed to be turning Bob's way. Although there had been several winter storms, for the most part Lake Champlain had not iced over so the ferry was still operating well into winter. An operating ferry meant customers could access the island. Granted, most people came to Christmas Island and Christmas Town during November and December, but there were always people who seemed drawn to a year-round Christmas attraction even during the summer months. Christmas had that effect on people.

Then reports started coming in over the little weather radio Bob kept bungeed to one of the shelves in the kitchen of ice bound conditions up north, near Canada and the St. Lawrence Seaway. There, in the south islands, the waters remained relatively clear. Occasionally a random sheet of ice wandered down the lake but they were so small that ferries plowed right through them, pulverizing the ice in its wake. Every morning Bob narrated and opined the daily ice report to Linda before he left the house. Linda was through arguing. She would let him bloviate, and then go back what was important to her: The kid's needs and her own.

After a thorough vetting, Bob had hired another part-time cook for the duration of the holiday season. Mercifully, this new hire got along well everybody, including Paco.

Paco had returned to his job a different man. He still wore his hair long. But it would no longer be swept up into a ponytail. Instead, the cook preferred to let it fall across his horribly scarred face, to obscure the scars. Paco still refused to wear a hairnet; Bob didn't argue with him about it.

Paco was a man afflicted with post-traumatic-stress-disorder. He flinched at loud noises. Often, Bob would catch Paco staring off into the distance, food burning under his spatula. Bob found himself in the difficult position of needing his cook to return to his old form or having to consider letting him go. He was a legacy hire. Mr. Murray was mad enough with the Suttons over the incident, and Bob wasn't certain what the fallout would be if he fired the frazzled cook. Bob dealt with Paco's shortcomings through gritted teeth. He found that he had to help Paco in the kitchen most days. As a result, Bob asked Jenn to stay on after the holidays.

Jenn was unsure of how she could manage a job while attending school full-time. Bob begged her to stay. She could work part time, a few days a week. He appealed to her better nature, imploring her to "do it for Paco." Jenn was a tremendous help for Bob. He came to look forward to the days that she was scheduled, and not only because of the lighter load. She only agreed to come back after Bob profusely apologized for his inappropriate kiss the night of the incident. That, and the twenty percent raise, didn't hurt as well.

Christmas came and went and so did the crowds. Once the New Year's ball dropped, and the champagne was uncorked, the Christmas season ended.

The drop off was dramatic in the first half of January. Thankfully, because of unseasonably pleasant weather. In the latter half of the month, there were still people making the trek across the lake. Not enough for Bob's liking. He began to regret begging Jenn to stay on. He had told her that once the lake iced up, he wouldn't need her, but the open water held out longer than the stream of customers. He resolved to sit her down on Friday and break the bad news to her.

That night, the phone rang at 4:30 am. Linda groggily picked it up and wordlessly handed it to Bob. The voice was gruff on the other line.

"Sutton, is that you?"

"Yes, Mr. Murray," Bob said, even while shaking the fog of sleep, he recognized the rough baritone of his boss.

"You heard about the storm?"

"Yes. I was listening to the news…" Bob glanced out the window, in the dim twilight he could see the snow had started. It was not particularly heavy yet. It would probably be nothing, the hyperbolic warnings of weatherman rarely came to fruition.

"Well, the ferries are running. You know what I say, Sutton?" Bob did know what Mr. Murray was saying. He had heard it almost every day during the holiday season.

"If the ferries are running, so are we," he muttered into the phone.

Linda glared at Bob from her side of the bed.

"That's right," Mr Murray said. "Even if there's one customer. We'll be open." The phone line went dead as Mr. Murray hung up before Bob could say goodbye. He held it in his hand for a minute then decided to just get up and get ready. He didn't bother saying goodbye to Linda, the phone call had already woken her so he knew she wouldn't be in any mood for goodbyes.

Things were strained between them. It irked him she didn't understand that he was under immense pressure. Linda didn't seem to care, in fact she seemed downright hostile to him sometimes. A thank you would go a long way. These days, with all the tension in the house, what was the point of disturbing her?

Bob groaned as he rose. He looked back at Linda in the bed; she had wrapped herself in the comforter. Her feet dangled over the edge of the bed. That goddamn dwarf bed, Bob griped to himself.

He'd grown to envy the freedom he thought Linda enjoyed. Many times, while flipping hamburgers or cleaning filthy toilets Bob would ruefully imagine what he could do with all the free time Linda had. She's lucky to have me to take care of her, she's lucky to have time to herself, he thought as he navigated the dark bedroom.

"OW!" Bob shouted, stubbing his toe.

"Everything ok?" Linda said groggily, looking up from the bed.

"No.," Bob replied sulkily. "It's not." He looked down. Linda had left her toolbox right in the middle of the floor.

"How many times do I have to tell you to put away your things?" Bob replied testily. "Jesus, you're worse than the kids, no wonder this house is a pigsty."

"Ok. have a nice day," Linda said.

God forbid I wake the Queen, Bob thought bitterly. He picked up the toolbox and threw it on a pile of clothes next to the laundry basket. It made a huge clatter. Linda stirred again, her eyes fluttered open for a moment, then she turned away, pulling the blankets over her head. Somehow, this only made Bob madder.

It would be tolerable if she were appreciative, Bob thought as he walked to the bathroom to take a shower. Bob had given Linda the room to grow into their new life. In the process, he felt he had been too lenient. The robust sex life that they had enjoyed in the halcyon days of their relationship had disappeared. Ever since they had come to Vermont it was practically nonexistent. Bob stopped asking. The very notion seemed to upset Linda.

Bob stooped into his tiny shower, bending his head down to get wet. Bob reached down and grabbed his flaccid penis and started his routine masturbation. As Bob's mind wandered to the storm and the house and Linda, he became aware that nothing was happening. Not even motivated to finish, he got out of the shower and resigned himself to the rest of the day. Bob walked outside, the wind blew gently as the snow fell around him, creating miniature whirlwinds and spirals on the cold hard snow already on the ground Alone in his thoughts, Bob did not even notice that it had already grown heavier than when he had woken up that morning.

*   *   *

The winter of 1978 was already shaping up to be a difficult one, even by New England standards. On January 21st, a record storm, dropped a surprise 21 inches of snow. The storm had caused a great deal of damage already. Power outages spread across the region in its wake. So much heavy snow had fallen, it collapsed the roof of the Hartford Civic Center. Forecasts in New England had been notoriously difficult to get right. Weathermen were viewed by the average New Englander as something of a joke. Weather segments were often used as an opportunity to inject levity into broadcasts. Already battered and weary from bungled snowfall prognostications, residents of New England disregarded all warnings and went about their daily lives. After all, weren't weathermen typically and hilariously wrong most of the time?

On February 5th, 1978, a storm cycle formed off the coast of South Carolina. It started its life as an extra-tropical cyclone and merged with an Arctic cold front. This created the ideal winter storm conditions. Compounding the strength and impact of the storm was the fact that it was a new moon, which meant atypically higher tides that would only exacerbate storm surge. Forecasters issued warnings across New England for blizzard conditions, but didn't they always?

On the 6th of January, the storm hit New England with a ferocity that took everybody by surprise. The storm battered the unsuspecting residents of New England with hurricane-force winds that reached recorded speeds of almost eighty-six miles per hour with gusts reported up to one hundred and eleven.

Bostonians went about their usual morning routine, ignoring the first flakes that began to fall around ten in the morning. By one o'clock, the snow started falling heavily enough for people to become concerned. The storm rolled across New England leaving devastation in its wake. In Boston, drivers got buried in their cars. Some poor souls suffocated when their tail pipes became blocked with snow. Snow laden trees and power lines snapped and plunged scores of communities into darkness. Schools were closed, businesses shuttered, and cities became ghost towns. Massachusetts Governor Michael Dukakis declared a state of emergency as people were told to shelter in place and weather the storm that rolled across the northeast. Trees uprooted; lines were down for miles.

In the age before the Internet and social media, news spread slowly across the region. Slower than the storm that rolled across it, seemingly unimpeded. Most New Englanders had no idea what was coming until it was too late.

*   *   *

The snow had already begun to accumulate as Bob trudged to work. In the darkness, with only a flashlight and the growing dawn to illuminate his way, the world felt alien and eerie. Bob arrived at the snack stand and fumbled with his keys until they slipped from his frozen fingers and landed in the new snow.

"God DAMN it!" Bob swore, bending down to pick them up.

"Ahem." Bob stood up quickly, blood rushing to his head. As spots and stars circled his vision, he saw Jenn standing in front of him.

"Oh, hello." Bob stammered.

"Man, it is *really* coming down" Jenn said.

"Oh, yeah. It is." Bob hadn't noticed, but he had to agree, the flakes were falling much faster. He unlocked the door and held it open for Jenn to walk through.

"I'm surprised you came," Bob said, flicking on the lights.

"I couldn't leave you in the lurch, could I?" Jenn said. She put on her uniform, which was nothing more than an apron with a pocket for a notepad and pen, and a name tag adorned with cheery little candy canes.

"So far it's just me and you."

"Paco?" asked Jenn leaning over the counter to pick up a spare pen from under the register. In the process she grazed her shoulder against Bob's hand.

"He said he's coming, but who knows with this snow. I don't even know if we'll get any customers," Bob replied.

"It wasn't so bad this morning when I left my apartment," Jenn said, sitting in a booth, filling the salt and pepper shakers. She looked at Bob and smiled. "Besides, would it be so bad if it was a slow day?"

"I would hate to waste your time," Bob replied.

"Nonsense," Jenn said. "It won't be wasted time, even if it's just us. It'll be a snow day! We'll find ways to entertain ourselves, right?" Jenn had a way of talking that made Bob feel at once attracted and uncomfortable.

"Right," said Bob staring at the snow outside, which had now become so thick it was almost like a fog. He thought about having to shovel the walkway and how much time it would take to clear. The snow would keep coming, and he'd just have to keep on shoveling. A thought crossed Bob's mind. Nick has a snow-blower. Bob had seen him with the gas-powered beast impressively clearing out huge banks of snow from the pathways of Christmas Town. Bob wondered if he could persuade Nick to lend it to him.

The morning was as slow as Bob feared it would be. Paco still hadn't shown up, but that was fine since they had yet to have one customer walk through the doors. The snow was falling thicker. The winds had started up as well. He made up his mind to take the trip to Nick's maintenance shed. He asked Jenn to watch the store and said he'd be back soon.

As he stepped outside, snow crystals stung and bit his face. Unable to see, Bob returned to the stand. He checked behind the counter for the Lost & Found box under the register. Most of the time items went unclaimed, but every once in a while, there would be a frantic phone call from a parent looking for a cherished stuffed animal or dental retainer. Bob rummaged around in the box, sifting through 8-track tapes and lost credit cards. He found what he was searching for. Someone had left a pair of swim goggles behind last summer. As he put them on, he caught a glimpse of his reflection in the window. He looked ridiculous, but at least his vision would be protected.

"See you later, Jenn," Bob said, walking out the door.

"Stay safe!" Jenn replied. Bob put his hand up to shield his face against the wind. The snow whipped around him, already thicker in the few moments since he had gone back into the stand. Bob turned down the path that led toward his home and the shed. Bob squinted into the distance. There was another person out. The figure was indistinguishable in the snowflakes. As he moved closer, he recognized Linda's jacket. Linda?

Why is she out in weather like this? he thought.

"Linda!" Bob shouted; she showed no sign of hearing him. "LINDA!" Bob cupped his gloved hands around his mouth and called again. His words were lost, caught on the wind. She did not see or heard Bob as she walked forward against the gale, head down to protect against the storm.

Linda arrived at the shed before Bob. She glanced around furtively but didn't seem to see Bob. She pounded on the door and shuffled from foot to foot to keep herself warm. The door opened and warm light shone from the interior. Linda walked in, shutting the door behind her.

Bob tramped the rest of the way to the shed. He was about to knock when a small voice in his head told him to wait. Linda was friends with Nick. There would normally be nothing particularly out of order in her stopping by. Why in this crazy weather, though? Where were the kids?

His curiosity and suspicions piqued, Bob creeped his way around the shed, stepping through a snow drift in the process.

"Shit!" Bob cursed at himself. His socks getting cold and wet with snow.

Bob looked for a window. He spotted one around the back. It was high up. Just too high for him to spy through it, even on his tiptoes. Bob looked around for something to stand on. He found a galvanized bucket. He turned it over, put it on the ground and awkwardly stepped up.

Bob saw his wife. Sitting on an old cot in the corner, she had removed her coat. In fact, she had removed most of her clothes. Nick was kissing her milky-white stomach. She laughed at his affections, his hands moving deftly across her body. Bob felt sick to his stomach. He lost his balance and fell into a snowbank. He felt the snow slide down the back of his shirt, freezing cold.

Bob stood up in a daze, his mind reeling.

"That bitch," Bob mumbled. "No wonder she doesn't want to have sex. She's holding out on me. With a fucking dwarf?" Bob shouted against the din of the storm.

Humiliation burned brightly in Bob's mind. He staggered back to the front door and put his hand up to knock. He stopped. The thought of facing this little man galled him.

"A fucking dwarf." Bob fumed. Everyone would laugh at him. His wife with a freak.

Backing away, Bob's feet carried him to the path to the snack stand. His mind unspooled every interaction with Nick, with Linda. Linda had cast him as the cuckold. He stumbled through the snow, dimly aware of the cold wetness in his boot making his toes to throb. Before he realized it, Bob was at the front door of the snack stand, moving on rote memory.

He pushed the door open. Like a zombie, he lurched in and sat at the counter, not even bothering to wipe his boots or take off his winter coverings. Jenn looked up and instantly saw that something was amiss.

"Mr. Sutton? Are you ok?" she asked, sitting next to him.

"You can call me Bob," he said. He forced a smile, trying to hide his humiliation.

"Okay…Bob. Are you alright?" she replied, unsure.

Bob turned to Jenn, leaning over to kiss her.

"Wait, what are you doing—"

"It's okay," Bob said, moving his head closer.

"I don't think this is a good idea," Jenn said, backing into the counter, finding she had nowhere to go. Bob pressed on with intent burning in his eyes. "No," she said, squirming under his grasp.

Bob grabbed both of her arms to steady her. A look of panic flashed across her eyes as Bob moved his face closer to hers. Bob closed his eyes and pressed his mouth to her unwilling lips, her body rigid as he tried to invoke her to reciprocate. Bob pulled away to see her wide eyes staring back at him. She wore a look of disgust, not desire. She broke free of his grip and walked to the door. Bob followed after her and grabbed her by the wrist.

"No!" Bob said, forcefully yanking her from the door. The ripple of kinetic energy whipped her back. He drew her closer.

"Ow! You're hurting me!" she exclaimed, wrenching her wrist free of his grip. "What's the matter with you?" Jenn looked at Bob, terror building in her face. She glanced desperately at the door. Bob followed her eyes and lunged in front of her to block her passage. Bob seethed. He could see her shrinking away from him, yet he still advanced.

"Please let me go," she said, holding up her hands in supplication. "I just want to go home. Let me go."

Bob saw tears rolling down her face and found himself disgusted. "All your flirting? The late nights, what was that?" Bob asked incredulously.

"I was trying to be nice," Jenn pleaded, tears in her eyes.

Slut. He was being played the fool and now everybody was having their fun with him. He looked at her cowering in front of him, and it made him angry. She had humiliated him. *No, Linda had humiliated him.* Bob stepped aside. Jenn grabbed her jacket and ran out of the snack stand into the heart of the storm, not even bothering to button up her parka.

Bob sat at the counter and stared at the wall, checked out. Absolutely no thoughts running through his brain. Rage and indignant humiliation were growing from a seed planted long ago that was only now starting to bear fruit. His disquiet reverie interrupted by a thought. All the times he had served that little dwarf over the past few months. He thought back to their first meeting, how that *little shit* had humiliated him even then. Bob stood up and walked over to the register. After the incident with Paco and Carl, Bob had stashed a George Brett Louisville Slugger baseball bat behind the counter. Bob picked up the bat and turned it over in his hands, stroking the surface absent-mindedly as he tried to get his head to quiet.

The storm raged on, and so did Bob. The wind was picking up now, the snow flying more furiously by the moment. Bob walked out of the snack stand, bracing himself against the stinging snow that was swirling around in an ever-increasing cloud. He put the swim goggles back on to protect his eyes. At his feet were two sets of footprints in the snow. One trail led toward the ferry, the other led toward the maintenance shed and the Sutton home. Bob lingered for a moment on Jenn's trail, then turned to the other one. His fifteen minute-old footprints were already disappearing in the deluge of snow. Fighting the wind, Bob staggered toward the road that led home, bat in hand. Under his scarf, he bore a look of grim determination.

*   *   *

The jangling ringing bell of the phone had woken Linda up that morning. She stayed in bed and counted the rings. One, two, three... She was certain that this was, yet again, another phone call for Bob. It was always for Bob. It was invariably Mr. Murray. She stared at Bob, who was blissfully ignorant of the ringing. She nudged Bob with her leg to try to wake him. Finally, Linda gave in and wearily reached over to answer. She had half-hoped that whoever was calling would give up, it was now eight rings in by her count. She passed the phone directly to Bob, successfully waking him up this time. She turned over and tried to go back to sleep.

Linda could only hear Bob's end of the conversation, but it was clear he would have to go in to work. She rested on her side, unable to go back to sleep. Bob knew that the kids would not be going to school that day. The schools had sent advance word that they would be closed in anticipation of the approaching storm. Linda had been looking forward to having Bob home so he could share the burden. The kids would be cooped up with nowhere to go and would likely be bouncing off the walls by mid-day. Once again, she would not have any time to work on her personal projects. It would all have to wait until the storm passed.

Bob got up and walked out the door without even saying goodbye. Even though Linda had been having an affair with Nick Summers for months now, any guilt she felt was mitigated by these small moments of neglect.

Linda heard the door slam as Bob left for the day. There was no use trying to sleep anymore, she was fully awake. Linda bent down to look out of the window as she walked to the shower. There were some flakes, but nothing to be too worried about. She had heard on the radio of the storm that had already hit Boston. Part of her wondered if it would be another false alarm and she'd be stuck with the kids for nothing.

After her shower she got dressed and prepared to wake the kids. She wondered if Kathleen Lakeland was working today. If Mr. Murray had called them in, as he had Bob, there was a good chance that they would both be here today. In this weather, it was a certainty that it would be a light attendance day. Kathleen may be available to watch the kids. If she could be persuaded, then Linda could go see Nick.

In the beginning, Linda felt terrible about cheating on Bob. She had avoided both Bob and Nick for days, throwing herself into the inside projects she could do during the wintertime. She kept coming back to the shed. Her mind would drift back to it, unbidden. She would close her eyes, and the wood shaving smell would come back her, she could feel the rough wool of the blanket on her back, feel his hands running over her skin, it excited her, in various ways. Linda went up to her room, the kids were gone and laid down on the bed. Unbuttoning her jeans, she slid her hand down. She closed her eyes. Suddenly, she was not at Nick's shed. She was standing in front of the door to the snack stand. She thought about Bob and Jenn kissing. She imagined Bob's hand on her ass, moving his way up to her tits. Jenn looked at her and laughed.

Mood killed and furious at Bob and his latest affair, Linda had had enough. Fuck propriety. Fuck being the good wife. Bob was a selfish asshole, why shouldn't she be one too? So, she went back. Many times. Tonight, with the snow falling down and Bob being at work, the thought of going to her lover excited her. It was bad, and dirty, just what she and Bob deserved. Hiding the affair was surprisingly easy, she found for the most part, she felt little guilt. In the end, she had to admit that it turned her on. A lot.

Phone calls were made, plans were set. Linda went about the process of getting her children ready for a snow day at home with a sitter. Jim was particularly difficult this morning. Linda had let the kids sleep in. Why is it every time I let them sleep in, they act the worst? she wondered to herself as she struggled to strip Jim's pajamas off him. Lyndsey was only marginally better. She lay in Linda's arms like a limp rag doll. Linda glanced at her watch. Kathy said she'd be over at nine. That left an hour to get the kids fed and ready. An hour seemed impossibly long. Once she made her plans for her morning tryst with Nick, it consumed her thoughts. She enjoyed the sex very much; Nick was a generous and tender lover.

What Linda was *really* addicted to was that feeling of being desired. She felt like a woman again with Nick, not just a mom. Bob was off in his own world these days. He hardly talked to her anymore. She was sure he was fucking the young waitress he hired. The fact she stayed on after Christmas only confirmed Linda's suspicions.

Linda busied herself cleaning up the house. It was a Sisyphean effort keeping the house clean. As soon as she cleaned, it seemed that the kids would mess it up anew. As she carried some dirty laundry to the stairs, she suddenly tripped. Looking down, she saw a pile of Jim's books. He was a lover of reading but had an annoying habit of leaving his books around the house wherever he happened to be.

"Jim, pick up your darn books."

"Ok mom!" Jim called from the couch where he was watching TV.

"Now!" Linda called, shaking her head.

When the doorbell rang at 9:15 am, Linda was already dressed in her winter gear. Part of her wondered if this was a good idea to leave her kids alone. They're not alone, a voice in her head reassured her. Linda opened the door with a pop, partially due to her eagerness to leave, mostly because the winds were blowing so strongly. Kathleen practically fell into the house, trailing a flurry of snow and ice. Linda apologized for calling Kathleen out on such an ugly day and set out on her "errands."

Even on the short trip down the road toward Nick's maintenance shed, the snow grew more and more intense. The wind blew furiously, kicking up the snow that had already fallen. She felt trapped in a snow globe, as if some unseen giant was shaking the world vigorously. Snow seemed to be falling down and up. The effect was vertigo inducing. Linda's visibility was limited to only a few feet in front of her. To her distress, she had to walk into the wind. Halfway there, she thought about turning around. The storm was more than she anticipated it would be. She could actually feel the wind pushing her backward, toward the house, almost as if it didn't want her to go to Nick's.

Linda struggled the whole way to the shed. She had insisted that they restrict their rendezvous to his shed. She would feel strange making love in her own house. She knew she was a betrayal to Bob there, to do it in the marital felt a bridge too far, somehow. In the shed, it was removed. She pounded on the door and waited. It opened, and she was greeted by her lover. Linda's felt herself lighten a bit at the easy smile on Nick's face. Over the course of these months, she had grown to love his body. In fact, she didn't even see abnormalities anymore. All she saw were his beautiful eyes, his strong jaw and his charming smile.

Linda stepped into the comforting warmth of the shed. To her delight, she could smell the tea already steeping in anticipation of her arrival. Linda stepped in and held him to her, his head pressing against her belly. Linda took off her jacket and put it on the hook on the door. She turned around and wordlessly began to unbutton her blouse. Soon she was slipping out of her clothes and stood in front of him in her underwear. Nick pulled off his shirt and laid her down on the bed, placing little kisses on the familiar parts of her body he knew would make her squirm and giggle. Linda felt his hands over her body and surrendered to the moment.

Linda wrapped herself in a quilt and was quietly sipping her cup of tea. She smiled at Nick. Feelings of post-coital guilt had started creeping into her mind. She knew she deserved this. Bob was cheating on her. But is it right? the voice in her head spoke to her from time to time. Most times she would shake it off, today it lingered.

She turned to Nick, who had already dressed and was over at his workbench, tinkering. Sometimes she would just lie in bed and watch him. It was nice to be around another person for a while. It could get so lonely in that house. It didn't matter that it was a half scale house. When it was empty, it felt as big as a mansion.

"Nick," she said, her voice trailing off.

"I know," he said, his back turned to her.

"You do?" Linda said, shocked.

"I know you pretty well, Linda," Nick said,. "I know every inch of you."
She felt herself blushing. "I know what you're going to say."

"If you do, then what do you say?"

"Don't," Nick said.

"I don't know, Nick, it's just…" she said.

"Bob," Nick said, more as a statement than a question.

"Yes."

"He doesn't deserve you," Nick said.

She felt greedy and guilty. "Maybe," Linda said.

"I love you." Nick said.

The words hit Linda with a force harder than the winds of the storm
raging outside. He had never said them before. She was unable to speak. He
jumped off his stool and walked over to her. "I know you love me as well."
He planted a tender kiss on her lips.

"I don't know what to say," was the only thing Linda could manage.

"I know," said Nick. "You don't have to say anything. I know how you
feel." Linda was silent, still in shock. They had never said those words to
each other. It was an unspoken agreement, she thought. Do I love this man?
It scared her to think of the implications if she felt the same. It was silly to
think these things. She had already committed adultery, but it was just sex
and companionship, she had told herself. Now with love in the equation, it
became a betrayal.

"It's okay, I understand," Nick said, seeming to be able to read her mind.
He glanced out the back window. The snow was coming so intensely now, it
seemed like a white sheet was covering the window. "You better head back,
or else you might get stuck."

Linda looked outside and agreed, glad for the opportunity to exit the
awkward situation. She quickly pulled on her boots and clothes and started
out the door. Nick grabbed her hand gently. Linda turned around. Nick
climbed his stool, up to her level. Their gaze met eye to eye. Nick kissed her
again.

"Be careful," he said as the door closed behind Linda.

The wind hit Linda like a slap to the face. The storm had grown in
intensity and magnitude. Linda trudged slowly through the snow and biting
wind, struggling to get back to the house. Twice she fell into a snowbank
after being blown by the gale-force winds. In some places, the snow was up
to Linda's knees, and she had to wade through it. She heard a deep cracking

noise and looked up just in time to avoid a falling tree limb.

Slowly, the house came into view as if through a fog. The snow had blown against one side of the house. The drift was so deep it reached the second floor, completely covering the first-floor windows. She said a little prayer to God in thanks that the front of the house was not likewise buried. Linda continued slogging through the snow to the front steps. She looked over to see if the car was similarly entombed. To her relief, she saw the Volkswagen. The car was in the lee of the house. Kathleen's Jeep was parked next to the Volkswagen. It was not as buried but was quickly gathering snow.

She kicked and stomped her boots on the front porch to remove most of the snow. As Linda entered the house, she was greeted by an ashen-faced Kathleen Lakeland. She had been monitoring the storm on the television. Her husband, Tom, had called to tell her that the next ferry would be the last one of the day. The storm was too intense for normal operations, and there were concerns over visibility due to snow and pack ice. Linda offered Kathleen some money for her efforts, but she refused. Linda said goodbye and walked to the living room to see her children. They were sitting on the couch watching television with cups of hot chocolate. Lyndsey saw her mother, put the cocoa on the end table and gave her a big hug.

Linda heard thumping on the porch and the screen door opening. Thinking it must be Kathleen again, she got up and walked down the hallway, grabbing her coat she had slung over the banister. She probably needed help digging out her car. Zipping up her jacket, Linda twisted the deadbolt on the lock of the door and turned the knob.

* * *

Bob struggled against the wind and ice whipping past him. Using the bat like a blind man with a cane, he pressed on. The road home was only partially visible in an ever-shifting world of white. Home, he thought bitterly. Humiliation. He supposed everybody on the island knew. He was sure even Jenn knew. She was probably laughing about it right now with her college friends on the mainland. I guess I'll need to hire another waitress, he thought bitterly.

With each step, Bob became angrier. *She. She did this to me.*

Snow whipped into Bob's eyes, he teared up. Shame racked Bob's body.

"Stop fucking crying!" Bob shouted into the storm. Resentment grew with each passing moment, burning so hot that the cold and wind chill seemed to have no effect.

Before he knew it, Bob again arrived at a crossroads. To his right, the little road led to the maintenance shed, to the left, home. Bob chose the road to the shed. He arrived at the door, but this time his hand did not falter. He pounded three times with his gloved hand.

It seemed an eternity before he heard the slide of a lock from the other side. Light peaked out from the crack in the door around Nick Summers' face. The sight of this ugly, stunted man rankled him. The thought of this troll touching his wife, much less penetrating her, sickened Bob. He stood there and said nothing, the bat in his hand.

"Bob, what are you doing out in weather like this?" Nick asked, opening the door wider. Bob could see that Nick was alone. "Come in out of the cold," Nick offered. "I'll put on some tea, perhaps you'd prefer coffee?"

Bob stepped through the door. The musky smell of sex still hung heavy in the air. Without saying a word, Bob gripped the bat in his gloved hands, bringing it back far behind his shoulders like a baseball player in the batter's box. Bob took a hard swing at Nick's head. The sound was darkly comical to Bob at the time. He noted it was the same sound as a bat hitting a ball. He watched Nick's body fall, taking pleasure in its descent. Nick fell to the floor, motionless. Bob left, not bothering to close the door behind him.

Every part of Bob Sutton was numb as he walked home. He had watched himself attack Nick almost as an out-of-body experience. He supposed he was in shock. A gust of wind blew Bob back on his heels, as he steadied himself. He felt cold. The air was running right through his winter jacket like icy knives. The anger was rising again. Bob's rational mind told him he should feel bad about hitting Nick. What his heart told him ran contrary. He didn't feel bad. He felt good. Bob supposed Nick had gotten an immense sense of satisfaction having his meals served to him by the man whose wife he was fucking. Just thinking about it, he felt the rage rise again.

Bob found his way back to the house—this ridiculous dwarf-sized house. A house that would mock him every day he spent in it, a constant reminder of his wife's transgressions. Had she fucked him in their bed?? *I bet it felt just like home to him.* The door opened and Kathleen Lakeland walked out, struggling against the wind, walking to the driveway.

"So, she's in on it too," Bob said to himself, watching her get into her car. "Bitch." He waited for her to drive away. As the Jeep slowly disappeared into the blizzard, Bob walked up to the porch. He looked inside. Linda was buttoning up her jacket and walking to the door. She must be going back for round two. He heard the door unlock and saw the doorknob turn.

As the door opened and Bob saw surprise on Linda's face. *Good*, thought Bob. *I'll have the upper hand in this argument. For once.*

*　*　*

"Bob?" Linda said, looking at him standing in the doorway. "You're home early." Bob walked through the door and stood the front hallway.

"Were you expecting someone else?" Bob said in a cold voice.

"No, it's just…did you shut down the stand because of the storm?" Linda wondered why he wasn't removing his winter clothes. The snow on his jacket and hat had already started melting in the warmth of the house. Bob pulled the scarf down from his face and pushed the goggles up on his forehead. Linda saw something strange burning in his eyes, something alien. Unconsciously, she took a step backward.

"I know Linda," he said in a quiet voice. Linda felt her stomach sink.

"Know what?" she asked.

"I KNOW!" Bob roared. She took another step back. "I know you fucked that fucking piece of shit troll."

Linda's first thought was of the kids. She looked toward the living room. They stood in the doorway, their mouths agape.

Her hands started to shake. "Okay, kids, go upstairs. Mommy and Daddy need some grown-up time," Linda said.

"Mommy, is everything ok?" Jim asked.

"Yes baby, everything is fine. Take your sister. Go upstairs." Linda herded her children out of the living room to the stairs. Bob was in the way. He was pacing back and forth like a wild animal. At least he has to have the presence of mind to let the kids go upstairs, she thought. She needed time to gather her thoughts, find a way to defuse the situation.

Terrified, the kids ran upstairs. Relieved, Linda then heard the door close to their room. Good. She started to say something when she felt all the wind rush out of her lungs. Gasping for air against her spasming diaphragm, she looked up and saw Bob standing over her. He had hit her. He had actually hit her. To her horror, she realized he must have used the bat that he held in his hands.

Linda struggled to get up, wheezing and sucking for oxygen.

"How could you?" Bob howled.

"How could you?" wheezed Linda.

"I didn't fuck a dwarf, Linda."

"You fucked that waitress," Linda retorted, knowing full well in her heart that two wrongs did not make it right. This seemed to confuse Bob. Then the humiliation of his clumsy advances from this morning came back to him.

"I never fucked her," he spat.

"I saw you. I saw you kissing her," Linda said, her own anger rising.

"What you think you saw…you didn't see. I saw you and that *freak*, together," Bob raged, gesturing at her with the bat.

"You've been spying on me?" Linda shouted at him, still clutching her stomach. It hurt to breathe.

"You've been fucking around on me," Bob said, moving toward her as Linda backed away. "You've got no right to be upset about this."

"I've got every right to be upset," Linda screamed back at him. "I hate my life. I hate what I've become. I used to be young, and pretty and smart…I was going to be a doctor, or a lawyer until I met you." Tears of pain and hurt streamed down her cheeks. "YOU did this to me! I HATE you!" She backed into the wall and had nowhere else to go. Bob took a step forward. In a fit of panic, Linda took a swing at him. She found purchase, her fingers raking his cheek. Bob bellowed like a wounded animal and grabbed his face. Linda had drawn blood. She tried to run around him but tripped over one of Jim's books he had piled all around the house.

Bob stood over her. She scrambled backwards. He looked down and then to his own blood on his hands. He gripped the bat and brought it over his head. Linda closed her eyes and covered her head with her arms. A panicked thought ran through her mind. Will my kids remember what their mommy looked like when they grow up? This fleeting thought brought more tears. She winced in anticipation of the blow that was certainly on its way. When the blow did not come, Linda opened her eyes and cautiously looked up. Bob stood frozen with the bat over his head. The rage had drained from his eyes. All she saw now was pain and hurt. In this moment of hesitation, Linda saw her opportunity.

"Bob," she said, her voice quavered as she tried to sound calm.

She heard a loud "THWACK." Bob collapsed in a heap. Linda had to scramble back to avoid him falling on top of her. Nick stood in the hallway holding a snow shovel. He was bleeding from his head. *Did Bob do that to him?* Linda thought, feeling sick.

"Come on, we don't have much time," Nick said, offering Linda his hand to help her up. Bob was moaning on the floor.

"Time for what?"

"We need to take the kids, catch the last ferry. It leaves in 20 minutes," Nick said, moving Linda toward the stairs.

"But what about the storm?"

"It's not safe for any of us here. We need to go. NOW!" Nick said. He pulled her up the stairs.

Bob recovered his wits. Seeing Nick and Linda together gave him an adrenaline boost. He groped for his bat and shakily rose from the floor.

"I KNEW IT! This is what you planned, isn't it? To take my family from me?" Bob bellowed, running at them. Linda and Nick had already climbed most of the way up to the second floor. They hurried into Jim's room to find both children cowering under the covers. Linda slammed the door and locked it. She ran over to the closet and flung it open, grabbing some of Jim's jackets and sweaters. There's not enough time to grab Lyndsey's, Linda thought looking back at the door. She could see the light from the hallway through the crack at the bottom of the door. A shadow passed in front of it. Linda knew that Bob was on the other side.

"Come on now, put these on," she said, pressing the coats into her scared and confused children's hands.

"This is not mine," Lyndsey said, staring at Jim's blue jacket.

"I know baby, just put it on" Linda said, trying to sound calm and reassuring.

She could see the shadow of Bob's feet as he stood in front of the door. BANG! The wooden door shuddered and flexed from the force of a blow. Whether it came from a kick or Bob throwing himself against the door, Linda could not tell. Linda recoiled from the pounding and drew her children closer as she frantically looked around the room for a way out.

The door shuddered from the weight of Bob slamming his body into it, cracking and creaking in protest. Linda screamed, not a scream of terror, but of shock and surprise. Her head whipped around the room, looking for something. She stopped at the window—she flipped open the sash lock and tried to open it but it wouldn't move.

"Why won't this open?" Linda said, as the window was stuck, whether it was from the cold, or from the accumulation years of paint, she could not say.

"Do you need help?" Nick asked woozily leaning against the wall, holding a wooden Nutcracker in his hand like a cudgel, one of Jim's toys.

WHAM! The door seemed to be pushing in with every hit from Bob's body.

"Watch the door!" Linda shouted putting her fingers under the sash. She could feel something moving, so she pulled with all her might, screaming in pain as she tore a nail. The wood groaned in protestation, and finally relented.

"Hurry!" Linda screamed to be heard above the roaring storm that raged outside. A cold gust of wind whipped snow and ice into the room, instantly plunging the temperature to freezing. The thudding on the door continued. Jim looked at the door jamb. The spot where the lock met the frame was starting to splinter. It would break at any moment.

Linda grabbed Jim by the shoulders. She pushed him across the room to the window, pulling a sweater over his chest and wrapping another as a makeshift hat around his head. Jim looked in surprise as his mother threw one of her legs out of the window. Straddling it, half in, half outside.

"Come on Slim-Jim," she said. She picked Lyndsey up and perched her on her hip. Jim looked over the edge to the outside. Below him was a wall of snow. The wind had blown the snow clear up to the second story. It sloped away from the wall. Jim hesitated, afraid to jump. He felt a hand on his back. Nick was behind him.

"I'll show you," he shouted against the raging wind and snow. The door started to make crunching noises as the wood split up the casement. Nick climbed onto the windowsill. Without hesitation, he jumped out into the whiteness. Jim stuck his head out to see what happened. Nick was waving from the bottom of the slope. He shouted something up to Jim, but his words were lost on the wind. Linda grabbed him and pushed him out the window.

He was weightless in a white void. The wind whipped and burned his face as he tumbled in space, unable to tell up from down. Jim landed in the snow and slid downward. Jim put his bare hands out to steady himself. The cold wet chill made his fingers throb. He slid toward Nick, who was waiting at the bottom, his arms open wide, bracing for impact. And he caught him.

"It's okay, I've got you," Nick shouted to Jim. He was barely audible over the storm. Jim looked back up the snowbank to his room. His mother was silhouetted in the window. She took a last look inside, grabbed Lyndsey and jumped out The two of them tumbled down the snowbank in a tangled mess of arms, and legs. Nick ran over when they settled at the bottom. Jim could see his mother struggling to stand up. Lyndsey was crying, Jim could hear that plainly over the howling wind. Linda gestured toward the half-buried car in the driveway. Jim knew what she was asking him to do. He ran as best as he could, fighting through snow that at times was up to his neck.

Linda held Lyndsey tight against her chest as she waded through the snow. All she could think about was reaching the car. She looked to her left and saw Nick struggling in snow almost above his head.

"Get on!" she shouted to him over the howling wind.

"What?"

"Get on my back. There's no time to argue." She looked back at the window of Jim's room and her heart skipped a beat. Bob was leaning out the window, brandishing the bat. Their eyes met, even over this distance. She saw the rage still simmering in his face. They were so close to the car now. She grabbed Nick's hand and picked him up in one motion and hurled him onto her back. Jim had already made it to the car. He was digging the snow out from around the tires. Good boy, she thought. You're doing mommy proud. A surge of adrenaline coursed through her body. Linda pushed forward, her child in her arms and her lover clinging to her back. She fell into the snow by the car, exhausted. Every muscle in her body was crying to stop. *No, not yet,* she thought to herself. *Not yet.*

Linda mustered her will and rose to her feet. She felt for the keys. For one moment she panicked. I've lost them. Then, like a miracle, she felt them, cold and hard in her pocket. Jim was already in the back seat with his seat belt fastened. She opened the door to put Lyndsey in the back.

"Don't wanna sit in the back," she wailed. Linda had no time to argue. She looked down to Nick, who was standing outside the passenger-side door.

"I'm so sorry," Linda said, and she meant it on every possible level. This was all her fault that Nick was involved. "Are you okay sitting in the back?"

"It's okay, let's go," Nick implored her, climbing into the back seat with Jim. Linda put Lyndsey in the front seat of the car and buckled her in. She ran back around to the driver side and jumped behind the wheel. She turned the key. To her relief, the car started. It turned over sluggishly, but it started. She or Bob must have left the radio on. It was louder than she expected. From the tinny speakers of the Volkswagen, the Carpenters' *"On Top of the World"* blared at her, causing her to jump. She reached out to turn it down and the volume knob came off in her hand. With more urgent things to deal with, she put the car into gear and pressed her foot to the gas pedal. The sound of whirling wheels failing to make purchase greeted her ears, an unwelcome guest. Crying, she pumped the gas and prayed to God for any help, any forward movement at all.

Linda balled her hands into fists and hit the steering wheel, screaming in frustration. She stomped her foot down, pressing the pedal to the floor.

The car roared in protest. Then, miraculously, something caught, and the car lurched forward. Linda momentarily lost control of the station wagon, and it veered across the frozen driveway. Lyndsey started crying. Linda regained control of the car and righted its course.

*   *   *

Bob tried the doorknob to Jim's room. Locked, of course. Linda and her lover had retreated in there. It presented him with a quandary. His children were in that room. Should he knock down the door like he wanted to do, or should he wait it out? Bob rubbed the back of his head where the dwarf had hit him. When he removed his hand, there was blood. He probed the injury more closely. There was a definite gash there. He would probably need stitches. Another expense, another humiliation to have to endure. How dare that freak hit me? How dare he come to my wife's rescue? The thought caused his fury to boil over. That's right, MY wife. He'd had enough of this game. If the little man wanted to play, Okay, let's play.

Bob took a step back and hurled himself at the door. This was a well-built Vermont oak door with strong Vermont ash casings. Bob could feel how solid it was as he hit it. It barely yielded, but it did yield. Bob heard Linda scream from the other side. Good, he thought, I hope she's scared. He didn't know what he would do when he got to the other side of the door. But he thought the two of them could use a good scaring. Especially the dwarf. Yes, something would have to be done about the dwarf. Bob heard the splintering sound of wood giving as he threw himself against the door again. It wouldn't be long now.

Bob moved back from the door and kicked at it with all his might. The jamb ripped, and the lock flew out of the wrecked wood. The door slammed open, then bounced back, not quite closing because of the broken casement. Bob pushed the door and triumphantly strode in.

It was cold in the empty room. Snow was pouring through the open window and already accumulating on the floor in a pile. Bob stalked around his child's room in disbelief, then ran to the window. Sticking his head out into the storm, he saw how they had escaped. There were fresh trails leading from the snowbank outside the house. Bob craned his neck to see several small bundled figures struggling through the snow. They were headed for the...No. No! thought Bob, realizing their intended destination. Linda looked back. Their eyes met. Through the snowstorm and wind and swirling biting ice, Bob swore he saw a smirk on her face.

Infuriated anew, Bob pulled himself inside the window and slipped on dusty pile of snow. Cursing as he got up, Bob grabbed for his bat and ran out to the hallway. If he made it down the stairs, he could stop them before they would be able to drive the station wagon out of the snow. He had meant to install the snow chains but had procrastinated. Without them, they would have a difficult time getting traction on the icy roads. Bob stood up. With his mind on what he was going to do to Linda and the dwarf, he forgot about the perils of living in a half-sized house. Bob's head slammed into the top of the doorway with an audible crack. *Curious, just like the sound of a bat.* The thought randomly drifted through Bob's mind before the intense pain and throbbing white lights brought him to his knees.

He wasn't knocked unconscious, but his faculties were disabled. For a few seconds, Bob's mind went blank, like a computer rebooting after a crash. He shook his head and moaned. He could already feel the throbbing of his forehead, like a heartbeat. The little lights and the high-pitched whine subsided. Bob regained his senses. Rising to his feet as quickly as he dared, Bob stumbled down the stairs cursing damned dwarf house.

Bob ran to the driveway just in time to see the Volkswagen fishtailing out onto the road that headed to the ferry. Bob ran, bat in hand, off the porch and toward the car. He misjudged a bank of snow and plunged into it, disappearing into an expanse of frozen whiteness. As he struggled to right himself and climb out of the snow, he could see the Volkswagen driving away. The dull orange red of the car stood out strikingly against the white of the blizzard. As he rose, he watched it vanish into a white wall of snow and wind. Defeated, the bat dropped from Bob's hands as he sank to his knees into the snow.

*   *   *

Linda got her bearings; she turned the windshield wipers to high. The Carpenter's song ended and Led Zeppelin's *"When the Levee Breaks"* started. Linda noted in the back of her mind that the wipers were beating in perfect time to the song. This observation made her laugh darkly to herself. She had to get to the ferry. There was only one more today. It was leaving in minutes, if it had not left already. It was growing dark, Linda turned on the high beams to see if it would help. It only made things whiter and worse.

Linda's thoughts turned back to Bob. Certainly, he must be out by now. She looked in her rear-view mirror as the house behind her grew ever smaller. She saw a solitary figure stagger out into the road. She put the car into a higher gear and pressed the accelerator. The figure in the mirror grew smaller and smaller. To her relief, he did not seem to be following them. Concerned about the snowy conditions, she took her eyes off the mirror and on to the road in front of her. When she looked back again, he was gone.

Under normal circumstances, Linda was a cautious driver, especially during bad weather. The prospect of missing the ferry and having to stay on this island until the storm passed filled Linda's heart with dread. As a result, Linda drove like a woman possessed. The car rocketed around corners, sliding and skidding. Linda came close to running off the road, but a preternatural desire to protect her kids seemed to be guiding her actions.

Through the white screen of ice and snow, a sign for the dock appeared. Linda turned the wheel with a jerk, cutting the corner. Jim and Lyndsey laughed in delight at this fun new game. Linda looked ahead, focused on only one thing. *Was it still there? Please, Please, Please God, let it still be there.* Linda was not a particularly religious woman. She had been raised Lutheran, had gone to church Sundays. In this moment, she reached out with all her heart, to a supreme being, any supreme being to help her. A shape emerged at the edge of the water. Tears began to form in Linda's eyes. She smiled as they streamed down her face. To her relief, the ferry slowly came into focus, the instrument of their exodus.

Linda skidded to a halt at the tollbooth. A man in a parka came running up to her car. "Just made it!" he shouted, struggling to be heard over the blizzard. he retorted "Good thing, too. This is the last one out."

Linda happily parted with the fare, just grateful to be boarding. Reflexively, she looked in her rear-view mirror. Rationally, she knew there was no way Bob could have made it on foot, but she still looked, just to make sure. Reassured that no-one had followed them, Linda pulled her car onto the ferry. It was a full boat, and she was the last one on board. Linda put the car into park and set the emergency brake. It wasn't until the gate went down and she felt the ferry shudder away from the dock that she finally let herself relax. Linda realized she had been holding the wheel with a vice-like grip the whole time. She let go and exhaled, comforted that she and her family were finally safe.

*   *   *

The ferry between Burlington and Christmas Island was not so much a boat, but rather a flat piece of road that would shuttle cars back and forth. There was a Captain's nest and an area above where people would go and sit on wooden benches to get out of the weather, relax and enjoy the view, but for all intents and purposes, the deck was just a floating piece of highway. It was actually surfaced with asphalt, cracked and patched like any road; with the same yellow painted stripes you might see on any typical street. The cars that took the ferry sat on their little piece of road, made the trip across the water, then disgorged to meet more macadam. The whole trip, wheels never met actual deck or boat.

Linda sat for a while as the ferry pulled away from the dock. She felt around on the floor for the knob to the radio. Her shaking fingers found it. Just in time. The radio was still blaring music loudly. Its current selection was *"Go Your Own Way,"* by Fleetwood Mac.

"A little too on the nose" Linda muttered to herself. She replaced the knob and turned off the radio. Merciful silence filled the car.

"Wasn't that fun?" she said with a smile, turning to the kids. Jim looked at her face. She seemed to be happy, but there was something that didn't sit well with him. He nodded, mostly because it was what he thought she wanted to see.

"Want some hot chocolate?"

They nodded yes.

"Great!" She forced a smile. Linda turned to Nick. "Can you stay and watch the kids? I don't want them out in this."

"Do you think that's a good idea?" Nick asked, looking from Linda to the kids and back.

"I think the kids need this. Don't you?" Linda replied, her eyes wide as if to say *I need this.*

"I understand" Nick nodded.

"Don't go mommy!" Lyndsey cried. "I'm scared." Linda froze. Keep it together, she told herself.

"Come on kids, hot chocolate sounds great! Nick replied, looking from Jim to Lyndsey. "Don't worry, you'll be safe with me." For a moment, there was a fine crack in his Linda's smile. Don't cry, Linda told herself, not in front of the kids. She closed her eyes, and swallowed, the grin returned even bigger.

Jim watched his mother walk away from the car, struggling to keep her footing on the icy deck as the boat rolled in the growing storm. She turned up her collar and staggered up the stairs to the upper deck and out of view. He knew in a few minutes she would return with hot chocolate in those little cups with the poker cards printed on the bottom.

The ferry was packed with Christmas Town staff fleeing the fury of the storm. Like the Sutton's, they had been ordered by Mr. Murray to proceed with business as usual. Kathleen and Tom Lakeland waved nervously at Linda from the upper level as the ferry pitched up and down on the roughening waters. Next to them stood John Roebling, still dressed in his full Santa garb, and why not? It provided ample protection from the cold and snow.

Around North Burlington, a thin rim of ice had formed over the last few days. The ice extended out a few hundred feet from the shore, but it was nothing that the ferries couldn't muscle through. Farther north, the lake had frozen over, in some places several feet thick. The storm had hit with such fury that ice had broken free and was pushed south by the wind and water. The ferry rocked and pitched with the waves as the Captain valiantly steered it around ice floes and through worsening conditions and visibility. The normally placid lake swelled like an ocean. The wind whipped the waters into a frenzy. Visibility on Lake Champlain was the same as it was on the island, almost nothing. The ferry ride was normally a twenty-minute journey, but the ferryboat captain was forced off course by strong winds and currents.

The crew members manned searchlights and scanned back and forth across the surface of the water in order to spot any rogue ice in their path, most of which could be rammed and deflected by the sheer bulk of the boat. The lights converged on a large white mass, right in front of the ferry. It was too close to avoid. The boat pushed forward. For a minute it seemed like they would ride right over the ice, but a strong gale-force wind in concert with a wave pitched the ice up. The boat reared back like a horse, the front deck rising out of the water.

Jim sat in the car waiting for his mother to return. He had grown accustomed to the ferry rocking back and forth in the storm. It was almost fun, like a roller coaster. But then, the boat rocked farther than he expected. A shock of fear ran through him as the deck rose higher and higher, like a drawbridge. Just as it seemed like it would tip the whole ferry over, it stopped. Then he felt the car move ever so slightly. Spray from the lake had coated the cars and deck with a growing layer of ice that formed almost on contact. The car, without any traction or snow-chains, found itself victim to the forces of gravity. Even with the emergency brake engaged, the car started inching backwards. Jim looked to Nick. His face grim, he had already unbuckled his seatbelt. Through the rear window Jim saw they were slowly sliding toward the slender chain that separated the deck from the open water.

A cold gust of air raced through the car. Nick had opened the door. The snow and spray from the lake blew in. Lyndsey was crying for her mommy. Jim felt small hands fumbling at his waist. He heard the click as the seat belt came free.

The car was picking up speed, and now the pickup truck in front of the station wagon was starting to slide as well. Jim felt a strong force grip him and push him out the door. As Jim fell to the deck, he saw Nick standing on the seat, struggling to maintain his balance.

"Get to the stairs!" Nick shouted at Jim. He then started to climb into the front seat where Lyndsey was still buckled. "GO!" he shouted. Snapped out of his shock, Jim tried to get on his feet, only to slip on the ice of the deck. He slid down the slope of the ferry, hurtling toward the edge and the inky black water beyond. Jim flailed his arms and legs, trying to make purchase on the icy surface, unable to get a grip. Jim waved his arms in desperation, sensing he was almost to the edge of the boat. His hand hit something hard and metal. He grabbed at it, and with a jerk, he arrested his fall. Jim had managed to grasp a side safety rail. The cold burned his hand, but he dared not let go. He looked down at his feet which were inches from the cold water lapping beyond the edge. The back of ferry was partially under water, tilted up by the ice wedged under the bow of the boat.

Jim turned his head towards the bow of the ship, which was still up in the air. To his horror, the Volkswagen was still sliding down the ramp, right toward him. If he didn't get out of the way, it would crush him or plunge him into the freezing cold waters of Lake Champlain. To make things worse, Jim did not have gloves. He felt frostbite stinging his fingers as he gripped the bare metal pole for his very life. The wind was howling and the snow blowing. Jim heard a familiar voice carry to him over the roar of the storm. He looked beyond the station wagon. His mother was clutching the rail on his side of the boat. She was several cars up and appeared to be inching toward him. Behind her, with his arm locked around her waist was Santa himself, John Roebling. He gripped one of the railings with his strong gloved hand, helping Linda make her way down the incline of the icy deck. Jim could see his mother's mouth open and shut but could not hear her. Wind and noise carried her words away, he could only catch random syllables in between the waves and spray that were soaking him.

At the angle the boat was, he would have to climb the railing like a ladder, knowing that in a few seconds the car would come crashing into the rail, then him. Jim put his right foot against the rail and pushed upward, screaming as skin ripped from his hand. Linda and Santa moved closer; she was calling for him to climb faster. He looked at his torn hand, it was starting to bleed. The cold dulled the pain, but he pulled the sleeves of his jacket over his hands as makeshift mittens.

The red Volkswagen scraped its way down the deck, its tires little use against the ice. Jim climbed out of the way, with just enough time to avoid the sickening crunch of metal on metal. The car crashed into the railing, closing the back door and denting the whole right side of the car. The metal shrieked and wailed in concert with the wind as the car scraped along the metal railing. The ferry listed to the left, and the car inched away from the rail, dangerously close to the flimsy chain at the back of the boat.

He couldn't hear anything from the car with the doors closed. Even if they were open, the wind howled around his ears with such ferocity, any words or sounds would have been scattered to the fury raging around them. Nick had climbed to the front seat and had managed to get Lyndsey's seat belt off. He held her in his arms and put his hand on the handle of the door to open it. It was stuck. He tried it again. Stuck. The crash with the railing had deformed the door, and it wouldn't move. SNAP. The chain, the one thing that had kept the car from the unthinkable, broke and gave way. It whipped around. Jim ducked, narrowly avoiding being hit. Jim clung to the side railing, watching in horror. He looked into the front of the car as the rear wheels slipped off the ferry and into the water. Nick pulled at the door with all his might as the car slipped into the lake. The station wagon floated, then turned, submerging the driver's side. Jim screamed for help, not knowing who or what could come to their aid.

Santa and Linda were still half a deck away. She screamed, her wails rising louder than the howling winds. Clawing at Santa, Linda tried to wrench herself free, but he held her tightly. It was too late.

One of the defining characteristics of Volkswagens is that the engine is in the back of the car. The heavy rear end of the Sutton's station wagon sunk first, the nose pointing up out of the water like a bobber. Nick stopped his struggling to open the door and held Lyndsey. Lyndsey looked around, confused. Nick got the little girl's attention as reached his small hand behind her ear and drew back a bright shiny quarter. Lyndsey clapped her hands in delight. Nick's eyes met Jim's own. The car dipped up and down below the surface. Jim felt a desperate clawing at his back and heard the unintelligible screams of his mother as she grabbed him. She had finally traversed down the rail to her son. Santa held her by the belt of her jeans as he gripped the railing. Santa's once jolly face was still apple cheeked, but now it was etched with grim determination.

"JIM!" Santa shouted, his basso profundo voice rising over the cacophony, reaching out to him. Jim stretched his arm as far as it would go. He felt the tight grip of a gloved hand around his own. A powerful force pulled him up.

"IT'S GOING TO BE OK!" Santa shouted, holding him tight in a bear-hug embrace. The snow and water still whipped around them both, stinging their faces like a swarm of angry hornets. Jim looked back and saw his mother crawling down the frozen railing toward the churning water.

"JIM!" Santa shouted. "Take this, it will make you feel better." Santa pressed a chocolate bar into his hand. "DON'T LOOK BACK, JIMMY," Santa said holding Jim tight to his red and white costume. "Just don't look back."

Jim did not heed Santa's words, he looked back at his mother. She had made it to the end of the ferry. Jim's mother held the rail, her hair whipped in the wind, her mouth open. Shrieking filled the air. Was it the wind or the wailing of his mother? Jim could not tell. Beyond his mother Jim could see the spot where the car had been bobbing. There was nothing, just the wild undulations of the surface of the lake. He stared into the deep. Far below, in the clear churning water of Lake Champlain, despite the ferocity of the storm, he could see two headlights glowing in the darkness.

VISITING AN OLD FRIEND

2000

Twin beams of light from the resurrected Ford Festiva illuminated the velvety blackness of the winding road leading out of Strawberry Falls. Jim leaned forward, as if perhaps it could help him see beyond the reach of the beams. Navigating by instinct, trying to anticipate the curves of the country road, the car seemed to be floating in an inky void.

Outside of clinging to the curves of the road that undulated and slithered through the dark valley like a snake, Jim had no purpose. His book was gone, held hostage to his time in Strawberry Falls. He was grateful to have escaped that town with his life. His book wasn't going to light the literary world on fire, but it gave him a reason for being in Vermont. Without that shield, he felt naked and adrift.

Jim glanced at his rear-view mirror and saw the flashing lights of a police car. Then he heard the siren. *Deputy Avery, come to finish the job,* Jim thought grimly.

He thought about flooring it, but he was sure if he went much faster, he'd run into in a ditch or ravine. That's how I ended up here in the first place, he thought. He started to pull over to the side of the road. I'll be ready, Jim thought. There was a tire iron in the trunk. But how would he get it?

Suddenly, a black and white Crown Victoria careened around the bend. It was right on top of him faster than he could react. Jim pulled over in expectation and was surprised to see the police car pass him by without a second thought. Jim watched the lights wind their way back and forth until they disappeared into the enveloping darkness.

Just for a minute, Jim told himself. He turned off the engine and felt himself drift away.

It hurt to open his eyes. It hurt to keep them closed, so what was the difference. Dazed, Jim blinked in the harsh morning light. He moved his arm up to shield his eyes from the piercing rays of the impertinent sun. As he did this he heard and felt his clothes crackling. Oh yeah, the mud. Jim grimaced. He had fallen asleep in the car, caked in the stuff.

Jim tilted the rear-view mirror to look at himself. The right side of his face seemed to have gotten the worst of the beating from the night before. Scraping off some dried mud, he saw a wicked black eye that had swollen to just a slit. He was surprised he could see anything out of it at all. Wincing, he touched his jaw, the bruises felt like they went deeper than skin, bone deep. He grimaced as he removed his seatbelt and felt the sharp pain in his side. Jim's hair was still slicked to his head, but now the mud had cured to a crusty veneer, which gave his whole appearance a "lost tribes of Vermont" look. Jim picked at a flake of mud with his fingernail, it was stuck tight. He'd need a shower, a long one. He felt a desire for something to eat. *Something sweet.* His stomach grumbled in approval of the plan.

"I guess we should go" Jim said to no-one in particular. His had went to turn the keys in the ignition. They were not there. He looked around and found them sitting on the dashboard. Must have taken them out last night, he thought. He didn't remember. Reaching for them he fumbled, the keys dropped to the floor.

Groaning, Jim reached down. He felt something next to the keys. Picking them both up, he saw the AbaZaba bar from Cammy's garage. Just looking at it made him sick. Maybe it was the stale crackers. He threw the candy bar into the back of the car, it bounced off the seat and onto the floor once again.

It was hard to muster the same enthusiasm for onion rings after all that had transpired, but he didn't know what else to do. Luly's was as good a place as any to start. It was the reason he had detoured into Strawberry Falls in the first place. Maybe if he went there, it might not seem a total loss.

"Yeah right," Jim muttered.

To Jim's relief, the drive to Luly's proved to be uneventful. He saw the big red and yellow neon sign that spelled out "Luly's" in looping cursive appear around the bend. Jim turned into the gravel parking lot and parked his maroon Festiva in front.

Jim creakily stepped out of the car, shedding flakes of mud in his wake. He stood in the parking lot and looked up at the restaurant.

"It probably would have made for a great review" Jim sighed.

The sign in the window read "CLOSED: ON VACATION- LULY." He got back into his car and drove further north into the Champlain Valley.

On the drive up Route 89. A sign read, "MONTPELIER, 12".

"As good as place to stop as any" he muttered to himself.

Montpelier is a French name, like many others in the Green Mountain State. This area was colonized by French explorers, and the area still has many elements of French culture but with a Vermont twist. For instance, Montpelier, which in French means "bald mountain," is pronounced Mont-PELL-EE-AY. Vermonters pronounce it thusly: Mont-PEEL-EE-ER.

Jim found a place across from the capitol with some half-decent onion rings. The waitress gave Jim a wide berth in his current mud be-speckled state, but he didn't care. After lunch, he bought a spiral bound notebook at the Ben Franklin general store across the road.

I'll never get back those lost reviews, Jim thought bitterly. The book was dead but writing something was better than facing the literal and metaphorical beating he had taken. He had compiled from memory a handful of the destinations he had intended to visit and kept it on the passenger's seat, his only companion now. Completing his itinerary brought no real comfort. Every location, and review checked off his impromptu list only brought him closer to the last entry. It was becoming something he simply could not avoid anymore. As he drove, he passed a sign that read: BURLINGTON 38. He looked down at his list again. There was only one name left.

CHRISTMAS TOWN

Jim stood in the shower, methodically washing all the caked mud and filth off his body. He had found a little motel outside of Middlebury, close to a place he had remembered from his old notes, called The Dog Team Tavern. He'd heard nothing but good things about the restaurant, especially something mysteriously called a relish wheel.

Jim probably could have pushed on through to Burlington the day before, but in the state he was in, the bruises were enough of a conversation starter. He'd rather not have to explain why he was covered in dried mud as well. Truth to be told, the delay was welcome, not only for the relief from the mud and dirt, but also as a way to forestall the final stop on his journey.

After a hot shower Jim felt human again, he thought he might as well cross one of the few names off his revised list. The Dog Team Tavern did not disappoint. The restaurant was charming, with its rustic Vermont farmhouse decor. Jim had a burger with rings. They tasted amazing, maybe the best thing he had ever had. Jim knew that this was because of his brush with death, but it didn't matter. It was like the food of the gods. He was advised to try the sticky buns, and while they were sticky sweet and so very good, he could not help it when he spied apple pie on the menu, he had to order a piece.

"Cheddar cheese?" The waitress asked.

"What, why?"

"For the pie," she replied.

"People order that?" Jim raised an eyebrow.

"Oh yeah. Besides it's the law now."

"Really?"

"Yep," the waitress answered. "Act passed last year. 'When serving apple pie in Vermont, a "good faith" effort shall be made to serve it with: (a) with a glass of cold milk, (b) with a slice of cheddar cheese, (c) with a large scoop of vanilla ice cream.' So, I guess you could have the milk or the ice cream."

"I'll take the cheddar," Jim replied. "I don't want to break the law."

The pie was good, even (especially) with the cheese. His belly more than full, Jim retired to his room and fell straight asleep, dead to the world.

The next day, as Jim drove past the University of Vermont, memories came back, unbidden. The Burlington of his childhood only existed in his mind now. Where a comic bookstore once stood, there was now a coffee shop. A head shop was now a coffee shop (strangely the one coffee shop from his childhood was currently replaced by a head shop). There had been a camera store where Jim saw his first Polaroid picture, it also had vanished, replaced by a coffee shop. They were all ghosts now. All the people who knew these places, as they passed on one way or another, that Burlington grew fainter. One day it would be gone. One day all Jim's personal memories of his childhood, of Vermont, Christmas Town and his family, they'd be gone too. As he drove down the hill leading toward the lake, he passed a building with a neon "Nectar's" sign out front. Jim remembered that Nectar's (at the time) was the hot new spot to listen to up and coming local bands and live music.

Jim's journey through Burlington was a trip down memory lane, but it was truly a detour from his final destination. Jim drove out of town and headed to Colchester. As he passed Mallet's Bay, he remembered overhearing Carl bragging to Paco about seeing a "titty show" at the drive-in. The Mallet's Bay Drive-In had shown adult selections al fresco from the early seventies through the mid-eighties.

Jim gripped the wheel tighter as the port came into view. He fought the compulsion to turn the car around and drive back to Brooklyn. Subconsciously, he rubbed the scars on the palm of his right hand. Jim shook it off. He had wondered what he would do when he got to this point. He had come too far to turn back now. It was the true reason why he had made the trip in the first place. He admitted what he never could have before this point, the book was the excuse. Christmas Island was the reason. Jim pulled up to the gate for the ferry where an old man stood, taking fares.

"Whoa, what happened to you buddy?" The man said, staring at Jim's face. The black eye was still prominent, though most of the bruises had transitioned from dark purple to bluish and a sickly yellow.

"You should see the other guy," Jim said.

"You're not from here, are you?" he asked, eying Jim quizzically.

"No," Jim said with a forced smile.

"You visiting someone?" The ferry attendant pressed, glancing at Jim's New York plates.

"Yes, an old friend," he said, smiling.

"Okay, good. Some folks think they can still go to Christmas Town, but that area's closed and fenced off. No reason to go to the island anymore unless you live there. If you're lookin' for a good time, that place's long-gone buddy."

"I used to live there, years ago," Jim offered.

"Really?" The ferryman's face brightened. "No kidding. Your family worked on the island?"

"My father ran the snack stand at Christmas Town," Jim replied.

"Oh...okay...well, have a nice trip." The man abruptly ended their conversation and raised the gate.

Jim pulled the car forward and drove onto the ferry. A feeling of dread took him as the rubber of the wheels met the surface of the deck. His chest tightened as the gate clanged closed, *a gate*, Jim reassured himself, *not just a chain*. Safety improvements had been made since he last took this ferry boat ride. Jim put the car into park, got out, and walked up to the second level.

Christmas Town closed for good in 1982. In a sense, the long slide to its eventual extinction began on the night of the blizzard of 1978. The storm did impressive damage to the park. Ironically, the blizzard destroyed all the remaining snow machines. It was too costly to replace them. Without actual snow, Christmas Town lost a great deal of its off-season appeal. Mr. Murray had not printed new promotional materials in almost a decade. Tourists would find hotel pamphlets advertising "real snow" only to be informed upon arrival, that it was "outdated information." Some took this in stride, but most asked for their money back.

The attraction fell quickly into disrepair. When the oil crisis of 1979 hit, it was the proverbial nail in the coffin. Skyrocketing gas and oil expenses forced Mr. Murray to shut down some rides indefinitely and fire much of the staff. The place held on for a few more years, but it shuttered for good after Glenn suffered a fatal heart attack riding the ferry back to Colchester after collecting rent. His heirs decided to close the park. They sold vast swaths of the land to real estate developers. By the year 2000, the island was home to some of the most desirable homes in Vermont.

The boat's horn sounded as they pulled into port. Jim started to make his way to the stairs when, by chance his gaze fell upon the parking lot. There were several nice-looking cars, including a Hummer and a Prius, de rigueur on an upscale residential island, but it wasn't the newer cars that caught Jim's attention, it was a black and red Ram truck, just like the one that Cammy and Dodge owned back in Strawberry Falls.

God, I hate pickup trucks, If I never see one again, it will be too soon.

Jim waited in his car and watched as the crew prepared to let them disembark. The gangway hit the deck with a loud clang. All you have to do is stay on the boat. Go back. He pressed brake pedal and put the car into drive. The Festiva slowly rolled toward the edge of the boat. As the wheels touched the asphalt parking lot, he looked around. He hadn't *expected* anything to happen. He just felt numb. As he was examining his lack of feelings, he saw something that almost made him drive off the pier into the drink.

Of the sights he could have expected upon reaching the shore, he never thought he would see Cammy Norman, leaning against the red and black Ram truck, her arms folded, a smile on her face. Impossible. He pulled the car around, driving into to the parking lot. As he made the turn, Jim was not entirely sure that she would be there. Part of him was certain that this was a hallucination. To Jim's astonishment, Cammy was still there, still leaning on the truck. Her wild curly hair blew gently in the wind. She was smiling, and he noticed that she wasn't alone. Lying on the hood of the car in a dark furry lump was Kaiser Bill. Jim's mind raced. *What will I say to her? What could I say? Why is she here?* He pulled his car into a parking space and walked over to the truck.

"What took you so long?" Cammy said.

"What are you...how did you find me?" Jim finally spluttered.

"You told me about your trip. I figured you might end up here. It was worth a shot. Besides, I had this." Cammy pulled a package from behind her back.

"My bag?" Jim stared at it in disbelief. Cammy handed it to Jim. "But your mother…you said you'd stay."

"I did tell her that," Cammy said. "But I'm not a prisoner. I'm free to come and go as I please, so I went."

Jim turned over the old satchel in his hands. He opened the bag and leafed through, as far as he could tell, every note he had written for his book.

"She didn't try to stop you?"

"She didn't. But then again, she didn't see me leave. She also didn't see me take that." Cammy nodded to the satchel.

"Are you going back?"

"No. No, I don't think so. I can't live there anymore."

"Where will you go?" Jim asked.

She walked closer to Jim. "I don't know, really. Maybe I'll go back to school."

"You should" Jim replied with a grin. The act of smiling made him wince, his face still swollen and tender.

"Yeah." Cammy winced in sympathy. "I'm really sorry about that."

"It's ok." Jim heard the platitude tumble from his still stinging lips. What else could he say really?

Kaiser Bill sniffed the air, his one good eye opened, and his tail thumped against the metal hood of the truck.

"I'm glad to see you too, boy," Jim smiled. "Wait!" Jim ran back to the car. He searched in the mess under the seat and felt it against his fingers. He grabbed it and trotted back to Kaiser Bill and Cammy. He opened his hand, in it an AbaZaba bar. It was mushed and melted, but it didn't seem to bother Kaiser Bill who wolfed it down in one gulp, wrapper and all. Cammy raised an eyebrow disapprovingly.

"It's alright," Jim explained. "There's no chocolate."

"I guess…" Cammy replied skeptically.

"How did you know I'd be here today?"

"I didn't. I had your notes and maps. I hoped you'd show up here eventually." She smiled and brushed her hair from her eyes. "Actually, I've been here every day for two days."

"Every day?" Jim blustered. "Why?"

"I owed it to you. I had to get you your notes. What my mother did…" Cammy shuddered. "…what she did was wrong, on so many levels. I did what I did to save your life. You helped me set myself *free* Jim. There's nothing holding me there anymore. I can finally leave Strawberry Falls. I sat here hoping you'd show up. I had your book to keep me company. You're a good writer, Jim." She smiled. "But you need an editor" Jim winced, then laughed.

"What about Dodge, won't he come looking for you?"

"I told him I was going to gets some parts in New Hampshire, he doesn't expect me back until next week, then I imagine he'll figure it out and come looking," Cammy replied. "But he's in the blind. He doesn't know where either of us are. Honestly, this would be the last place he'd look for me. Besides" she looked Jim in the eye "I know where the bodies are buried."

"So to speak." She hastily added with a wink, seeing Jim's slack jawed expression.

She stood and put her hands on her hips. "So, are you going to show me around, or do I need an engraved invitation?"

"Around the island?"

"Yeah. You did tell me you lived here once, right? I want to get the inside scoop on Christmas Town. I know you told me you were here to visit a friend. Is it okay if we take a little detour, or will he mind?" Cammy said, smiling at Jim.

"No, he won't mind waiting, but Christmas Town is closed. It's gone."

"You up for a little felonious trespassing, then?" Cammy winked at Jim.

"I am, if you are," he said, "Why don't we take my car?"

Jim and Cammy climbed into the cramped confines of his Ford Festiva. There was plenty of room in the back for Kaiser Bill who made himself comfortable in a pile of abandoned junk food wrappers.

He took the turn on the road that were once marked with many signs directing tourists to Christmas Town, now bare save for overgrown weeds. They navigated the rutted pavement for a stretch until they came upon a metal gate that barred the road. Jim got out of the car and walked up to the gate. It was chained and padlocked.

"We'll have to go the rest of the way on foot," Jim called back to Cammy.

"Its best if we leave Bill here!" Cammy shouted, tying his leash to the fence. Kaiser bill wagged his tail happily.

Jim began to climb over the rusty metal fence, he groaned and held his side. Cammy hopped the fence, throwing her legs over the top in a graceful leap despite her own shortcomings. After Jim shambled over the fence, the two of them walked down the road. The maple trees had grown tall since he last set foot here. They now formed a canopy that shaded the road, creating a patchwork of light and dark on the ground. The wind gently blew through the leaves, rustling them. They continued down the road in silence. Cammy moved closer to Jim, he felt her hand deftly move to his own and felt their fingers intertwine.

As they walked around the bend, they were greeted by a large scarred and pitted concrete Santa Claus holding a sign that at one time would have said "WELCOME TO CHRISTMAS TOWN." He currently held a prefab sign that read: "NO TRESPASSING."

Santa had clearly seen better days. The elements had not been kind to old St. Nick, the paint was faded and flaking. Lichen had taken hold and was growing like a rash on his face. Santa's nose was missing. If it had fallen off due to natural causes or to vandalism, Jim could not determine.

Christmas Town had deteriorated precipitously over the years. Most of the fiberglass figurines had been toppled, stolen, or shattered by trespassers and curiosity seekers. Santa's house at the North Pole was boarded up, but someone had pried the plywood door off its hinge, leaving it open for anyone to explore. Santa's old chair was still inside, the upholstery, long disintegrated leaving only bare rusty springs. Beer bottles tinkled underfoot everywhere. Graffiti covered every inch of the walls, written in pen and spray paint, indecipherable for the most part, save for the large "HO HO HO" scrawled in enormous red letters. It looked more like the lair of a Christmas-themed serial killer than Santa's house.

"Wow, this looks so different than when my family came when I was little," Cammy said.

"No kidding" Jim replied. He walked out the back door. The mailbox for letters to Santa lay on its side, door askew. Jim looked inside. There were no letters. He looked up from the mailbox, and there it was - the snack stand.

The snack stand had changed in the years after his father and mother sold it. During the divorce proceeding it was declared that they would split the marital assets. The stand was one of them. Bob needed the cash anyway. He had been charged with assault and attempted murder. The ferry tragedy and the events that led up to it became fodder for the press. From what his mother told him, it was sold for pennies on the dollar. The dark celebrity of the accident caused an uptick in attendance from people who came to gawk at the macabre. Mr. Murray had already reaped the benefit of the Sutton's naïveté. He rushed in like a vulture to pick over the corpse of their marriage. It was not until Christmas Town went belly-up that Linda let go of her bitterness at being taken advantage of by the Murray family. She felt some modicum of justice after she heard they went bankrupt.

The paint was cracked and faded. The windows had at one time been boarded up. Now the plywood lay on the ground warped and rotting from exposure to the elements. The glass in the front doors had long ago been shattered. Although the doors were chained, anyone could just walk through the empty panes. Jim carefully ducked inside. The restaurant had been stripped clean. There were no more booths or chairs, no register, or counter stools. Presumably, they had been sold as assets to creditors, along with all the kitchen equipment which was likewise absent. Light streamed through the hole in the roof. Dirty black water created an ominous looking pond in the middle of the restaurant. Black mold and lichen adhered to every surface.

"This used to be my father's stand," Jim said.

"It's seen better days, huh?" Cammy said. She ducked under a tree that bisected the room. Jim noticed her slight limp again.

"Even in its best days, it wasn't so good."

They walked through the center of Christmas Town, heading toward the path that led to the maintenance shed and the Sutton home. Several sections of the park had been sold off to developers and were now gone, replaced by luxury homes. The Ice Palace was converted to condominiums in the 1990s. The trees in that section of the park created a natural barrier to the rest of Christmas Town, the boardwalk ripped up and divided into lots. The current residents of Christmas Island were in perpetual battle over the remains of Christmas Town. However, litigation and competing claims of ownership plagued the developers. Only one section of the park was currently developed as planned

Though the live animals in the park had been presumably sold off during the closing, some children swore that there were still reindeer on the island. These reports were spotty. Most doubted the veracity of these tales as the island was too small to have any significant population of reindeer to remain hidden for any length of time. The location where they had been housed had been partially developed, but only as lots, not homes. A huge sound baffle fence stood on the perimeter of what use to be the Ice Palace section. It was painted forest green in an attempt blend into the natural surroundings.

Everything seemed smaller and sadder than he remembered it. It was very quiet in this part of the park, the only noises other than their footfalls were small, the creaking of trees, calls of song birds. An eerie silence permeated the lush green air. As they walked, Jim saw the little road to what was once Nick's maintenance shed. Choked with weeds and barely visible, Jim glanced toward it but decided not to take that path. He wanted to see the house where he lived, where they all had lived.

Standing in front of the house once again, Jim was struck by how small it was. As a child, this house seemed so perfect. It was just the right size in his eight-year-old mind, because everything was to his scale. He knew that his family lived in a house built for little people, but he was not prepared for what greeted him. The building was small, too small. What seemed like perfection to him as a child was obviously confined and constricted. The home had fallen into neglect like every other part of what the Murray's owned. All the careful work his mother had done on the building was gone, a victim to time and the elements.

"You lived here? In that?" Cammy said.

"Hard to imagine, isn't it? Jim said, walking up to the front door. Cammy followed behind him.

"This isn't a playhouse. It's a real one?" She said.

"Yes. It was built for the workers here. They were little people hired to be elves, if you can believe it." Jim walked up to the door. There was no knob. He pushed gently at the door and it creaked open on rusted hinges.

Jim had to stoop to get through the door. This was an experience he never had as a child. It made him keenly aware of the conditions his parents dealt with every day. The house had no furnishings. Like Santa's House at The North Pole in Christmas Town, the house had graffiti on the walls. It looked like the children of the neighborhood used the abandoned home as club house, judging by the quality and content written on the decaying walls.

Jim started up the stairs towards his room. To his surprise, the door to his room had not been fixed since the incident. Shattered and rent wood still remained where his father had kicked the door. Jim ran his fingers over the split casing, as if the memory could be drawn forth just by touching it. He walked into the room, now bare. The plaster on the wall had cracked and sloughed off in some parts, exposing the wooden laths.

"This used to be my room," Jim said tonelessly.

"Are you okay?" It was the only thing Cammy could think to say.

"Not really."

"Cammy took Jim's hand and lightly ran her fingers over the ghosts of the scars on his palm. They stood there for a while not saying anything. "We can stay as long as you want."

"No," Jim said, looking at her. "There's nothing here anymore. It's just a shell."

Jim bent his head down, to clear the doorway as they walked out his bedroom and down the stairs, then out of the house. Jim closed the door behind him and never looked back.

"Where to now?" Cammy asked as they walked away from the house.

"I think it's time we met up with my friend," Jim said. "He's on the other side of the island."

"That's great. I'd love to meet him," said Cammy.

"He saved my life, in more ways than one," Jim replied.

Jim walked down an old gravel road that had seen better days. Years of neglect and harsh Vermont winters had made deep ruts from frost-heaves, some of which were filled with standing water. Cammy could see mosquito larvae swimming in the dark fetid puddles. The road led to the edge of a thick wood. From there, a smaller dirt path led into the woods.

"This leads to the old Sloat place and the houses on the north side," Jim said ducking under a birch sapling.

The forest was old. A feeling of earthiness clung to the air, perceptible, tangible, as if it were something they could reach out and grasp. The path formed by countless scores of feet snaked its way through the dappled wood, winding and turning, seemingly without a defined purpose or sense of direction. At one point Cammy was sure they had doubled back.

"I explored these woods many times with my sister Lyndsey, trust me," Jim reassured Cammy.

It was a virgin wood, having never been culled or maintained by human hands, save the path worn through it. The trees were dense and thick. Shafts of light cut through the branches and leaves. In these shafts danced motes and dust, floating and chasing each other in an infinite spiraling dance. These woods had stood on Christmas Island when Ethan Allen stealthily rowed his Green Mountain Boys to New York, before there was a State of Vermont. They had stood untouched when Samuel De Champlain first laid eyes on the cold, clear water. Even back to the time when the Abenaki Indians held dominion over the lake and the valley, these woods had silently stood witness.

Cammy's eyes slowly adjusted to the bright light of day as they neared the edge of the woods. When they finally did, what she saw took her breath away. The view was spectacular. They stood on the edge of a small embankment that led straight down to the water. A rocky beach lay at the foot of this minor cliff face. Lake Champlain lapped gently at the shore, the water impossibly clear and bright.

"That way..." Jim gestured to a path that snaked to the right. "...leads to the Sloat Manor. There's a two-car paved road that goes around the other side of the island, it leads back to the ferry. It's a spectacular, three story house. Actually, it's pretty impressive. They shipped granite all the way from Barre to make it."

"Oh!" Cammy said.

"But we're not headed that way."

Jim led her to a small path that mean its way to the left, paved with bricks, old and worn by time and countless feet. The path meandered along the edge but steadily up the side of the cliff face. The peaceful waters of Lake Champlain lapped at rocky beach. As they crested the hill, Cammy saw trees and a wrought iron fence.

When the Sloats acquired Christmas Island, part of the appeal was its remoteness, that is was far from the mainland. Wealth purchased privacy, but that came with the price of isolation. All William Sloat ever wanted to do was to make his wife happy, he built her a magnificent house with a grand view of the Adirondack Mountains. He even built a little Unitarian Church for her and paid to have a pastor ferried out every Sunday for services. He gave her every amenity she could ever desire, but he could not buy her happiness, however how hard he tried.

When Mary Sloat died from complications from the Spanish Flu in 1918, William could not bear to be apart from her. He had constructed a little theme park for her happiness, he constructed a churchyard right next door to the little Unitarian Church in his grief. It was a short walk along the bluff of the north side of the island to the Sloat mausoleum. He had picked Mary's favorite spot, the one with the view of Vermont. The view *from* Vermont is widely considered the superior view, towards Plattsburg and the New York side, towards the Adirondack Mountains. Mary Sloat far preferred looking upon the shores facing Vermont and the hills and valleys she adored.

Over time the little churchyard grew, expanding from the family mausoleum, to plots and gravestones. Many of the employees who came to work and live at Christmas Town had no families, or simply had no desire or plans for their eternal resting places. The little graveyard grew again and again. The army of dwarves who populated the attraction found their eternal rest in the Sloat family graveyard too. As well intentioned as it seemed at the time, all the "elves" of the graveyard had miniature headstones to mark their graves. The effect was eccentric to say the least, the rows of tiny gravestones gave the macabre impression of children, rather than little people resided in those graves. Add to that the intermittent whimsy of a carven granite Santa Claus grave marker, one with an angel sitting on his lap, it lent the whole affair the feeling of a melancholy side-show.

Jim walked up to the iron gate and pushed it. It swung open with a squeal of metal on metal. Jim walked for a while, then stopped. Cammy walked to his side to see what he was looking at. In front of Jim, almost covered by long weeds, were two gravestones, and they read as follows:

LYNDSEY ANNE SUTTON
JUNE 8, 1975 – FEBRUARY 7, 1978
TAKEN TOO SOON

NICHOLAS CLAUS SUMMERS
MAY 17, 1949 – FEBRUARY 7, 1978
A GIANT IN LIFE

Reflexively, Jim reached into his pocket for a candy bar. Cammy moved closer to Jim and slid her hand into his, halting his search. Words failed her as tears glistened in her eyes. Jim's mouth felt dry and sticky, there was a lump in his throat. The words were there, but they seemed to be stuck. Every time he tried to speak, his throat constricted, as if to strangle the sounds before they became words. Then Cammy squeezed his hand. Jim felt her strength, and it emboldened him. He took a deep breath and swallowed.

"It was in the blizzard of 1978. Nick was having an affair with my mother. My father found out. My mother took us from the house to protect us from my father and his anger. We made the last ferry. We all thought once we were on that boat…" He trailed off, wiping a tear from his eye. "My mother was on the bridge getting us hot chocolate when the ferry capsized in the storm. Nick pushed me out the door. He could have climbed out and saved himself, but he went back to save my sister. The car went into the water…and…" Jim's voice was thick. He turned to Cammy.

"I can still see him holding my sister in his arms. They were trapped inside." He sank to his knees.

"I'm so sorry," Cammy said. She sat next to him and put her arm around him, her face was wet.

"His eyes…," Jim said, turning to Cammy "…I can see him pressing Lyndsey's face into his chest, cradling her. Then…" Jim stopped. "He looked at me. I couldn't hear him, but he looked in my eyes. I could see him mouthing the words, 'Everything is going to be okay.' I don't know if it was meant for me or Lyndsey, then the car sank under the waves. It was the last I saw of them."

"No one went in after them?"

"The storm was too strong. The ferry was in danger of sinking. The authorities eventually retrieved the bodies from the bottom." Jim ran his fingers across Lyndsey's grave, tracing the engraved letters.

"At least they had the respect to give Nick a full-sized gravestone" Jim gestured to the grave next to Lyndsey. "He deserved that." Jim stared at Nick's grave. "He deserved better."

"I don't I can say..." Cammy offered up lamely.

"If my parents' marriage wasn't over with the affair, it was destroyed by Lyndsey's death. My dad was arrested on assault and attempted murder charges. My mom filed for divorce. My mother got custody of me. She wanted to move out of Vermont forever. So, I went to New Jersey with her."

"What happened to your father?" Cammy asked.

"He was found guilty of the assault charge, acquitted of the attempted murder. Her served three years, then he was paroled. He moved to White River Junction."

"Your dad stayed here in Vermont?"

"It was a condition of his parole that he stay in the state for three years. He got a job at Pizza Hut. He was fired for having sex with an underage employee. He actually got her pregnant. She was *fifteen*. I have a half-brother around here somewhere," Jim said, looking out at the water of Lake Champlain.

"You don't know where he is?"

"I don't think even my father knows where he is. He had broken the conditions of his parole and went back to jail for another five years. He eventually moved to New Mexico in search of work. He tried his hand at real-estate. He remarried and started another family." Jim picked up a rock and threw it out over the cliff. "A girl and a boy."

"You don't see them, or him?" Cammy asked.

"No. I think I just remind him of what happened. He sends a birthday card every once in a while, when he remembers I exist."

"So, you and your mom must be pretty close, huh?" Cammy said.

"Yeah. I can only imagine how hard it was doing it all on her own. She moved us to New Jersey and took odd jobs until she stumbled into her own business."

"Really?" Cammy said.

"Yeah, she started a restoration company. She fixed up old houses, really old houses. It was a hobby here on the island, to keep her from going crazy from boredom, being alone all day when my dad ran the snack stand," Jim replied.

"That is so cool. Does she still do it?"

No. She's got arthritis in her hands. She says it was from all the power tools she used over the years. She just runs the business now. She threatens to sell it from time to time and move to Florida. She says she's had it with winter."

"I can hardly blame her," Cammy said. She looked at Jim, he was staring blankly at the water. "You okay?"

"I don't know," Jim replied. "I knew I had to come here. But now that I'm here, I don't know how to feel. I feel like a fraud."

"Don't say that," Cammy said.

"I can't even remember her face." Jim said turning his head down. "I try to. I want to. Sometimes, I think if I concentrate hard enough, I might be able to see her again."

"You don't have *any* family photos?" Cammy asked.

"No. They were all lost."

"Was there a fire?" Cammy prodded gently.

"No." Jim kept kicking at the ground. "It was my fault. When my mom moved us from Vermont to New Jersey, there was no point in moving the tiny furniture in the house on Christmas Island. Everything we owned fit in the AMC Pacer she had borrowed from the Lakelands." Jim turned to Cammy "They worked on the island as well."

"They were lost in the move?" Cammy asked. "That happens all the time."

"We stopped in New Paltz to gas up," Jim said. "I was cold, my mother left the keys in the car when she went inside to go to the bathroom. It took a long time, so I got out to find her. By the time we got back, the car was gone."

"What about your grandparents, surely they must have pictures of you and your sister," Cammy offered.

My father's family basically disowned my mother and me after they found out she had an affair, made infinitely worse by the fact slept with a little person."

"Your mom had an affair with a little person, like a dwarf?" Cammy's eyes bugged.

"Yes. He worked on the island." Jim looked out at the water. "He was the best man I ever knew. It didn't matter he was short."

"I can't believe your grandparents did that to you, to your mother."

"They threw everything out. My mother had burned that bridge right before we moved here. My dad's parents died before I was born. Every picture of my sister was in that car." Jim sighed. "We lost everything, and everyone."

"I'm so sorry," Cammy replied.

"I thought if I made the trip, I might be able to *remember* Lyndsey. But there's nothing. The only evidence she ever lived is this gravestone. I know I was young, but sometimes…" Jim's voice trailed off.

"Yes."

"Sometimes I forget I even *had* a sister," Jim said, his voice thick. "Last year, I realized that I had not spoken or even thought about her for eight months. She deserved better."

"Don't be so hard on yourself," Cammy said.

"There are no answers here," Jim replied with a sigh. "Nick's not here. It's just dirt. I can never tell him how much he changed my life. I can never repay him for his kindness. I can never thank him for saving my life or ask him why he chose me over my sister."

"You'll never know why. You'll never be able to do any of those things. All you can do is live your own life. He gave you a gift. Be worthy of it, you know?" Cammy said, standing up and looking at the horizon. "After all, I like you, and I'm an excellent judge of character."

"It's not that, it's just…" Jim began.

"You know what I think? I think we *both* need to stop living in the past." She looked back over her shoulder and walked out of the cemetery. Jim got up, brushed dirt off his pants and followed her down the path. He thought for a moment about turning around to get one last look, but he had had enough. To his surprise, he did feel better, as if a weight had been lifted from him.

"You like me, huh?' Jim said, walking up beside her.

"So, you did hear me, slim-Jim," Cammy replied. When she spoke his nickname, this time it didn't bother him.

"What does this mean?"

"Honestly, I don't know," she said, kicking at rocks as she walked. "But I know that I'd like to see where it goes."

"Where does it go? Does it go back to Brooklyn with me?"

"God, No," Cammy said. "Not yet. I'm still reeling from my own family crisis, you know. Thanks again for that."

"So, we just say our goodbyes? Exchange numbers and hope for the best?" Jim asked.

"That's exactly what we do. Like the movie once said, 'I think this is the start of a beautiful friendship.'"

"Friendship," Jim said.

"What, you can't be friends with a girl?" Cammy teased.

"No. Well, yes, I mean…'.

"It is called *girl*friend isn't it?" She leaned over and grabbed him by the waist, pulled him in tight, and kissed him. Jim breathed in deeply and caught a familiar faint scent of motor oil and gasoline in her curly brown hair.

"Is that what you are?"

"Yep," she said,. "Pleaase, you're a writer Jim. Don't you recognize a happy ending when you see one?"

Jim stopped for a moment, trying to comprehend the series of events that had led him to this exact moment, this peculiar place in time. Of all endings, this was certainly the most improbable.

Cammy was a good ten feet or so ahead of him when she turned around. She stood on the edge of the woods, the light filtering through the branches, dappling the ground and her body. The maple trees and pines swayed gently in the breeze, whispering their secrets to the wind. It struck him how *alive* the woods felt. The very air shimmered green, light and delicate. He watched the remarkable woman who stood before him, her wild hair blowing in the breeze. It seemed to Jim that she might be a mirage or an illusion. If she was, did it even matter?

Cammy smiled at him and waved.

"Come on," she said. "I know a place that serves some pretty damn good onion rings."

End.

ACKNOWLEDGMENTS

I would like to thank the following people who helped me greatly in completing and making this book far better than when I first started

DEBBI STONE

Your perspective on the Vermont experience was something I could never have found on my own. Thank you for helping me find my voice and give me the courage to put my thoughts into words..

GK DARBY

Thank you for believing in this book and whipping it into shape.

JULIE MACHIA RUNEZ

You took (a lot) of time to read my book. Thank you for helping me "kill some darlings."

To read excerpts from Jim Sutton's
The Onion Ring Lover's Guide to Vermont,
complete with real reviews,
please visit www.onionringlovers.com